The Fox & Little Tanuki
KORISENMAN

3

Mi Tagawa

Table of Contents

The Little Fox & Tanuki
KORISENMAN

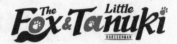

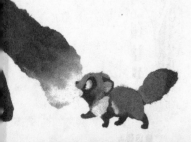

Chapter 14

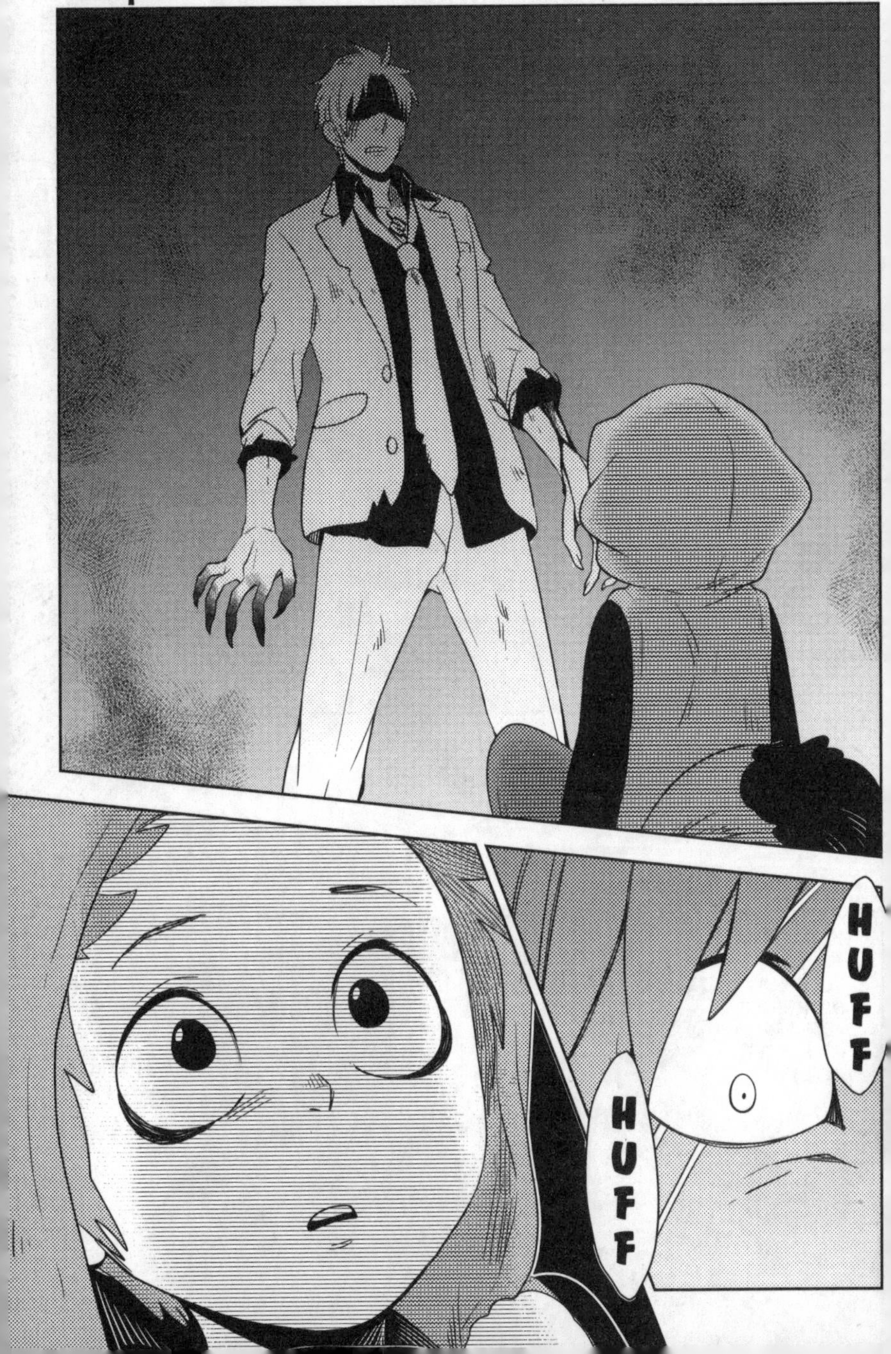
HUFF
HUFF

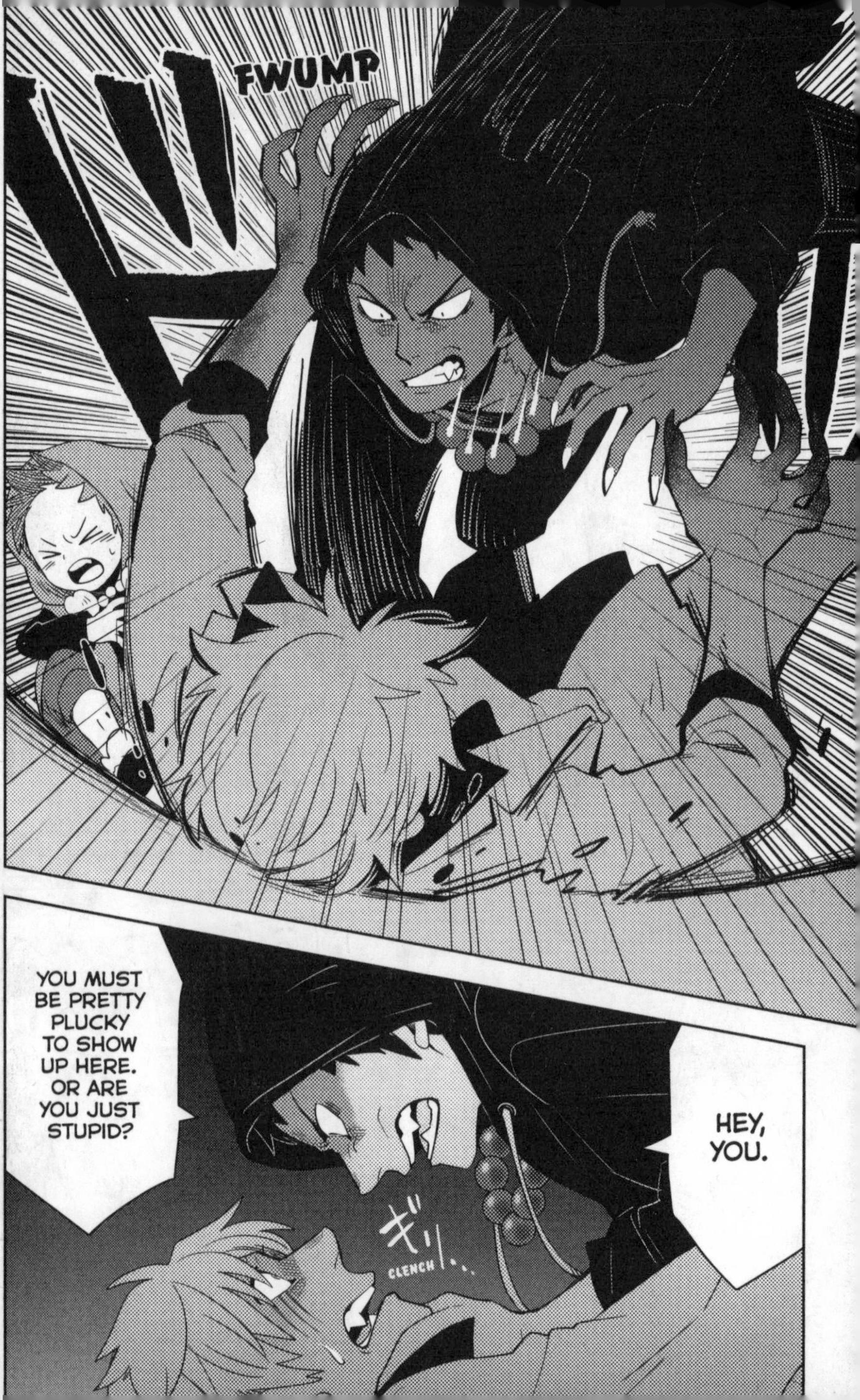
FWUMP
HEY, YOU.
ギリ…
CLENCH
YOU MUST BE PRETTY PLUCKY TO SHOW UP HERE. OR ARE YOU JUST STUPID?

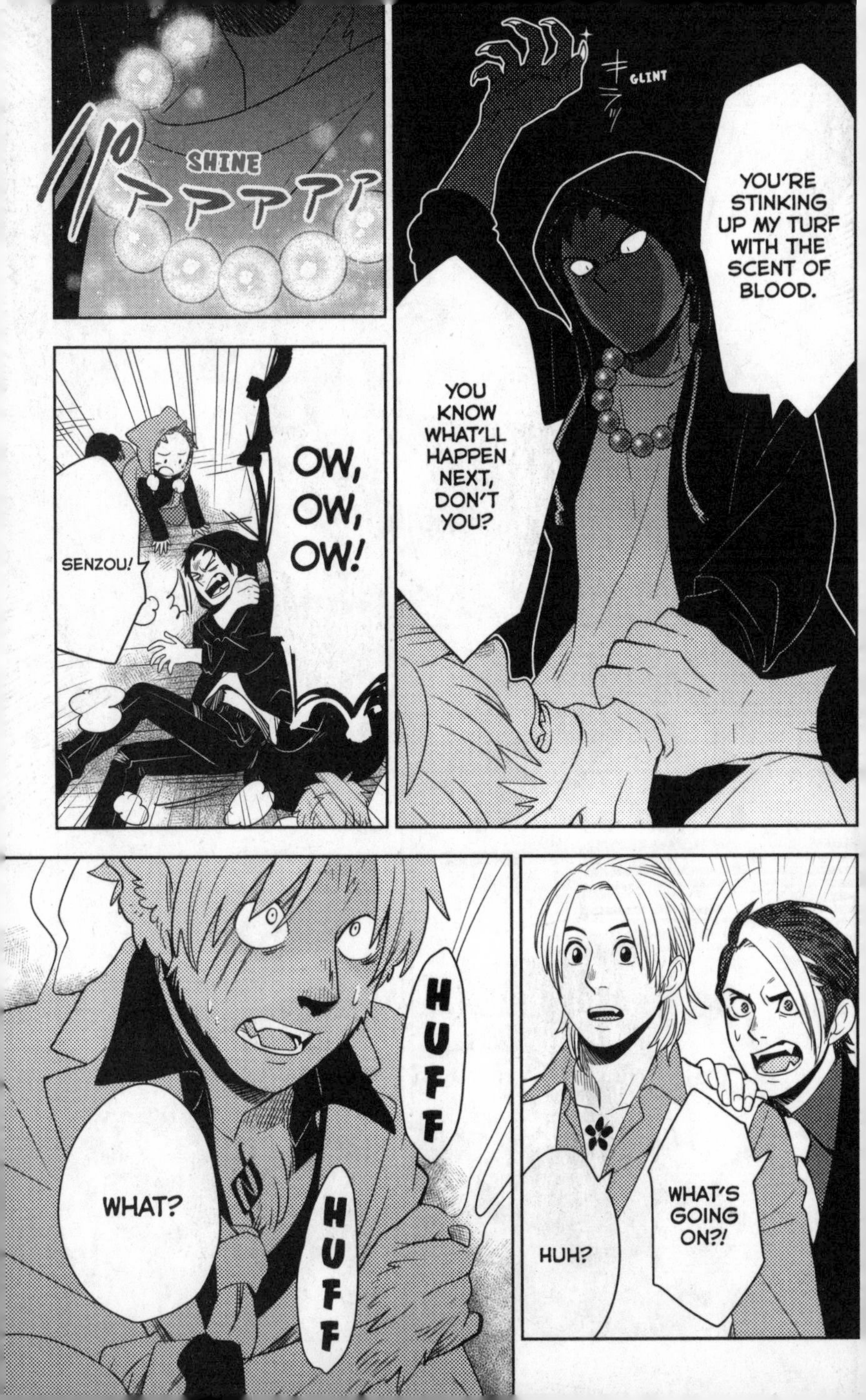
GLINT
YOU'RE STINKING UP MY TURF WITH THE SCENT OF BLOOD.
YOU KNOW WHAT'LL HAPPEN NEXT, DON'T YOU?
SHINE
OW, OW, OW!
SENZOU!
WHAT'S GOING ON?!
HUH?
HUFF
HUFF
WHAT?

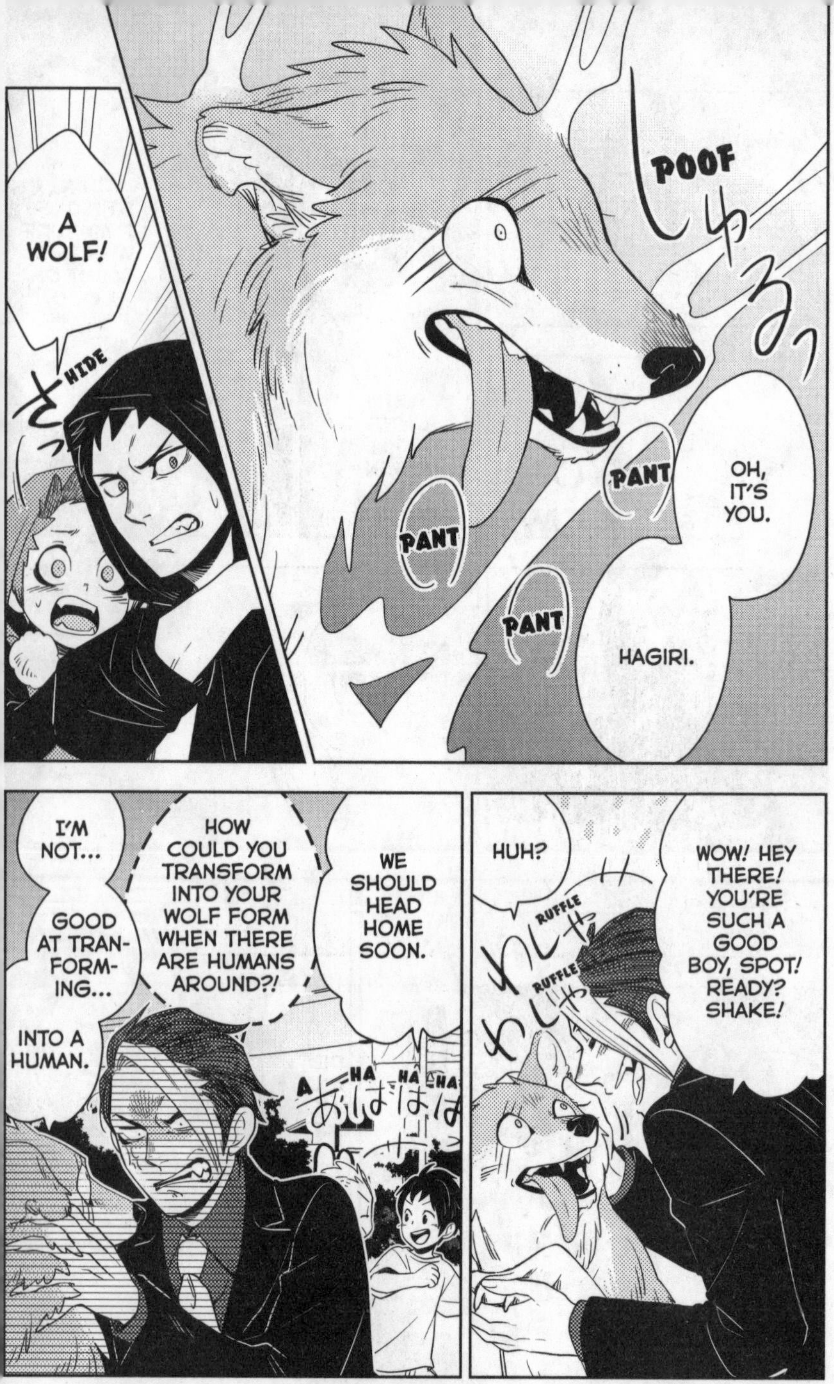
POOF
しゅるっ
PANT
PANT
PANT
OH, IT'S YOU.
HAGIRI.
A WOLF!
HIDE
さっ
WOW! HEY THERE! YOU'RE SUCH A GOOD BOY, SPOT! READY? SHAKE!
HUH?
RUFFLE
RUFFLE
わしゃ
わしゃ
WE SHOULD HEAD HOME SOON.
HOW COULD YOU TRANSFORM INTO YOUR WOLF FORM WHEN THERE ARE HUMANS AROUND?!
I'M NOT...
GOOD AT TRAN-FORM-ING...
INTO A HUMAN.
A-HA-HA-HA
あははは

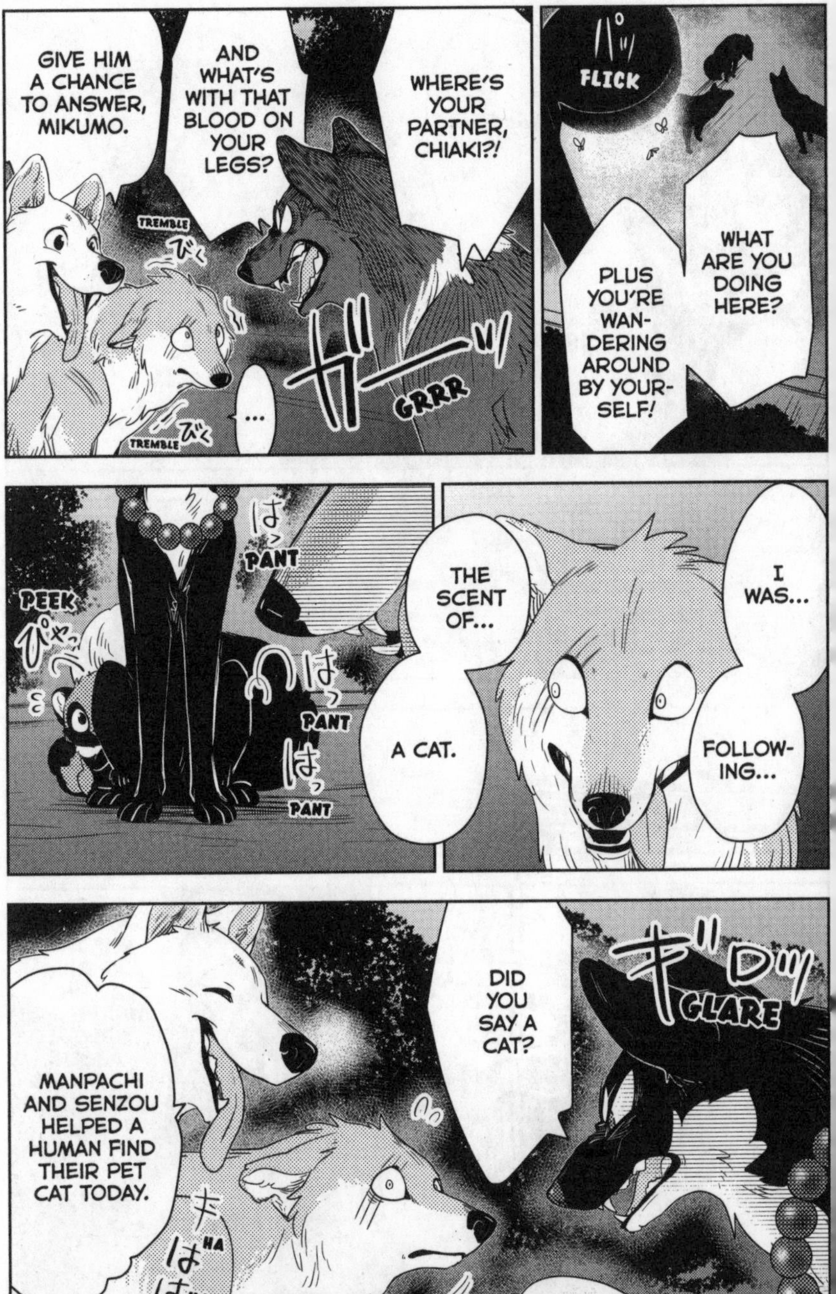
FLICK
WHAT ARE YOU DOING HERE?
PLUS YOU'RE WAN-DERING AROUND BY YOUR-SELF!
WHERE'S YOUR PARTNER, CHIAKI?!
AND WHAT'S WITH THAT BLOOD ON YOUR LEGS?
GIVE HIM A CHANCE TO ANSWER, MIKUMO.
TREMBLE
GRRR
...
TREMBLE
I WAS...
FOLLOW-ING...
THE SCENT OF...
A CAT.
PANT
PEEK
PANT
PANT
GLARE
DID YOU SAY A CAT?
MANPACHI AND SENZOU HELPED A HUMAN FIND THEIR PET CAT TODAY.
HA
HA

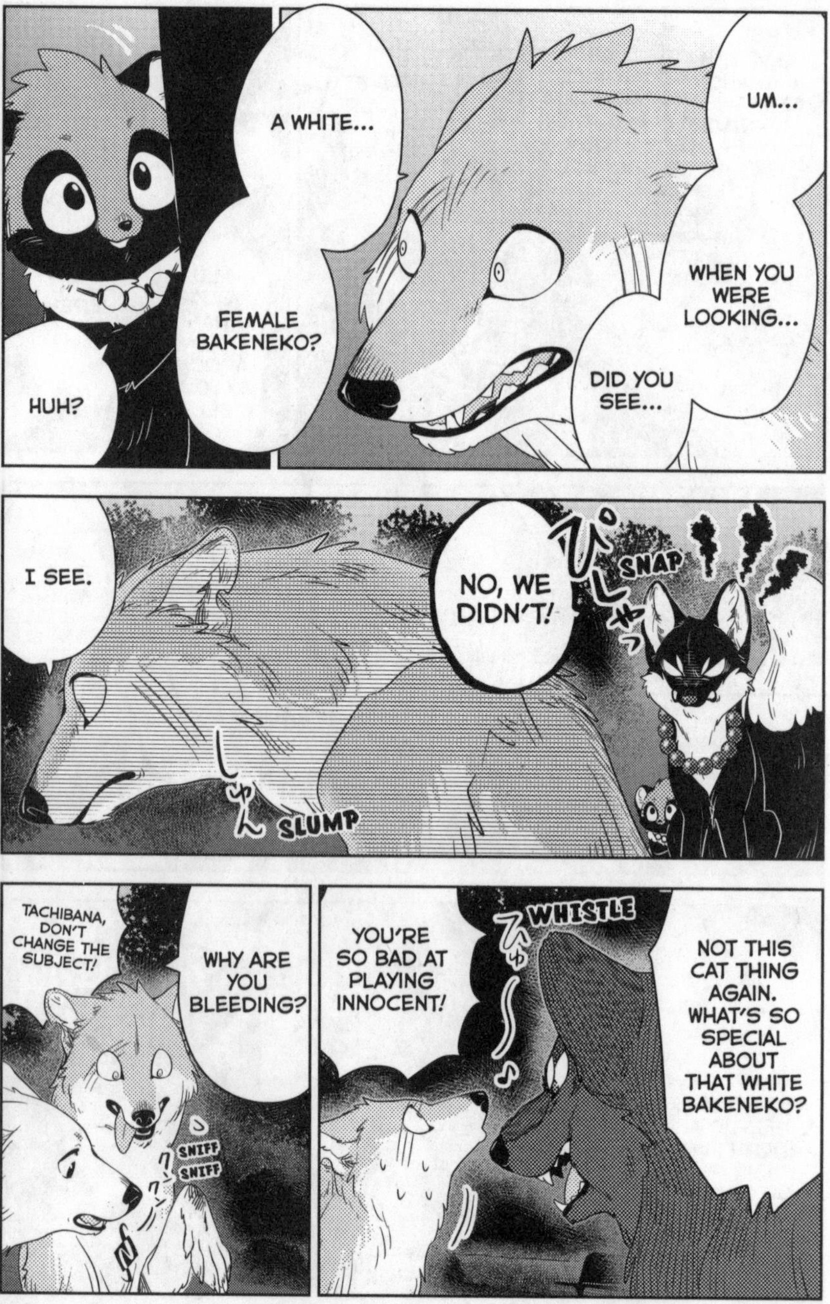
UM...
WHEN YOU WERE LOOKING...
DID YOU SEE...
A WHITE...
FEMALE BAKENEKO?
HUH?
NO, WE DIDN'T!
ぴしゃっ
SNAP
I SEE.
しゅん
SLUMP
NOT THIS CAT THING AGAIN. WHAT'S SO SPECIAL ABOUT THAT WHITE BAKENEKO?
WHISTLE
YOU'RE SO BAD AT PLAYING INNOCENT!
WHY ARE YOU BLEEDING?
TACHIBANA, DON'T CHANGE THE SUBJECT!
SNIFF
SNIFF

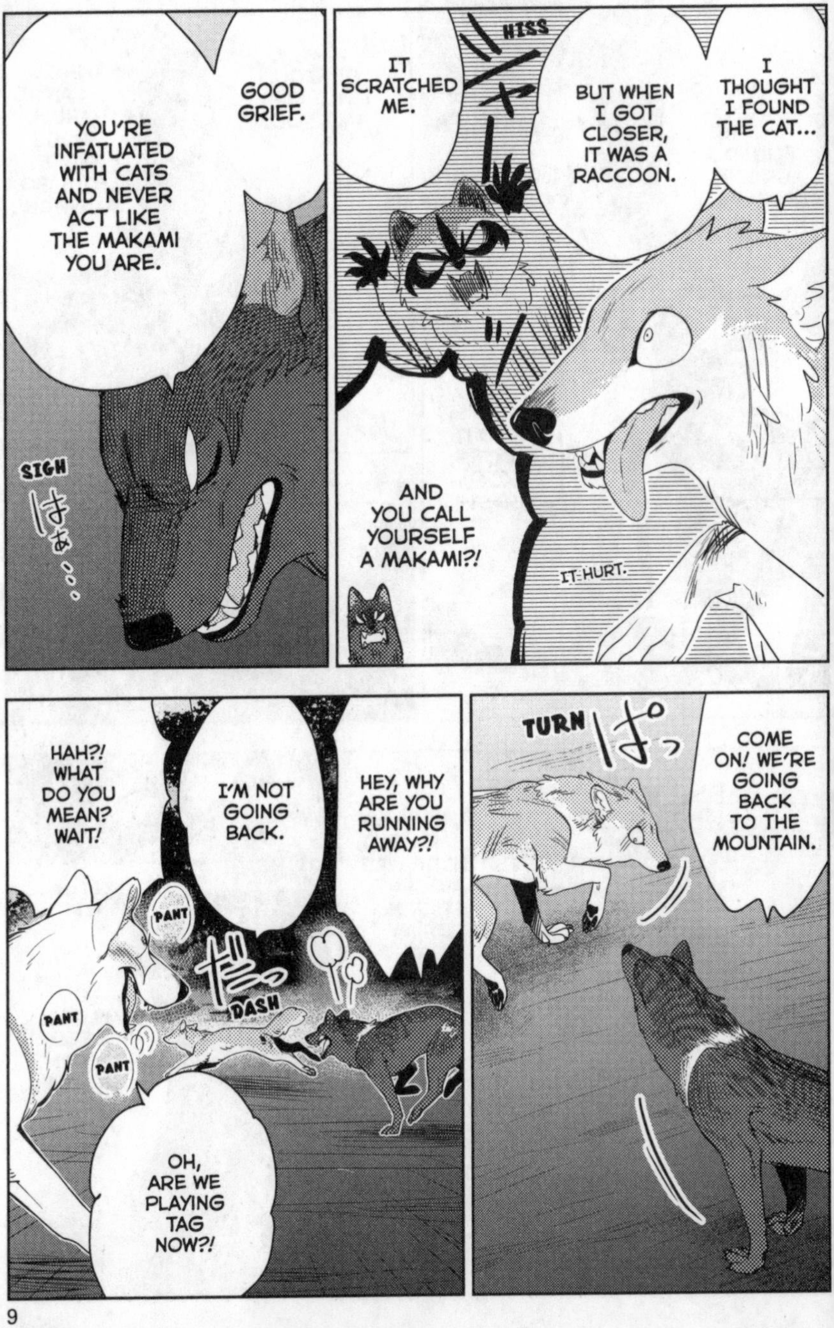
I THOUGHT I FOUND THE CAT...
BUT WHEN I GOT CLOSER, IT WAS A RACCOON.
HISS
IT SCRATCHED ME.
AND YOU CALL YOURSELF A MAKAMI?!
IT HURT.
GOOD GRIEF.
YOU'RE INFATUATED WITH CATS AND NEVER ACT LIKE THE MAKAMI YOU ARE.
SIGH
COME ON! WE'RE GOING BACK TO THE MOUNTAIN.
TURN
HEY, WHY ARE YOU RUNNING AWAY?!
I'M NOT GOING BACK.
HAH?! WHAT DO YOU MEAN? WAIT!
PANT
DASH
PANT
PANT
OH, ARE WE PLAYING TAG NOW?!

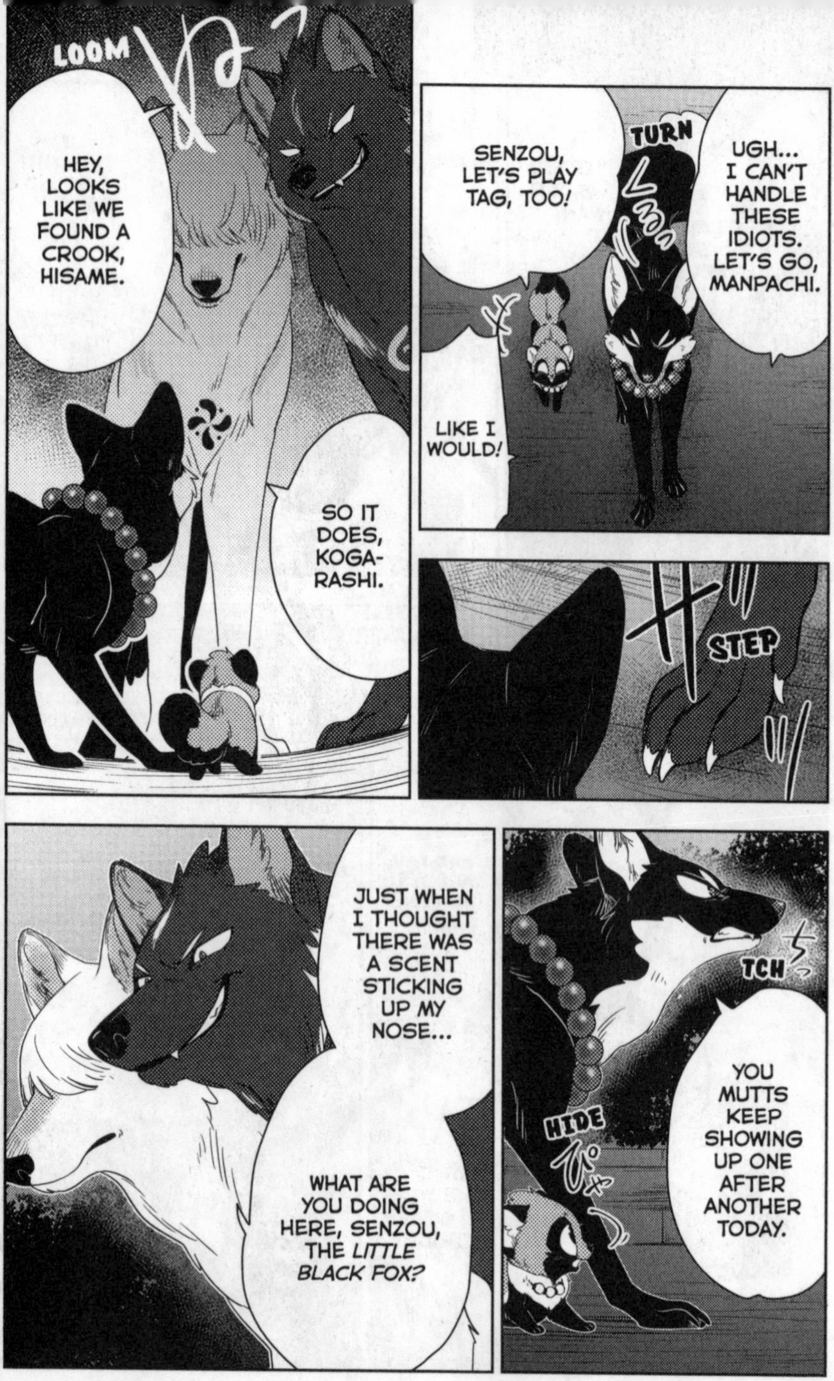
UGH... I CAN'T HANDLE THESE IDIOTS. LET'S GO, MANPACHI.
TURN
SENZOU, LET'S PLAY TAG, TOO!
LIKE I WOULD!
STEP
LOOM
HEY, LOOKS LIKE WE FOUND A CROOK, HISAME.
SO IT DOES, KOGARASHI.
TCH
YOU MUTTS KEEP SHOWING UP ONE AFTER ANOTHER TODAY.
HIDE
JUST WHEN I THOUGHT THERE WAS A SCENT STICKING UP MY NOSE...
WHAT ARE YOU DOING HERE, SENZOU, THE *LITTLE BLACK FOX?*

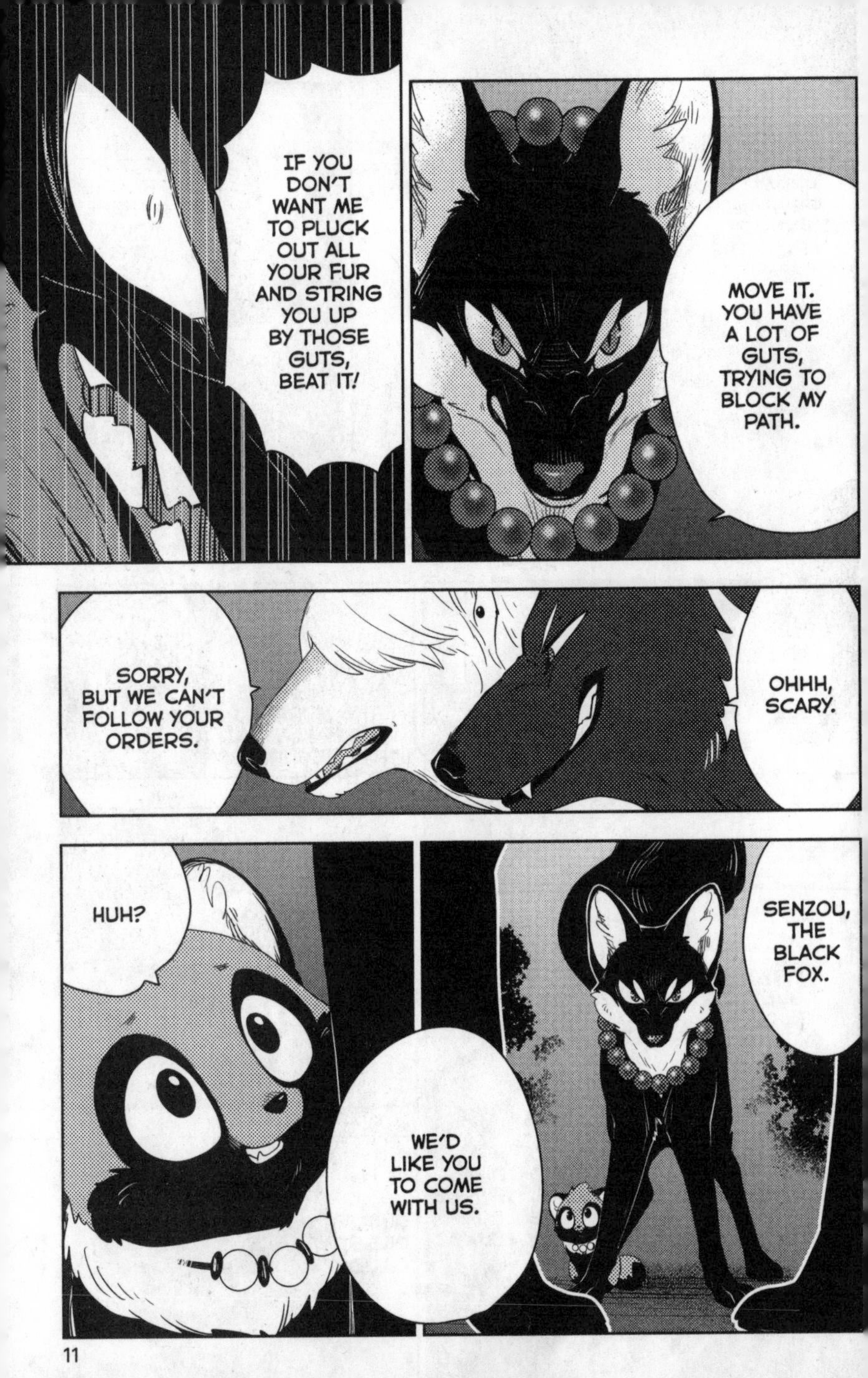
MOVE IT. YOU HAVE A LOT OF GUTS, TRYING TO BLOCK MY PATH.
IF YOU DON'T WANT ME TO PLUCK OUT ALL YOUR FUR AND STRING YOU UP BY THOSE GUTS, BEAT IT!
OHHH, SCARY.
SORRY, BUT WE CAN'T FOLLOW YOUR ORDERS.
SENZOU, THE BLACK FOX.
HUH?
WE'D LIKE YOU TO COME WITH US.

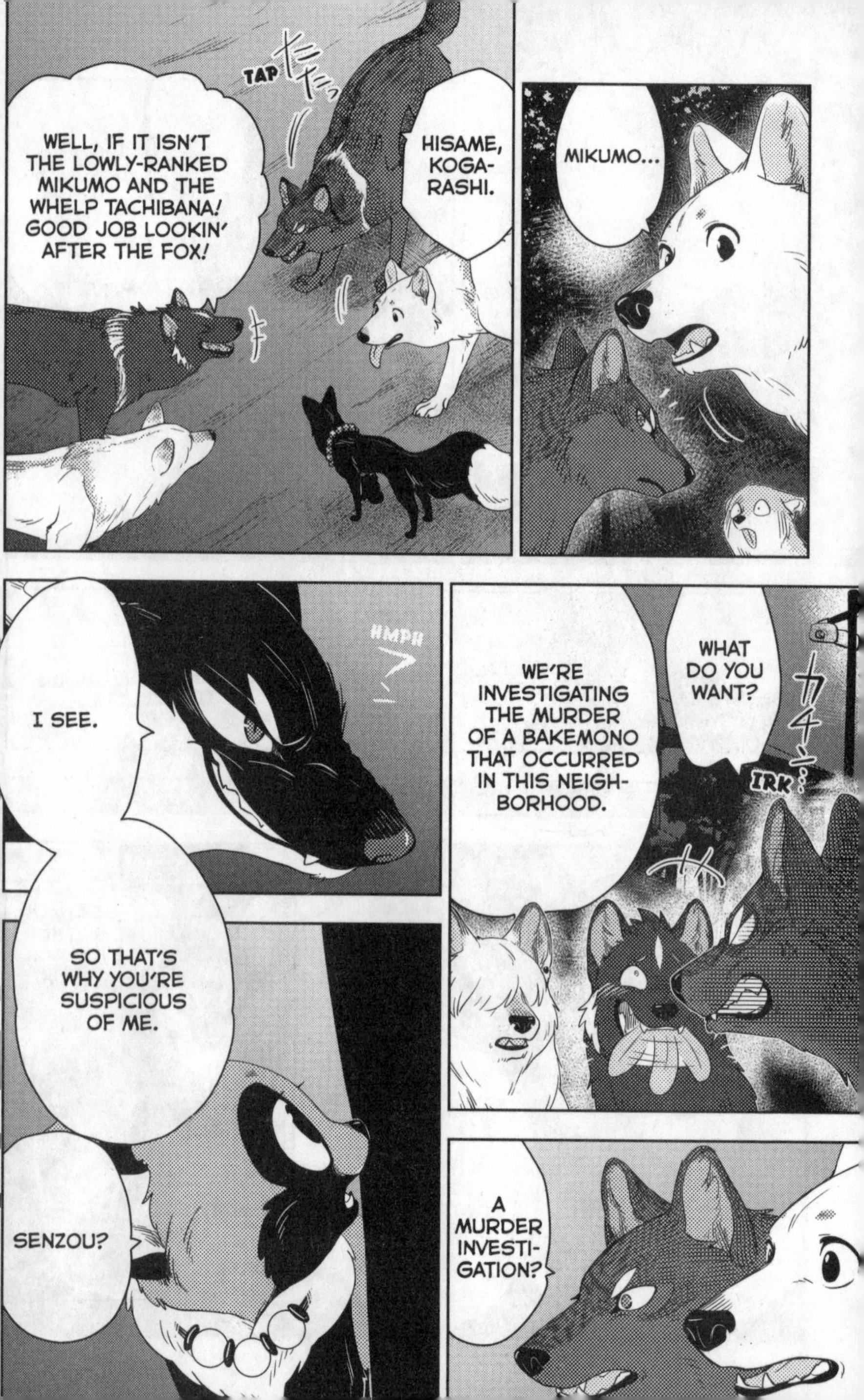
MIKUMO...
TAP
HISAME, KOGA-RASHI.
WELL, IF IT ISN'T THE LOWLY-RANKED MIKUMO AND THE WHELP TACHIBANA! GOOD JOB LOOKIN' AFTER THE FOX!
WHAT DO YOU WANT?
IRK
WE'RE INVESTIGATING THE MURDER OF A BAKEMONO THAT OCCURRED IN THIS NEIGH-BORHOOD.
A MURDER INVESTI-GATION?
HMPH
I SEE.
SO THAT'S WHY YOU'RE SUSPICIOUS OF ME.
SENZOU?

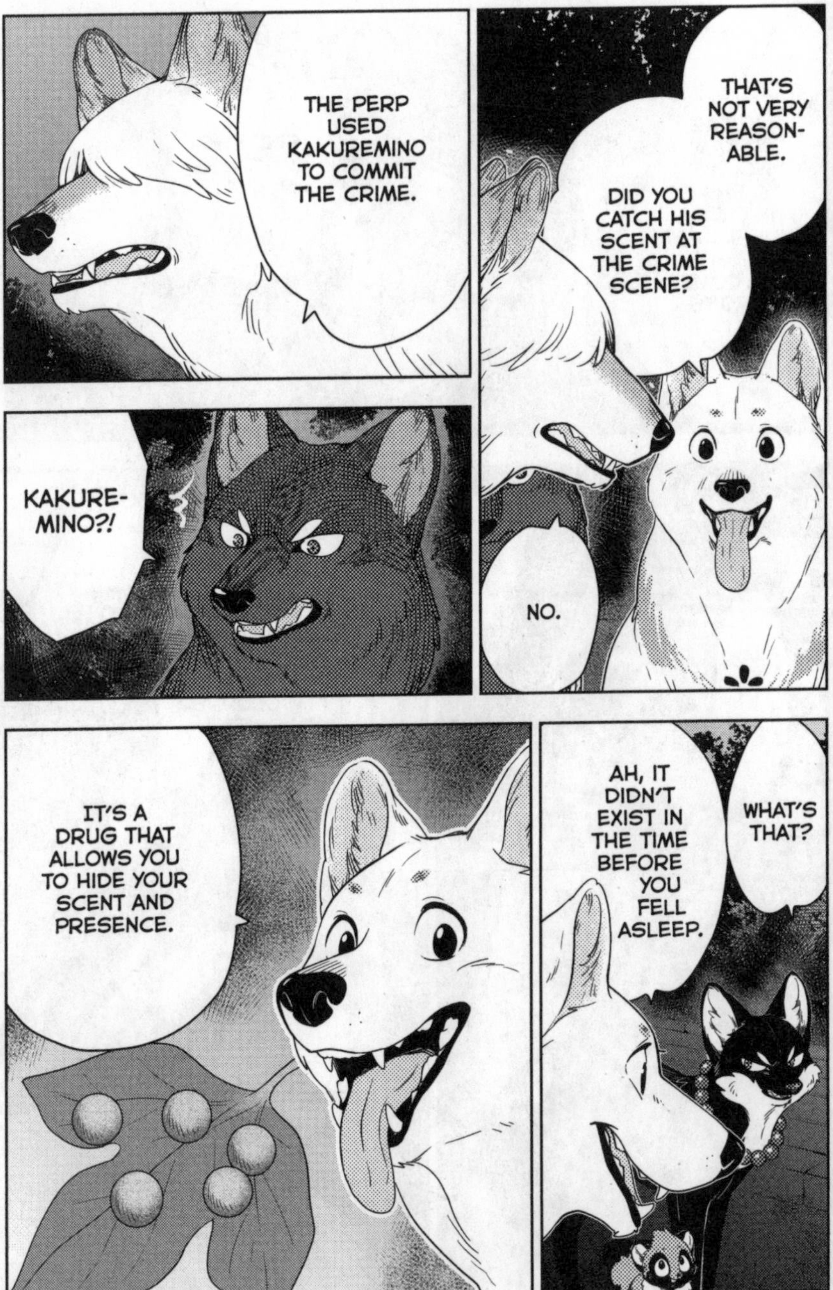
THAT'S NOT VERY REASON-ABLE.
DID YOU CATCH HIS SCENT AT THE CRIME SCENE?
NO.
THE PERP USED KAKUREMINO TO COMMIT THE CRIME.
KAKURE-MINO?!
WHAT'S THAT?
AH, IT DIDN'T EXIST IN THE TIME BEFORE YOU FELL ASLEEP.
IT'S A DRUG THAT ALLOWS YOU TO HIDE YOUR SCENT AND PRESENCE.

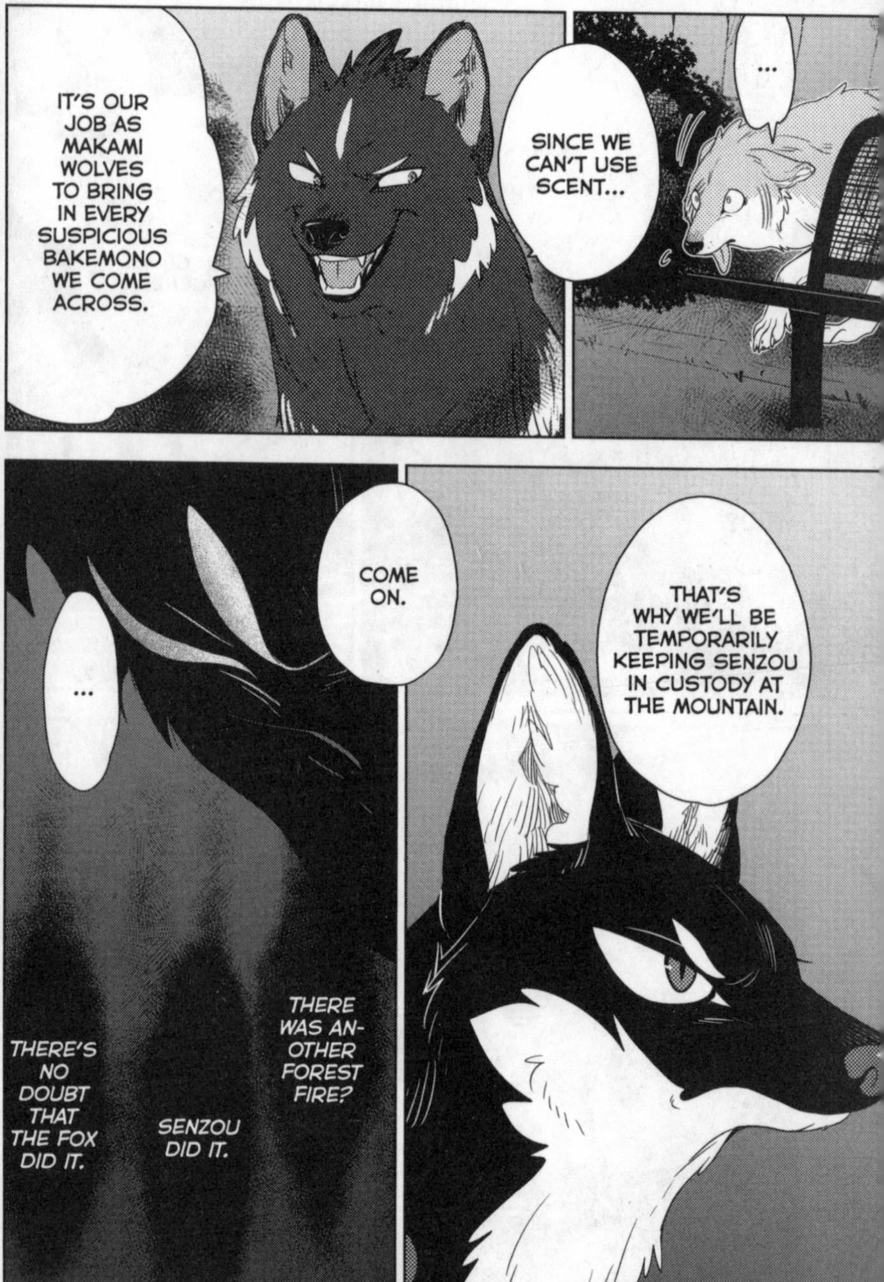
...
SINCE WE CAN'T USE SCENT...
IT'S OUR JOB AS MAKAMI WOLVES TO BRING IN EVERY SUSPICIOUS BAKEMONO WE COME ACROSS.
THAT'S WHY WE'LL BE TEMPORARILY KEEPING SENZOU IN CUSTODY AT THE MOUNTAIN.
COME ON.
...
THERE WAS AN-OTHER FOREST FIRE?
SENZOU DID IT.
THERE'S NO DOUBT THAT THE FOX DID IT.

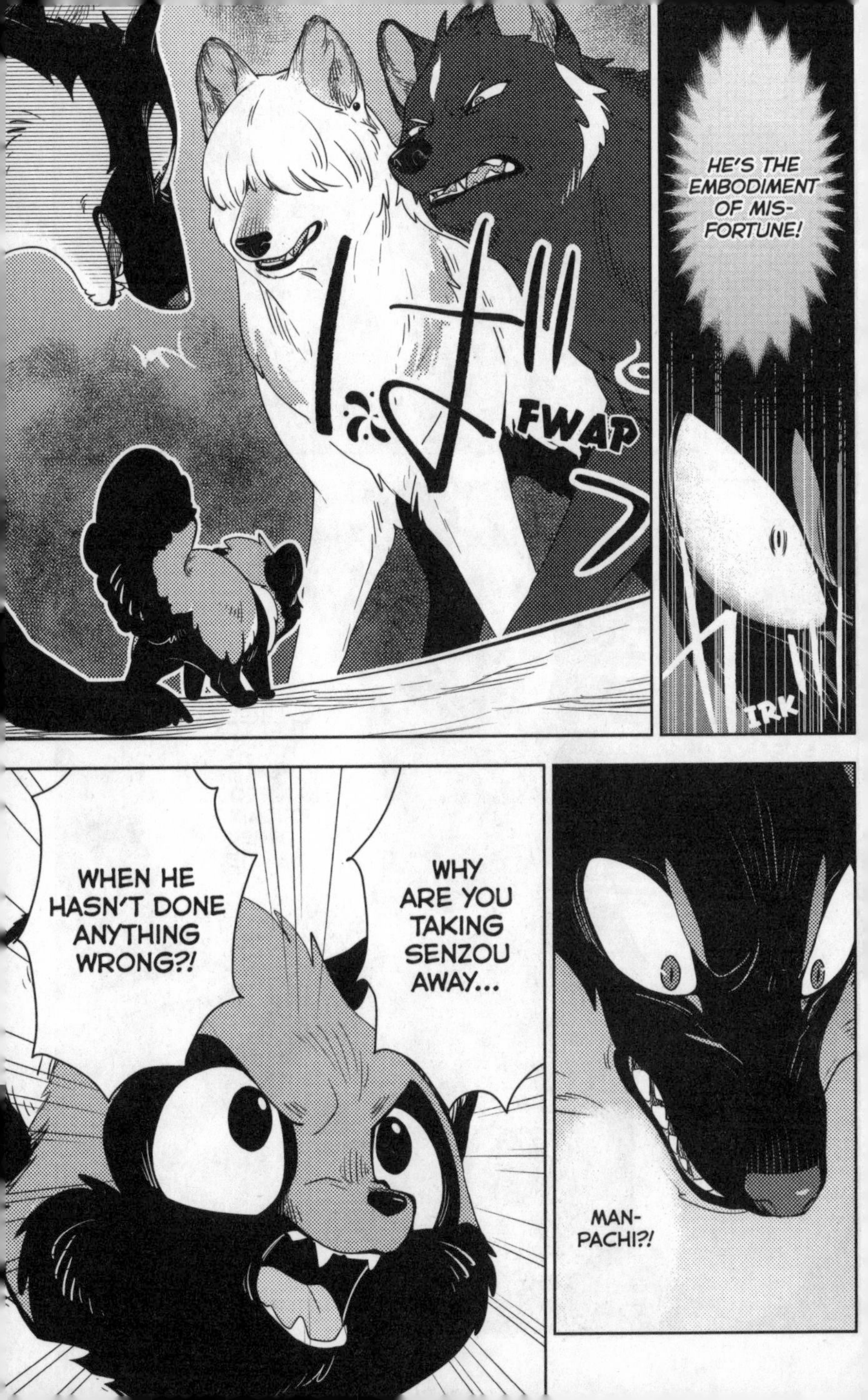
HE'S THE EMBODIMENT OF MIS-FORTUNE!
IRK
FWAP
MAN-PACHI?!
WHY ARE YOU TAKING SENZOU AWAY...
WHEN HE HASN'T DONE ANYTHING WRONG?!

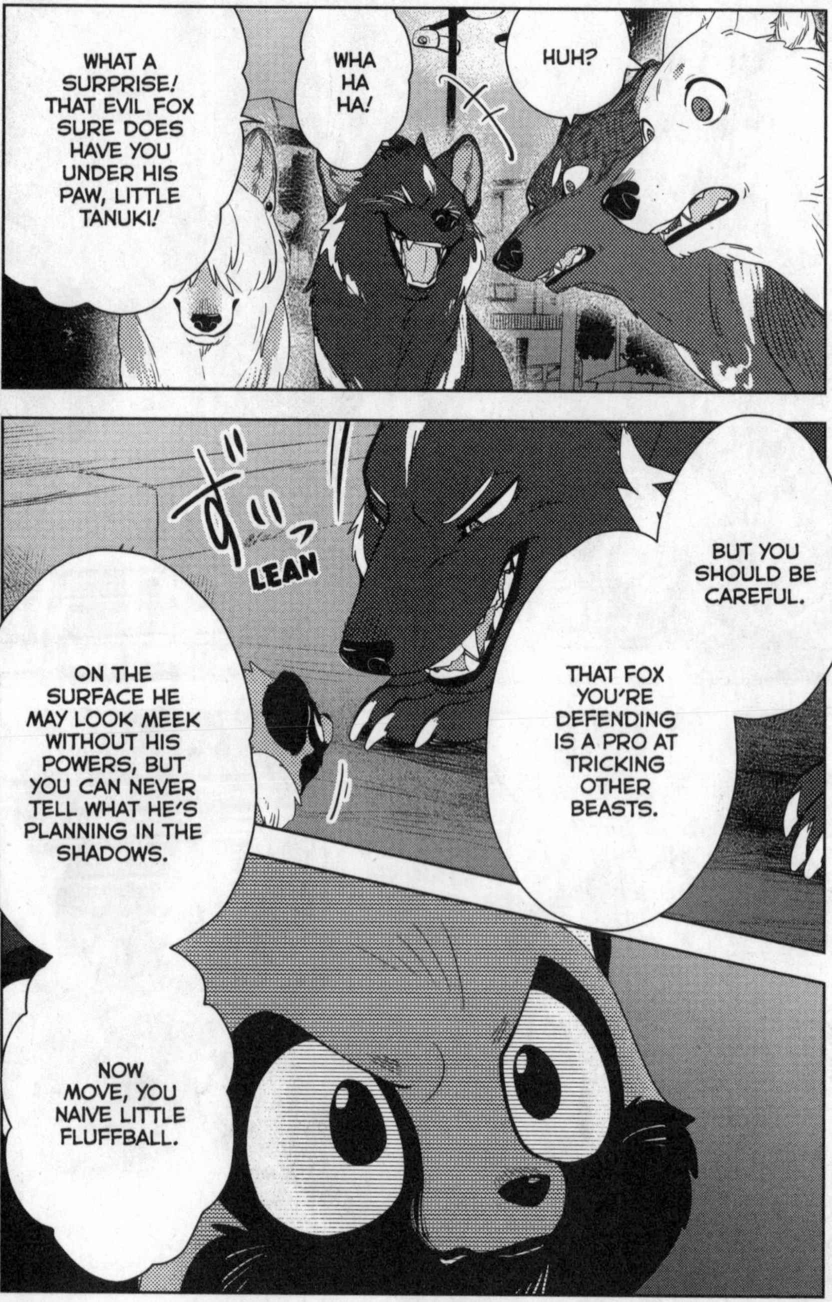
HUH?
WHA HA HA!
WHAT A SURPRISE! THAT EVIL FOX SURE DOES HAVE YOU UNDER HIS PAW, LITTLE TANUKI!
BUT YOU SHOULD BE CAREFUL.
THAT FOX YOU'RE DEFENDING IS A PRO AT TRICKING OTHER BEASTS.
ずいっ
LEAN
ON THE SURFACE HE MAY LOOK MEEK WITHOUT HIS POWERS, BUT YOU CAN NEVER TELL WHAT HE'S PLANNING IN THE SHADOWS.
NOW MOVE, YOU NAIVE LITTLE FLUFFBALL.

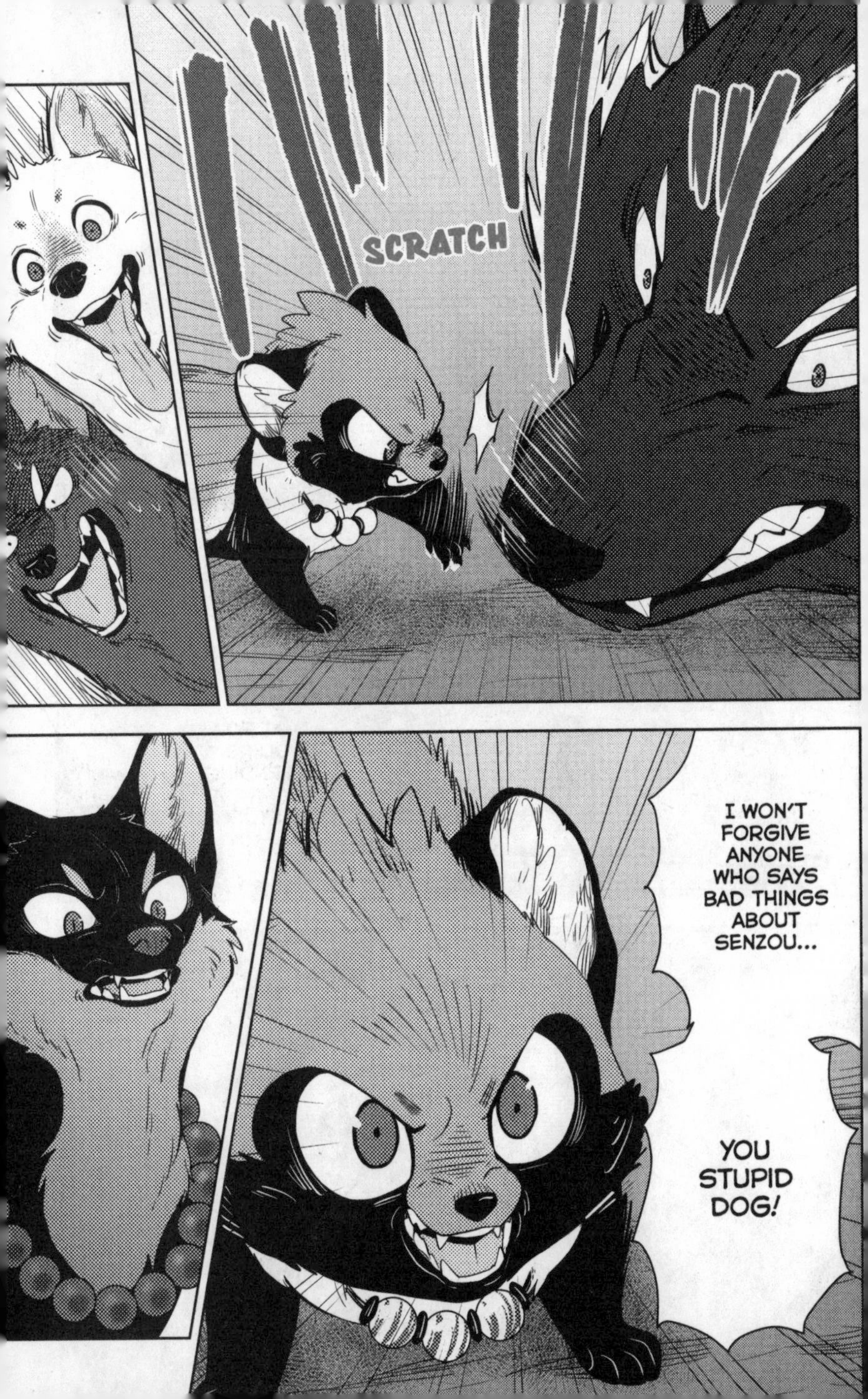
SCRATCH
I WON'T FORGIVE ANYONE WHO SAYS BAD THINGS ABOUT SENZOU...
YOU STUPID DOG!

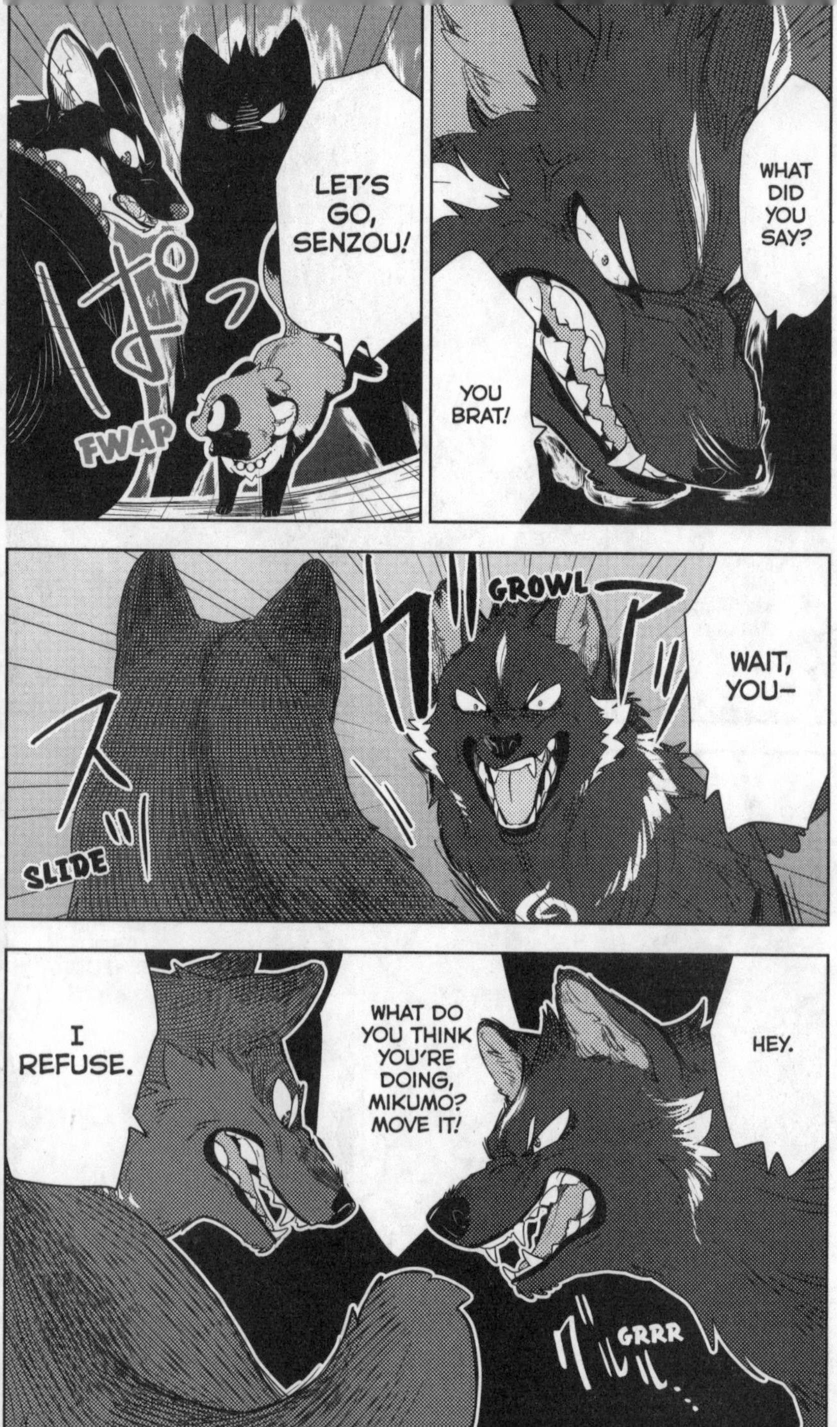
WHAT DID YOU SAY?
YOU BRAT!
LET'S GO, SENZOU!
FWAP
WAIT, YOU—
GROWL
SLIDE
HEY.
WHAT DO YOU THINK YOU'RE DOING, MIKUMO? MOVE IT!
I REFUSE.
GRRR

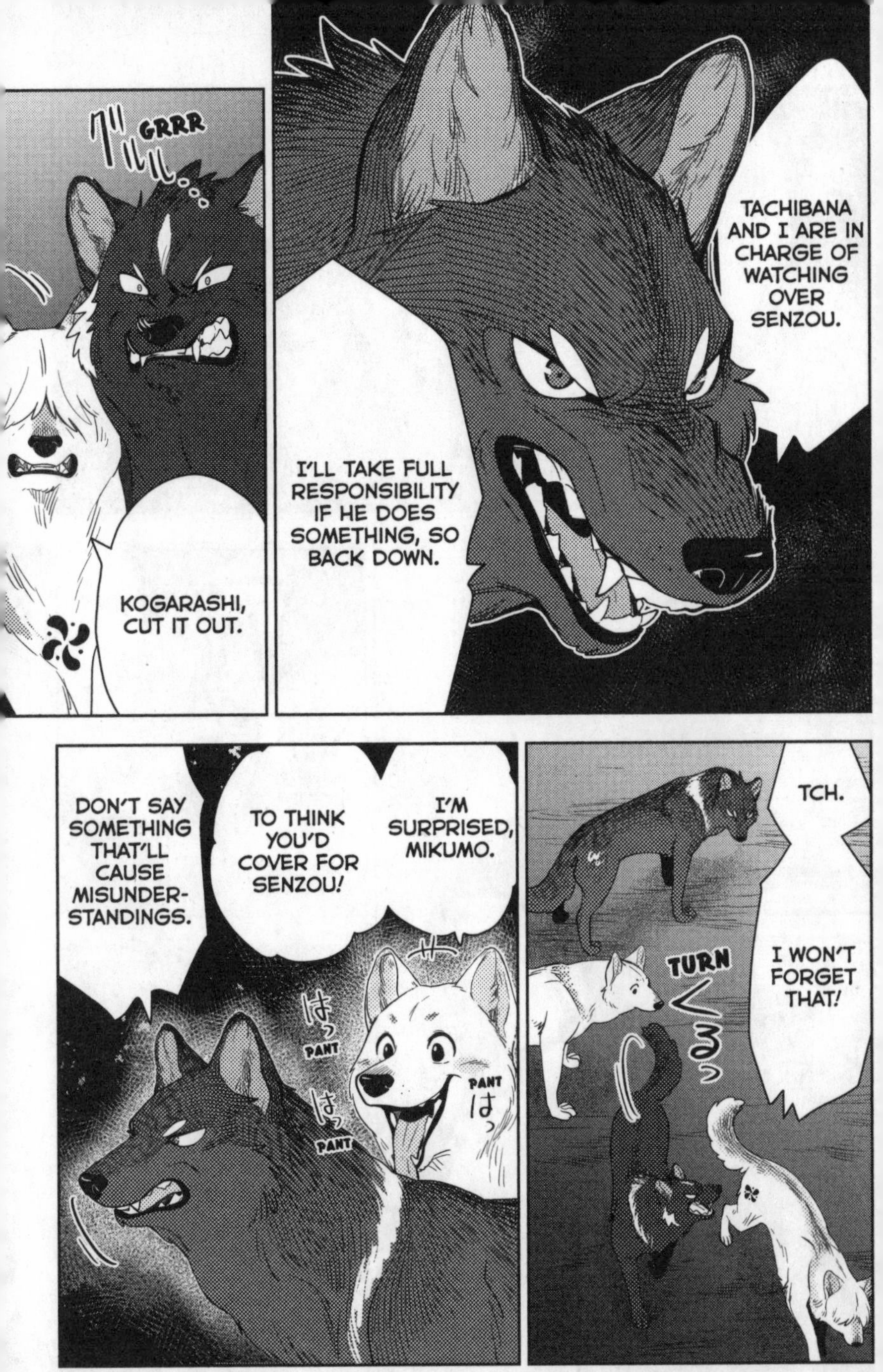
TACHIBANA AND I ARE IN CHARGE OF WATCHING OVER SENZOU.
I'LL TAKE FULL RESPONSIBILITY IF HE DOES SOMETHING, SO BACK DOWN.
グルル GRRR
KOGARASHI, CUT IT OUT.
TCH.
I WON'T FORGET THAT!
くるっ TURN
I'M SURPRISED, MIKUMO.
TO THINK YOU'D COVER FOR SENZOU!
DON'T SAY SOMETHING THAT'LL CAUSE MISUNDER-STANDINGS.
はっ PANT
はっ PANT
はっ PANT

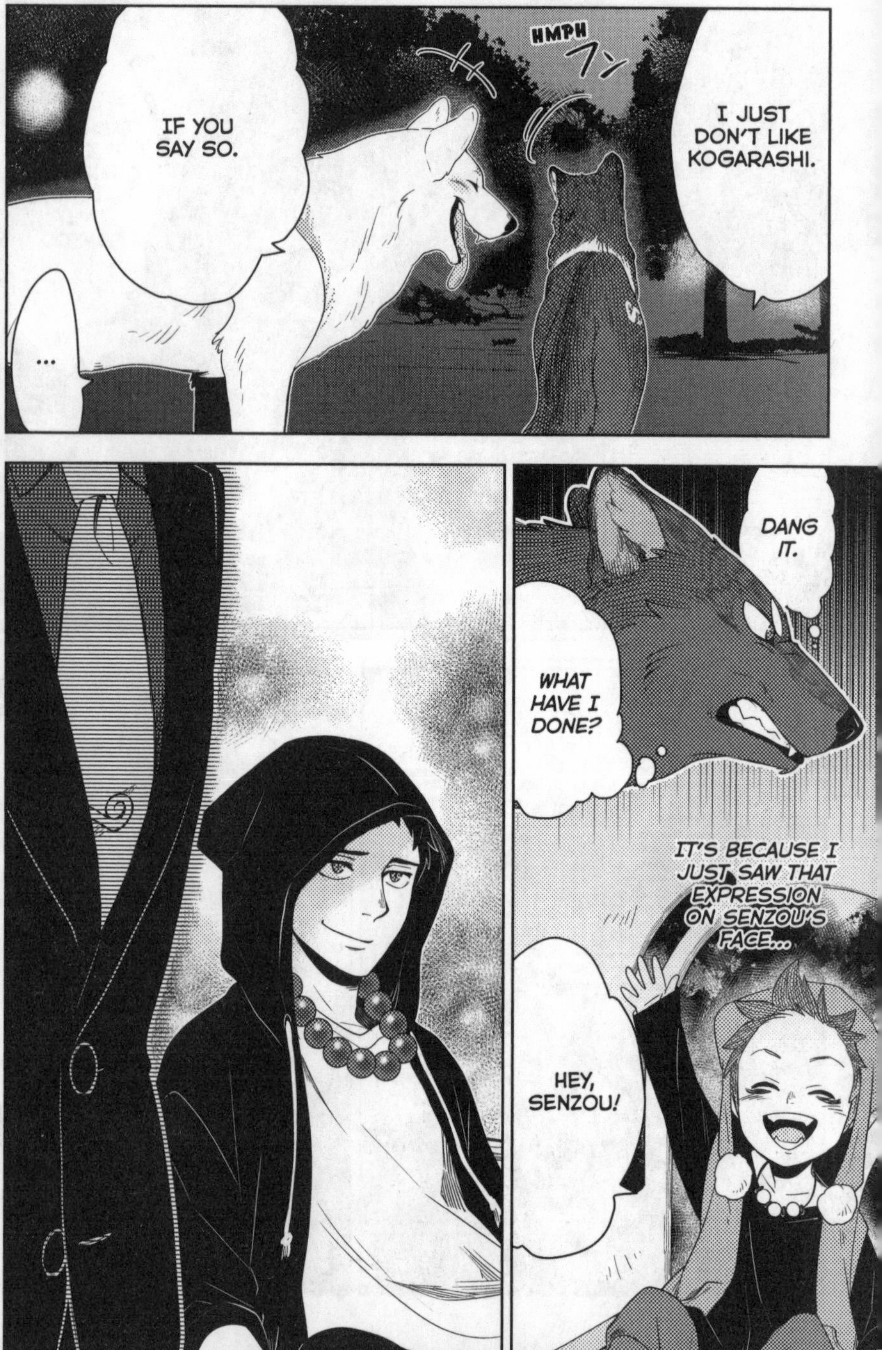
HMPH
フン
I JUST DON'T LIKE KOGARASHI.
IF YOU SAY SO.
...
DANG IT.
WHAT HAVE I DONE?
IT'S BECAUSE I JUST SAW THAT EXPRESSION ON SENZOU'S FACE...
HEY, SENZOU!

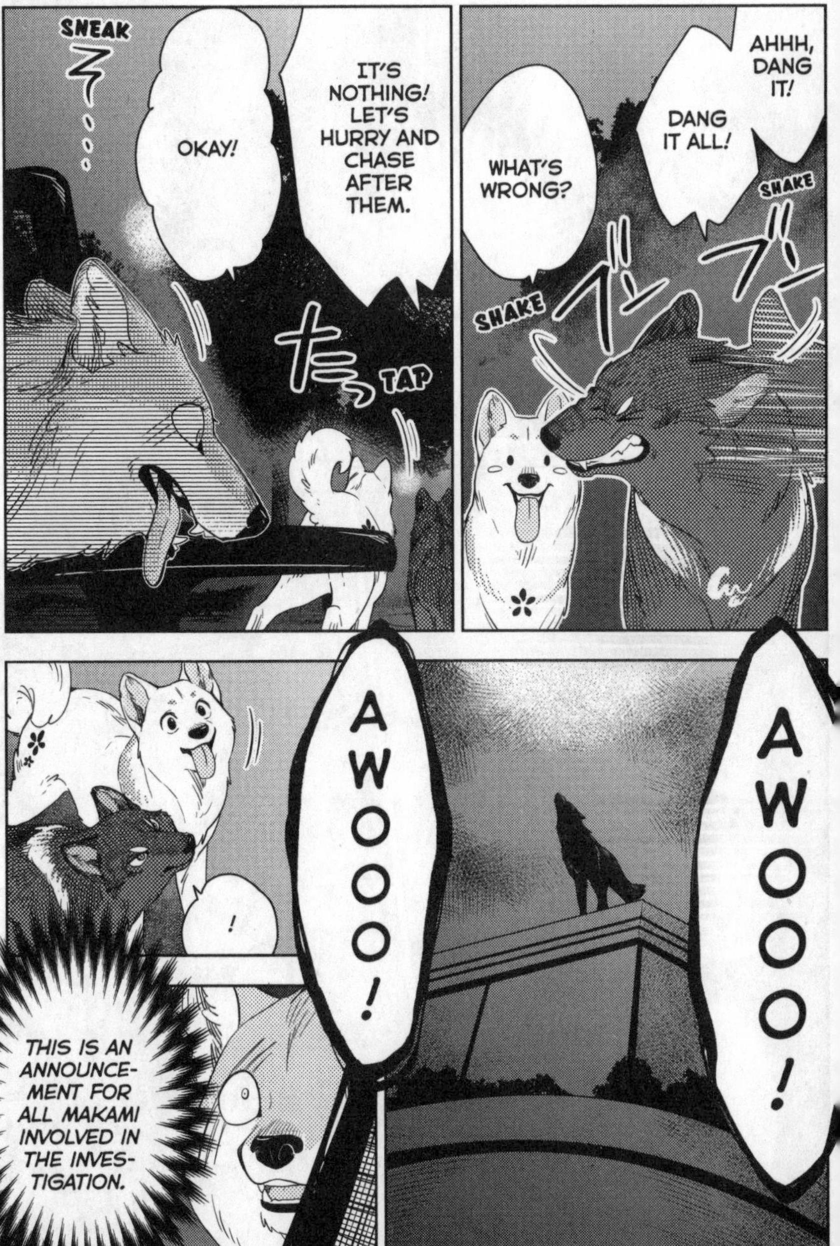
AHHH, DANG IT!
DANG IT ALL!
WHAT'S WRONG?
SHAKE
SHAKE
IT'S NOTHING! LET'S HURRY AND CHASE AFTER THEM.
OKAY!
SNEAK
TAP
AWOOO!
AWOOO!
!
THIS IS AN ANNOUNCE-MENT FOR ALL MAKAMI INVOLVED IN THE INVES-TIGATION.

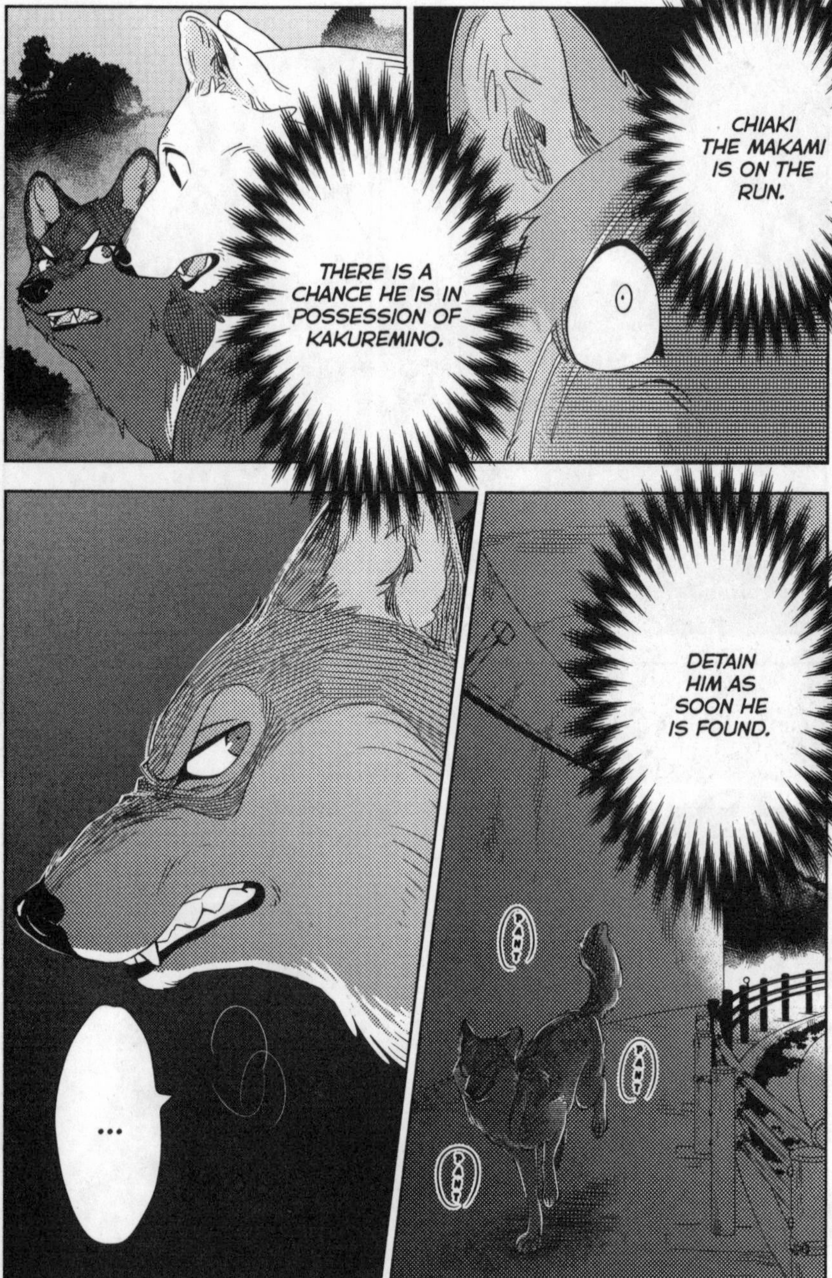
CHIAKI THE MAKAMI IS ON THE RUN.
THERE IS A CHANCE HE IS IN POSSESSION OF KAKUREMINO.
DETAIN HIM AS SOON HE IS FOUND.
PANT
PANT
PANT
...

Chapter 15

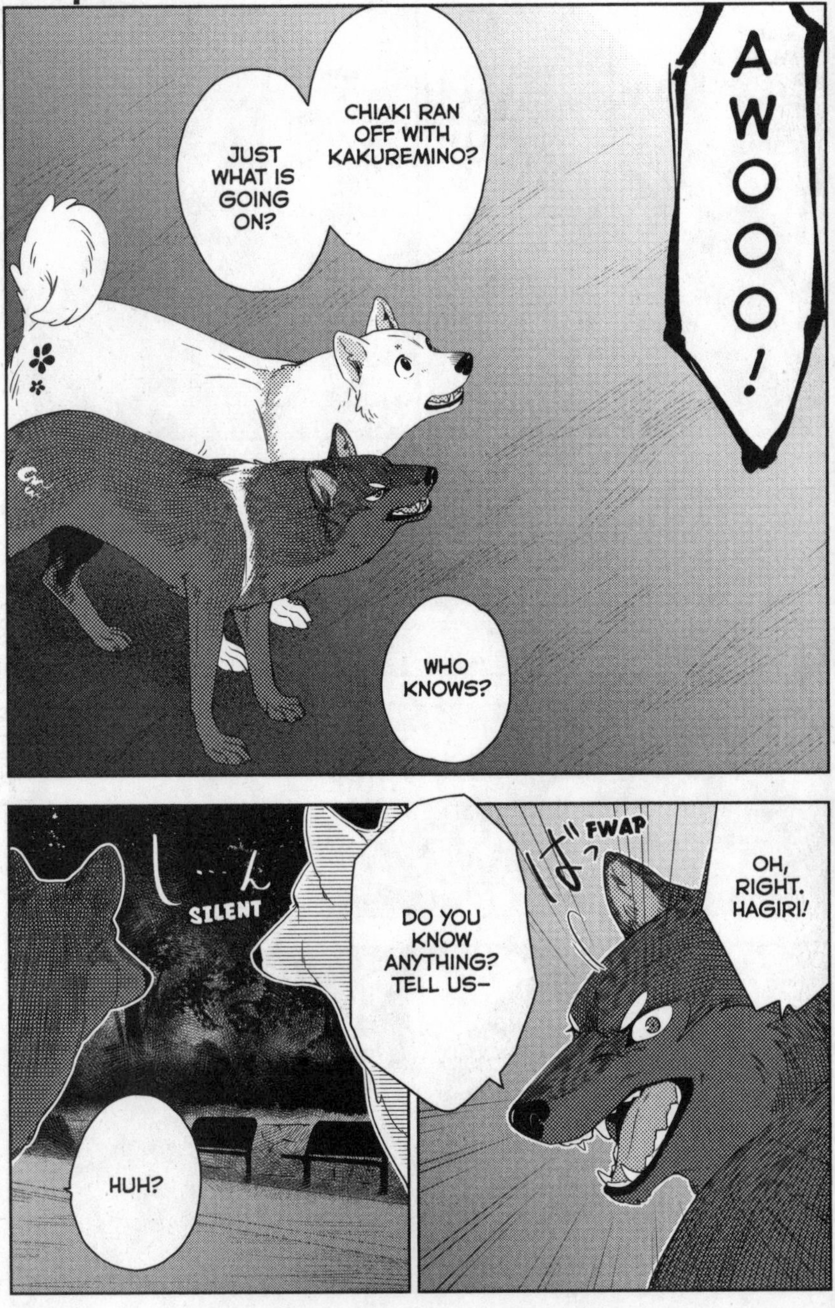

AWOOO!
CHIAKI RAN OFF WITH KAKUREMINO?
JUST WHAT IS GOING ON?
WHO KNOWS?
FWAP
OH, RIGHT. HAGIRI!
DO YOU KNOW ANYTHING? TELL US–
SILENT
HUH?

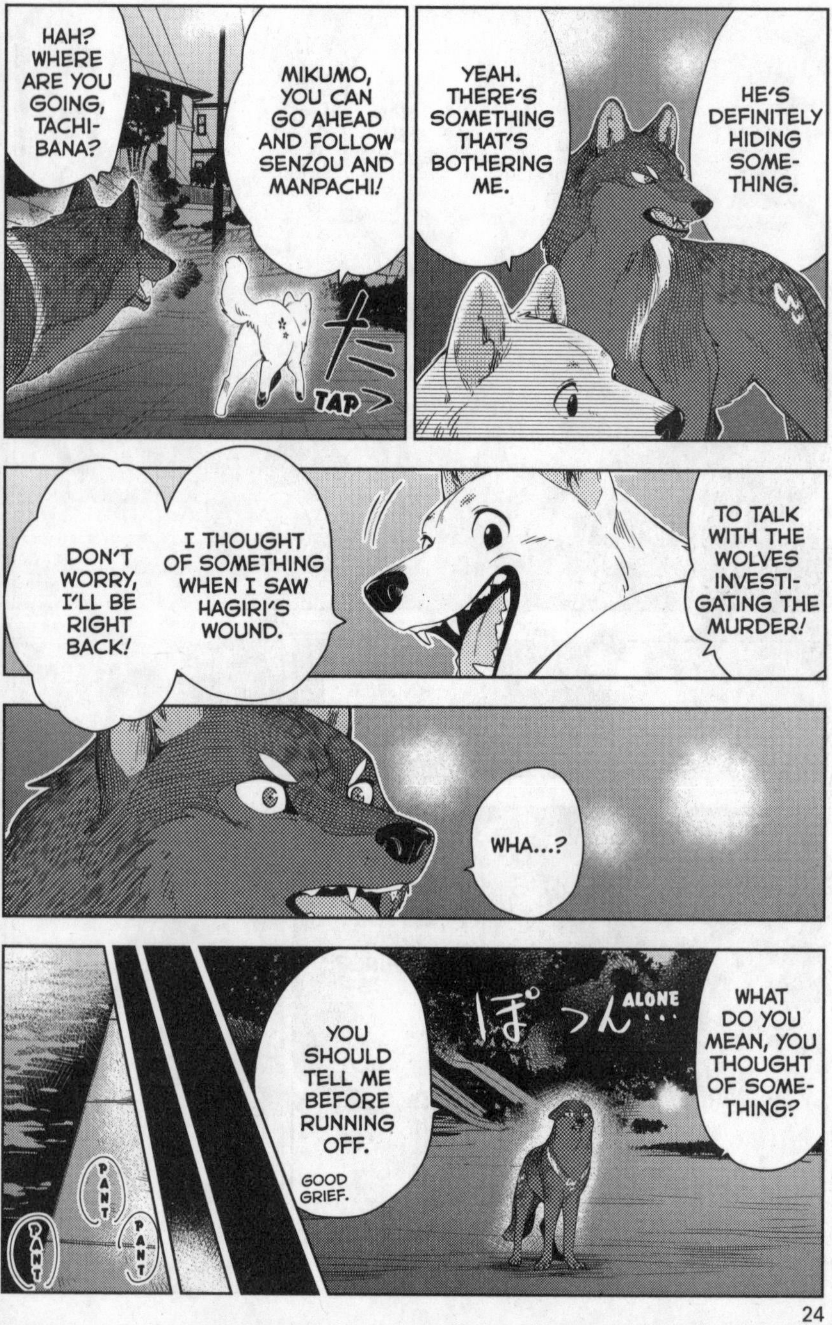
HE'S DEFINITELY HIDING SOMETHING.
YEAH. THERE'S SOMETHING THAT'S BOTHERING ME.
MIKUMO, YOU CAN GO AHEAD AND FOLLOW SENZOU AND MANPACHI!
HAH? WHERE ARE YOU GOING, TACHIBANA?
たっ
TAP
TO TALK WITH THE WOLVES INVESTIGATING THE MURDER!
I THOUGHT OF SOMETHING WHEN I SAW HAGIRI'S WOUND.
DON'T WORRY, I'LL BE RIGHT BACK!
WHA...?
WHAT DO YOU MEAN, YOU THOUGHT OF SOMETHING?
ぽつん
ALONE...
YOU SHOULD TELL ME BEFORE RUNNING OFF.
GOOD GRIEF.
PANT
PANT
PANT

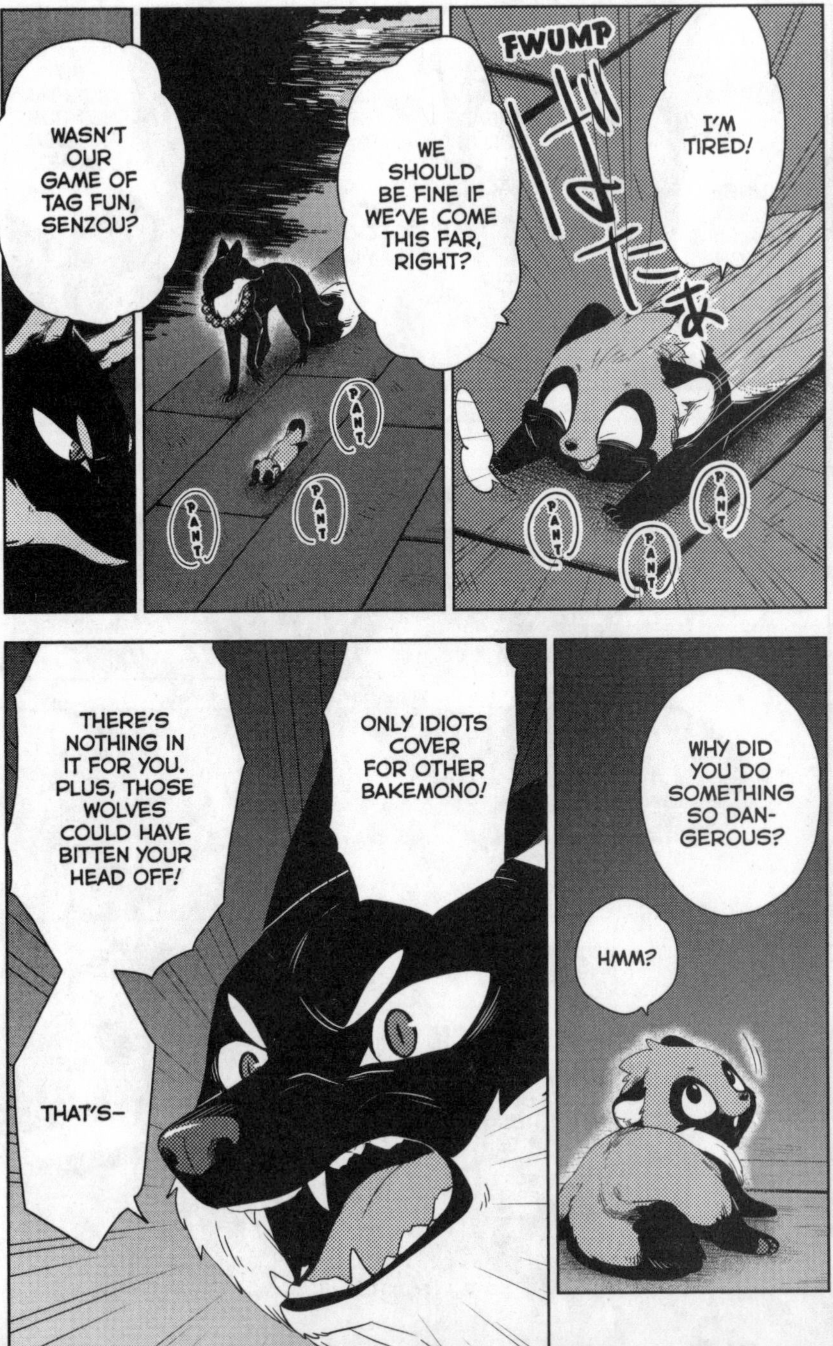
FWUMP
I'M TIRED!
PANT
PANT
PANT
WE SHOULD BE FINE IF WE'VE COME THIS FAR, RIGHT?
PANT
PANT
PANT
WASN'T OUR GAME OF TAG FUN, SENZOU?
WHY DID YOU DO SOMETHING SO DAN-GEROUS?
HMM?
ONLY IDIOTS COVER FOR OTHER BAKEMONO!
THERE'S NOTHING IN IT FOR YOU. PLUS, THOSE WOLVES COULD HAVE BITTEN YOUR HEAD OFF!
THAT'S—

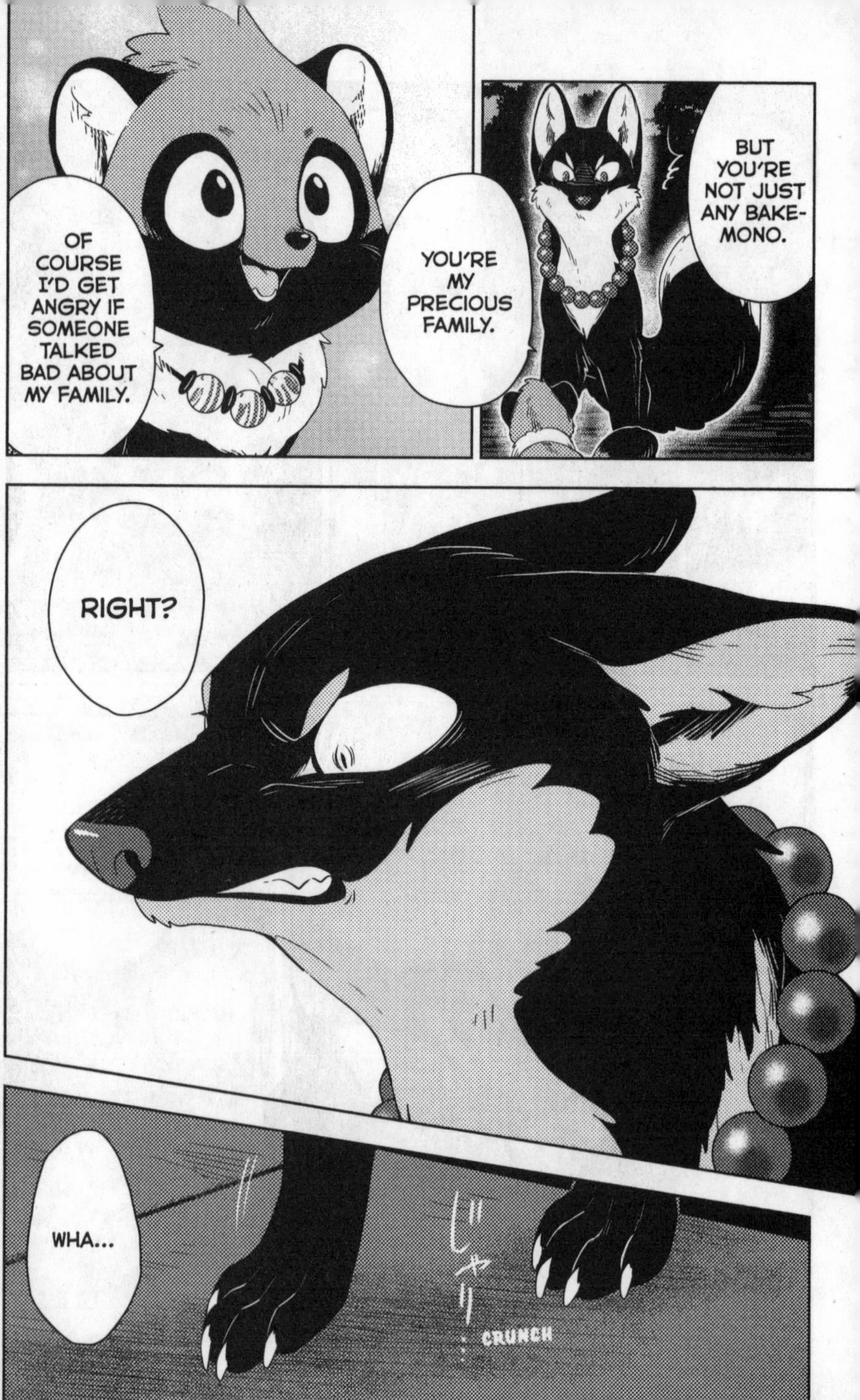
BUT YOU'RE NOT JUST ANY BAKE-MONO.
YOU'RE MY PRECIOUS FAMILY.
OF COURSE I'D GET ANGRY IF SOMEONE TALKED BAD ABOUT MY FAMILY.
RIGHT?
WHA...
CRUNCH

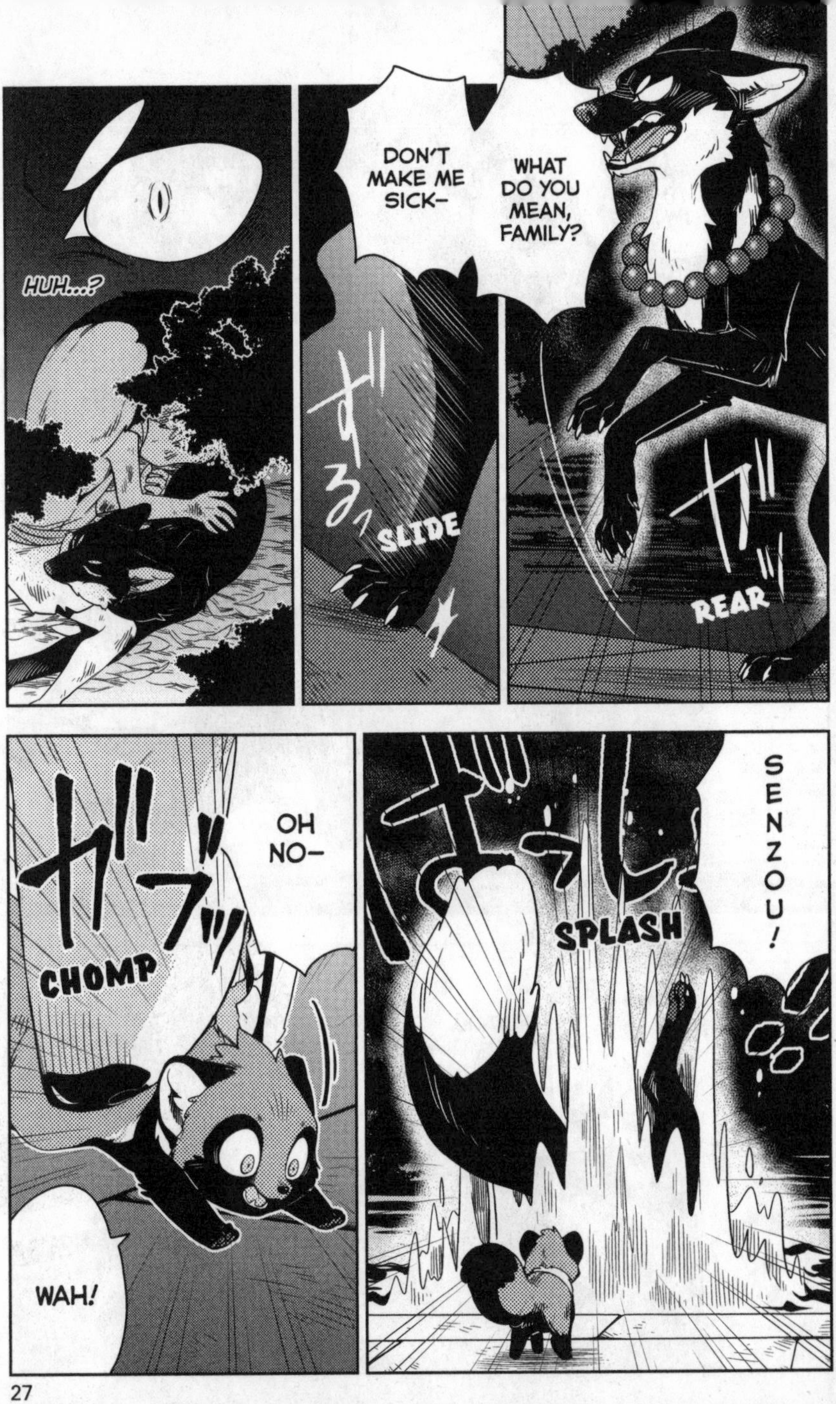
WHAT DO YOU MEAN, FAMILY?
DON'T MAKE ME SICK–
REAR
SLIDE
HUH...?
SENZOU!
SPLASH
OH NO–
CHOMP
WAH!

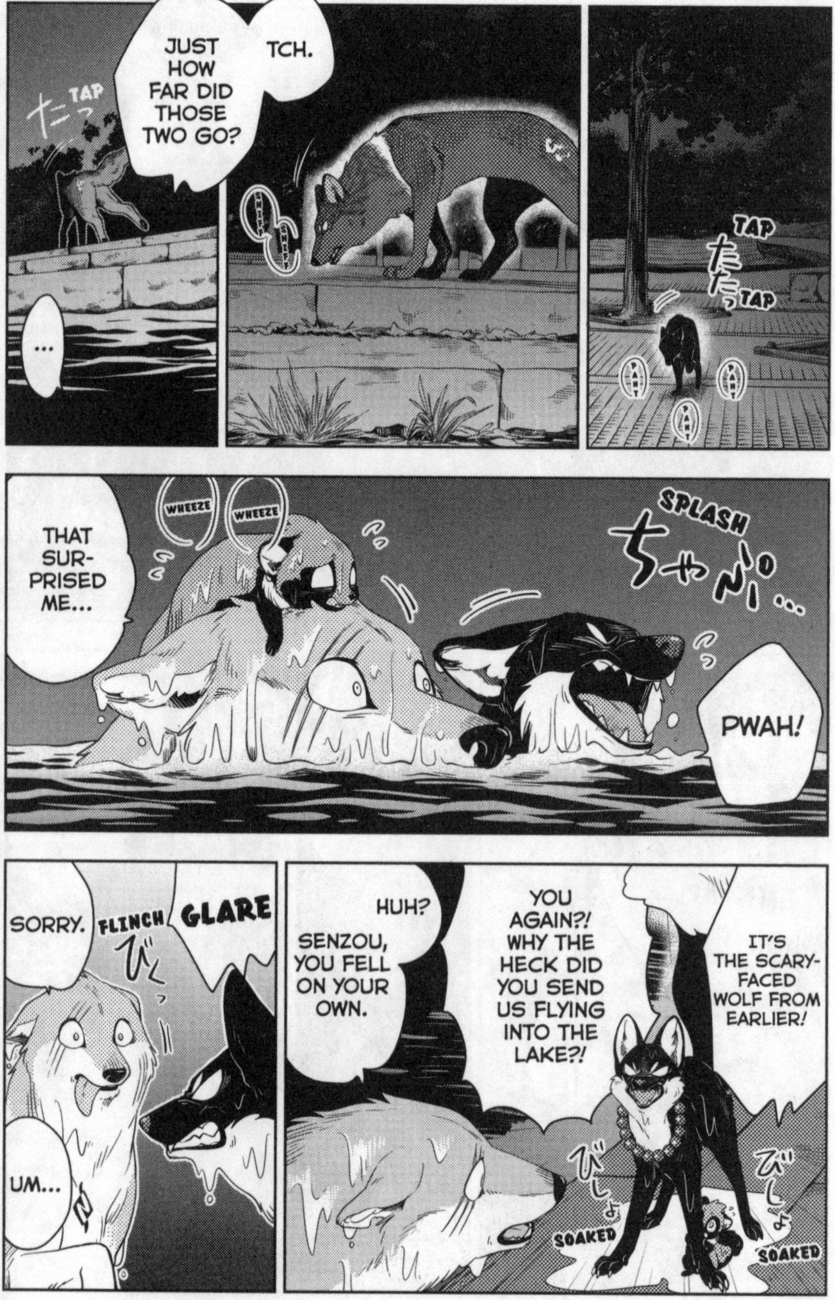
TAP
TAP
PANT
PANT
PANT
TCH.
SNIFF
SNIFF
JUST HOW FAR DID THOSE TWO GO?
TAP
...
SPLASH
PWAH!
WHEEZE
WHEEZE
THAT SUR-PRISED ME...
IT'S THE SCARY-FACED WOLF FROM EARLIER!
YOU AGAIN?! WHY THE HECK DID YOU SEND US FLYING INTO THE LAKE?!
HUH?
SENZOU, YOU FELL ON YOUR OWN.
SOAKED
SOAKED
GLARE
FLINCH
SORRY.
UM...

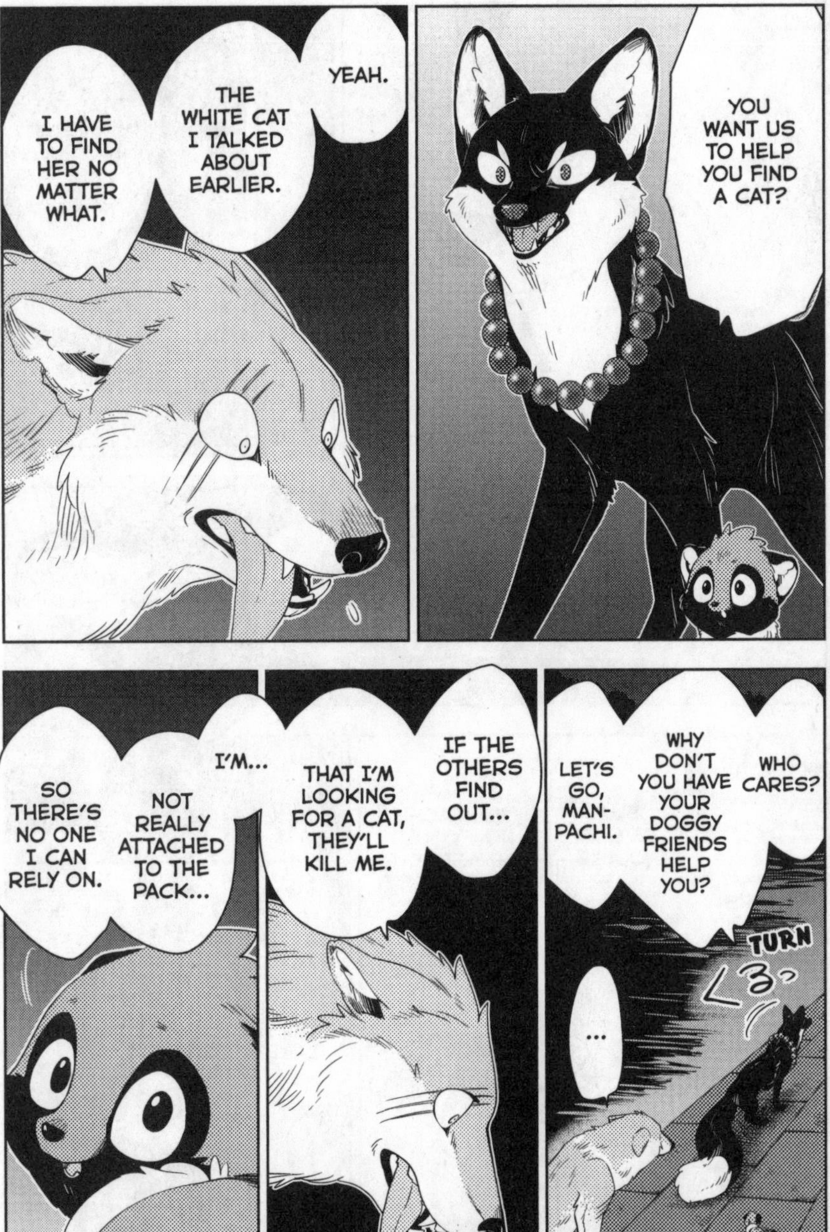
YOU WANT US TO HELP YOU FIND A CAT?
YEAH.
THE WHITE CAT I TALKED ABOUT EARLIER.
I HAVE TO FIND HER NO MATTER WHAT.
WHO CARES?
WHY DON'T YOU HAVE YOUR DOGGY FRIENDS HELP YOU?
LET'S GO, MAN-PACHI.
TURN
くるっ
...
IF THE OTHERS FIND OUT...
THAT I'M LOOKING FOR A CAT, THEY'LL KILL ME.
I'M...
NOT REALLY ATTACHED TO THE PACK...
SO THERE'S NO ONE I CAN RELY ON.

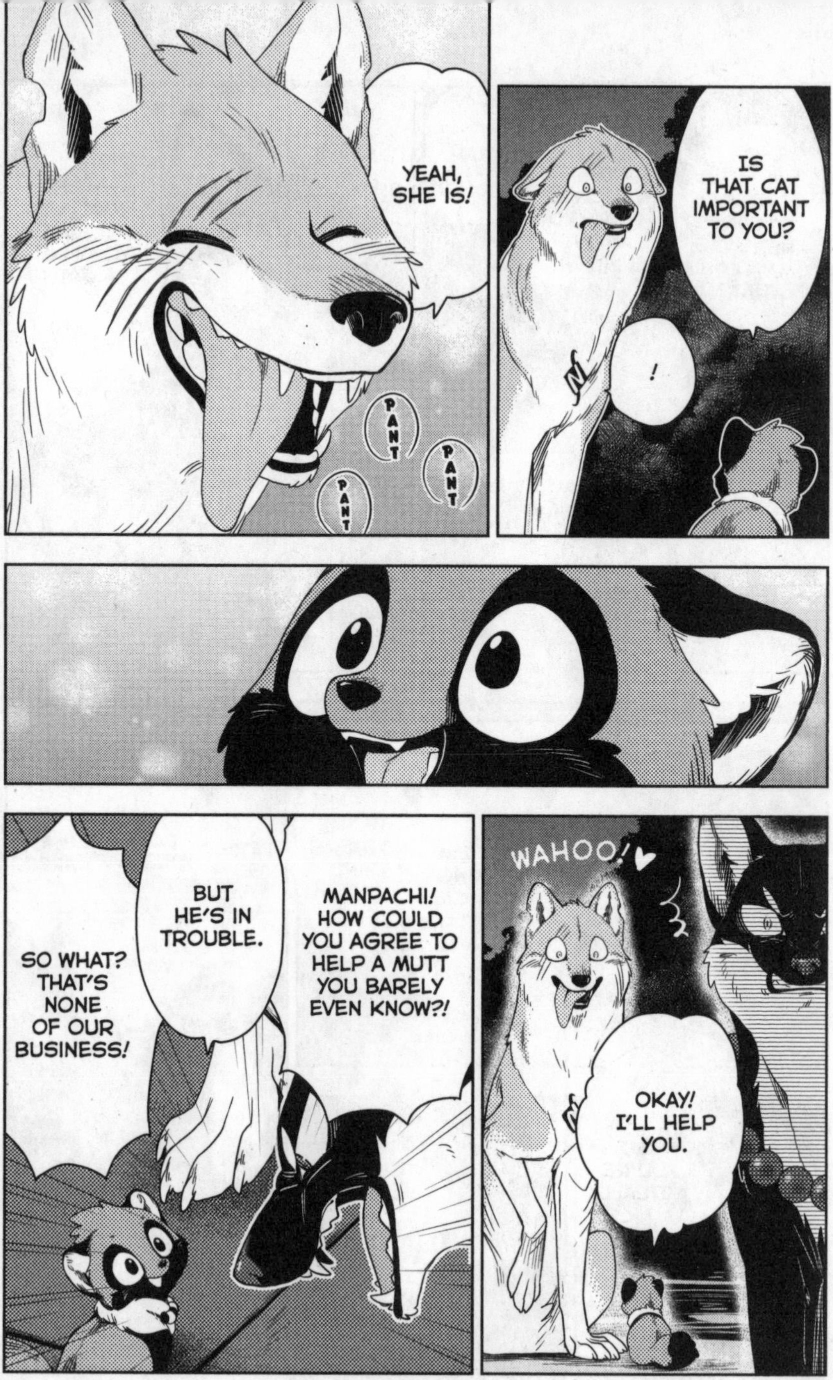
IS THAT CAT IMPORTANT TO YOU?
!
YEAH, SHE IS!
PANT
PANT
PANT
WAHOO! ♥
OKAY! I'LL HELP YOU.
MANPACHI! HOW COULD YOU AGREE TO HELP A MUTT YOU BARELY EVEN KNOW?!
BUT HE'S IN TROUBLE.
SO WHAT? THAT'S NONE OF OUR BUSINESS!

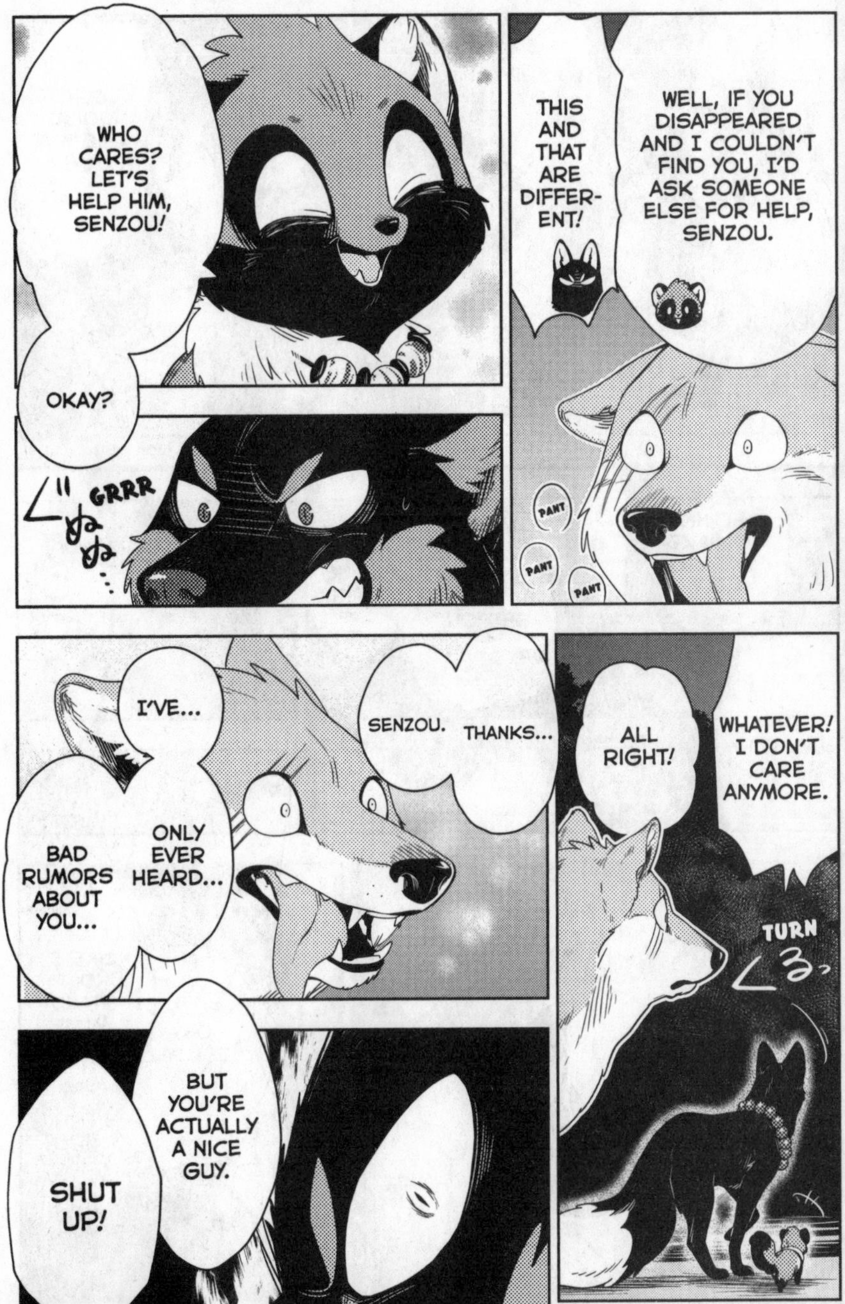
WELL, IF YOU DISAPPEARED AND I COULDN'T FIND YOU, I'D ASK SOMEONE ELSE FOR HELP, SENZOU.
THIS AND THAT ARE DIFFER-ENT!
PANT
PANT
PANT
WHO CARES? LET'S HELP HIM, SENZOU!
OKAY?
GRRR
ぐぬぬ…
WHATEVER! I DON'T CARE ANYMORE.
ALL RIGHT!
TURN
くるっ
THANKS...
SENZOU.
I'VE...
ONLY EVER HEARD...
BAD RUMORS ABOUT YOU...
BUT YOU'RE ACTUALLY A NICE GUY.
SHUT UP!

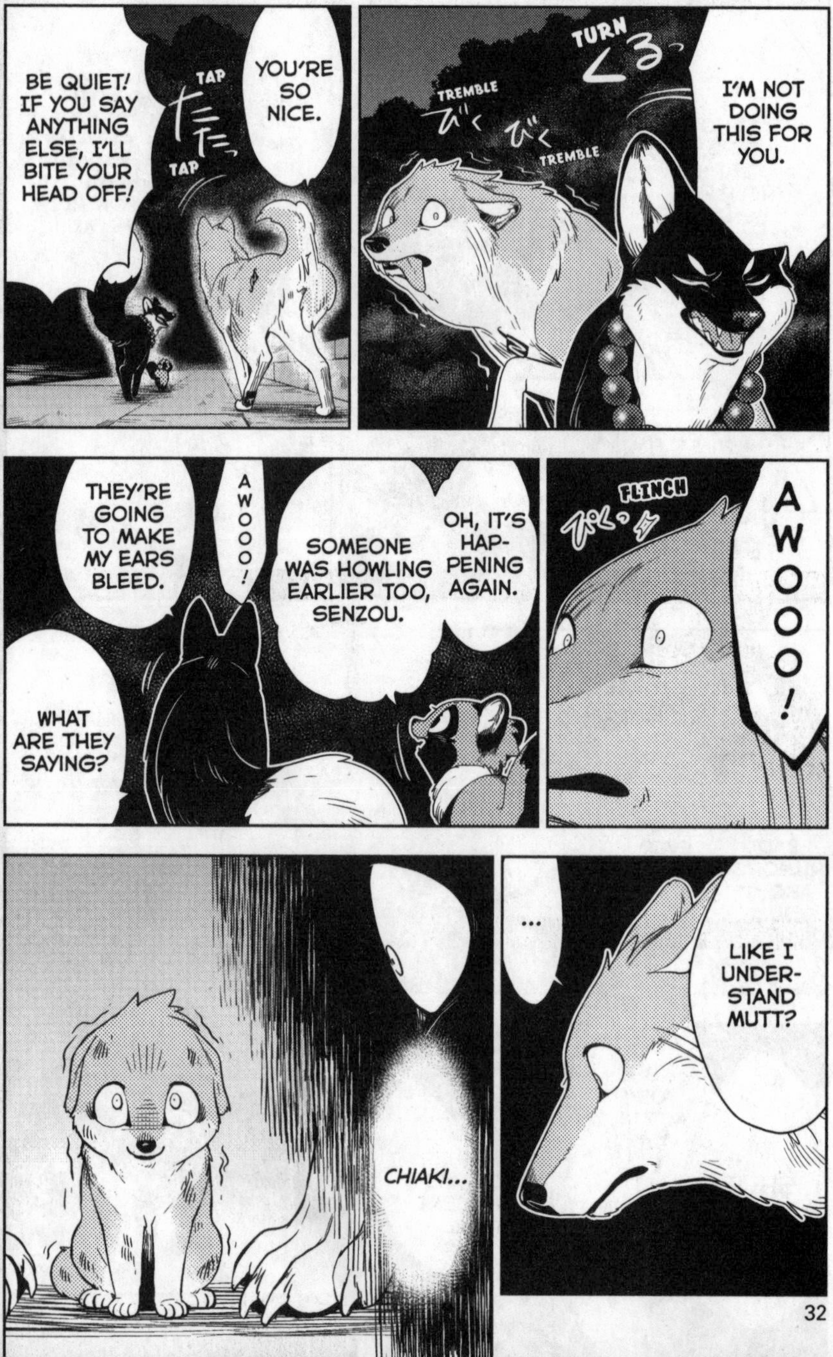
TURN
TREMBLE
TREMBLE
I'M NOT DOING THIS FOR YOU.
YOU'RE SO NICE.
TAP
TAP
BE QUIET! IF YOU SAY ANYTHING ELSE, I'LL BITE YOUR HEAD OFF!
FLINCH
AWOOOO!
OH, IT'S HAP-PENING AGAIN.
SOMEONE WAS HOWLING EARLIER TOO, SENZOU.
AWOOOO!
THEY'RE GOING TO MAKE MY EARS BLEED.
WHAT ARE THEY SAYING?
...
LIKE I UNDER-STAND MUTT?
CHIAKI...

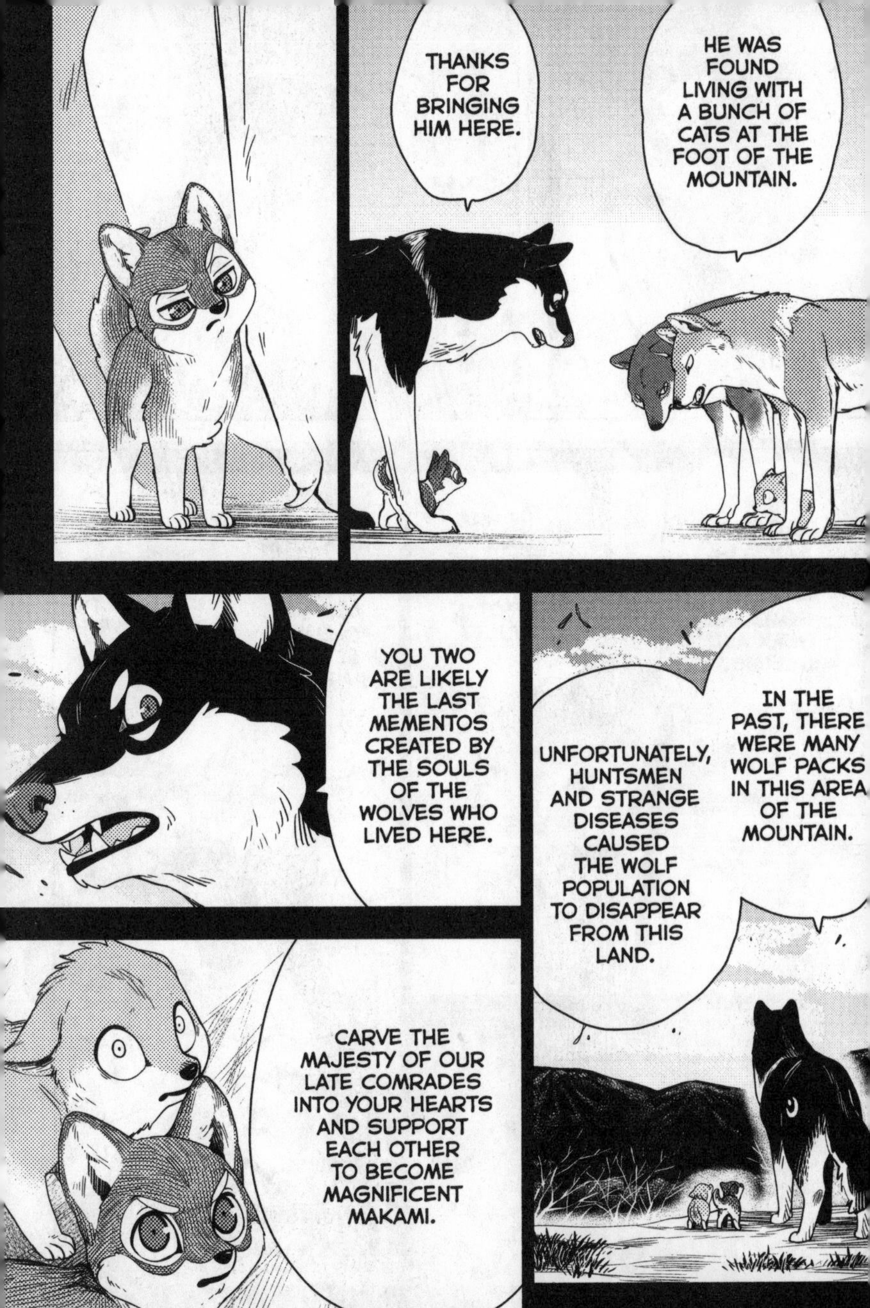
HE WAS FOUND LIVING WITH A BUNCH OF CATS AT THE FOOT OF THE MOUNTAIN.
THANKS FOR BRINGING HIM HERE.
IN THE PAST, THERE WERE MANY WOLF PACKS IN THIS AREA OF THE MOUNTAIN.
UNFORTUNATELY, HUNTSMEN AND STRANGE DISEASES CAUSED THE WOLF POPULATION TO DISAPPEAR FROM THIS LAND.
YOU TWO ARE LIKELY THE LAST MEMENTOS CREATED BY THE SOULS OF THE WOLVES WHO LIVED HERE.
CARVE THE MAJESTY OF OUR LATE COMRADES INTO YOUR HEARTS AND SUPPORT EACH OTHER TO BECOME MAGNIFICENT MAKAMI.

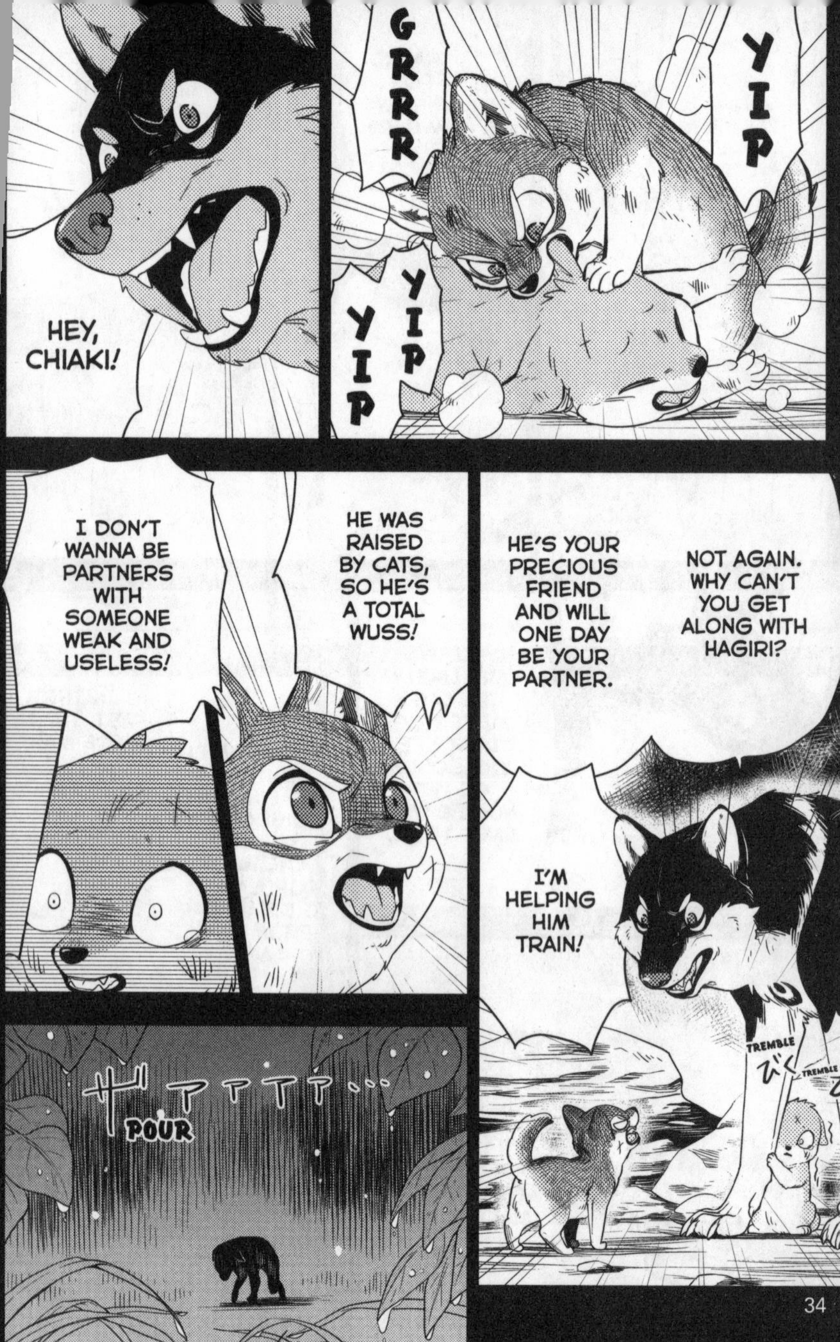

YIP
GRRR
YIP YIP
YIP
HEY, CHIAKI!
NOT AGAIN. WHY CAN'T YOU GET ALONG WITH HAGIRI?
HE'S YOUR PRECIOUS FRIEND AND WILL ONE DAY BE YOUR PARTNER.
I'M HELPING HIM TRAIN!
TREMBLE
びく
TREMBLE
びく
HE WAS RAISED BY CATS, SO HE'S A TOTAL WUSS!
I DON'T WANNA BE PARTNERS WITH SOMEONE WEAK AND USELESS!
POUR

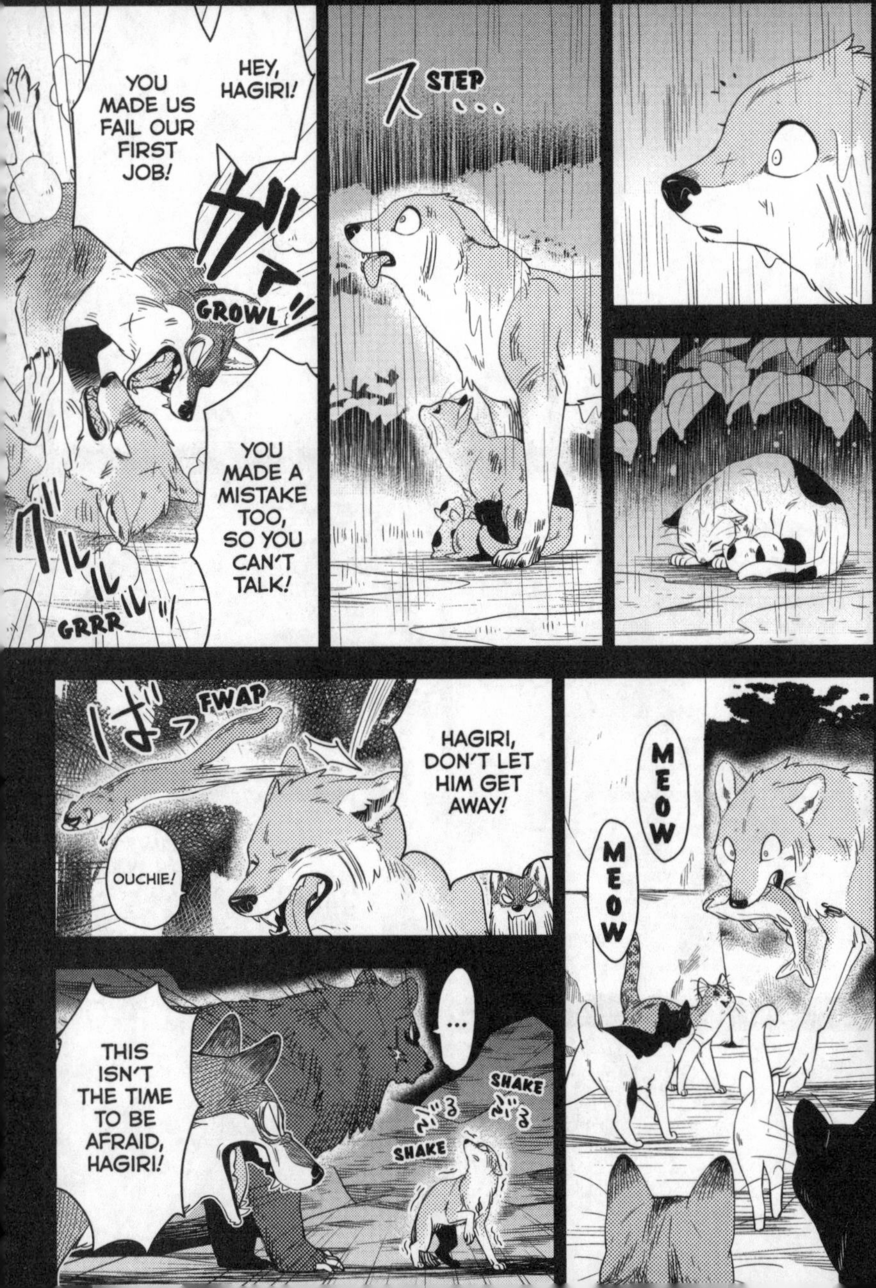
STEP . . .
HEY, HAGIRI!
YOU MADE US FAIL OUR FIRST JOB!
GROWL
YOU MADE A MISTAKE TOO, SO YOU CAN'T TALK!
GRRR
MEOW
MEOW
HAGIRI, DON'T LET HIM GET AWAY!
FWAP
OUCHIE!
...
SHAKE
SHAKE
THIS ISN'T THE TIME TO BE AFRAID, HAGIRI!

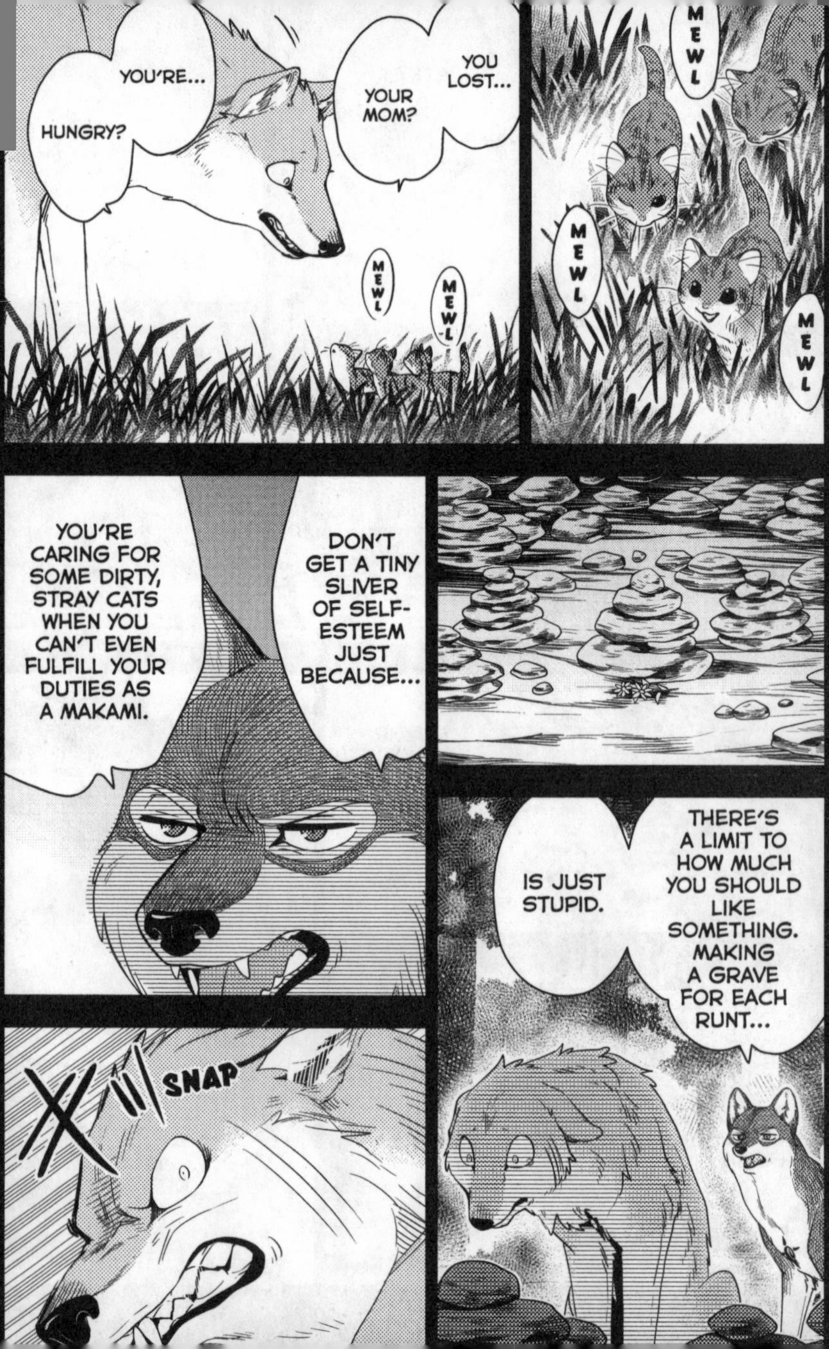
MEWL
MEWL
MEWL
YOU LOST...
YOUR MOM?
YOU'RE...
HUNGRY?
MEWL
MEWL
THERE'S A LIMIT TO HOW MUCH YOU SHOULD LIKE SOMETHING. MAKING A GRAVE FOR EACH RUNT...
IS JUST STUPID.
DON'T GET A TINY SLIVER OF SELF-ESTEEM JUST BECAUSE...
YOU'RE CARING FOR SOME DIRTY, STRAY CATS WHEN YOU CAN'T EVEN FULFILL YOUR DUTIES AS A MAKAMI.
SNAP

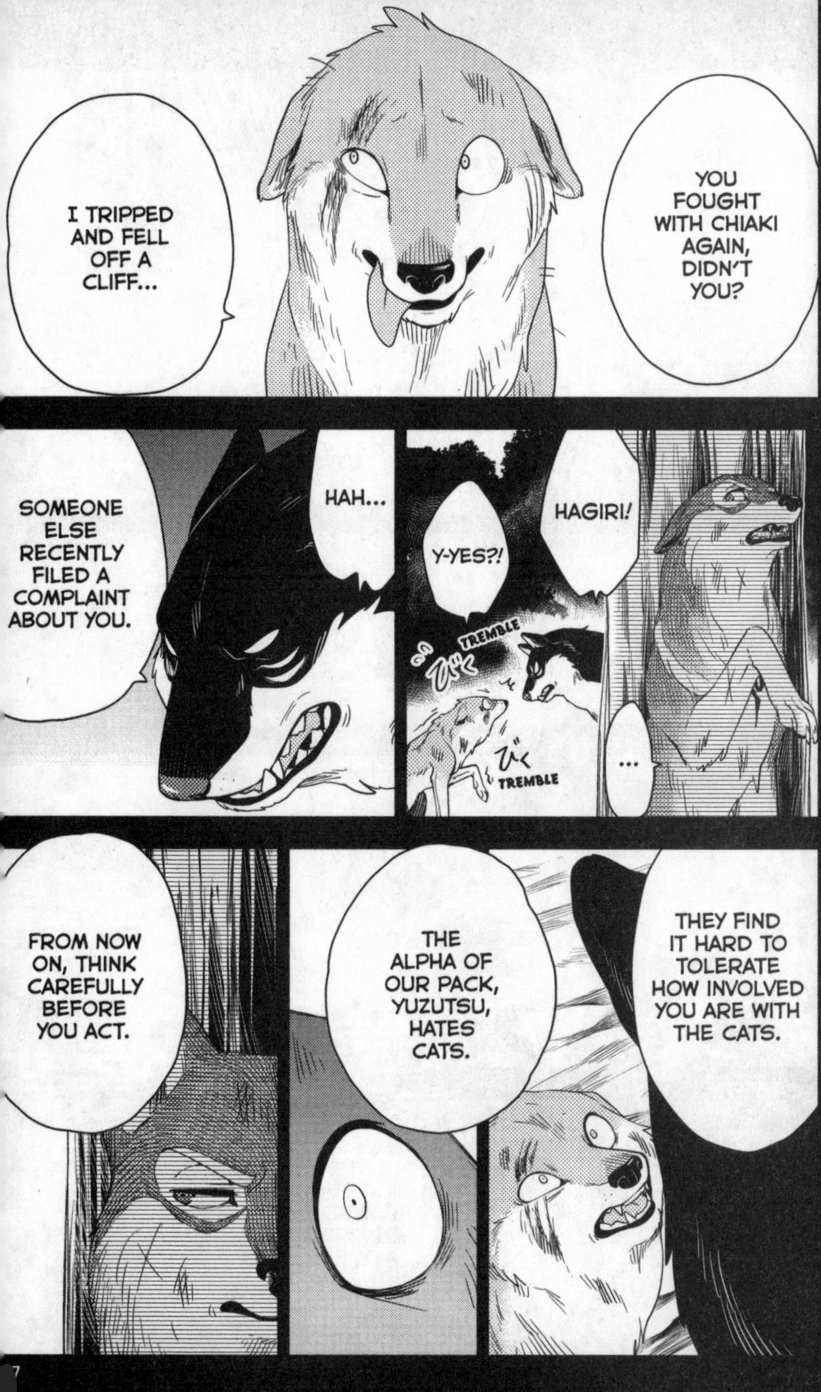
YOU FOUGHT WITH CHIAKI AGAIN, DIDN'T YOU?
I TRIPPED AND FELL OFF A CLIFF...
HAGIRI!
Y-YES?!
TREMBLE
びく
びく
TREMBLE
...
HAH...
SOMEONE ELSE RECENTLY FILED A COMPLAINT ABOUT YOU.
THEY FIND IT HARD TO TOLERATE HOW INVOLVED YOU ARE WITH THE CATS.
THE ALPHA OF OUR PACK, YUZUTSU, HATES CATS.
FROM NOW ON, THINK CAREFULLY BEFORE YOU ACT.

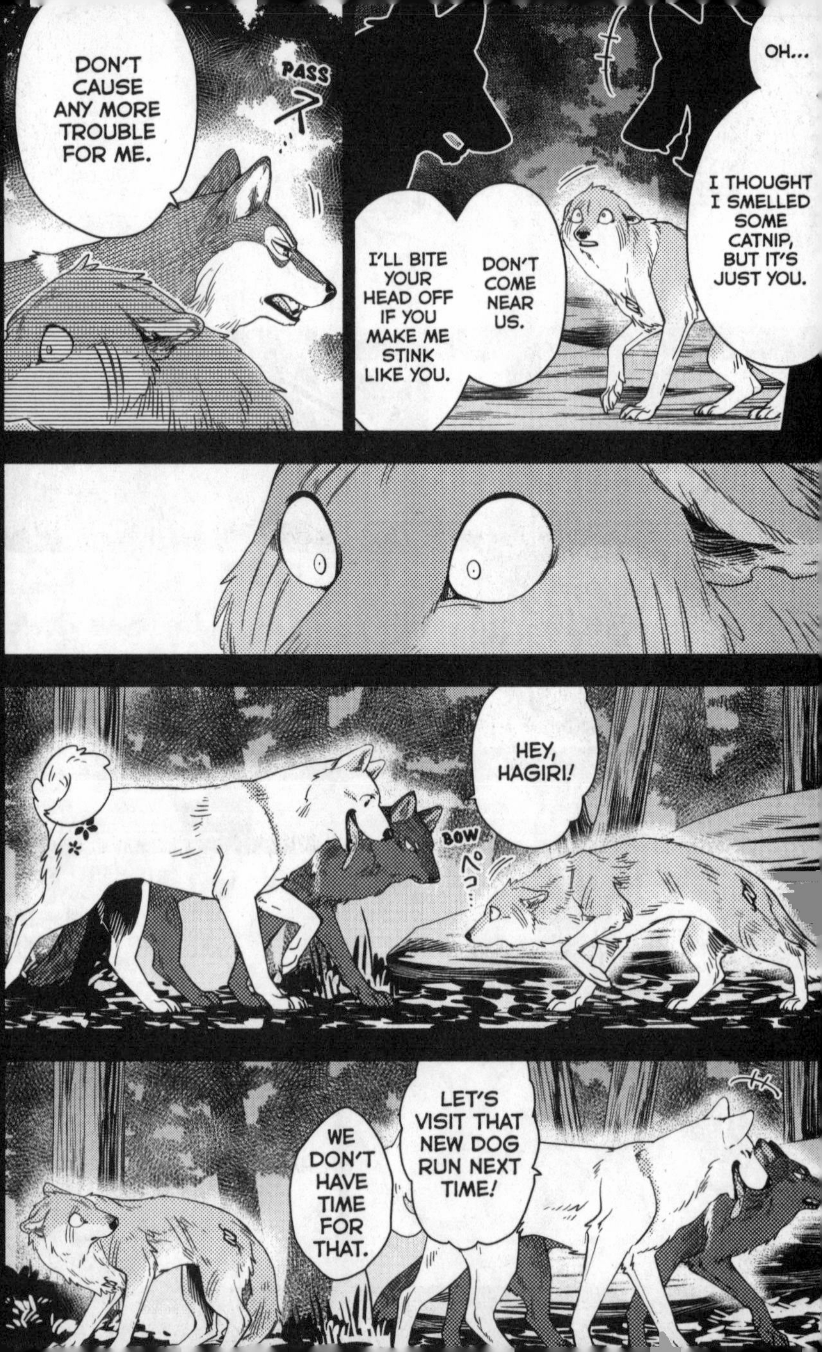
OH...
I THOUGHT I SMELLED SOME CATNIP, BUT IT'S JUST YOU.
DON'T COME NEAR US.
I'LL BITE YOUR HEAD OFF IF YOU MAKE ME STINK LIKE YOU.
PASS
DON'T CAUSE ANY MORE TROUBLE FOR ME.
HEY, HAGIRI!
BOW
LET'S VISIT THAT NEW DOG RUN NEXT TIME!
WE DON'T HAVE TIME FOR THAT.

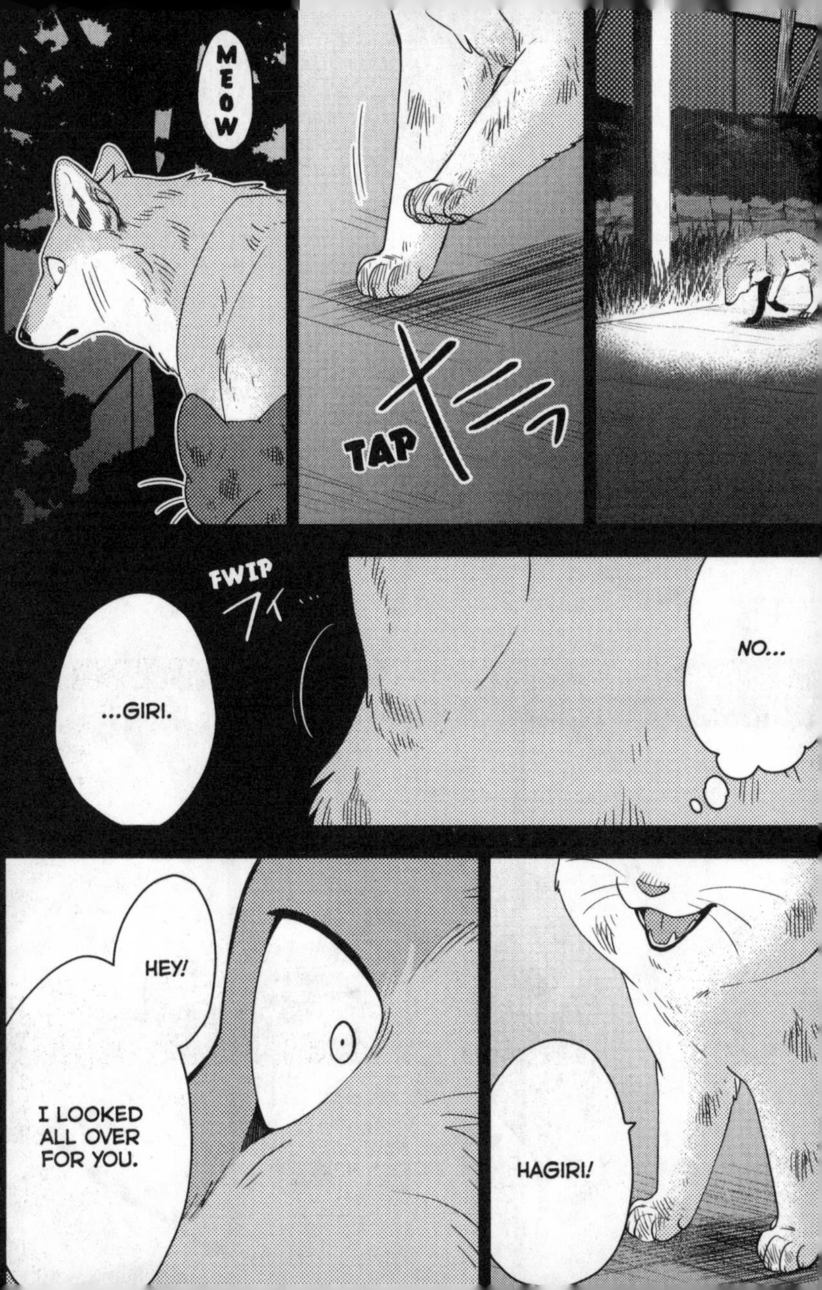
TAP
MEOW
NO...
FWIP
フィ...
...GIRI.
HAGIRI!
HEY!
I LOOKED ALL OVER FOR YOU.

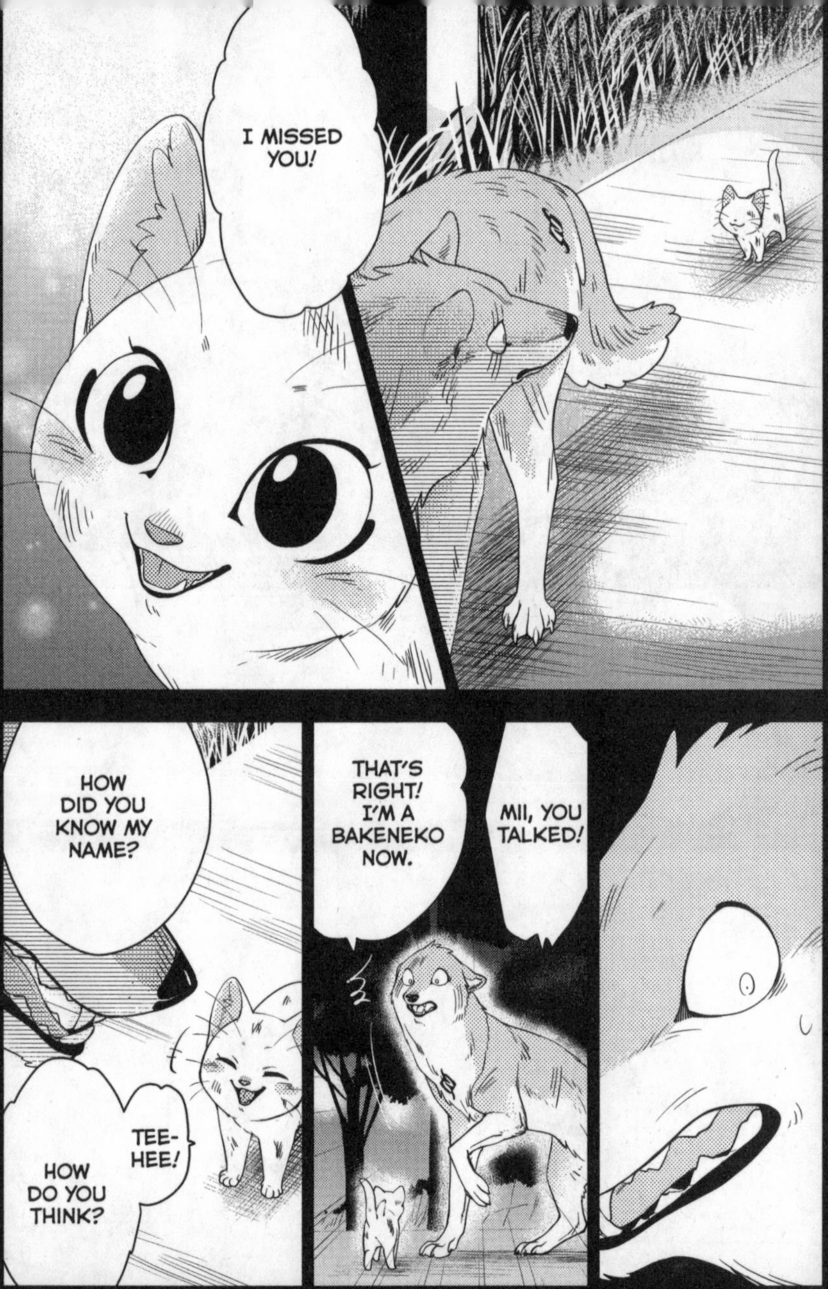
I MISSED YOU!
MII, YOU TALKED!
THAT'S RIGHT! I'M A BAKENEKO NOW.
HOW DID YOU KNOW MY NAME?
TEE-HEE!
HOW DO YOU THINK?

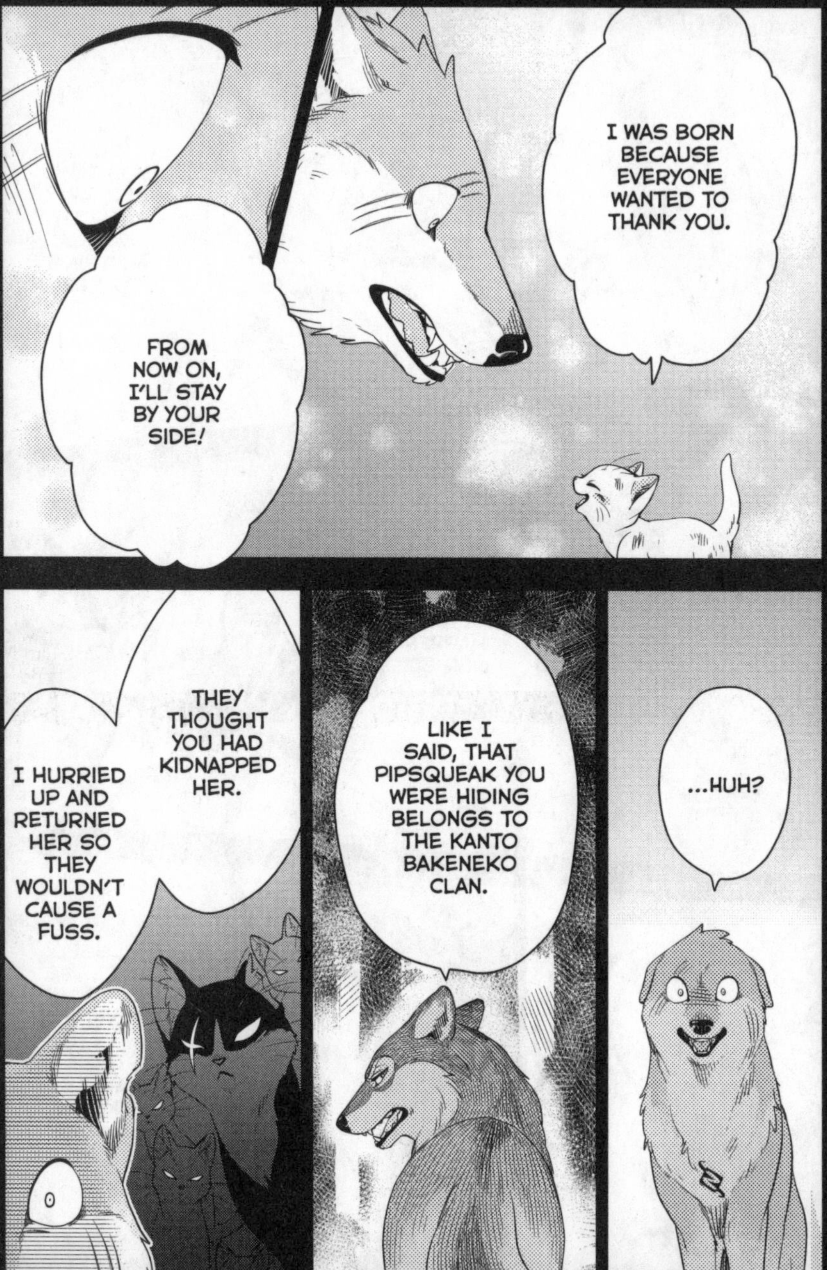
I WAS BORN BECAUSE EVERYONE WANTED TO THANK YOU.
FROM NOW ON, I'LL STAY BY YOUR SIDE!
...HUH?
LIKE I SAID, THAT PIPSQUEAK YOU WERE HIDING BELONGS TO THE KANTO BAKENEKO CLAN.
THEY THOUGHT YOU HAD KIDNAPPED HER.
I HURRIED UP AND RETURNED HER SO THEY WOULDN'T CAUSE A FUSS.

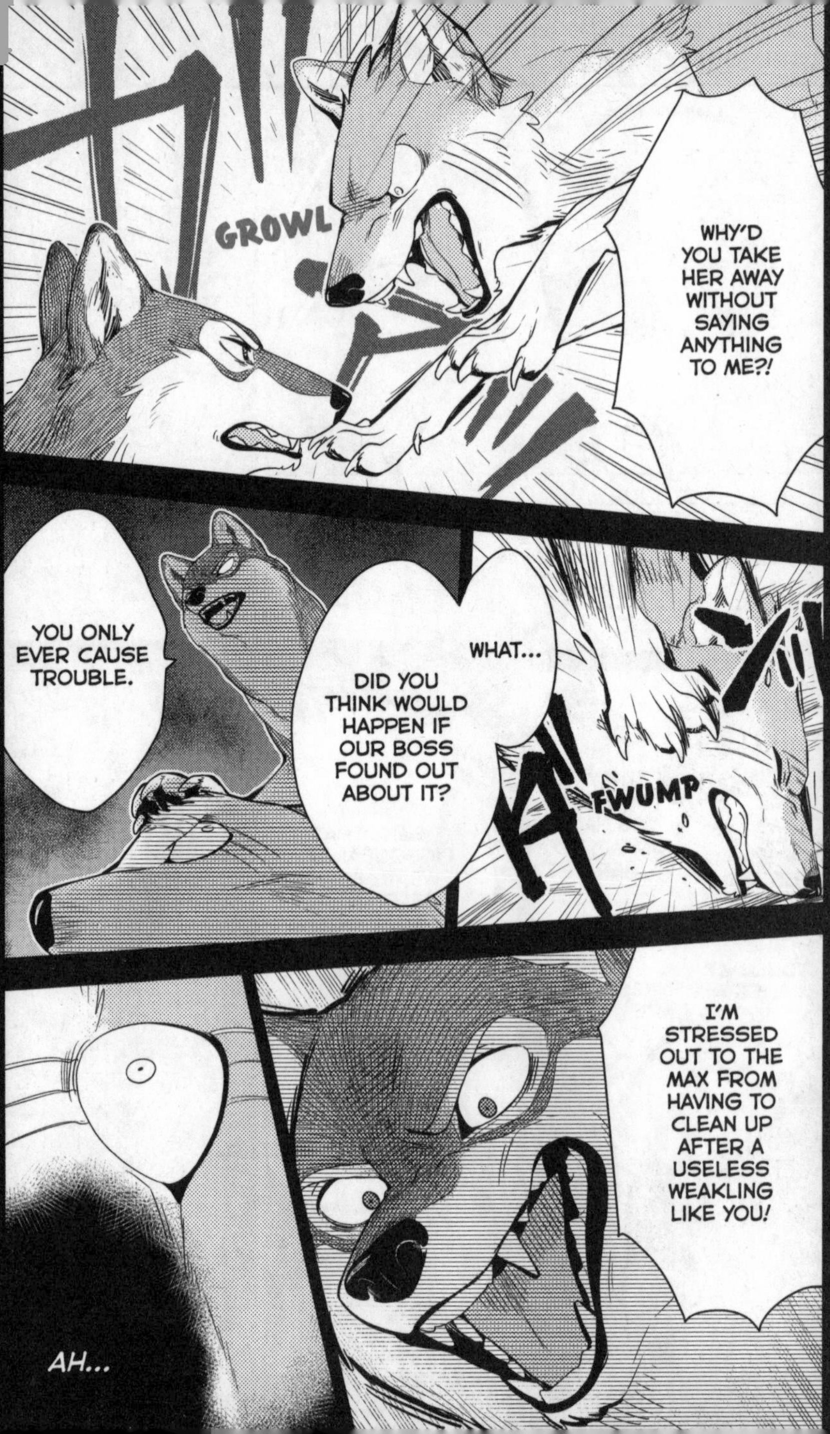
WHY'D YOU TAKE HER AWAY WITHOUT SAYING ANYTHING TO ME?!
GROWL
FWUMP
WHAT... DID YOU THINK WOULD HAPPEN IF OUR BOSS FOUND OUT ABOUT IT?
YOU ONLY EVER CAUSE TROUBLE.
I'M STRESSED OUT TO THE MAX FROM HAVING TO CLEAN UP AFTER A USELESS WEAKLING LIKE YOU!
AH...

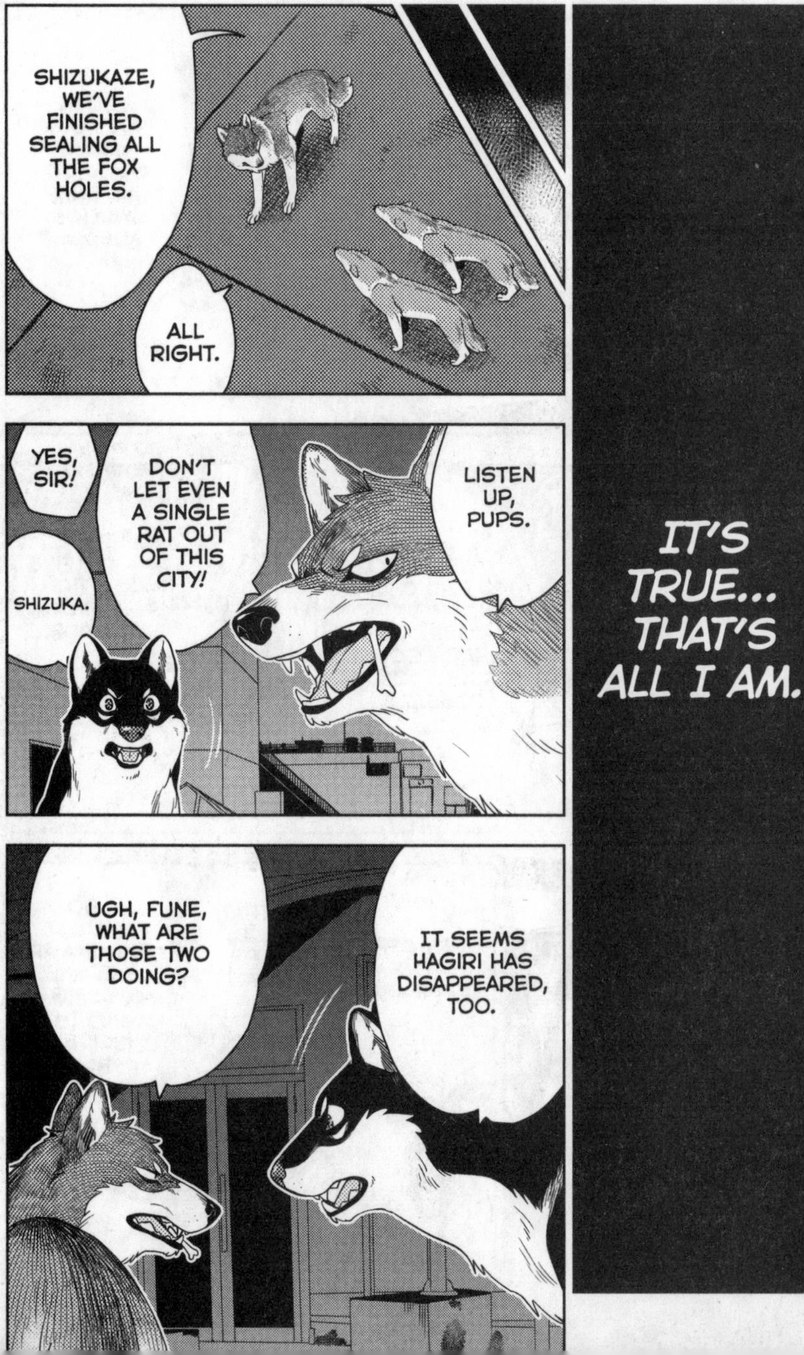
IT'S TRUE... THAT'S ALL I AM.
SHIZUKAZE, WE'VE FINISHED SEALING ALL THE FOX HOLES.
ALL RIGHT.
LISTEN UP, PUPS.
DON'T LET EVEN A SINGLE RAT OUT OF THIS CITY!
YES, SIR!
SHIZUKA.
IT SEEMS HAGIRI HAS DISAPPEARED, TOO.
UGH, FUNE, WHAT ARE THOSE TWO DOING?

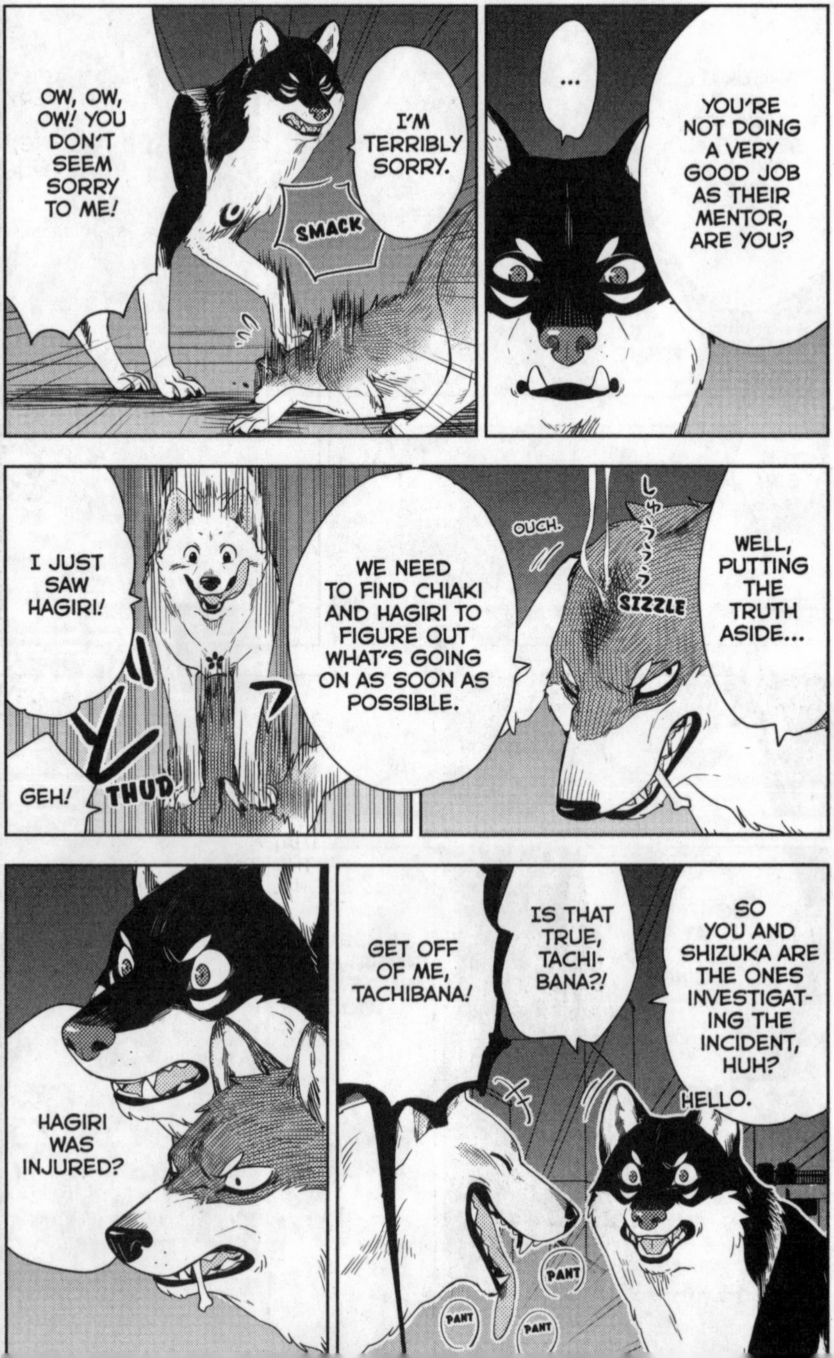
YOU'RE NOT DOING A VERY GOOD JOB AS THEIR MENTOR, ARE YOU?
...
I'M TERRIBLY SORRY.
SMACK
OW, OW, OW! YOU DON'T SEEM SORRY TO ME!
WELL, PUTTING THE TRUTH ASIDE...
しゅううう
SIZZLE
OUCH.
WE NEED TO FIND CHIAKI AND HAGIRI TO FIGURE OUT WHAT'S GOING ON AS SOON AS POSSIBLE.
I JUST SAW HAGIRI!
THUD
GEH!
SO YOU AND SHIZUKA ARE THE ONES INVESTIGAT-ING THE INCIDENT, HUH?
HELLO.
IS THAT TRUE, TACHI-BANA?!
GET OFF OF ME, TACHIBANA!
PANT
PANT
PANT
HAGIRI WAS INJURED?

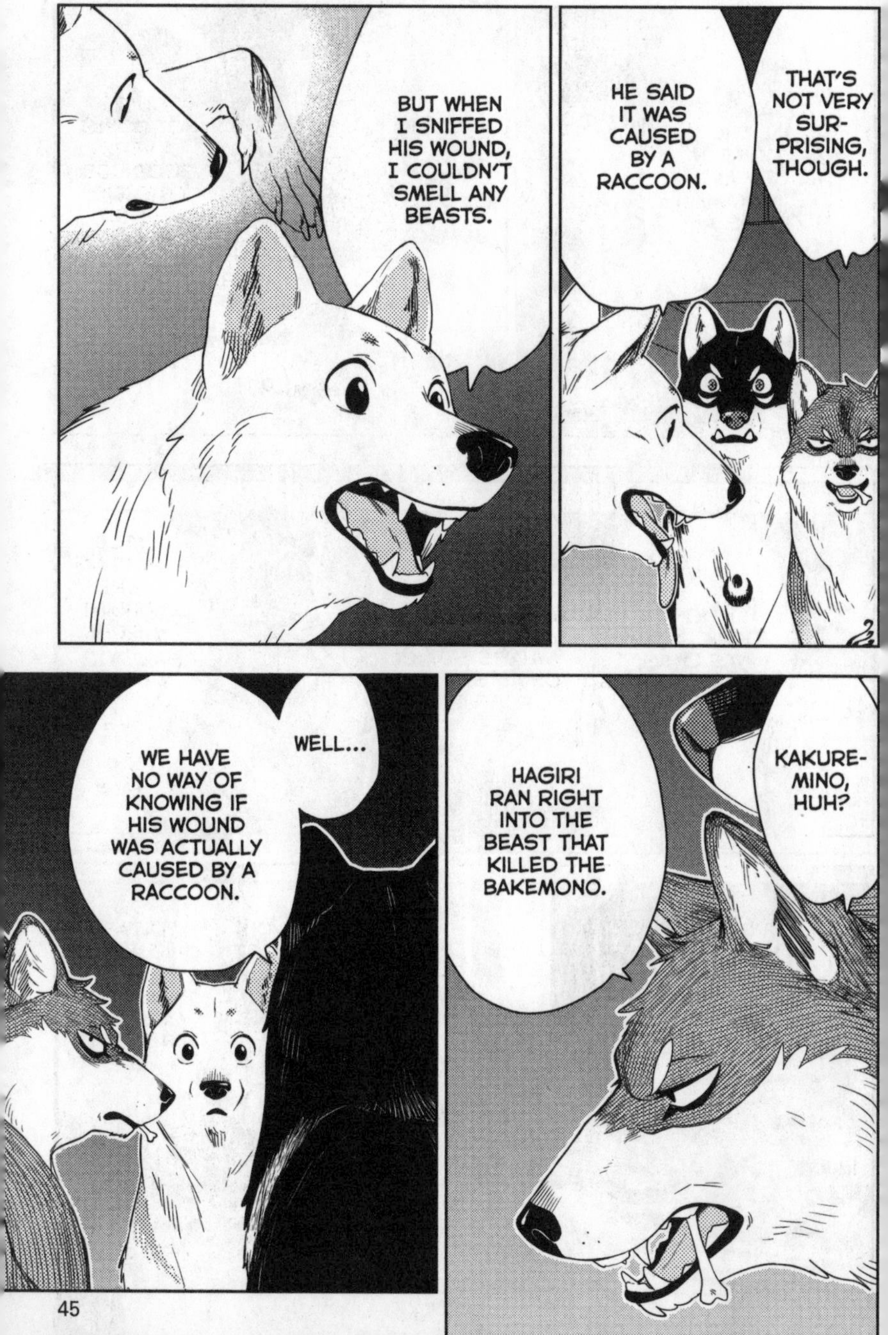
THAT'S NOT VERY SUR-PRISING, THOUGH.
HE SAID IT WAS CAUSED BY A RACCOON.
BUT WHEN I SNIFFED HIS WOUND, I COULDN'T SMELL ANY BEASTS.
KAKURE-MINO, HUH?
HAGIRI RAN RIGHT INTO THE BEAST THAT KILLED THE BAKEMONO.
WELL...
WE HAVE NO WAY OF KNOWING IF HIS WOUND WAS ACTUALLY CAUSED BY A RACCOON.

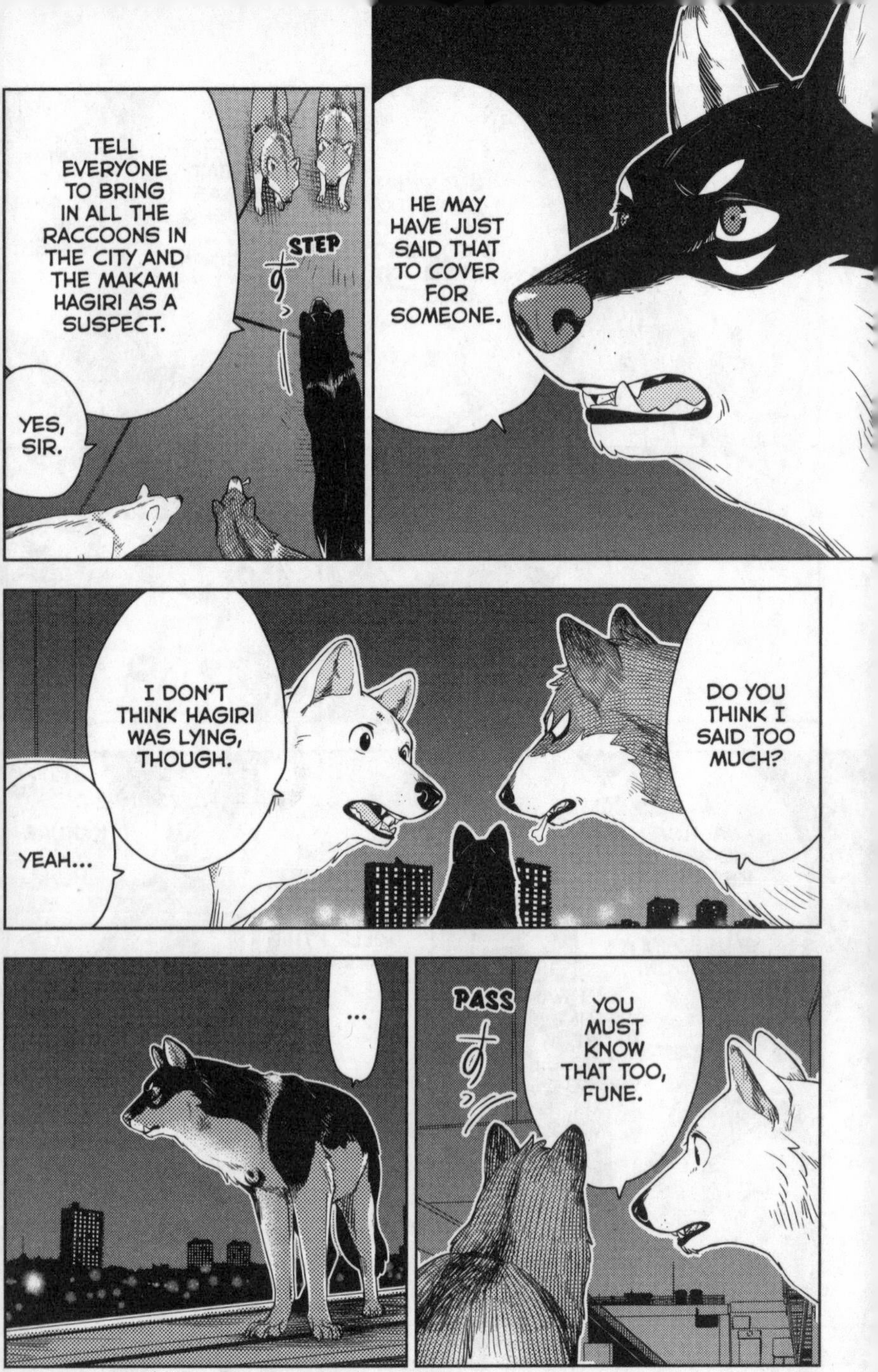
HE MAY HAVE JUST SAID THAT TO COVER FOR SOMEONE.
TELL EVERYONE TO BRING IN ALL THE RACCOONS IN THE CITY AND THE MAKAMI HAGIRI AS A SUSPECT.
STEP
YES, SIR.
DO YOU THINK I SAID TOO MUCH?
I DON'T THINK HAGIRI WAS LYING, THOUGH.
YEAH...
PASS
YOU MUST KNOW THAT TOO, FUNE.
...

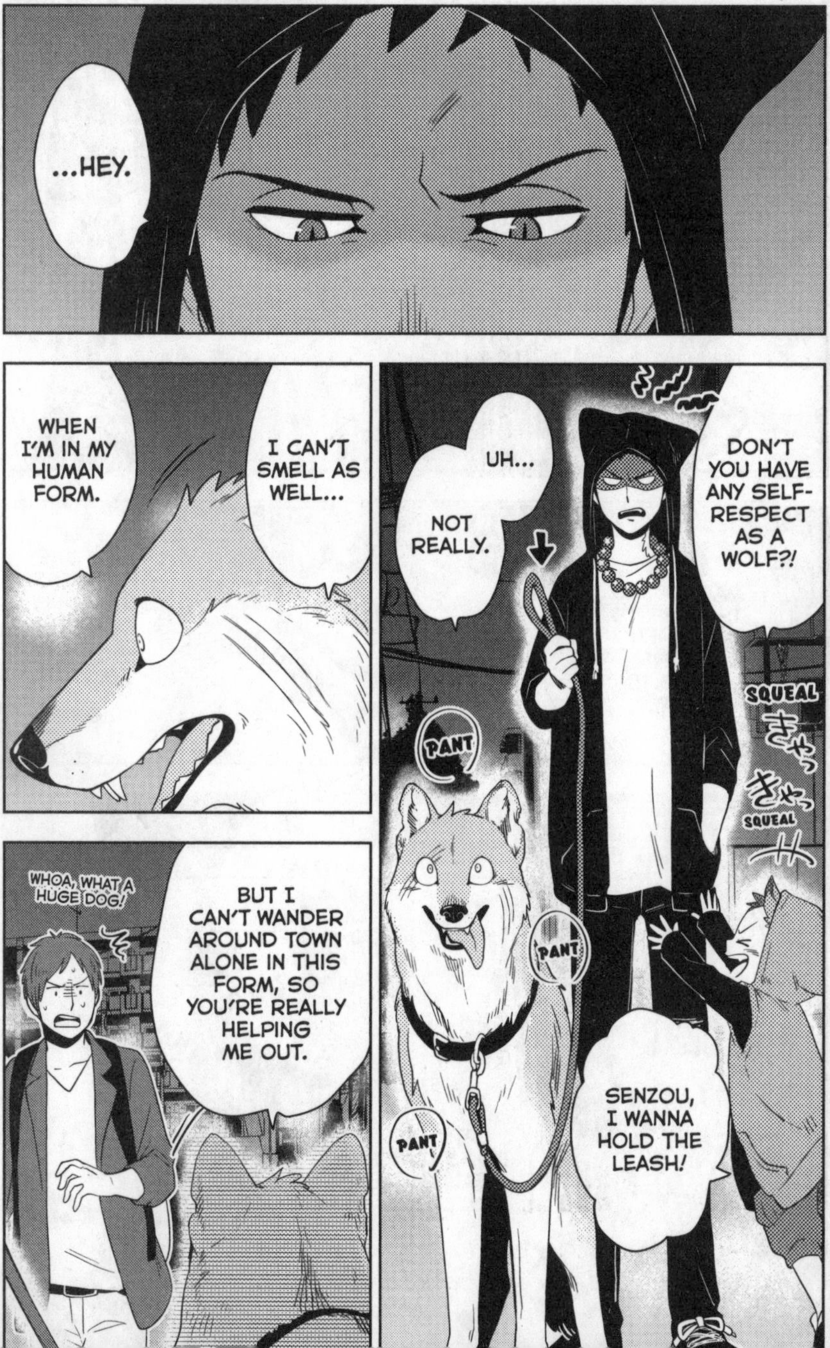
...HEY.
DON'T YOU HAVE ANY SELF-RESPECT AS A WOLF?!
UH...
NOT REALLY.
SQUEAL
きゃっ
きゃっ
SQUEAL
PANT
PANT
SENZOU, I WANNA HOLD THE LEASH!
PANT
I CAN'T SMELL AS WELL...
WHEN I'M IN MY HUMAN FORM.
BUT I CAN'T WANDER AROUND TOWN ALONE IN THIS FORM, SO YOU'RE REALLY HELPING ME OUT.
WHOA, WHAT A HUGE DOG!

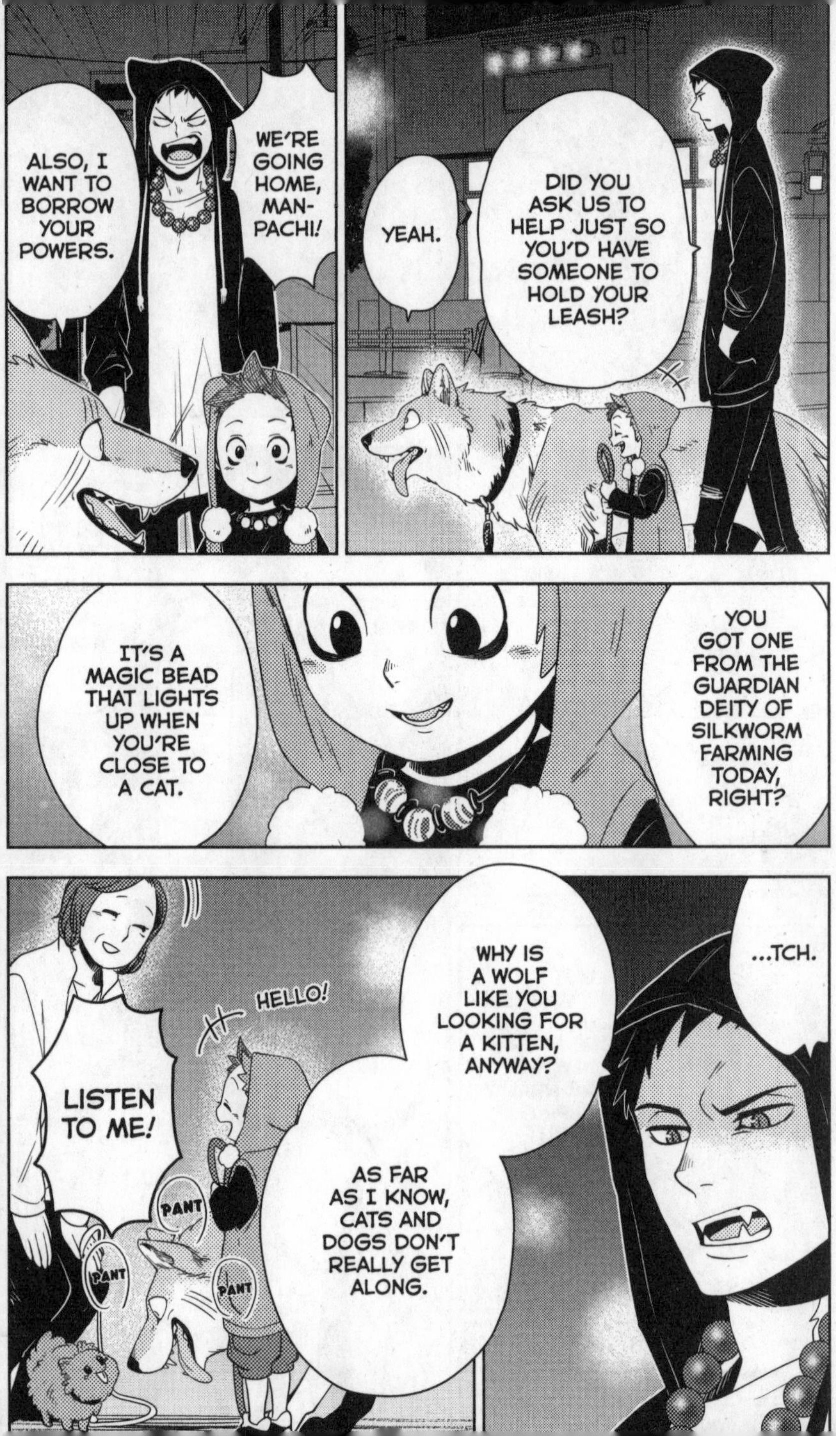
DID YOU ASK US TO HELP JUST SO YOU'D HAVE SOMEONE TO HOLD YOUR LEASH?
YEAH.
WE'RE GOING HOME, MAN-PACHI!
ALSO, I WANT TO BORROW YOUR POWERS.
YOU GOT ONE FROM THE GUARDIAN DEITY OF SILKWORM FARMING TODAY, RIGHT?
IT'S A MAGIC BEAD THAT LIGHTS UP WHEN YOU'RE CLOSE TO A CAT.
...TCH.
WHY IS A WOLF LIKE YOU LOOKING FOR A KITTEN, ANYWAY?
HELLO!
LISTEN TO ME!
AS FAR AS I KNOW, CATS AND DOGS DON'T REALLY GET ALONG.
PANT
PANT
PANT

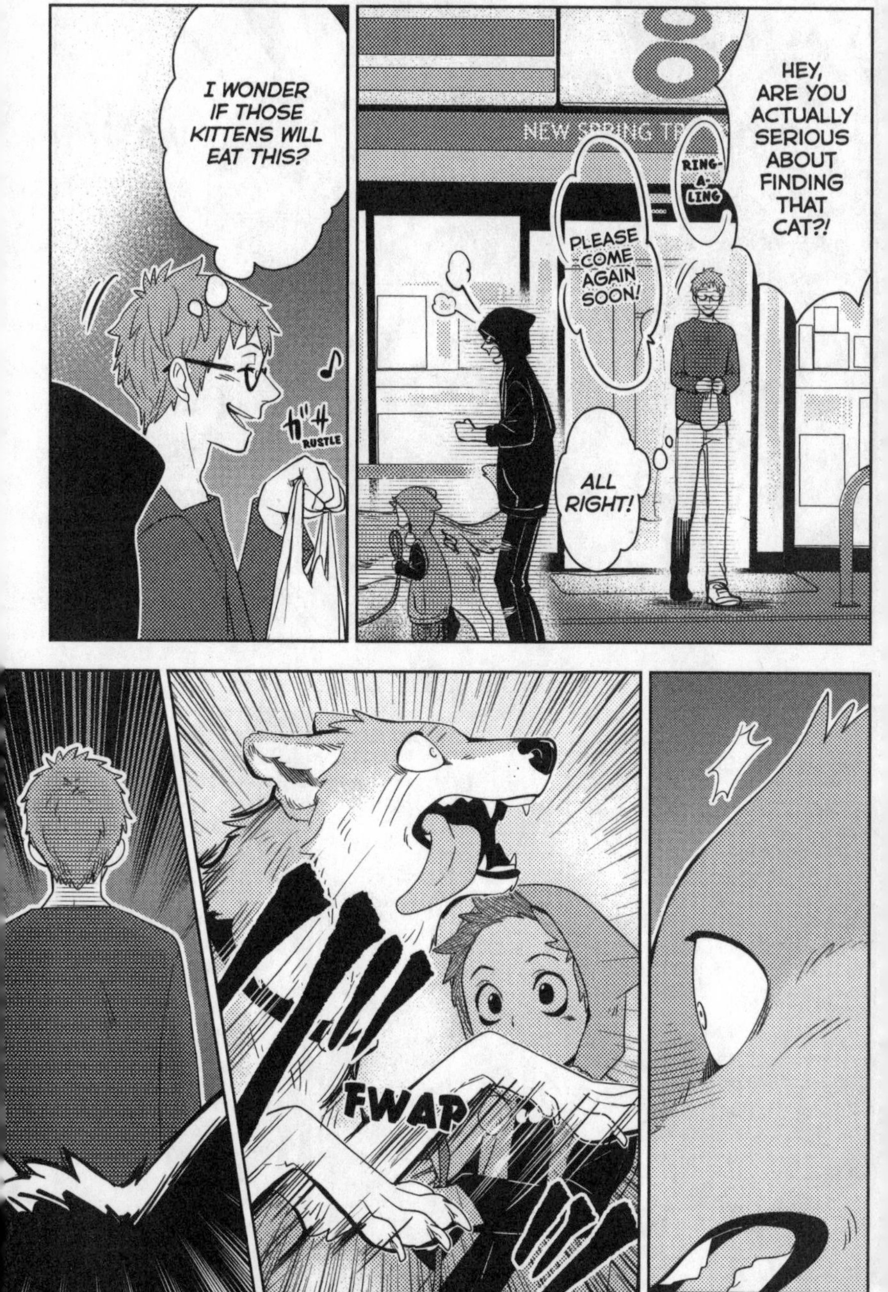
HEY, ARE YOU ACTUALLY SERIOUS ABOUT FINDING THAT CAT?!
RING-A-LING
PLEASE COME AGAIN SOON!
ALL RIGHT!
I WONDER IF THOSE KITTENS WILL EAT THIS?
ガサ
RUSTLE
FWAP

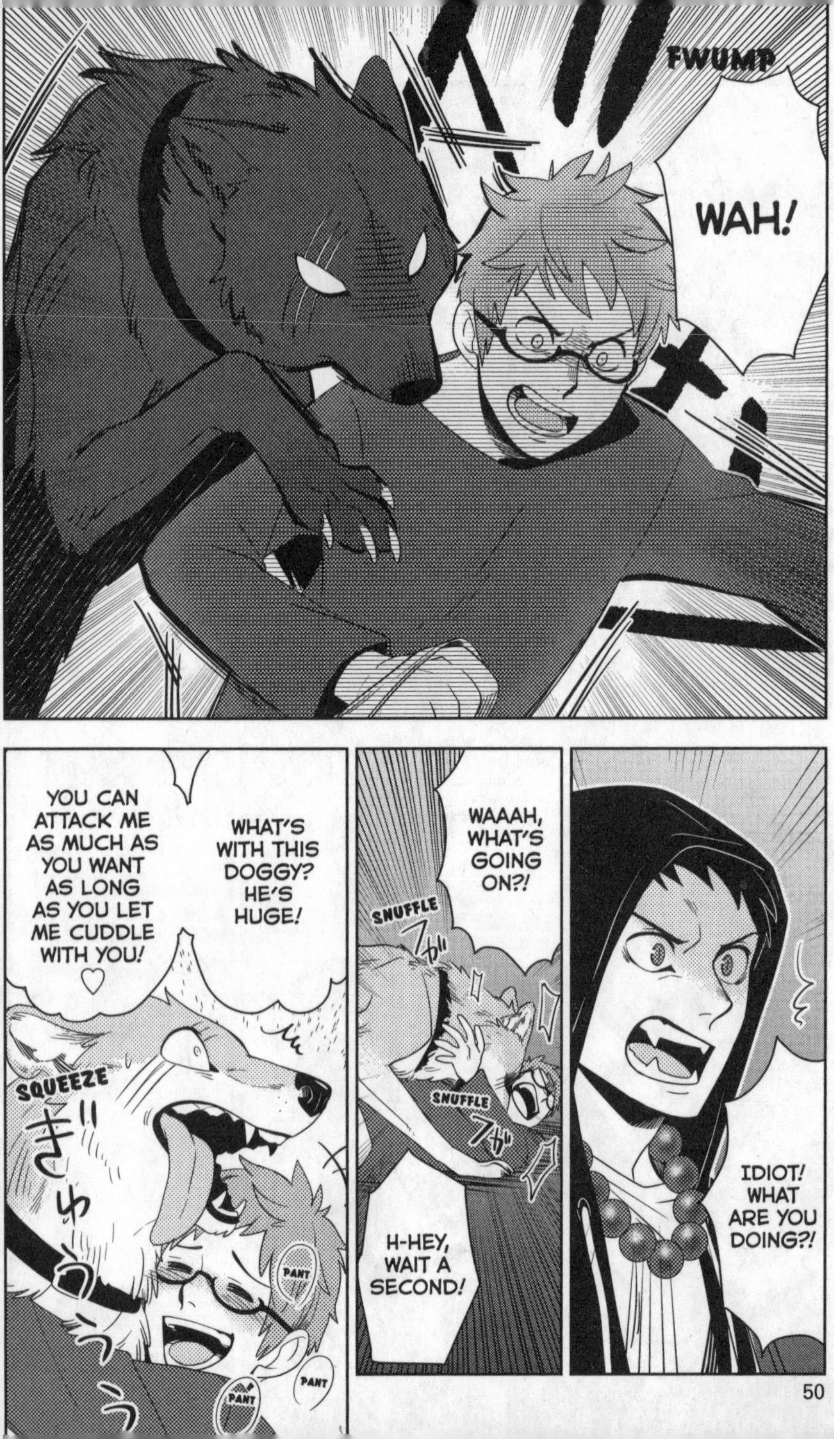
FWUMP
WAH!
IDIOT! WHAT ARE YOU DOING?!
WAAAH, WHAT'S GOING ON?!
SNUFFLE
SNUFFLE
H-HEY, WAIT A SECOND!
WHAT'S WITH THIS DOGGY? HE'S HUGE!
YOU CAN ATTACK ME AS MUCH AS YOU WANT AS LONG AS YOU LET ME CUDDLE WITH YOU! ♡
SQUEEZE
PANT
PANT
PANT

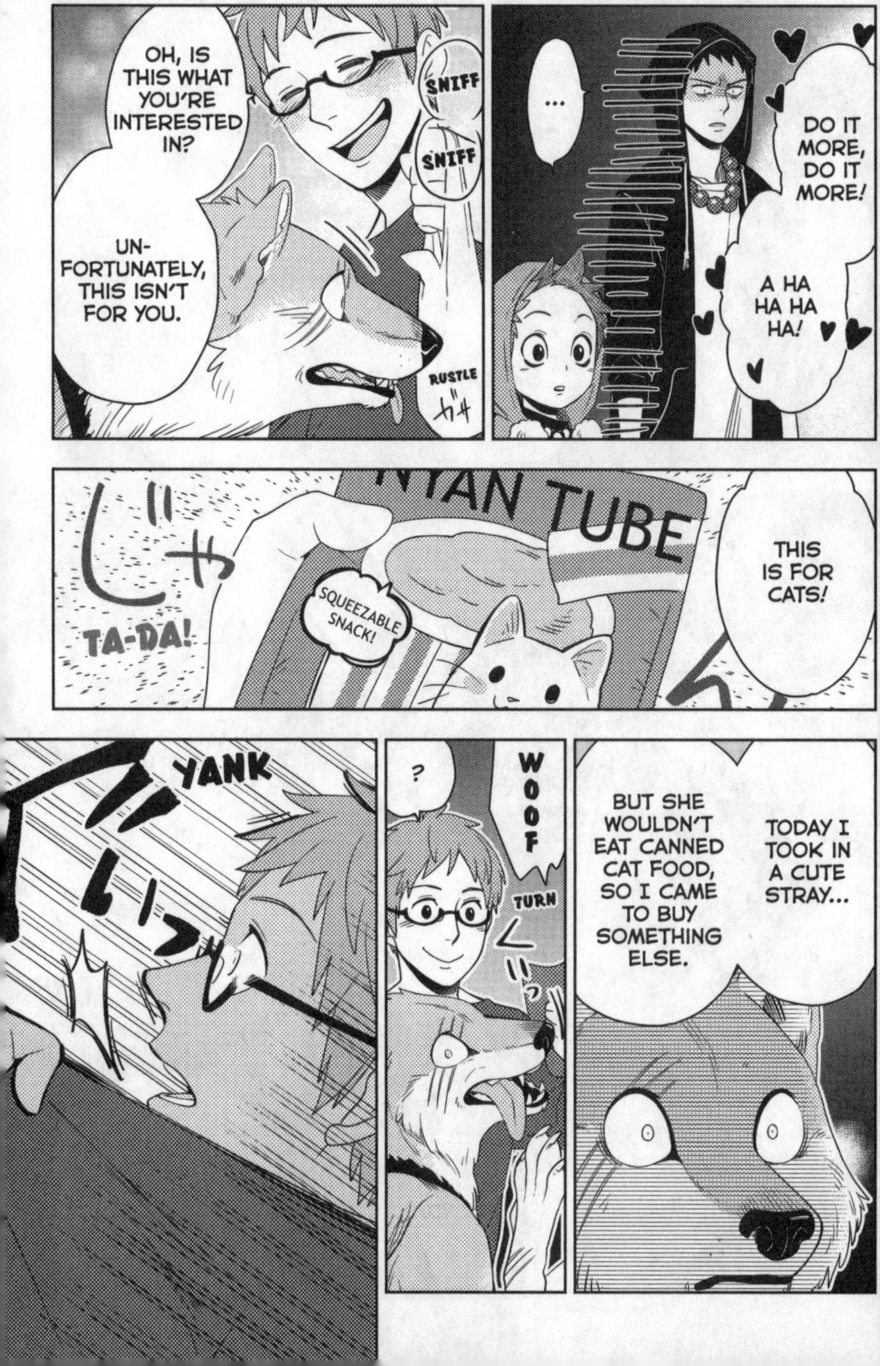
DO IT MORE, DO IT MORE!
A HA HA HA!
...
OH, IS THIS WHAT YOU'RE INTERESTED IN?
SNIFF
SNIFF
UN-FORTUNATELY, THIS ISN'T FOR YOU.
RUSTLE
THIS IS FOR CATS!
NYAN TUBE
SQUEEZABLE SNACK!
TA-DA!
TODAY I TOOK IN A CUTE STRAY...
BUT SHE WOULDN'T EAT CANNED CAT FOOD, SO I CAME TO BUY SOMETHING ELSE.
WOOF
?
TURN
YANK

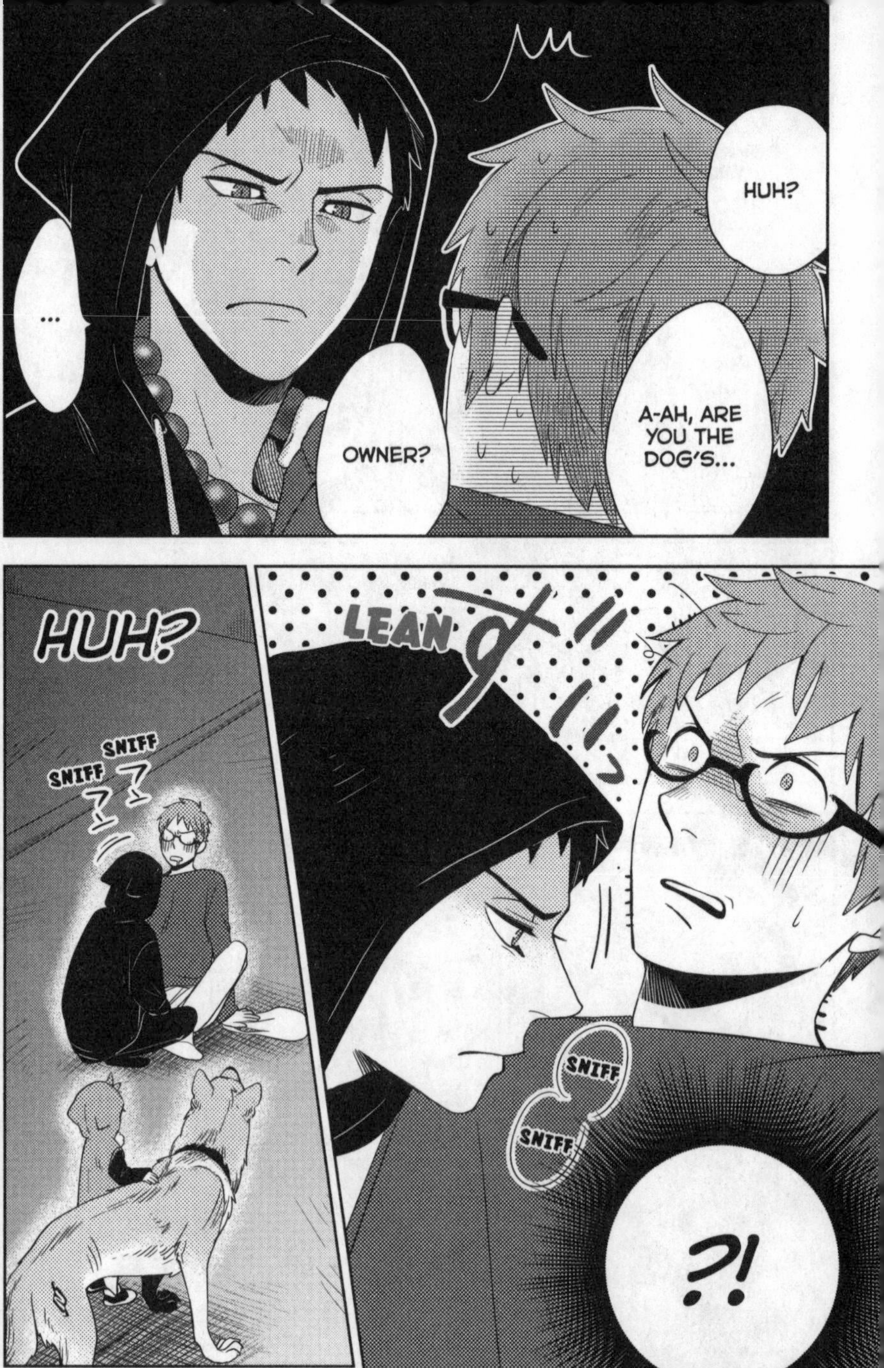
HUH?
A-AH, ARE YOU THE DOG'S...
OWNER?
...
LEAN
SNIFF
SNIFF
?!
HUH?
SNIFF
SNIFF

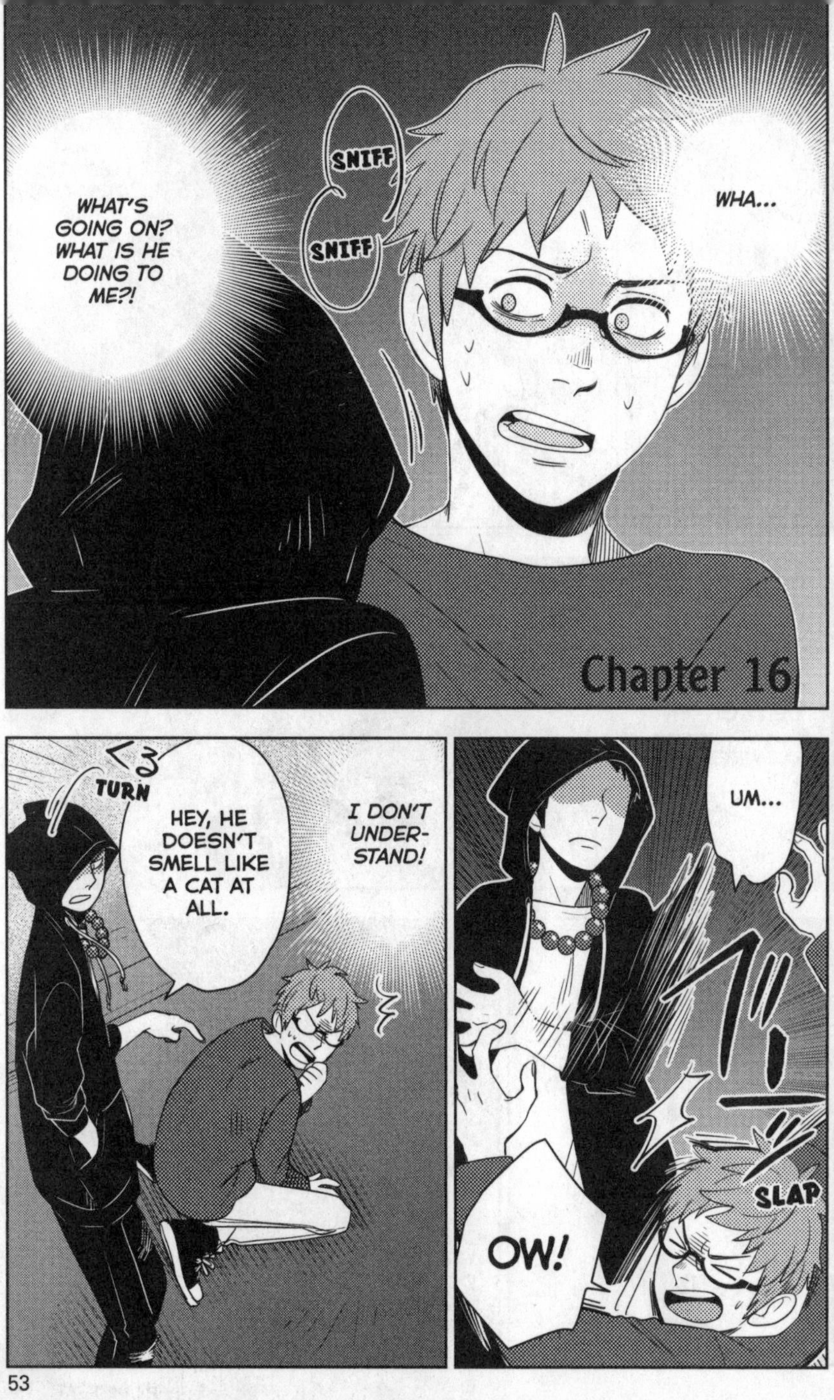
WHA...
SNIFF
SNIFF
WHAT'S GOING ON? WHAT IS HE DOING TO ME?!
Chapter 16
UM...
SLAP
OW!
I DON'T UNDER-STAND!
TURN
HEY, HE DOESN'T SMELL LIKE A CAT AT ALL.

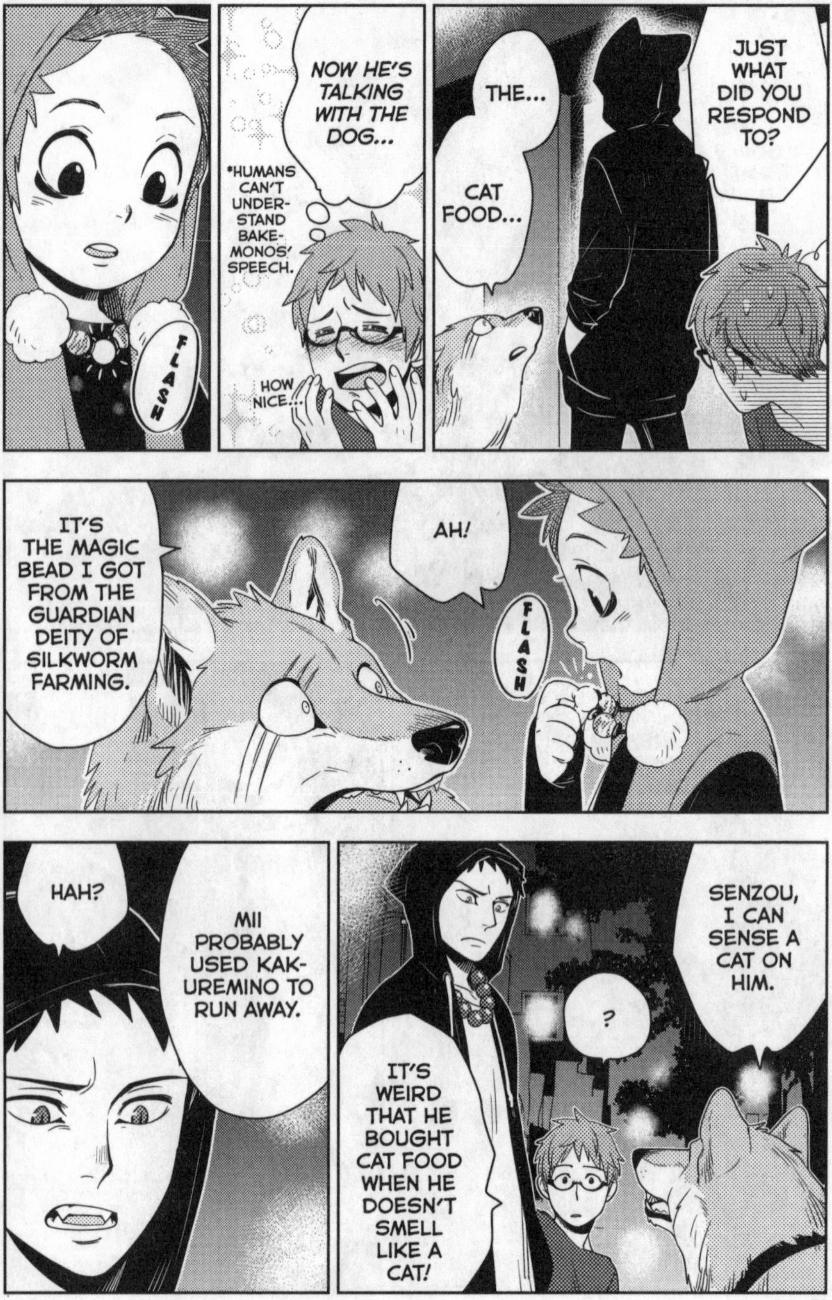
JUST WHAT DID YOU RESPOND TO?
THE...
CAT FOOD...
NOW HE'S TALKING WITH THE DOG...
*HUMANS CAN'T UNDER-STAND BAKE-MONOS' SPEECH.
HOW NICE...
FLASH
AH!
FLASH
IT'S THE MAGIC BEAD I GOT FROM THE GUARDIAN DEITY OF SILKWORM FARMING.
SENZOU, I CAN SENSE A CAT ON HIM.
?
IT'S WEIRD THAT HE BOUGHT CAT FOOD WHEN HE DOESN'T SMELL LIKE A CAT!
MII PROBABLY USED KAK-UREMINO TO RUN AWAY.
HAH?

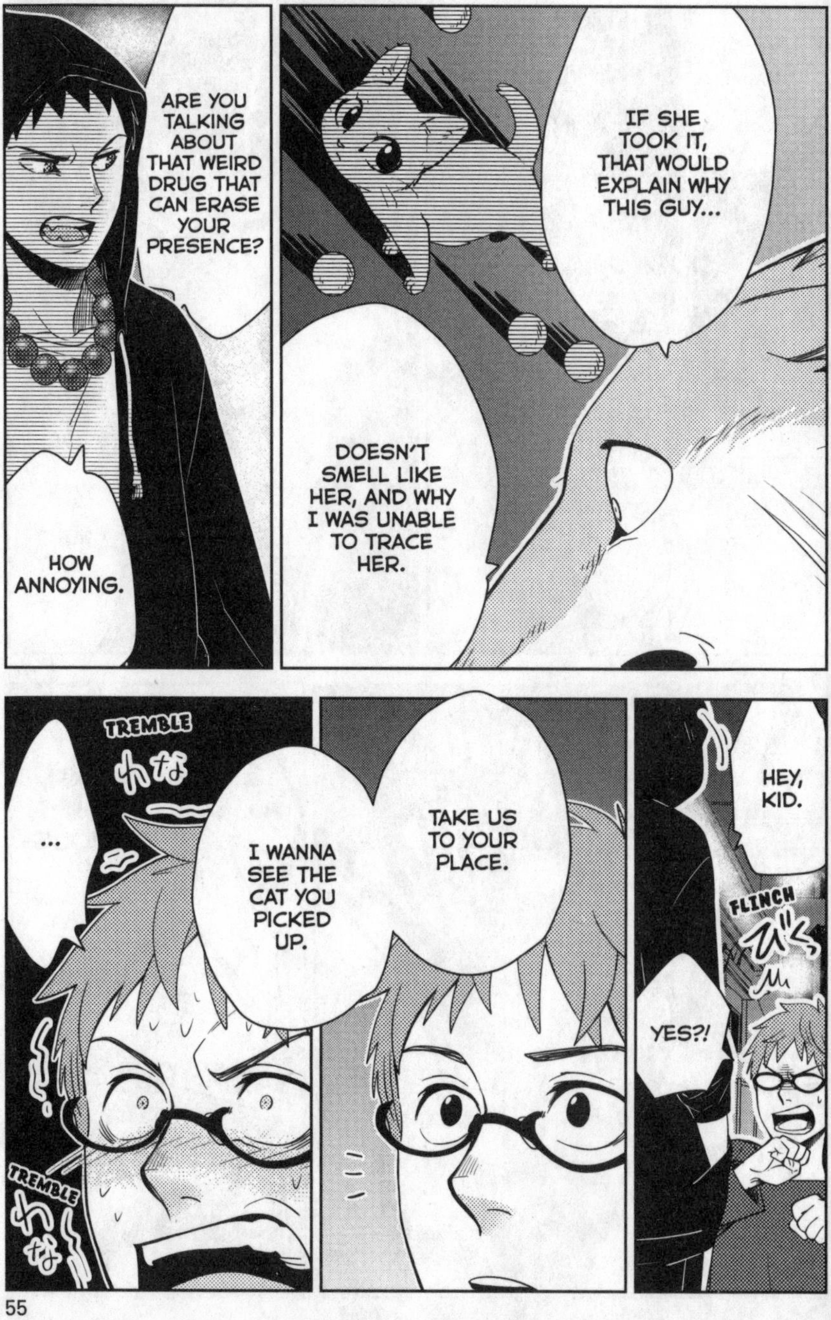
IF SHE TOOK IT, THAT WOULD EXPLAIN WHY THIS GUY...
DOESN'T SMELL LIKE HER, AND WHY I WAS UNABLE TO TRACE HER.
ARE YOU TALKING ABOUT THAT WEIRD DRUG THAT CAN ERASE YOUR PRESENCE?
HOW ANNOYING.
HEY, KID.
FLINCH
びくっ
YES?!
TAKE US TO YOUR PLACE.
I WANNA SEE THE CAT YOU PICKED UP.
TREMBLE
わな
...
TREMBLE
わな

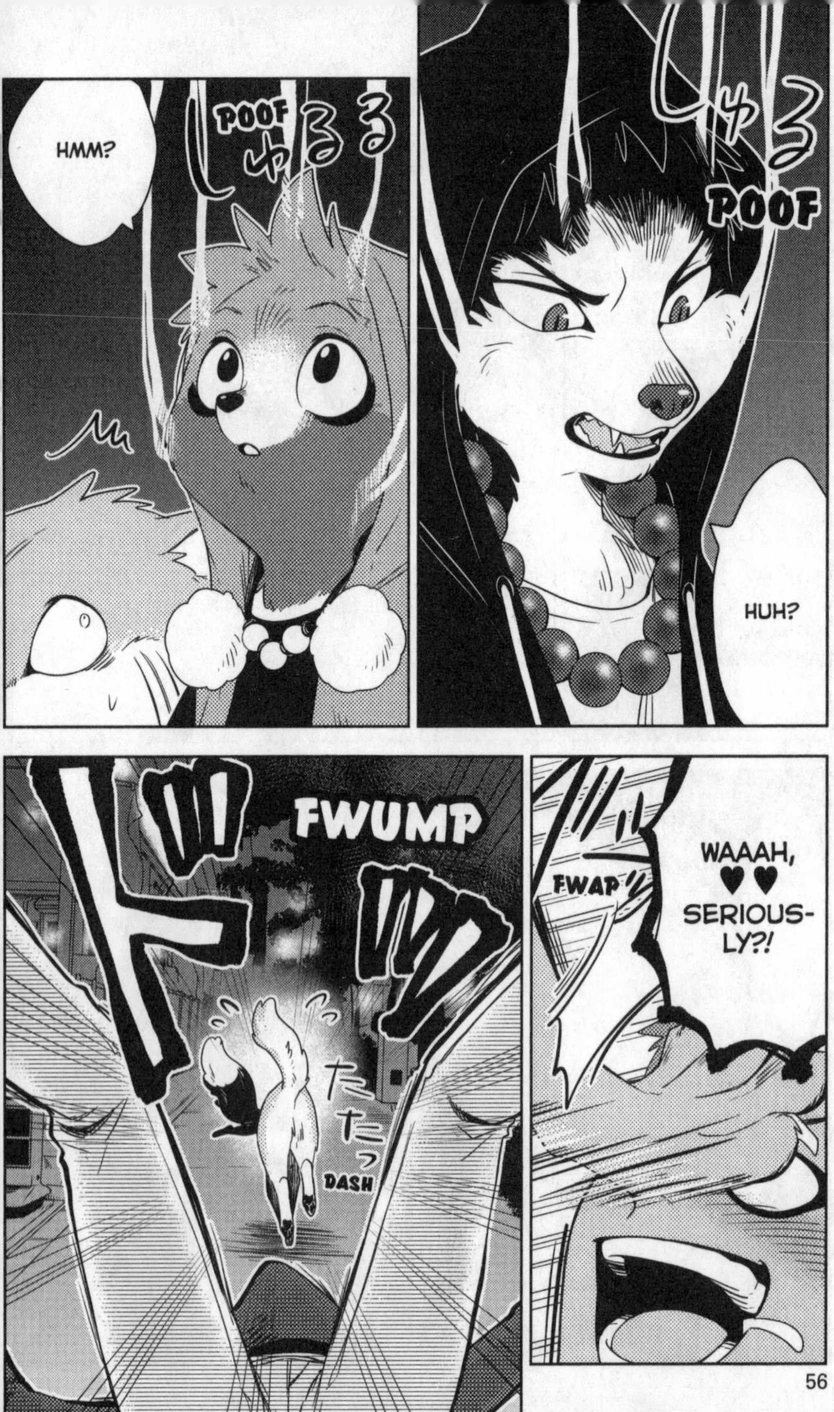
しゅる
POOF
HUH?
HMM?
POOF
しゅるる
WAAAH, ♥♥ SERIOUS-LY?!
FWAP
FWUMP
DASH

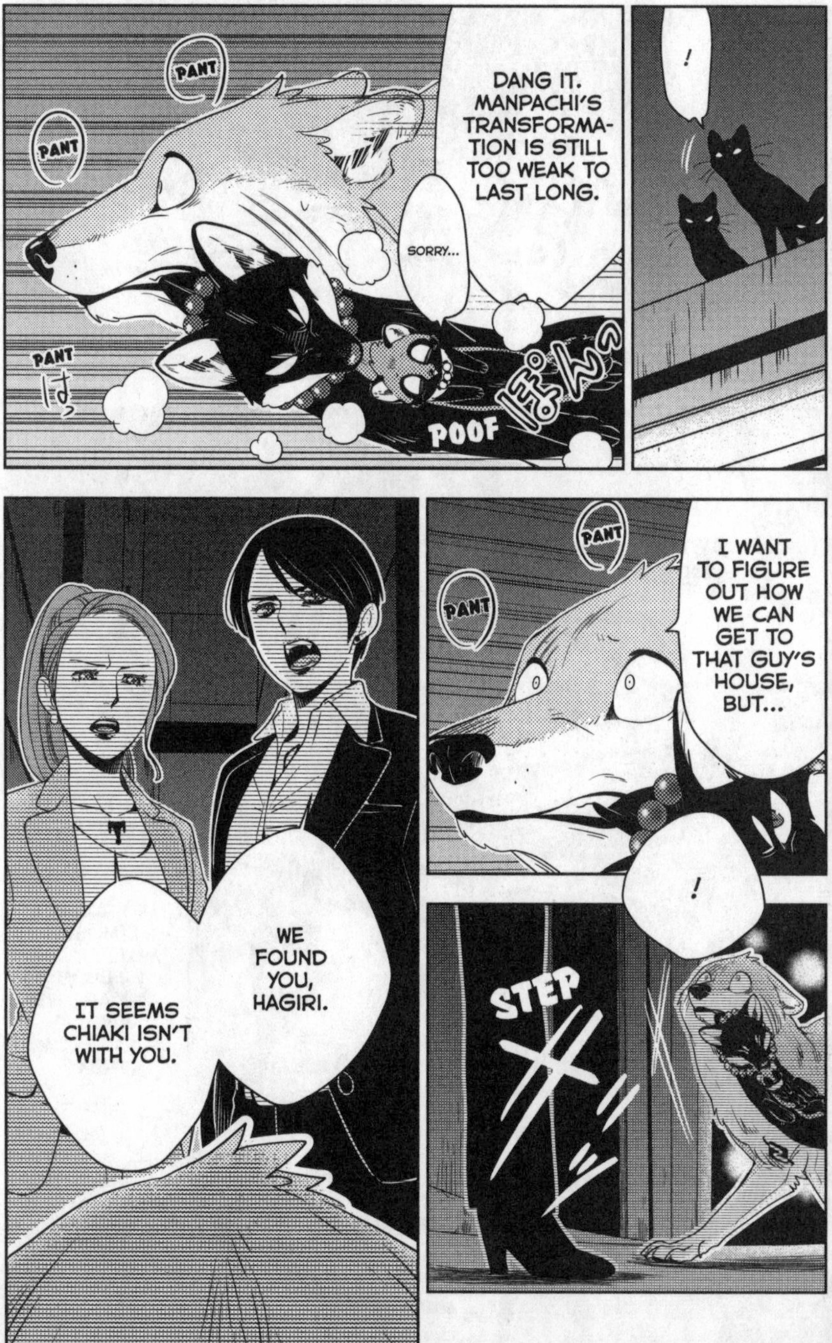
!
DANG IT. MANPACHI'S TRANSFORMATION IS STILL TOO WEAK TO LAST LONG.
SORRY...
PANT
PANT
PANT はっ
POOF ぽんっ
I WANT TO FIGURE OUT HOW WE CAN GET TO THAT GUY'S HOUSE, BUT...
PANT
PANT
!
STEP
WE FOUND YOU, HAGIRI.
IT SEEMS CHIAKI ISN'T WITH YOU.

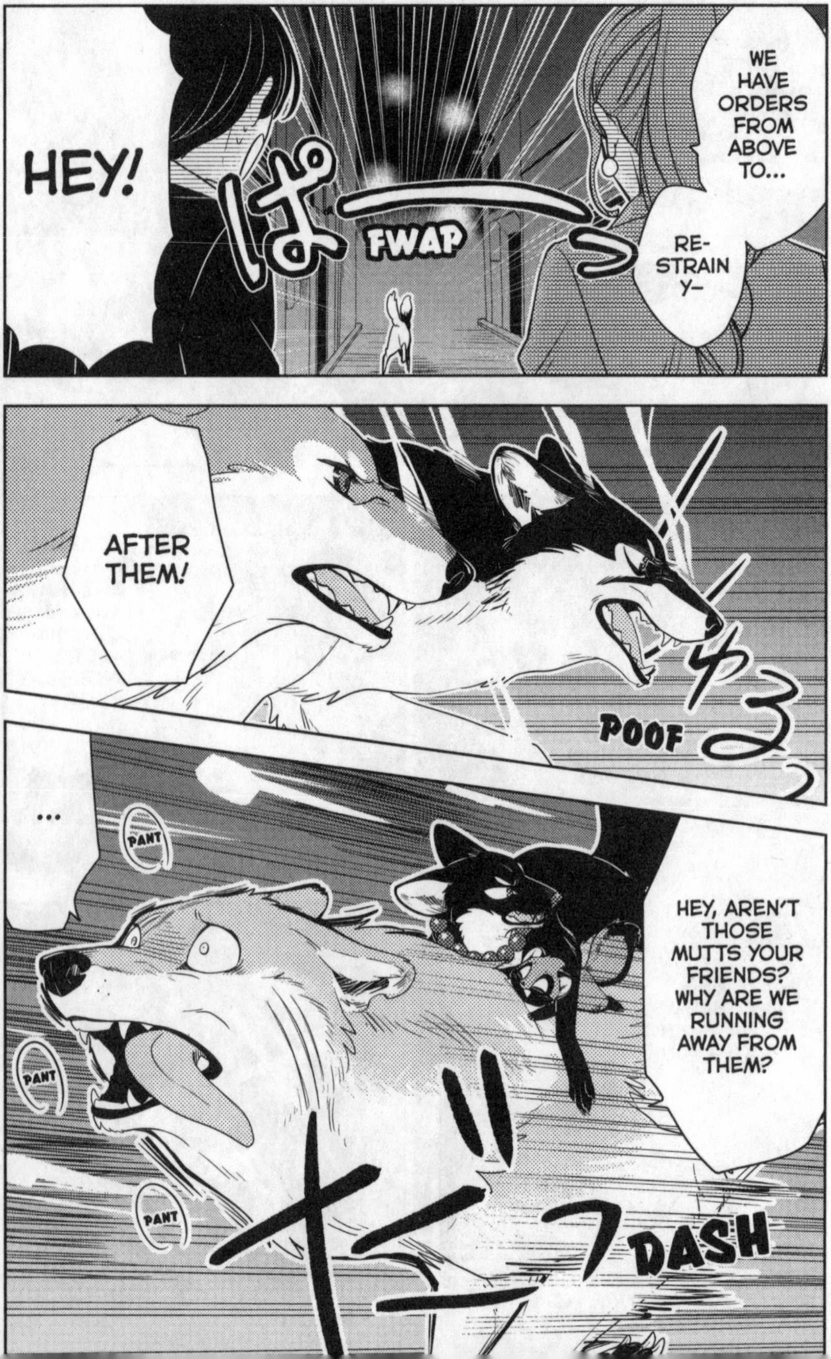
WE HAVE ORDERS FROM ABOVE TO...
RE-STRAIN Y—
FWAP
HEY!
POOF
AFTER THEM!
HEY, AREN'T THOSE MUTTS YOUR FRIENDS? WHY ARE WE RUNNING AWAY FROM THEM?
PANT
...
PANT
PANT
DASH

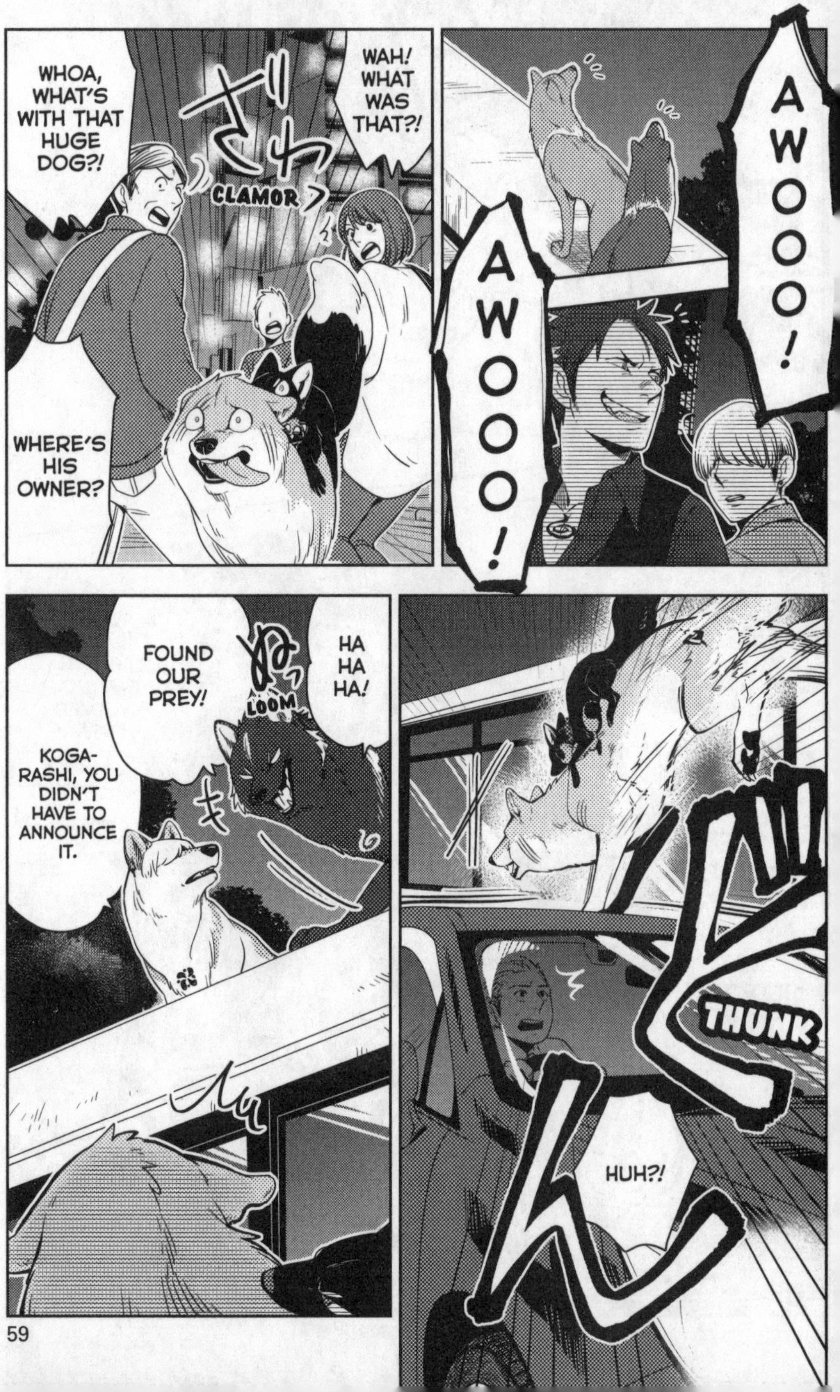
AWOOO!
AWOOO!
WAH! WHAT WAS THAT?!
CLAMOR
WHOA, WHAT'S WITH THAT HUGE DOG?!
WHERE'S HIS OWNER?
THUNK
HUH?!
HA HA HA!
LOOM
FOUND OUR PREY!
KOGA-RASHI, YOU DIDN'T HAVE TO ANNOUNCE IT.

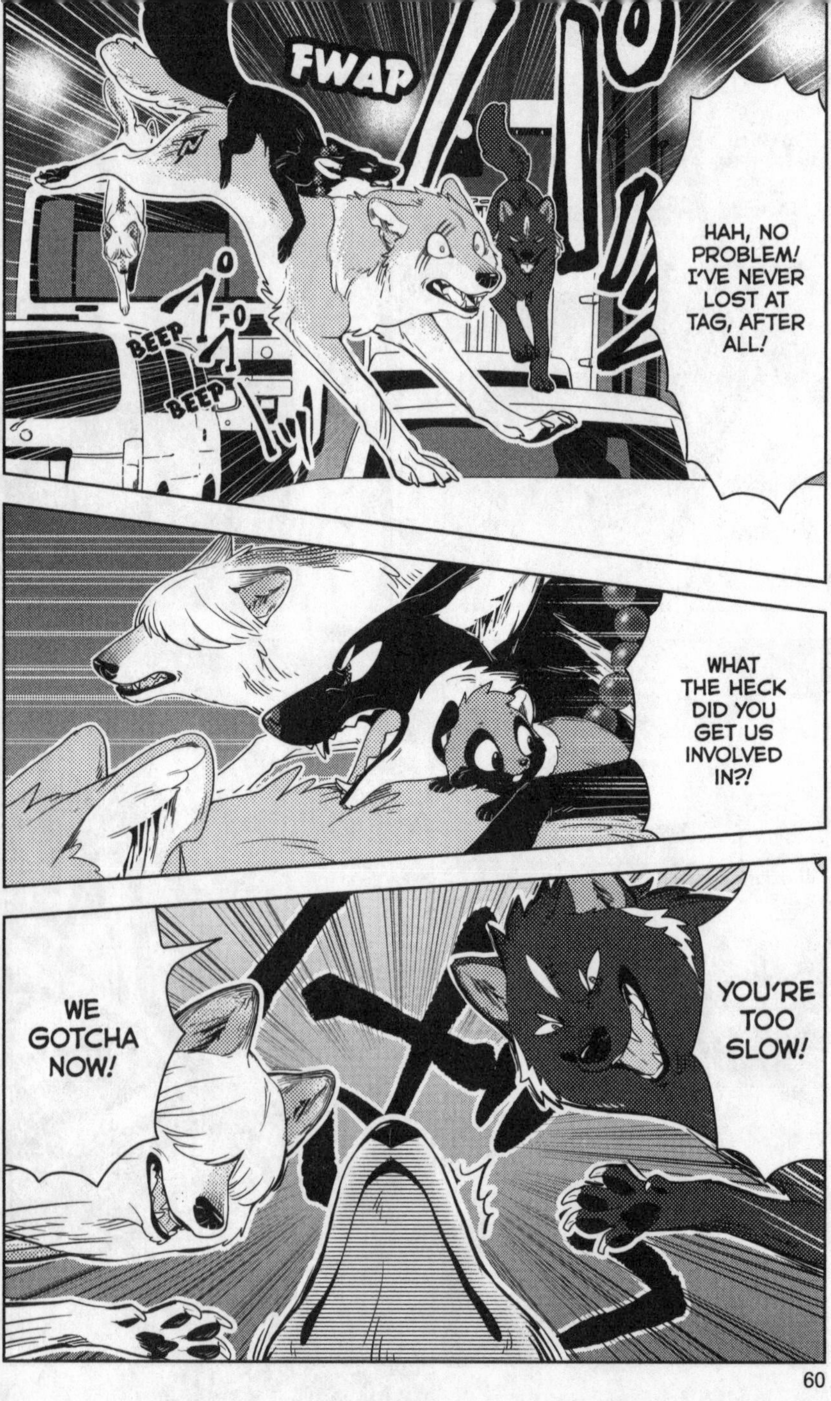
HAH, NO PROBLEM! I'VE NEVER LOST AT TAG, AFTER ALL!
FWAP
BEEP
BEEP
WHAT THE HECK DID YOU GET US INVOLVED IN?!
YOU'RE TOO SLOW!
WE GOTCHA NOW!

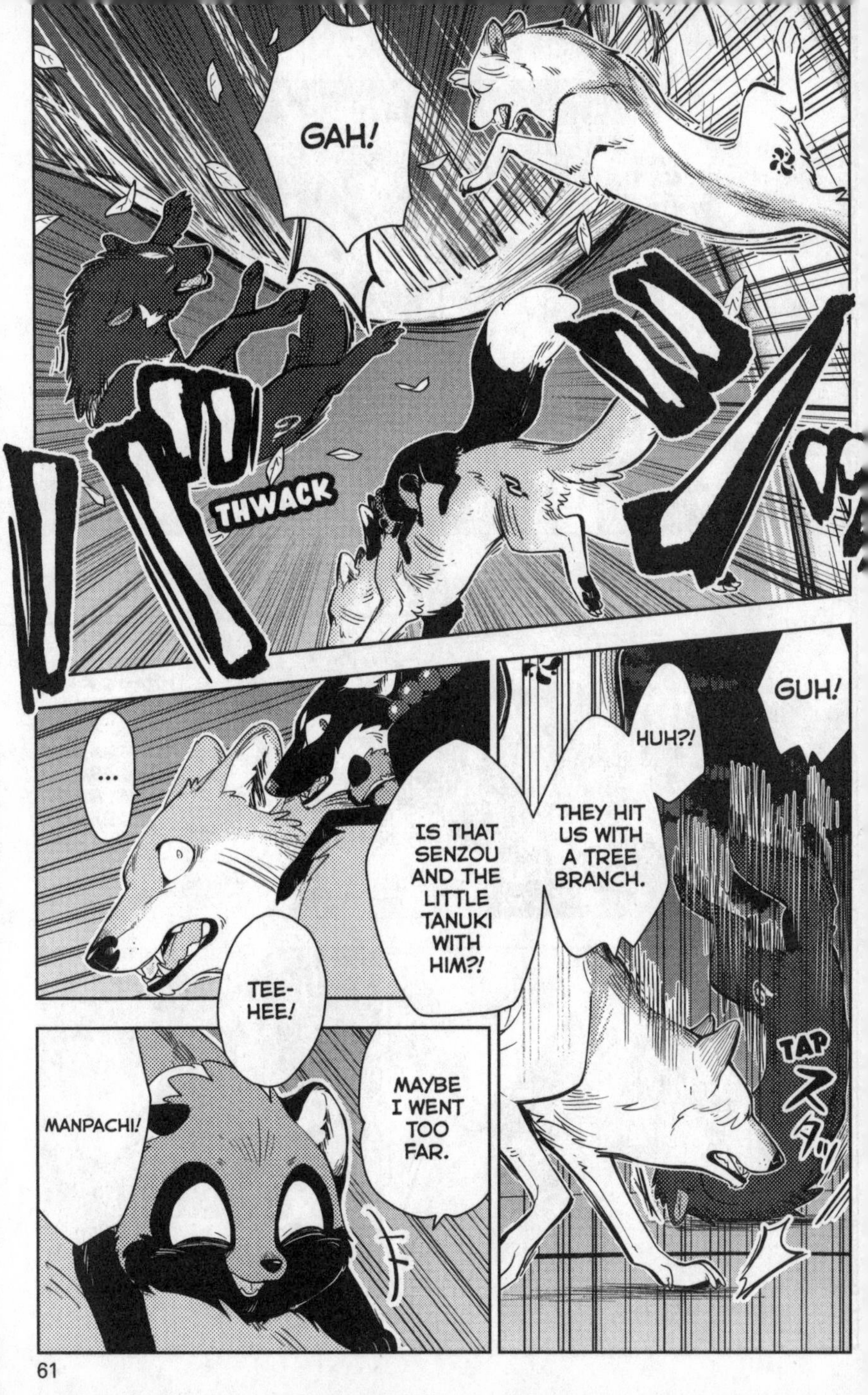
GAH!
THWACK
GUH!
HUH?!
THEY HIT US WITH A TREE BRANCH.
TAP
IS THAT SENZOU AND THE LITTLE TANUKI WITH HIM?!
...
TEE-HEE!
MAYBE I WENT TOO FAR.
MANPACHI!

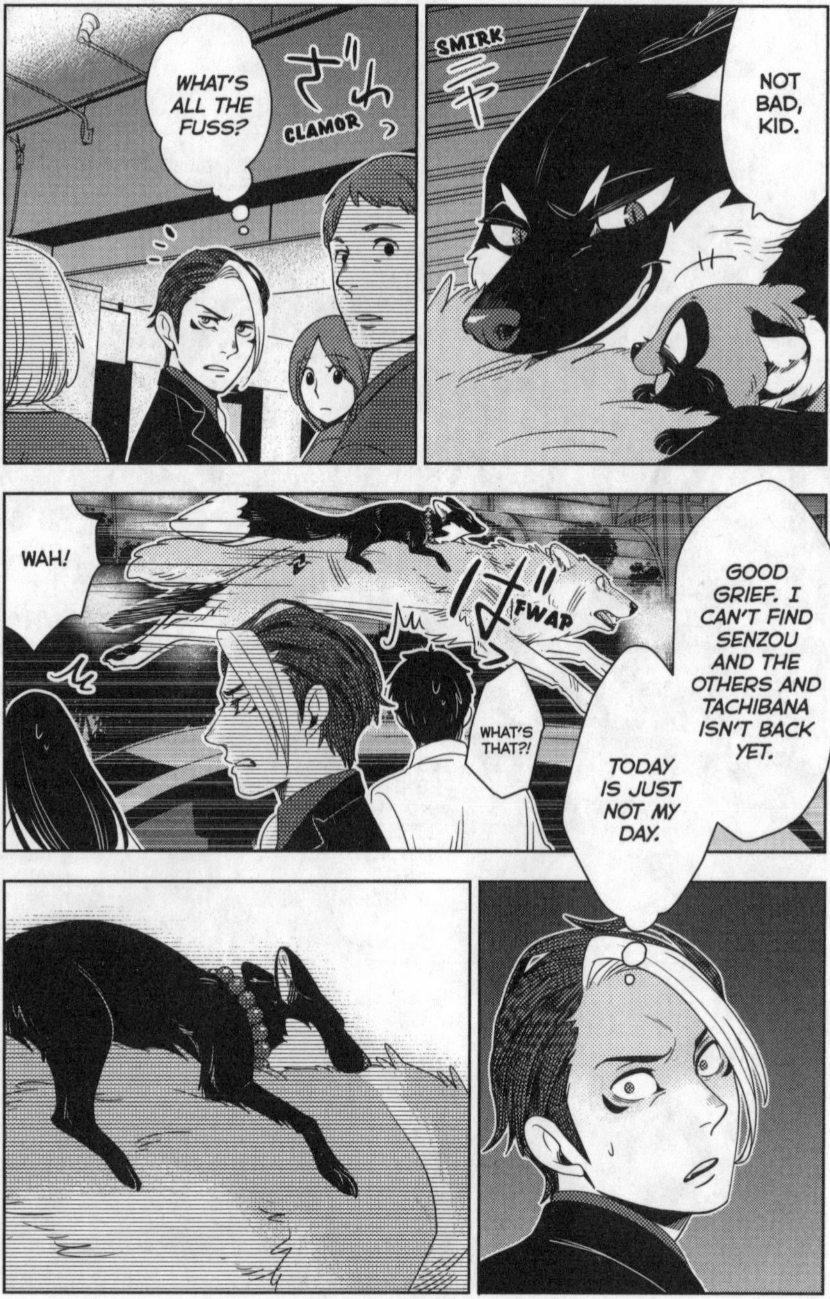
SMIRK
ニヤ
NOT BAD, KID.
ざわ
CLAMOR
WHAT'S ALL THE FUSS?
GOOD GRIEF. I CAN'T FIND SENZOU AND THE OTHERS AND TACHIBANA ISN'T BACK YET.
TODAY IS JUST NOT MY DAY.
FWAP
WHAT'S THAT?!
WAH!

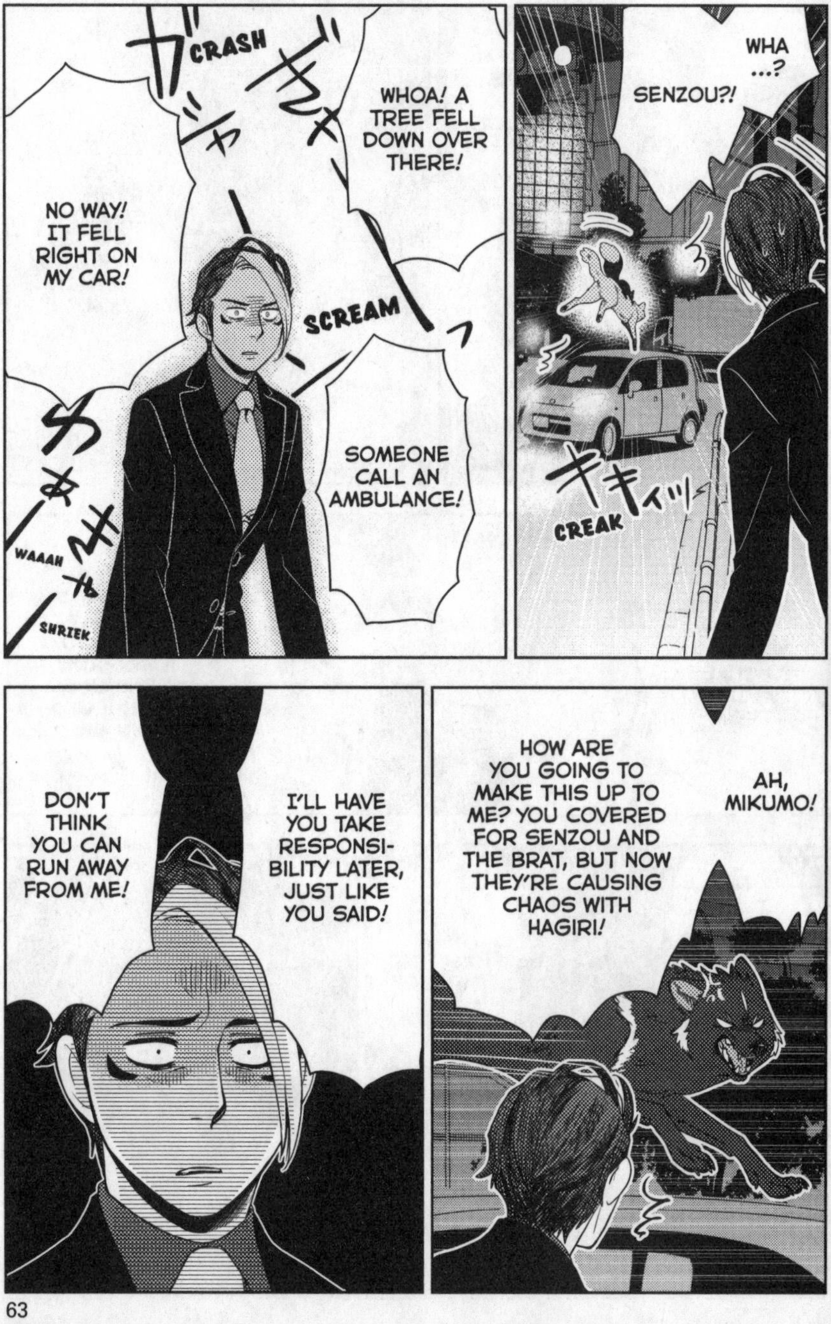
WHA ...?
SENZOU?!
CREAK
WHOA! A TREE FELL DOWN OVER THERE!
CRASH
SCREAM
NO WAY! IT FELL RIGHT ON MY CAR!
SOMEONE CALL AN AMBULANCE!
WAAAH
SHRIEK
AH, MIKUMO!
HOW ARE YOU GOING TO MAKE THIS UP TO ME? YOU COVERED FOR SENZOU AND THE BRAT, BUT NOW THEY'RE CAUSING CHAOS WITH HAGIRI!
I'LL HAVE YOU TAKE RESPONSI-BILITY LATER, JUST LIKE YOU SAID!
DON'T THINK YOU CAN RUN AWAY FROM ME!

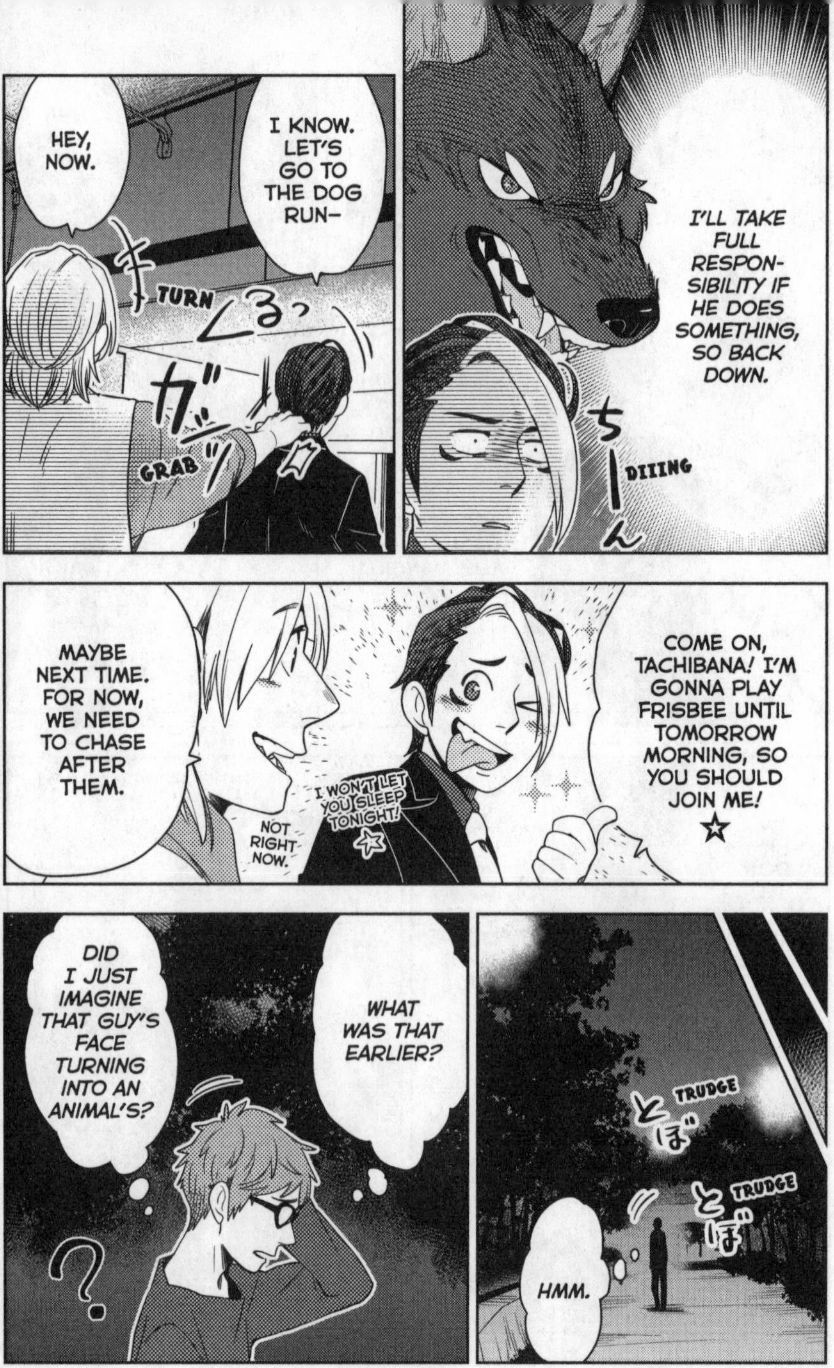
I'LL TAKE FULL RESPONSIBILITY IF HE DOES SOMETHING, SO BACK DOWN.
DIIING
I KNOW. LET'S GO TO THE DOG RUN–
HEY, NOW.
TURN
GRAB
COME ON, TACHIBANA! I'M GONNA PLAY FRISBEE UNTIL TOMORROW MORNING, SO YOU SHOULD JOIN ME! ☆
I WON'T LET YOU SLEEP TONIGHT! ☆
NOT RIGHT NOW.
MAYBE NEXT TIME. FOR NOW, WE NEED TO CHASE AFTER THEM.
TRUDGE
TRUDGE
HMM.
WHAT WAS THAT EARLIER?
DID I JUST IMAGINE THAT GUY'S FACE TURNING INTO AN ANIMAL'S?

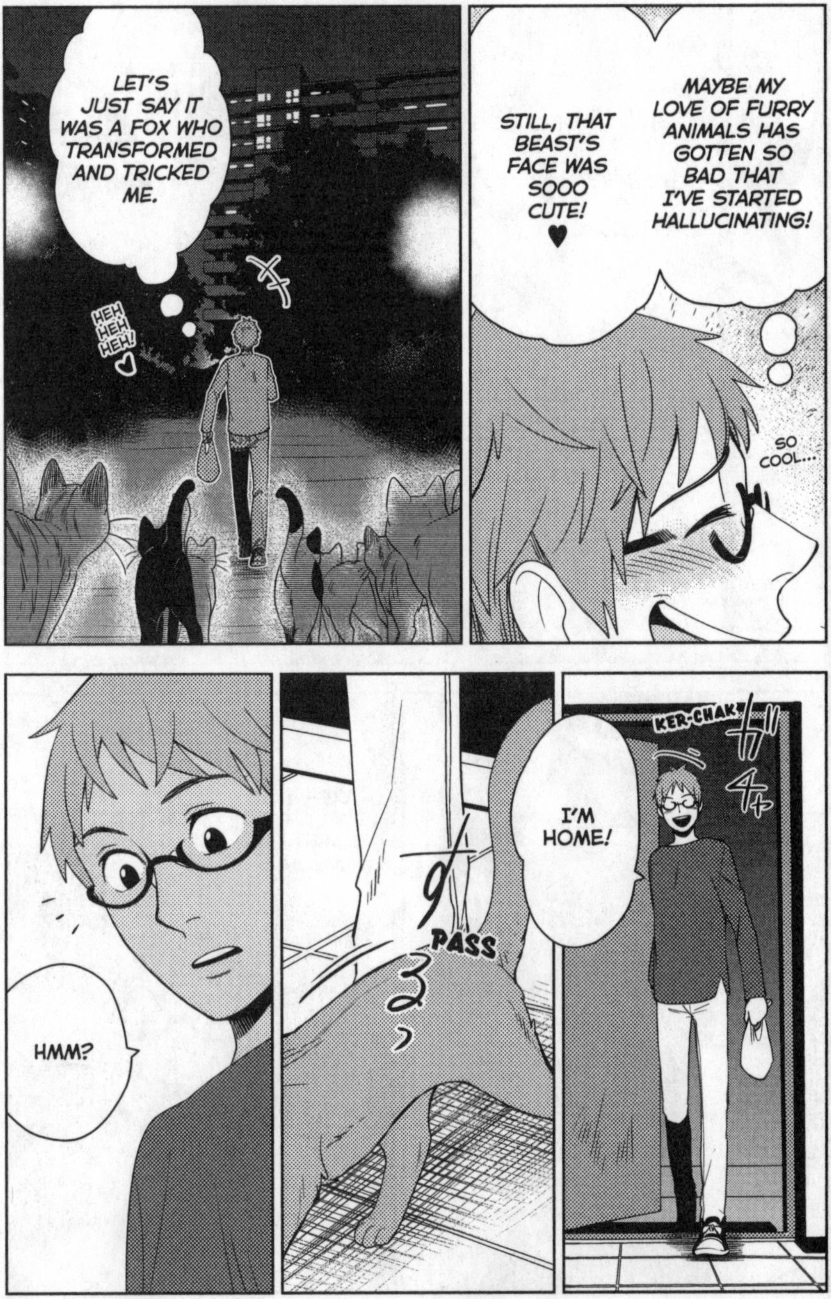
MAYBE MY LOVE OF FURRY ANIMALS HAS GOTTEN SO BAD THAT I'VE STARTED HALLUCINATING!
STILL, THAT BEAST'S FACE WAS SOOO CUTE! ♥
SO COOL...
LET'S JUST SAY IT WAS A FOX WHO TRANSFORMED AND TRICKED ME.
HEH HEH HEH! ♥
KER-CHAK
I'M HOME!
PASS
HMM?

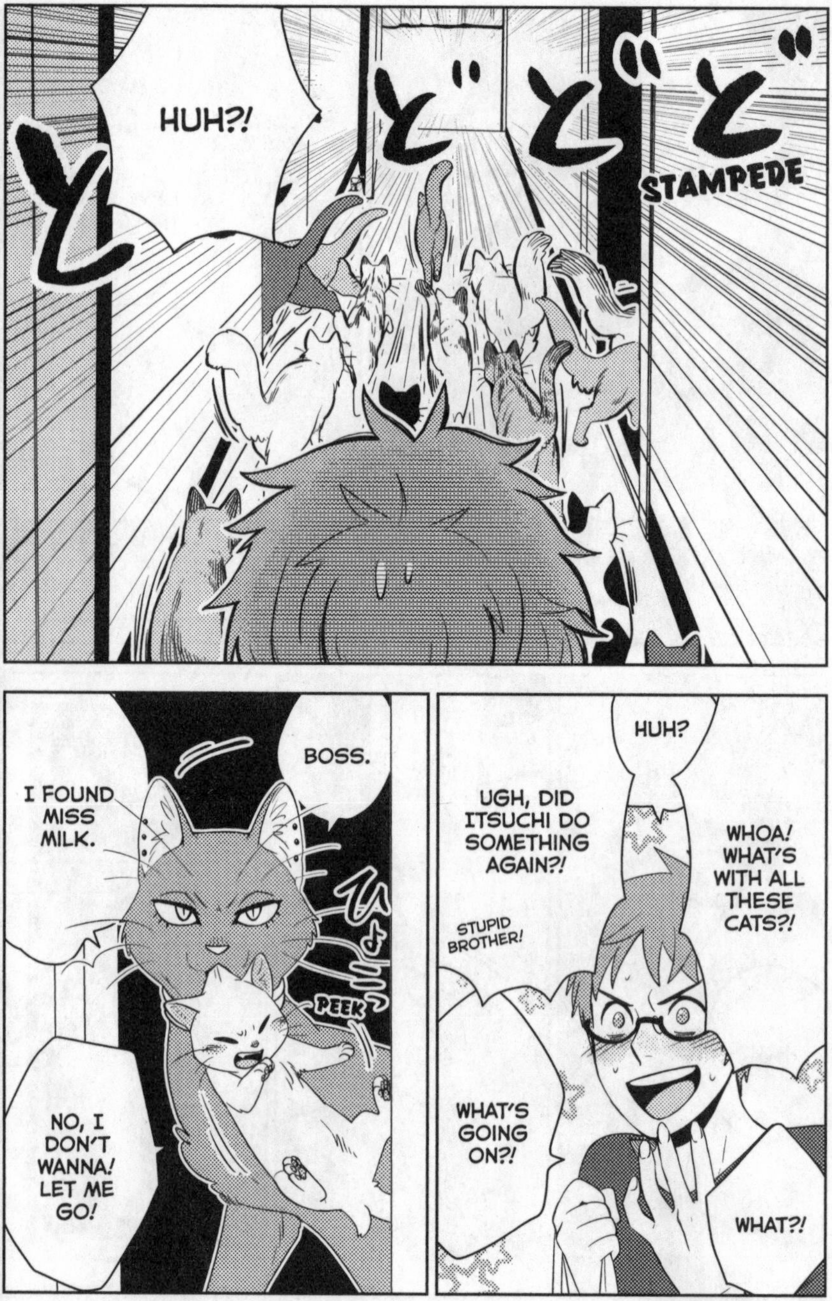
HUH?!
とどどど
STAMPEDE
HUH?
WHOA! WHAT'S WITH ALL THESE CATS?!
UGH, DID ITSUCHI DO SOMETHING AGAIN?!
STUPID BROTHER!
WHAT?!
WHAT'S GOING ON?!
BOSS.
I FOUND MISS MILK.
PEEK
NO, I DON'T WANNA! LET ME GO!

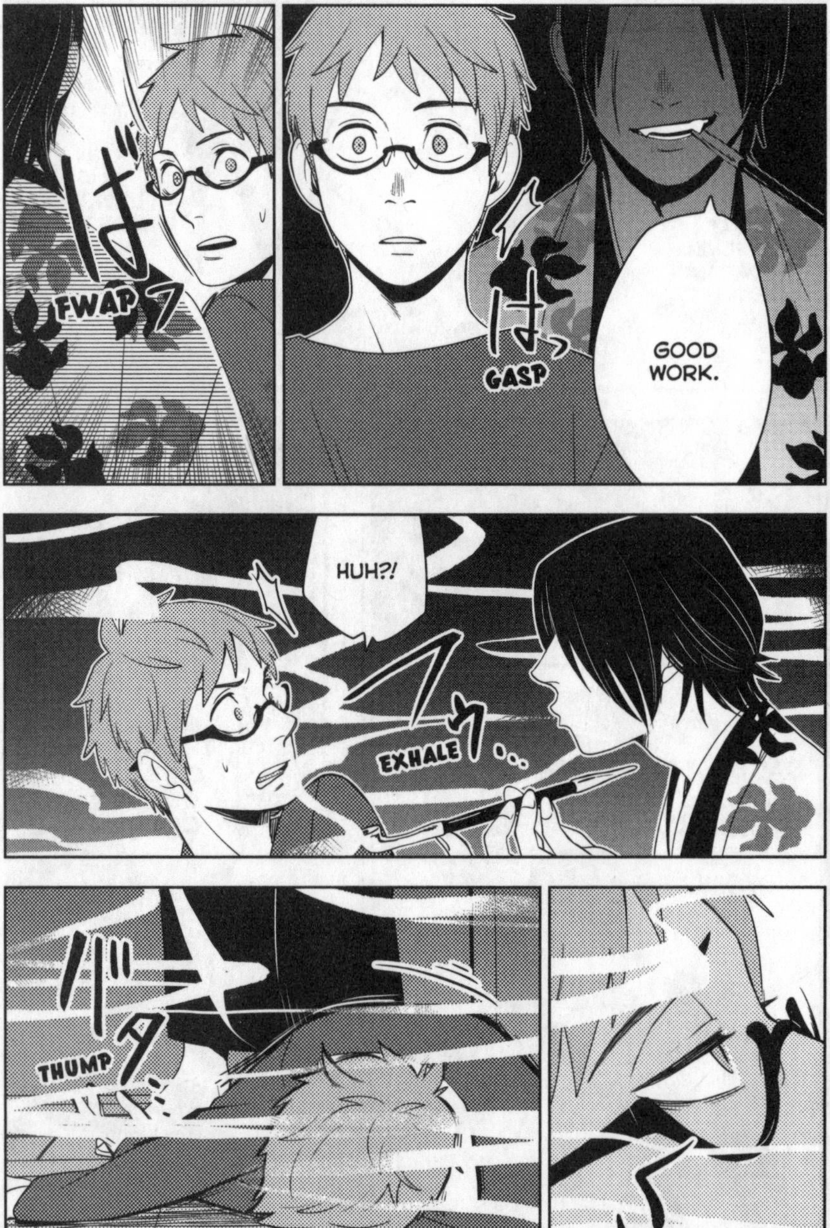
GOOD WORK.
GASP
FWAP
HUH?!
EXHALE
DIZZY
THUMP

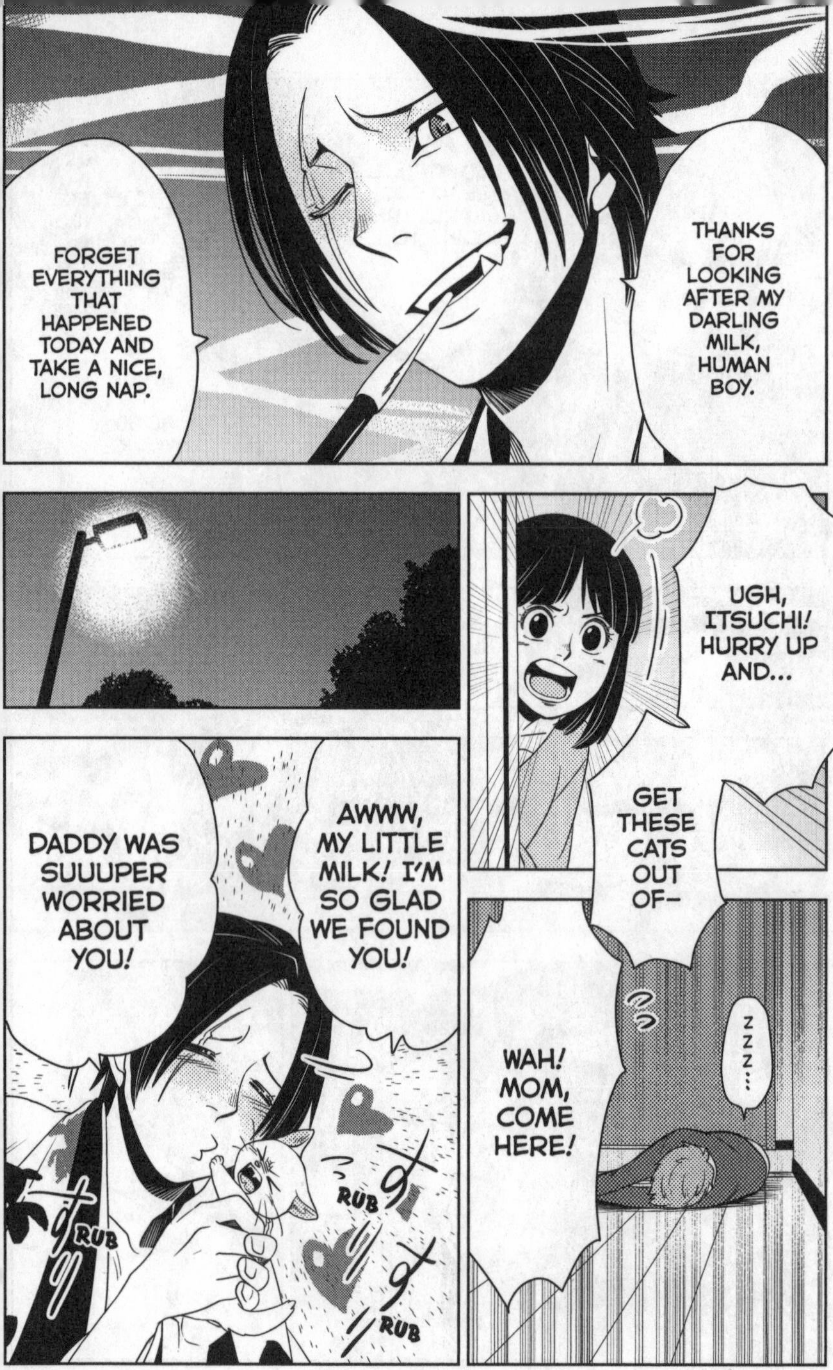
THANKS FOR LOOKING AFTER MY DARLING MILK, HUMAN BOY.
FORGET EVERYTHING THAT HAPPENED TODAY AND TAKE A NICE, LONG NAP.
UGH, ITSUCHI! HURRY UP AND...
GET THESE CATS OUT OF–
ZZZ...
WAH! MOM, COME HERE!
AWWW, MY LITTLE MILK! I'M SO GLAD WE FOUND YOU!
DADDY WAS SUUUPER WORRIED ABOUT YOU!
RUB
RUB
RUB

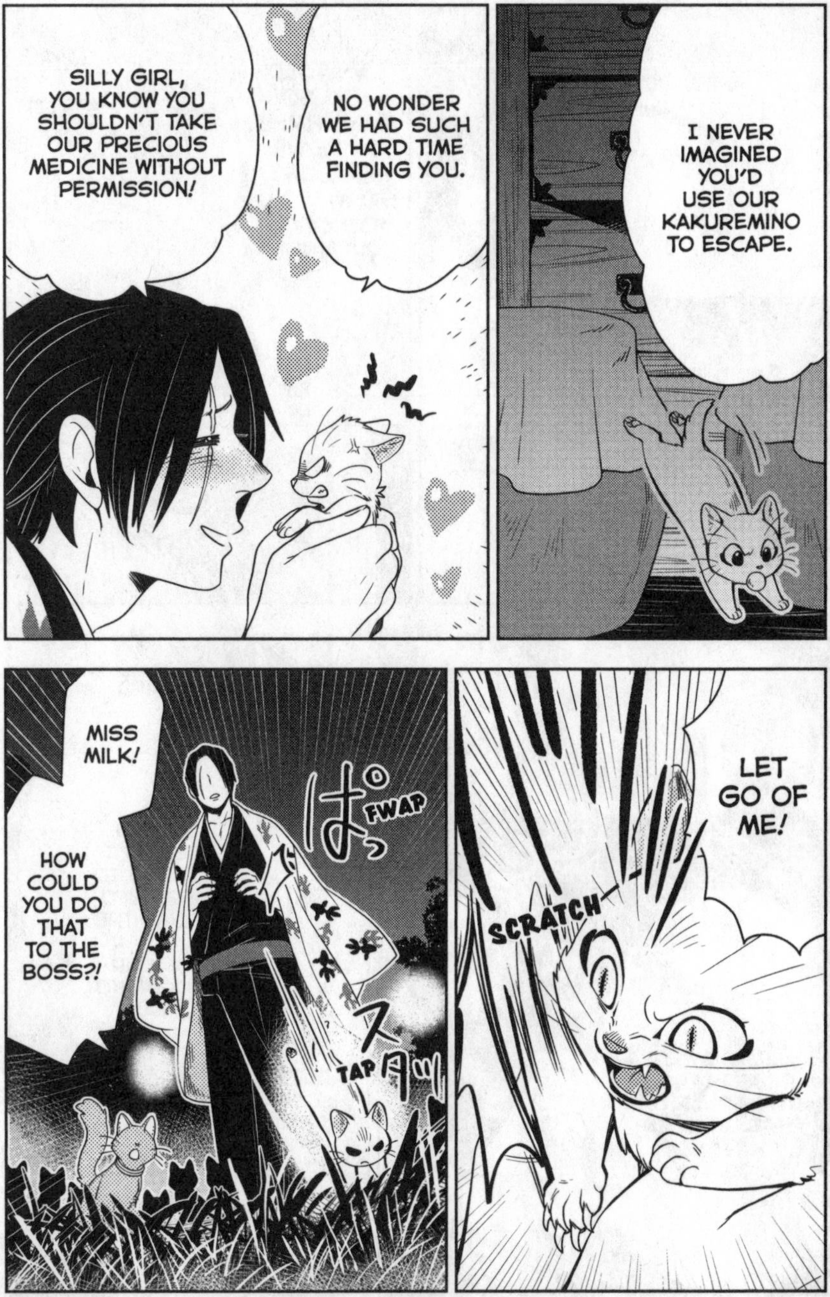
I NEVER IMAGINED YOU'D USE OUR KAKUREMINO TO ESCAPE.
NO WONDER WE HAD SUCH A HARD TIME FINDING YOU.
SILLY GIRL, YOU KNOW YOU SHOULDN'T TAKE OUR PRECIOUS MEDICINE WITHOUT PERMISSION!
LET GO OF ME!
SCRATCH
FWAP
MISS MILK!
HOW COULD YOU DO THAT TO THE BOSS?!
TAP

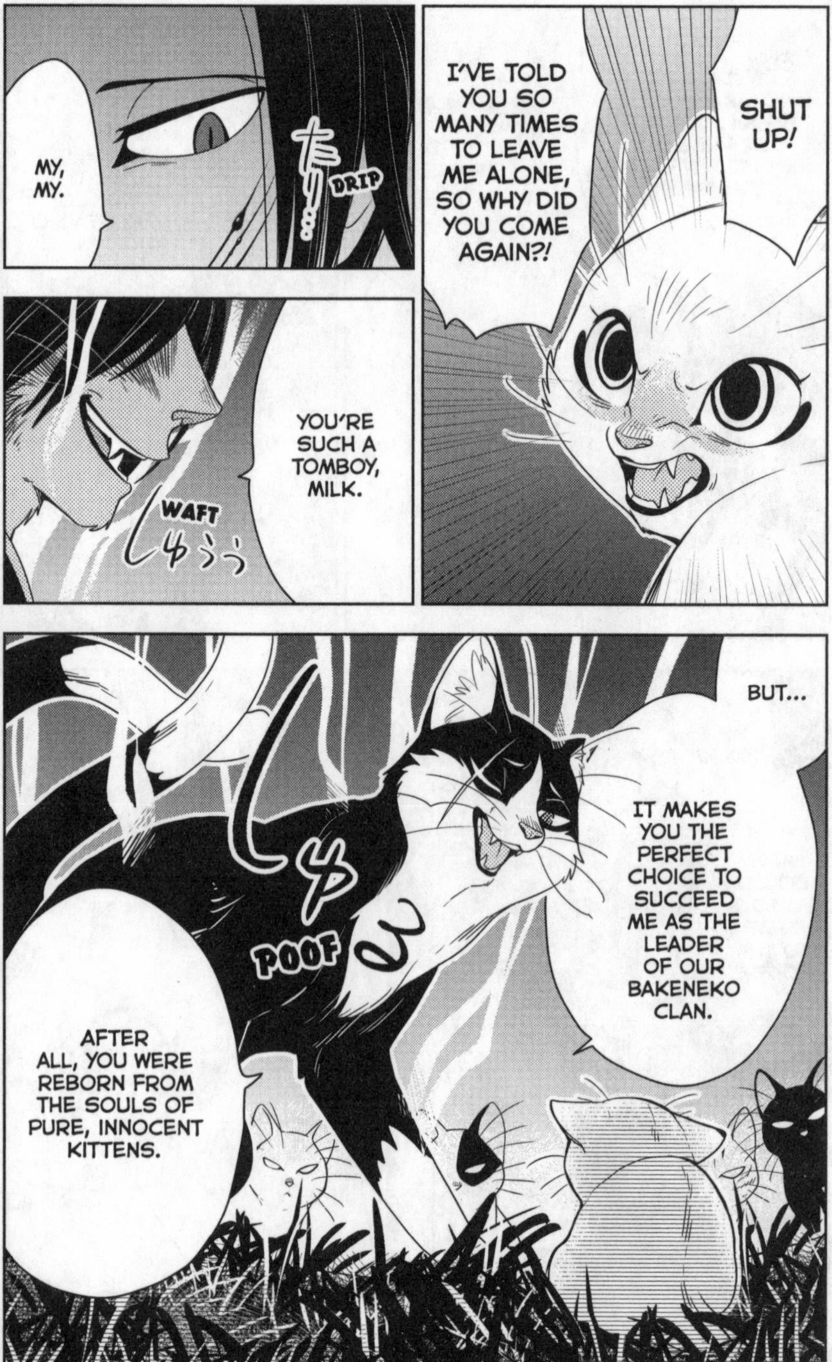
SHUT UP!
I'VE TOLD YOU SO MANY TIMES TO LEAVE ME ALONE, SO WHY DID YOU COME AGAIN?!
MY, MY.
DRIP
YOU'RE SUCH A TOMBOY, MILK.
WAFT
BUT...
IT MAKES YOU THE PERFECT CHOICE TO SUCCEED ME AS THE LEADER OF OUR BAKENEKO CLAN.
POOF
AFTER ALL, YOU WERE REBORN FROM THE SOULS OF PURE, INNOCENT KITTENS.

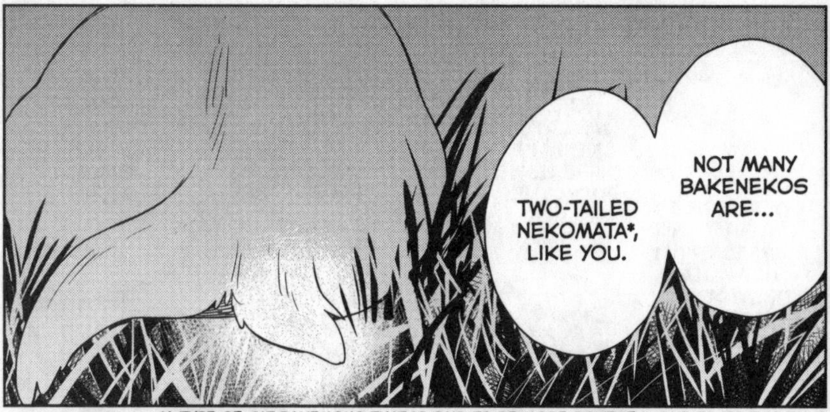
NOT MANY BAKENEKOS ARE...
TWO-TAILED NEKOMATA*, LIKE YOU.

*A TYPE OF CAT BAKEMONO THAT IS SAID TO BE MORE POWERFUL DUE TO ITS TWO TAILS

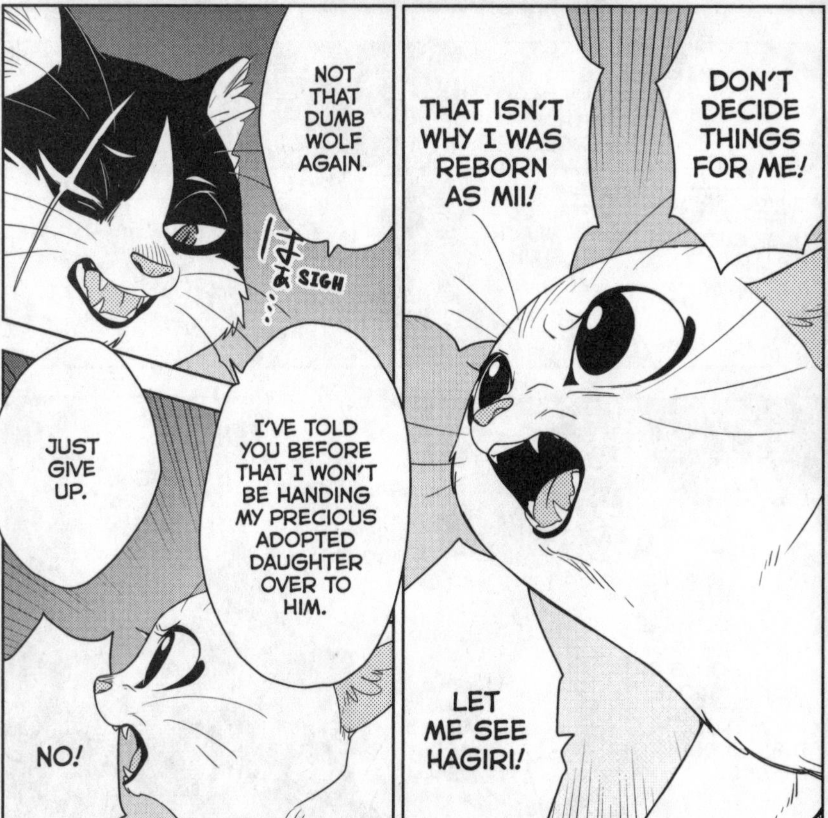
DON'T DECIDE THINGS FOR ME!
THAT ISN'T WHY I WAS REBORN AS MII!
LET ME SEE HAGIRI!
NOT THAT DUMB WOLF AGAIN.
はぁ… SIGH
I'VE TOLD YOU BEFORE THAT I WON'T BE HANDING MY PRECIOUS ADOPTED DAUGHTER OVER TO HIM.
JUST GIVE UP.
NO!

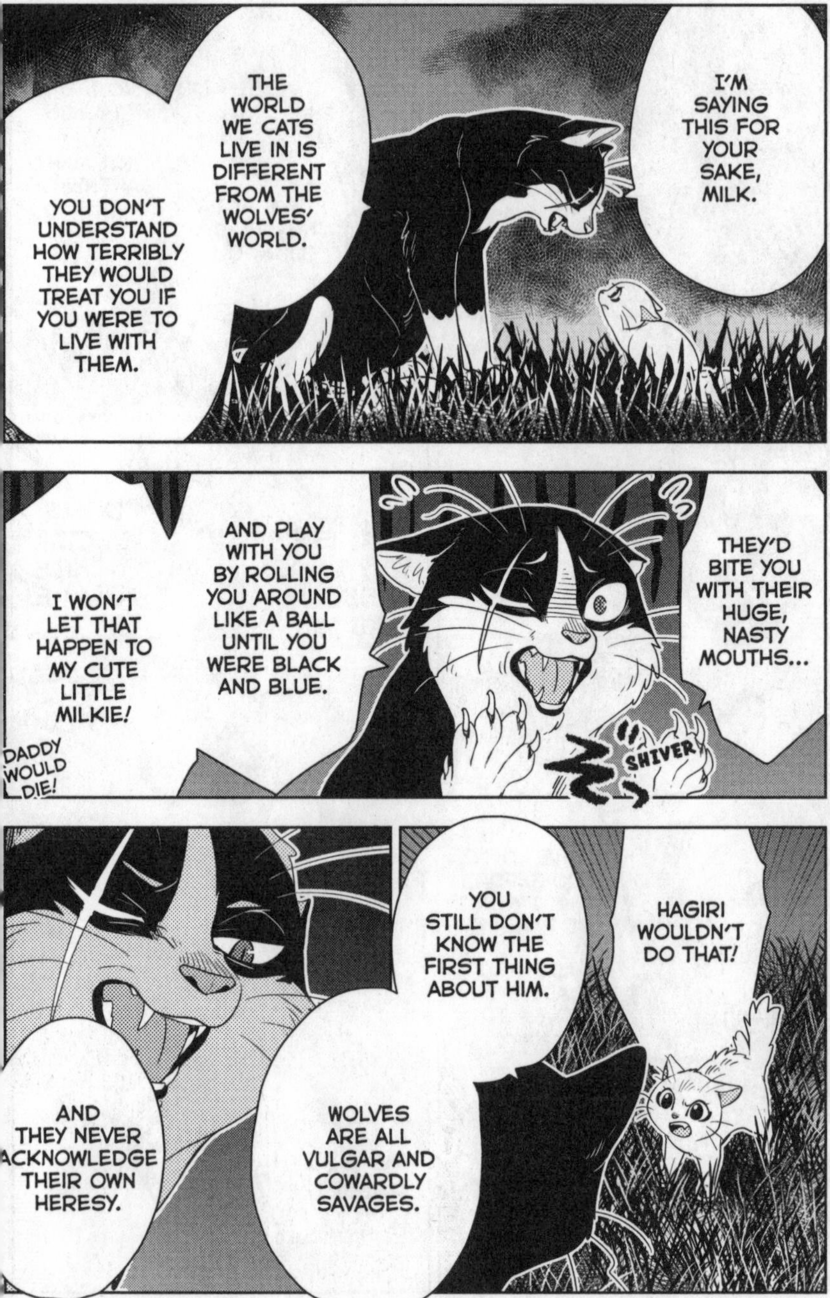
I'M SAYING THIS FOR YOUR SAKE, MILK.
THE WORLD WE CATS LIVE IN IS DIFFERENT FROM THE WOLVES' WORLD.
YOU DON'T UNDERSTAND HOW TERRIBLY THEY WOULD TREAT YOU IF YOU WERE TO LIVE WITH THEM.
THEY'D BITE YOU WITH THEIR HUGE, NASTY MOUTHS...
SHIVER
AND PLAY WITH YOU BY ROLLING YOU AROUND LIKE A BALL UNTIL YOU WERE BLACK AND BLUE.
I WON'T LET THAT HAPPEN TO MY CUTE LITTLE MILKIE!
DADDY WOULD DIE!
HAGIRI WOULDN'T DO THAT!
YOU STILL DON'T KNOW THE FIRST THING ABOUT HIM.
WOLVES ARE ALL VULGAR AND COWARDLY SAVAGES.
AND THEY NEVER ACKNOWLEDGE THEIR OWN HERESY.

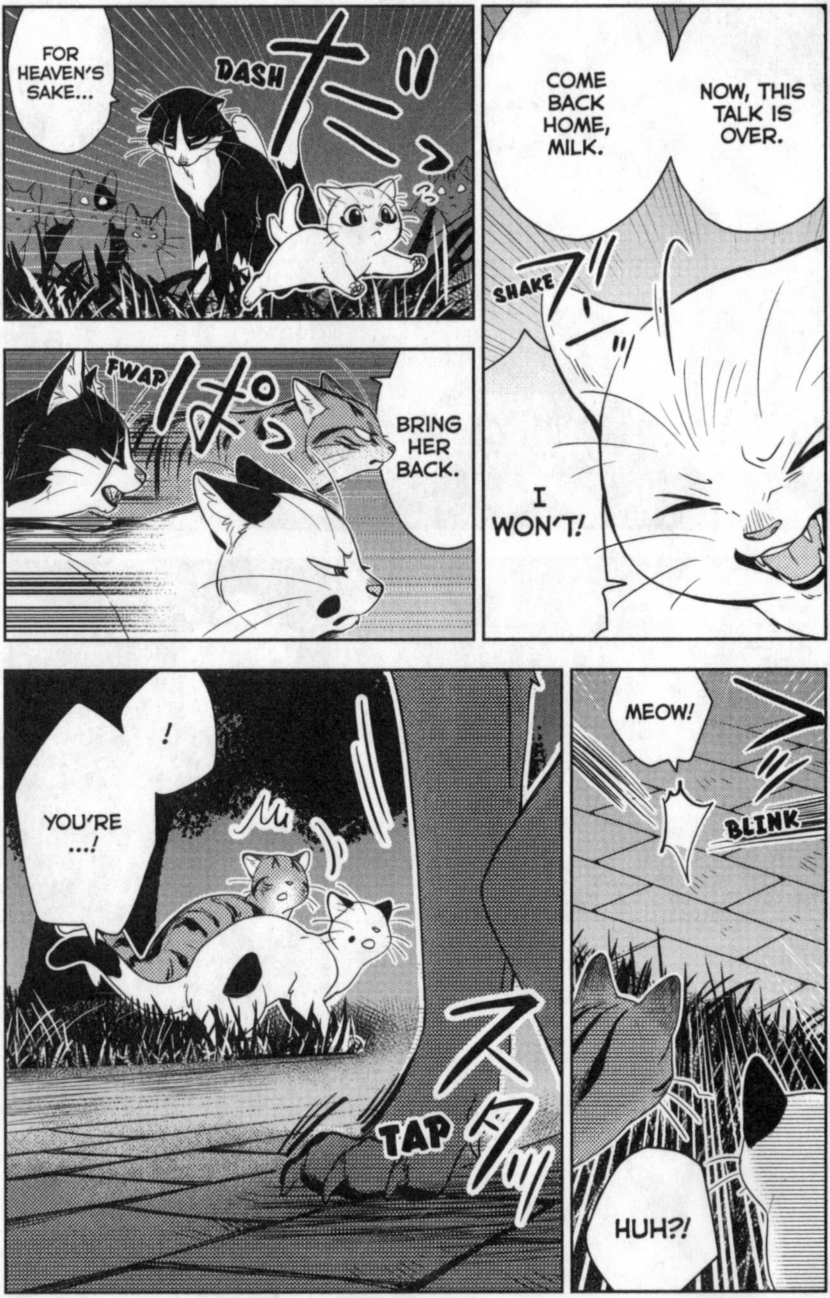
NOW, THIS TALK IS OVER.
COME BACK HOME, MILK.
SHAKE
I WON'T!
DASH
FOR HEAVEN'S SAKE...
BRING HER BACK.
FWAP
MEOW!
BLINK
HUH?!
!
YOU'RE ...!
TAP

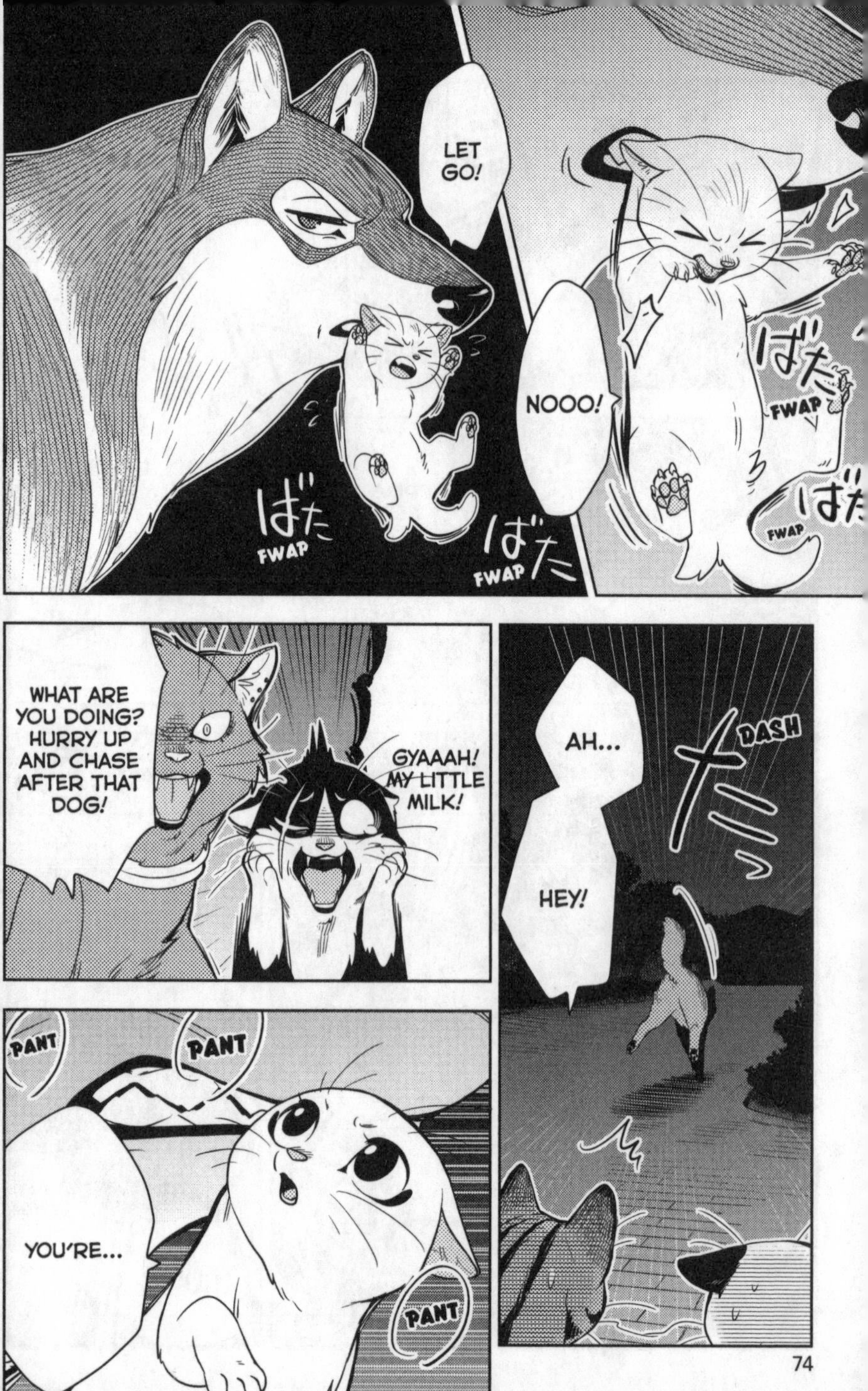
NOOO!
ばた
FWAP
ばた
FWAP
LET GO!
ばた
FWAP
ばた
FWAP
DASH
AH...
HEY!
GYAAAH! MY LITTLE MILK!
WHAT ARE YOU DOING? HURRY UP AND CHASE AFTER THAT DOG!
PANT
PANT
YOU'RE...
PANT

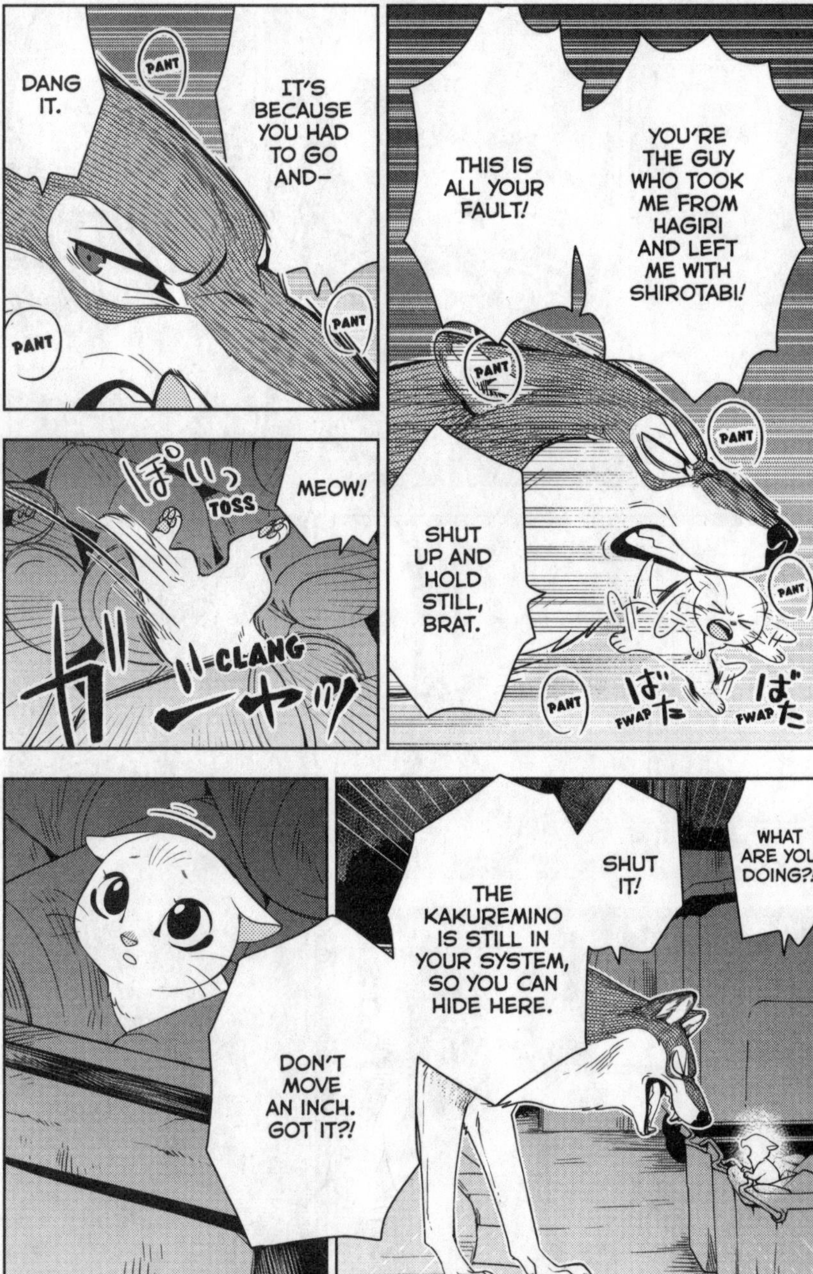
YOU'RE THE GUY WHO TOOK ME FROM HAGIRI AND LEFT ME WITH SHIROTABI!
THIS IS ALL YOUR FAULT!
PANT
PANT
SHUT UP AND HOLD STILL, BRAT.
PANT
PANT
ばた FWAP
ばた FWAP
IT'S BECAUSE YOU HAD TO GO AND–
PANT
DANG IT.
PANT
PANT
MEOW!
ぽいっ TOSS
ガシャッ CLANG
WHAT ARE YOU DOING?!
SHUT IT!
THE KAKUREMINO IS STILL IN YOUR SYSTEM, SO YOU CAN HIDE HERE.
DON'T MOVE AN INCH. GOT IT?!

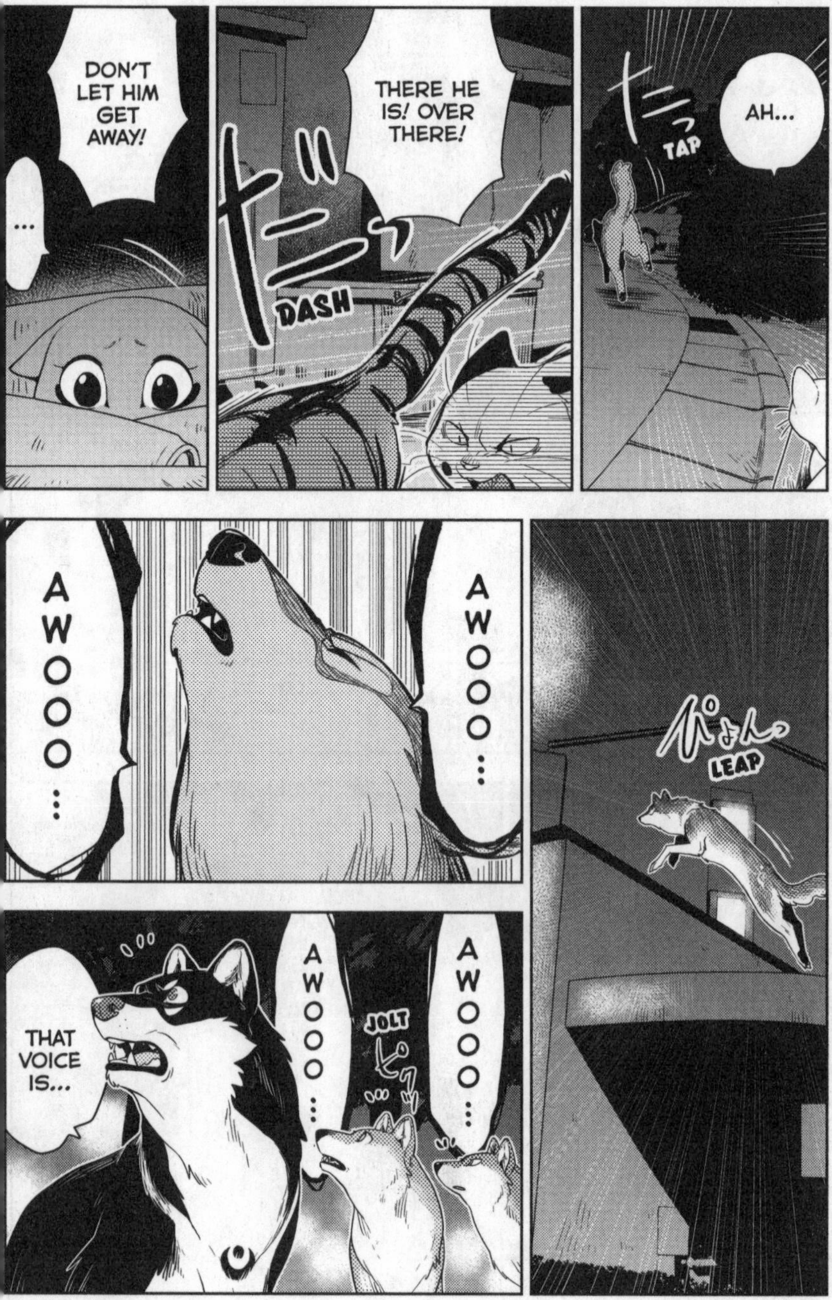
AH...
TAP
THERE HE IS! OVER THERE!
DASH
DON'T LET HIM GET AWAY!
...
LEAP
AWOOO...
AWOOOO...
AWOOO...
AWOOO...
JOLT
THAT VOICE IS...

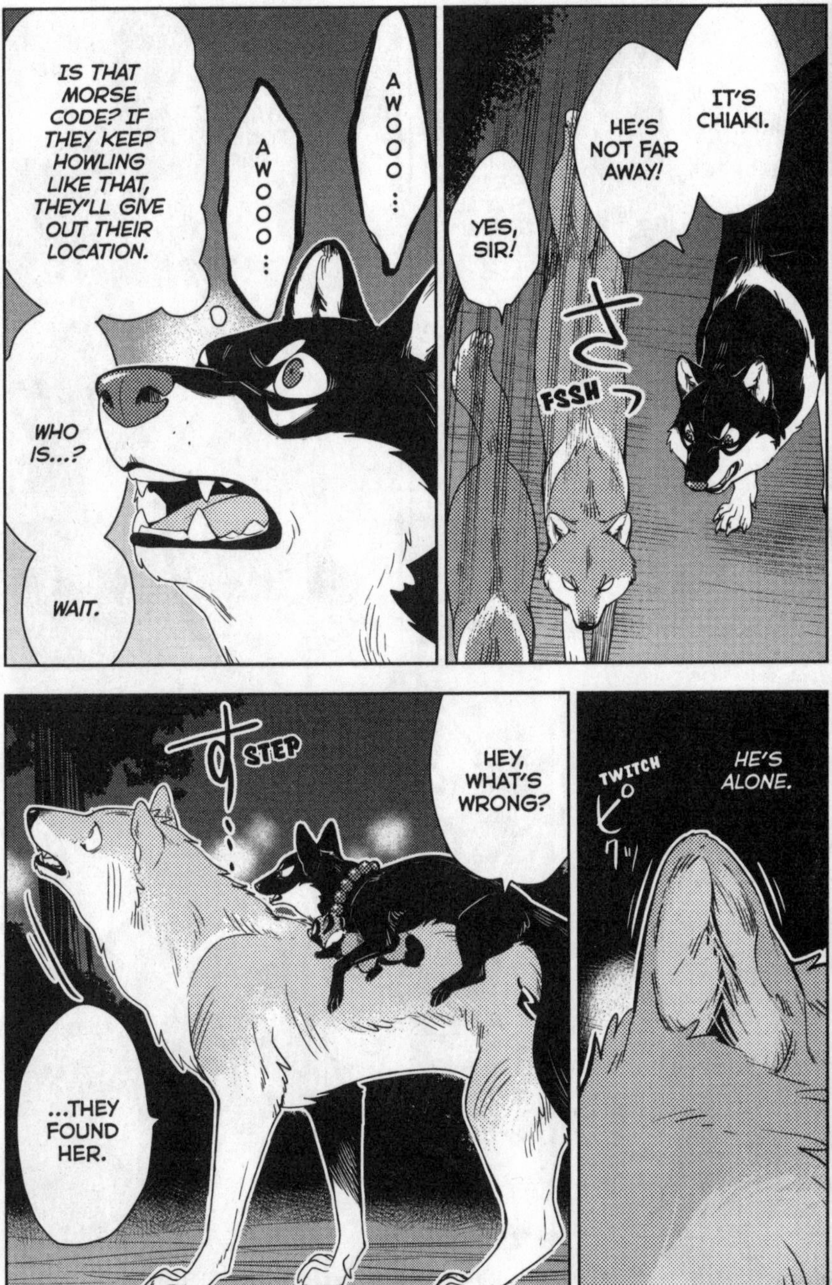
IT'S CHIAKI.
HE'S NOT FAR AWAY!
YES, SIR!
FSSH
AWOOO ...
AWOOO ...
IS THAT MORSE CODE? IF THEY KEEP HOWLING LIKE THAT, THEY'LL GIVE OUT THEIR LOCATION.
WHO IS...?
WAIT.
HE'S ALONE.
TWITCH
HEY, WHAT'S WRONG?
STEP
...THEY FOUND HER.

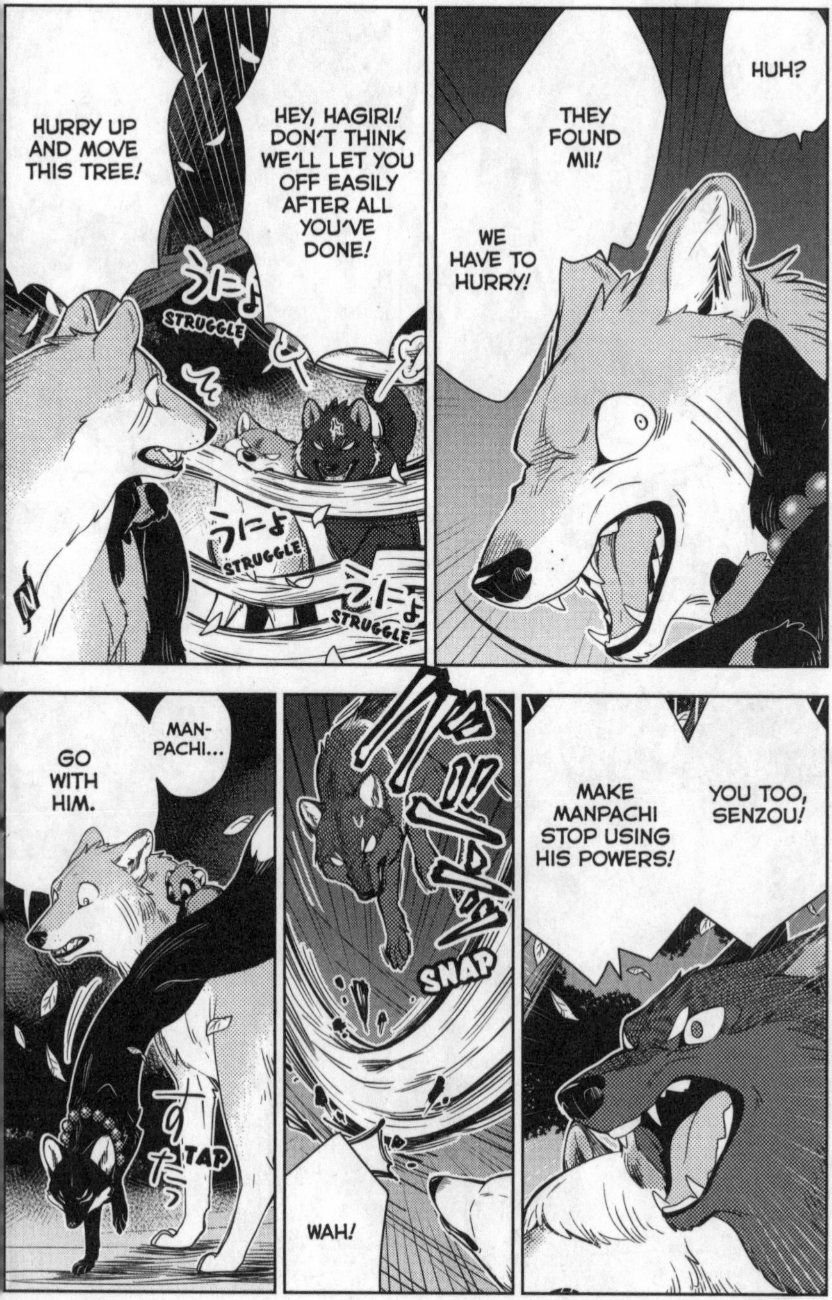
HUH?
THEY FOUND MII!
WE HAVE TO HURRY!
HEY, HAGIRI! DON'T THINK WE'LL LET YOU OFF EASILY AFTER ALL YOU'VE DONE!
HURRY UP AND MOVE THIS TREE!
うにょ
STRUGGLE
うにょ
STRUGGLE
うにょ
STRUGGLE
YOU TOO, SENZOU!
MAKE MANPACHI STOP USING HIS POWERS!
SNAP
WAH!
MAN-PACHI...
GO WITH HIM.
TAP

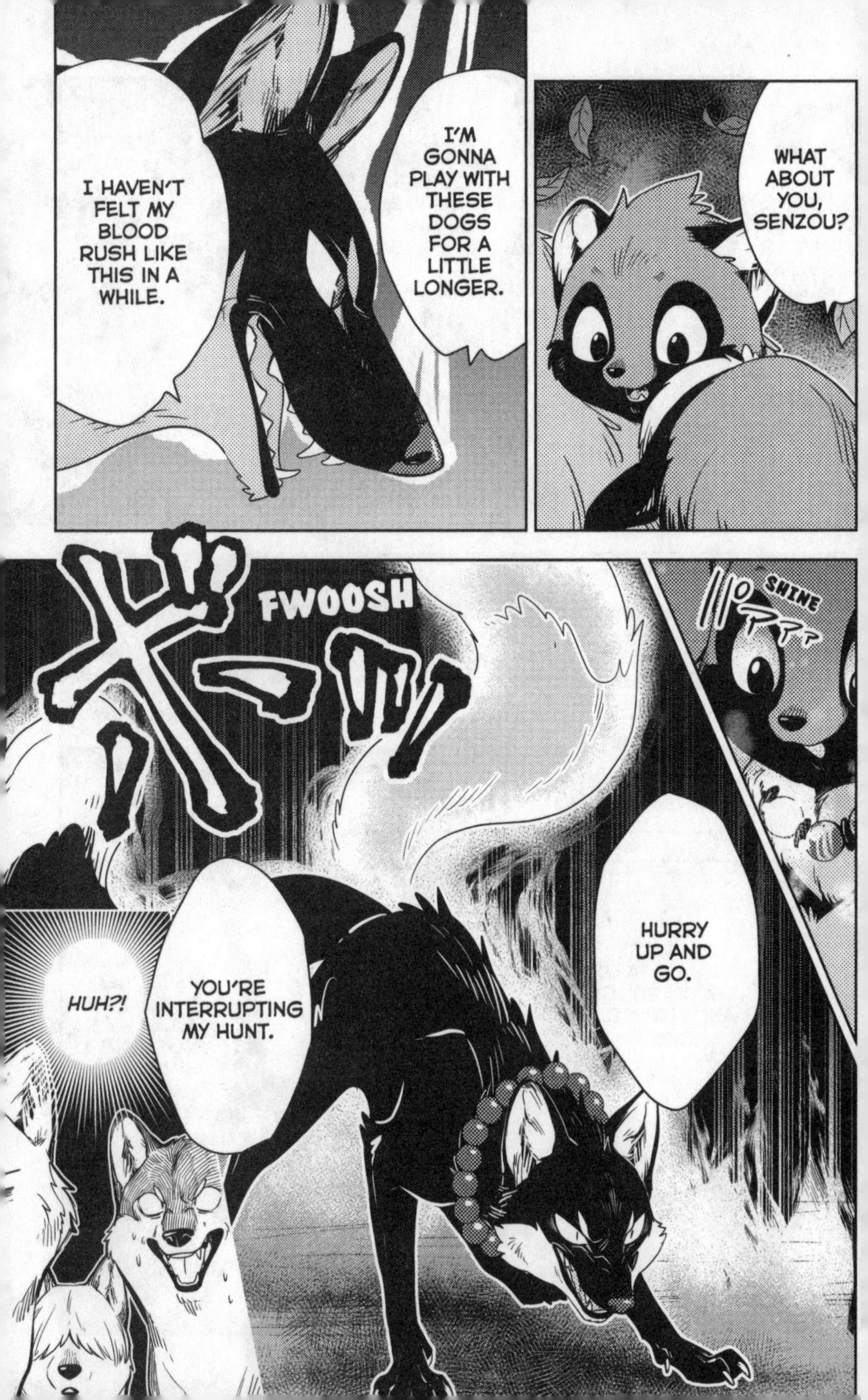
WHAT ABOUT YOU, SENZOU?
I'M GONNA PLAY WITH THESE DOGS FOR A LITTLE LONGER.
I HAVEN'T FELT MY BLOOD RUSH LIKE THIS IN A WHILE.
SHINE
FWOOSH
HURRY UP AND GO.
YOU'RE INTERRUPTING MY HUNT.
HUH?!

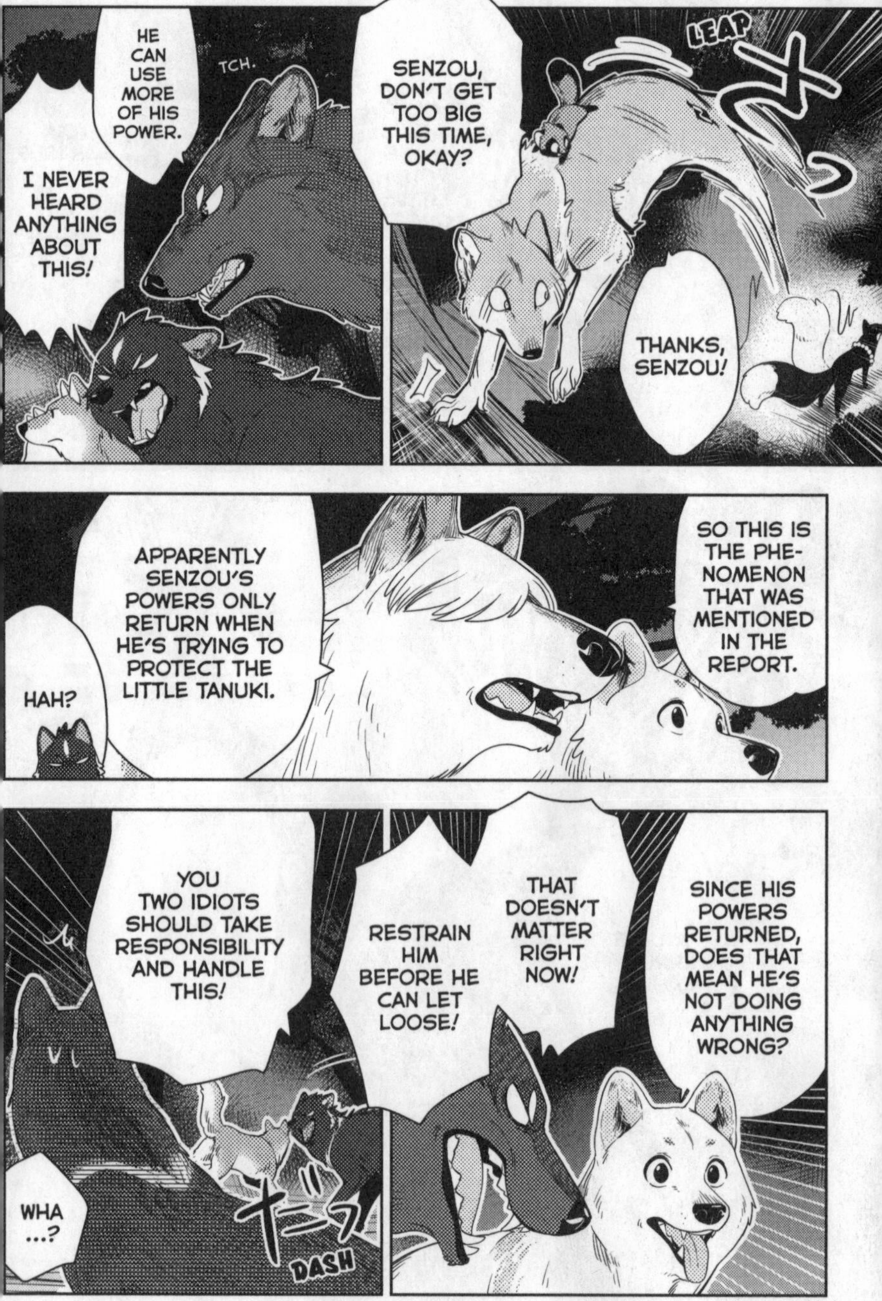
LEAP
SENZOU, DON'T GET TOO BIG THIS TIME, OKAY?
THANKS, SENZOU!
HE CAN USE MORE OF HIS POWER.
TCH.
I NEVER HEARD ANYTHING ABOUT THIS!
SO THIS IS THE PHE-NOMENON THAT WAS MENTIONED IN THE REPORT.
APPARENTLY SENZOU'S POWERS ONLY RETURN WHEN HE'S TRYING TO PROTECT THE LITTLE TANUKI.
HAH?
SINCE HIS POWERS RETURNED, DOES THAT MEAN HE'S NOT DOING ANYTHING WRONG?
THAT DOESN'T MATTER RIGHT NOW!
RESTRAIN HIM BEFORE HE CAN LET LOOSE!
YOU TWO IDIOTS SHOULD TAKE RESPONSIBILITY AND HANDLE THIS!
WHA ...?
DASH

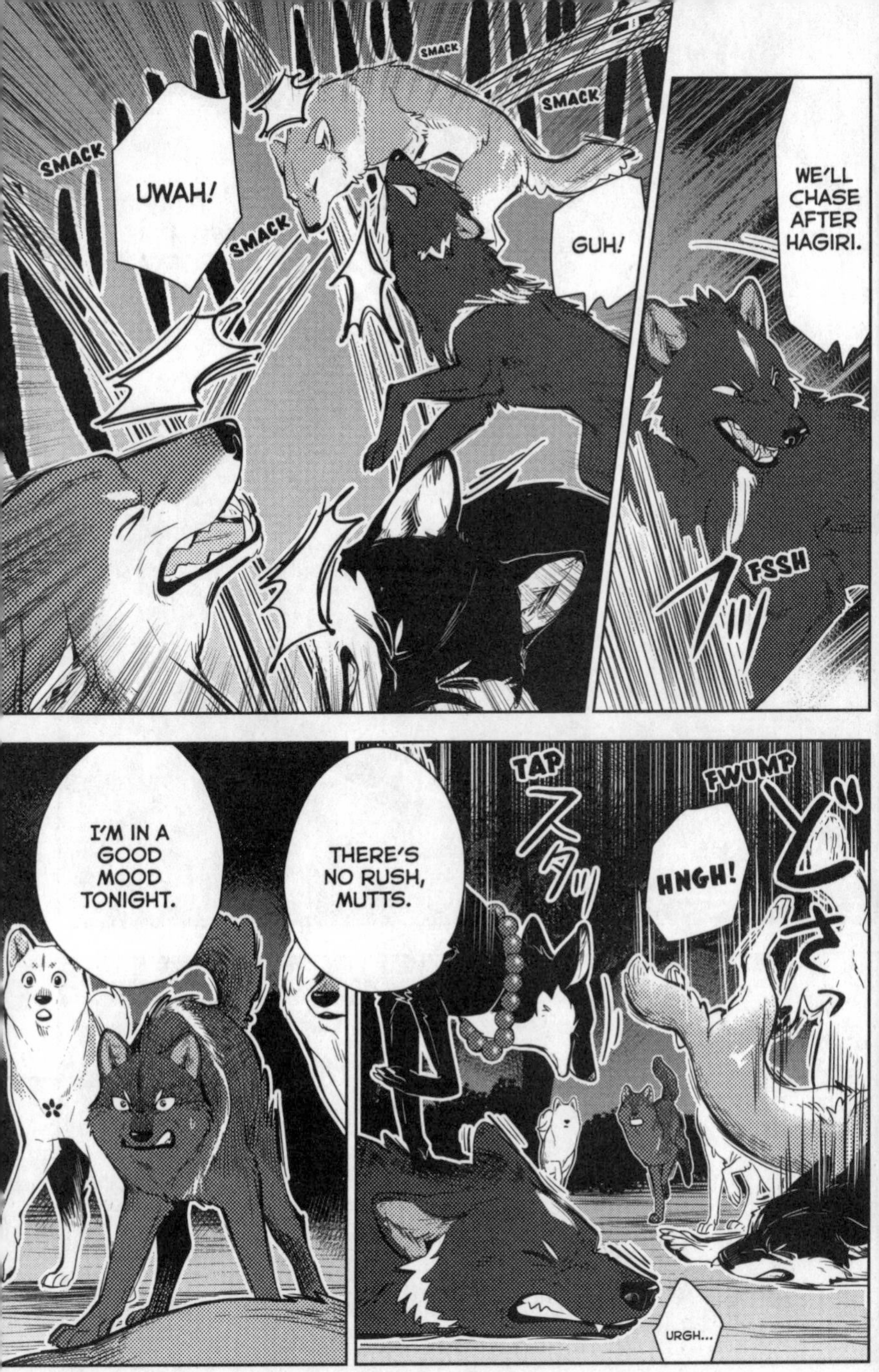
WE'LL CHASE AFTER HAGIRI.
FSSH
SMACK
SMACK
GUH!
UWAH!
SMACK
SMACK
FWUMP
どさっ
TAP
スタッ
HNGH!
URGH...
THERE'S NO RUSH, MUTTS.
I'M IN A GOOD MOOD TONIGHT.

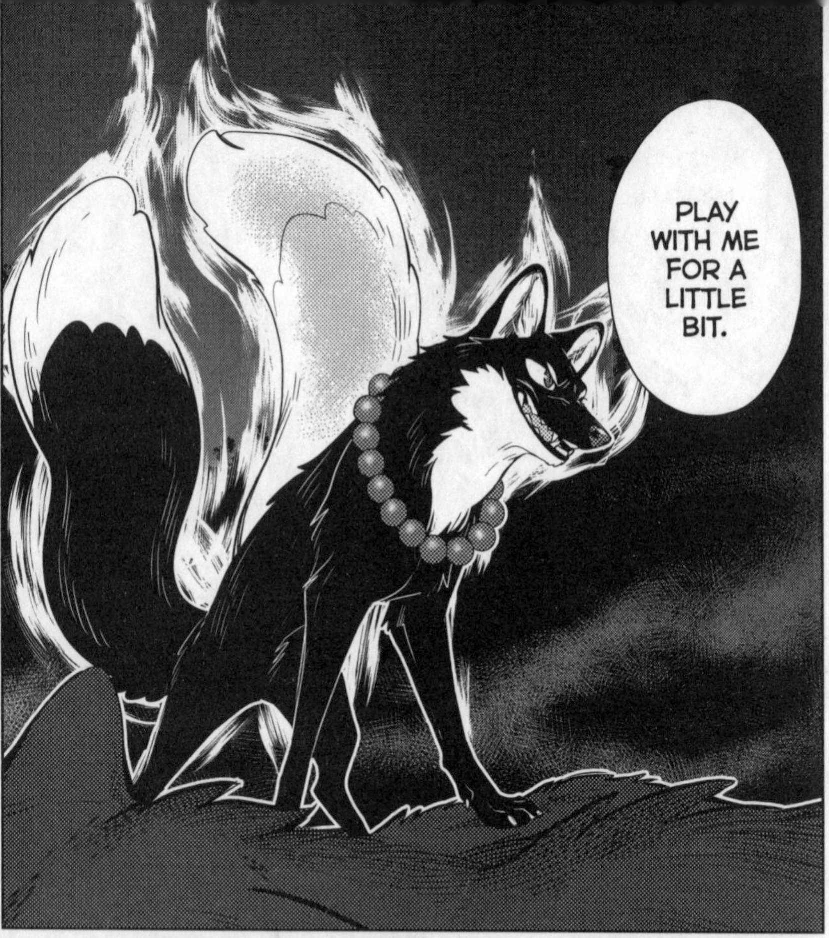
PLAY WITH ME FOR A LITTLE BIT.

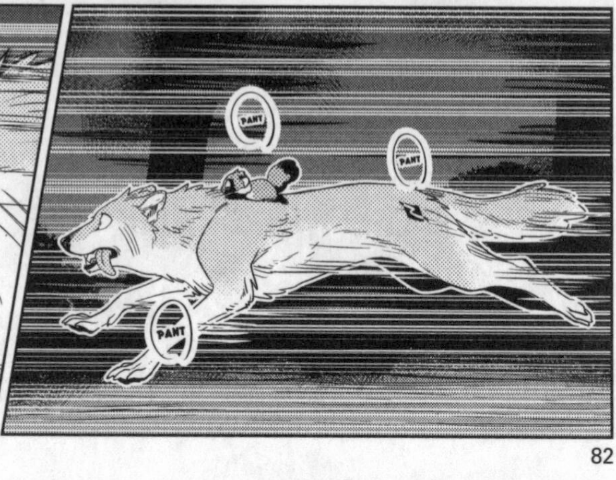
PANT
PANT
PANT

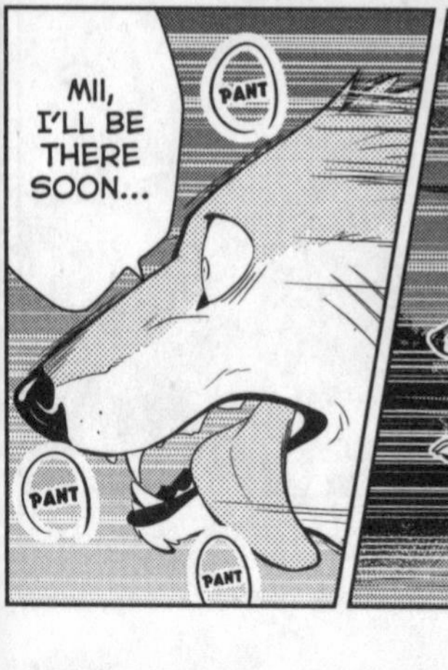
PANT
MII, I'LL BE THERE SOON...
PANT
PANT

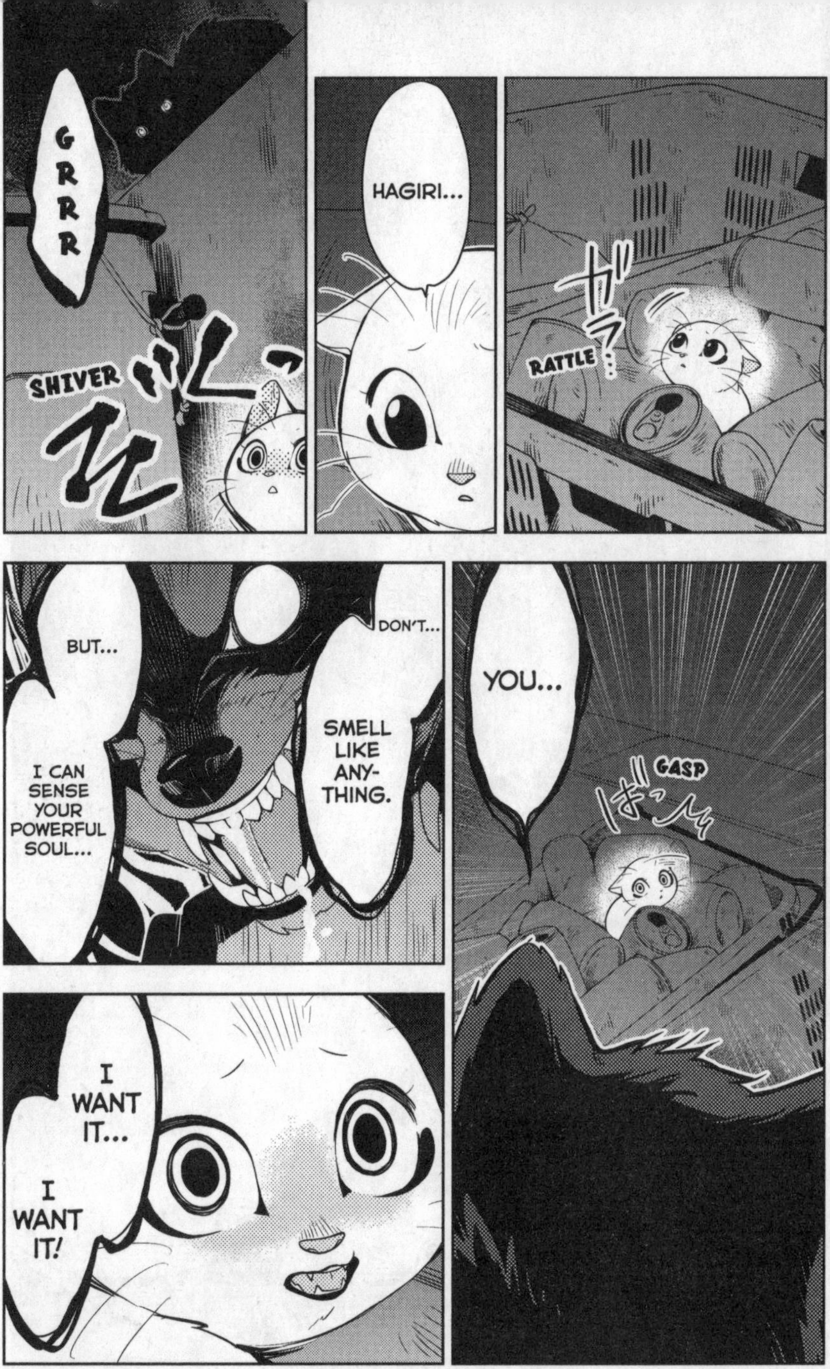

RATTLE
HAGIRI...
GRRR
SHIVER
YOU...
GASP
DON'T...
SMELL LIKE ANY-THING.
BUT...
I CAN SENSE YOUR POWERFUL SOUL...
I WANT IT...
I WANT IT!

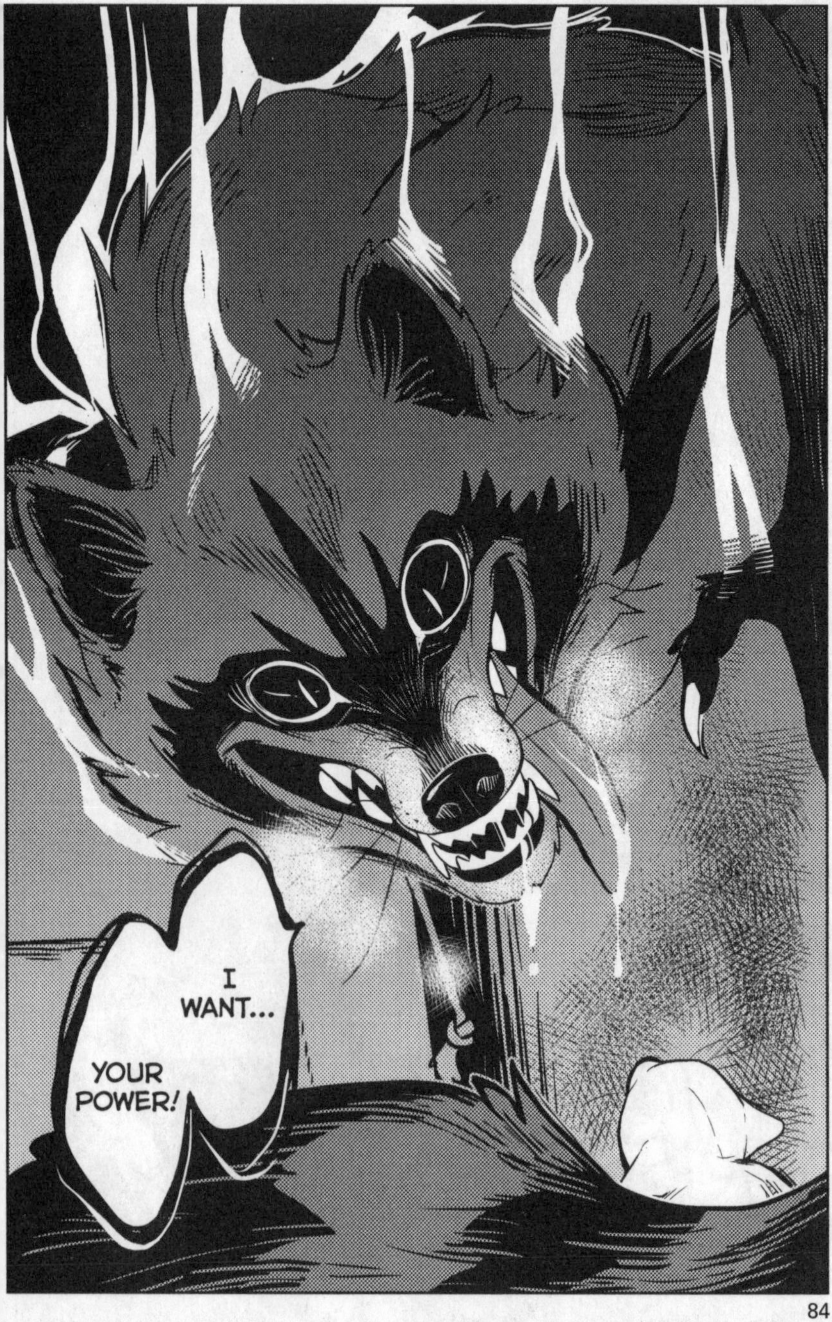
I WANT...
YOUR POWER!

Chapter 17

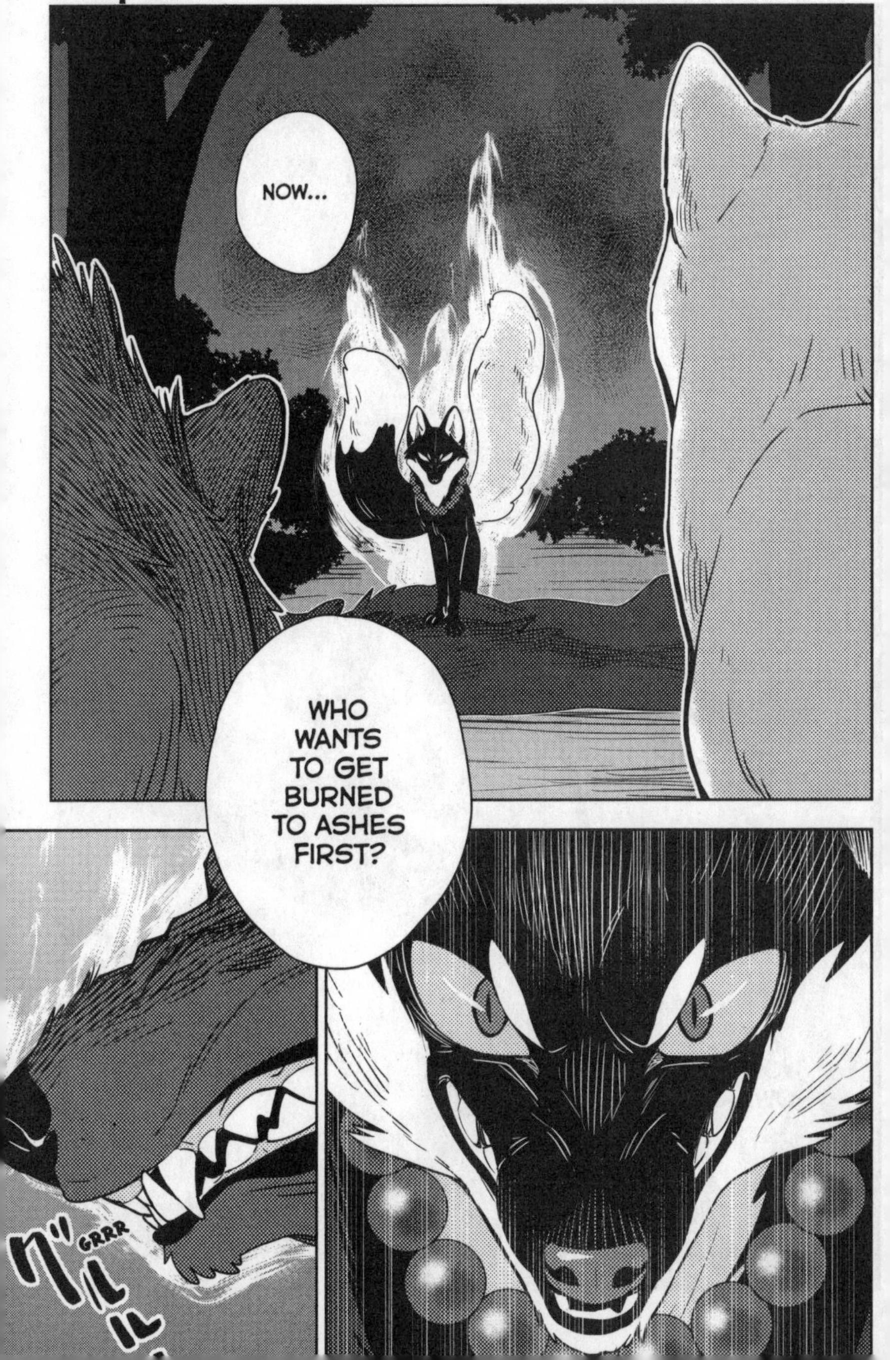
NOW...
WHO WANTS TO GET BURNED TO ASHES FIRST?
GRRR

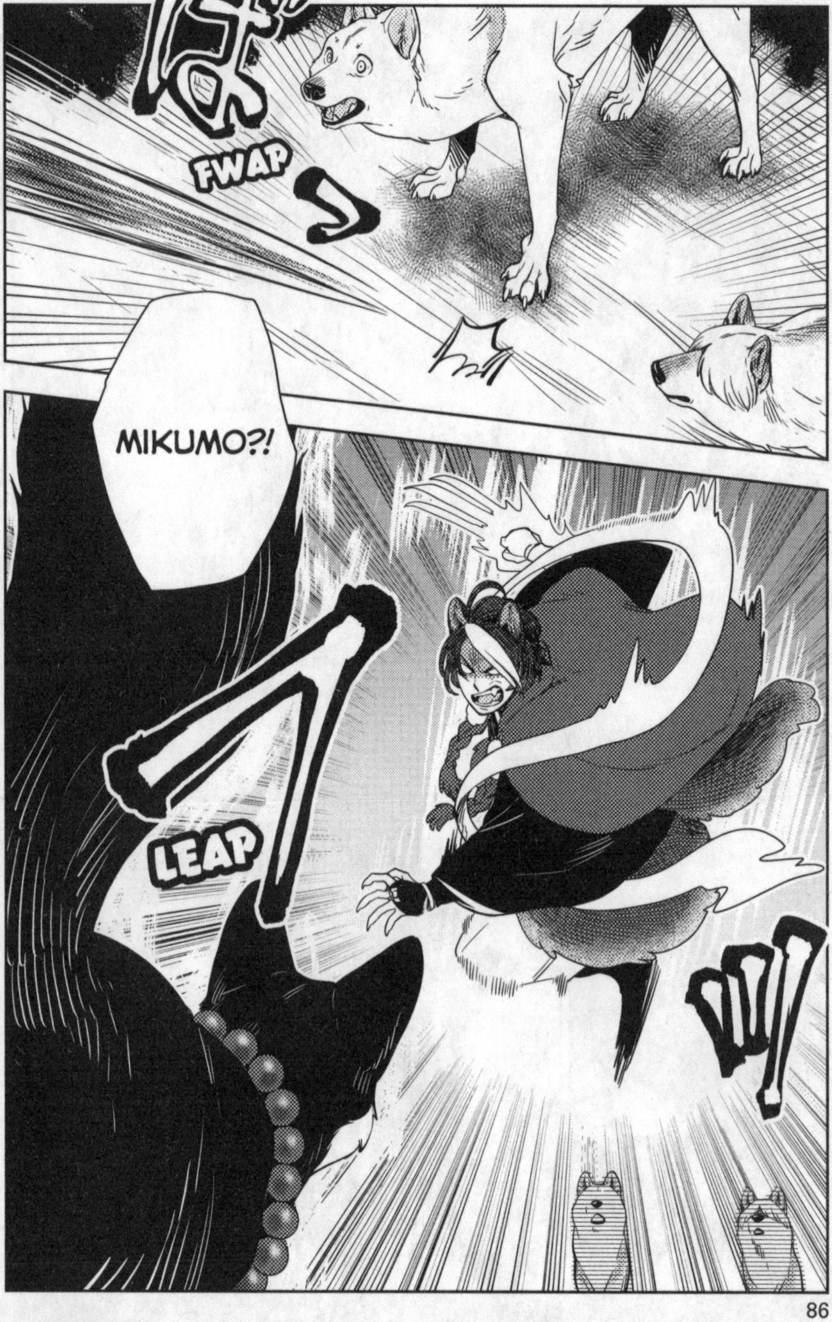
FWAP
MIKUMO?!
LEAP

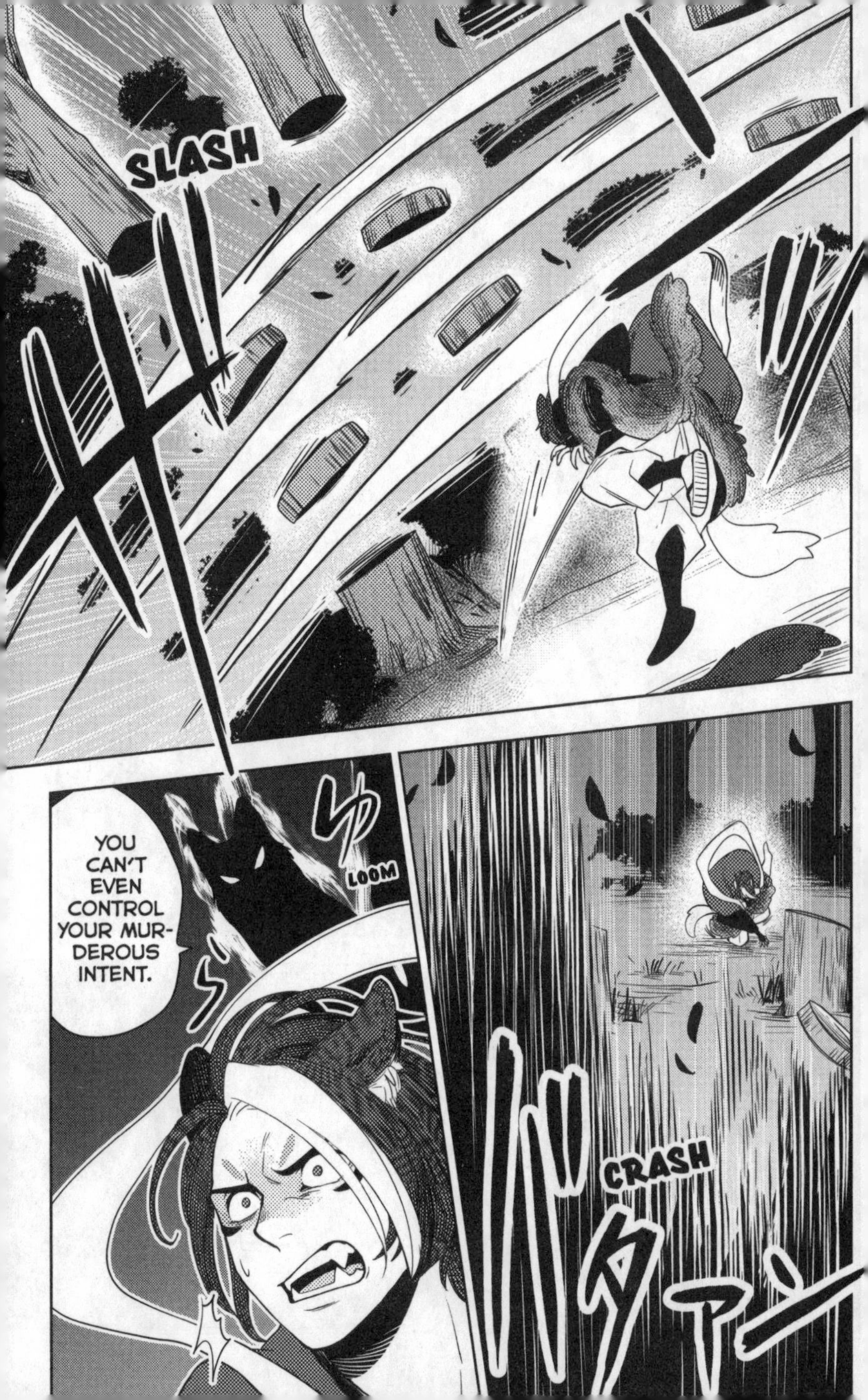
SLASH
CRASH
YOU CAN'T EVEN CONTROL YOUR MUR-DEROUS INTENT.
LOOM

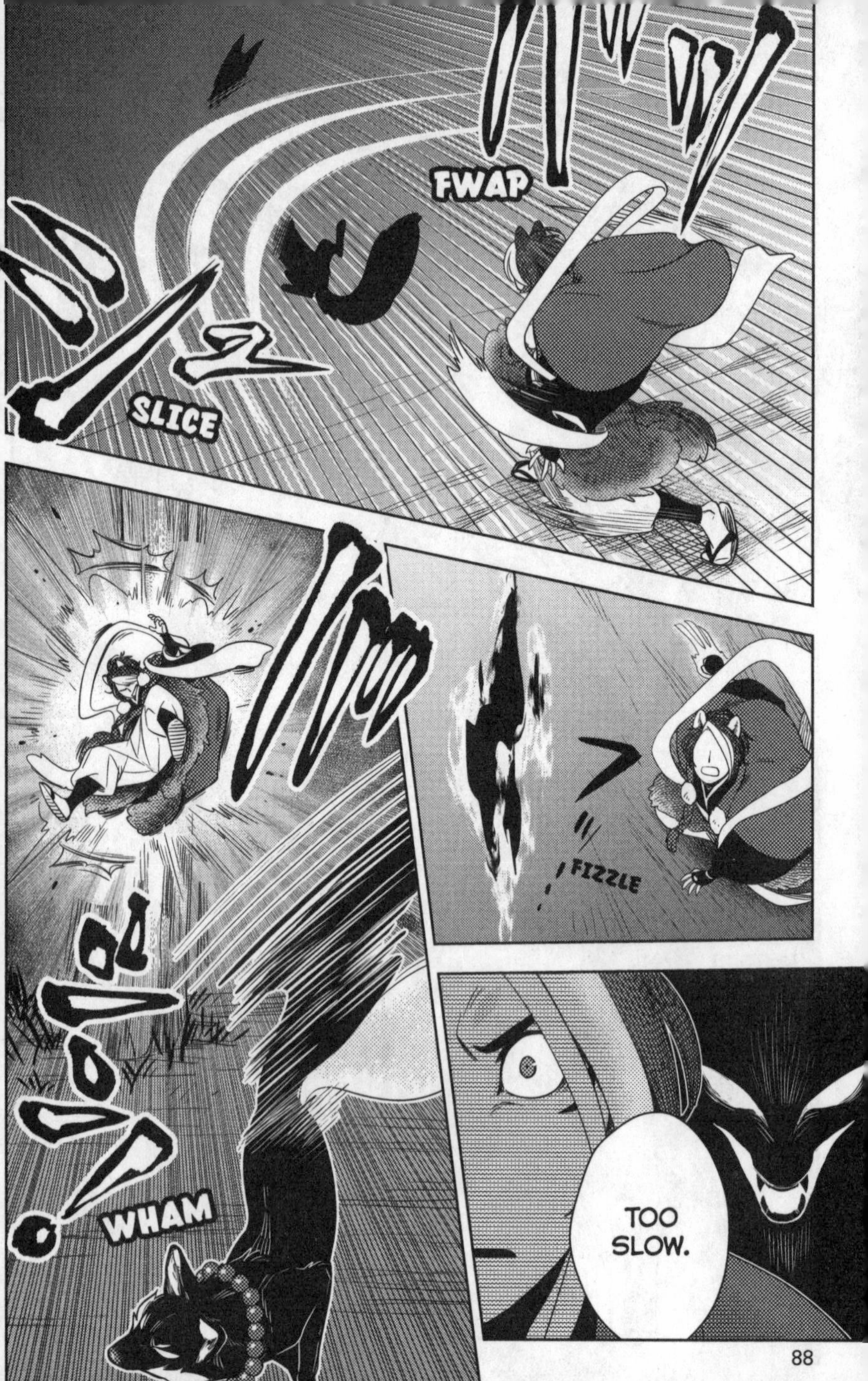
FWAP
SLICE
FIZZLE
TOO SLOW.
WHAM

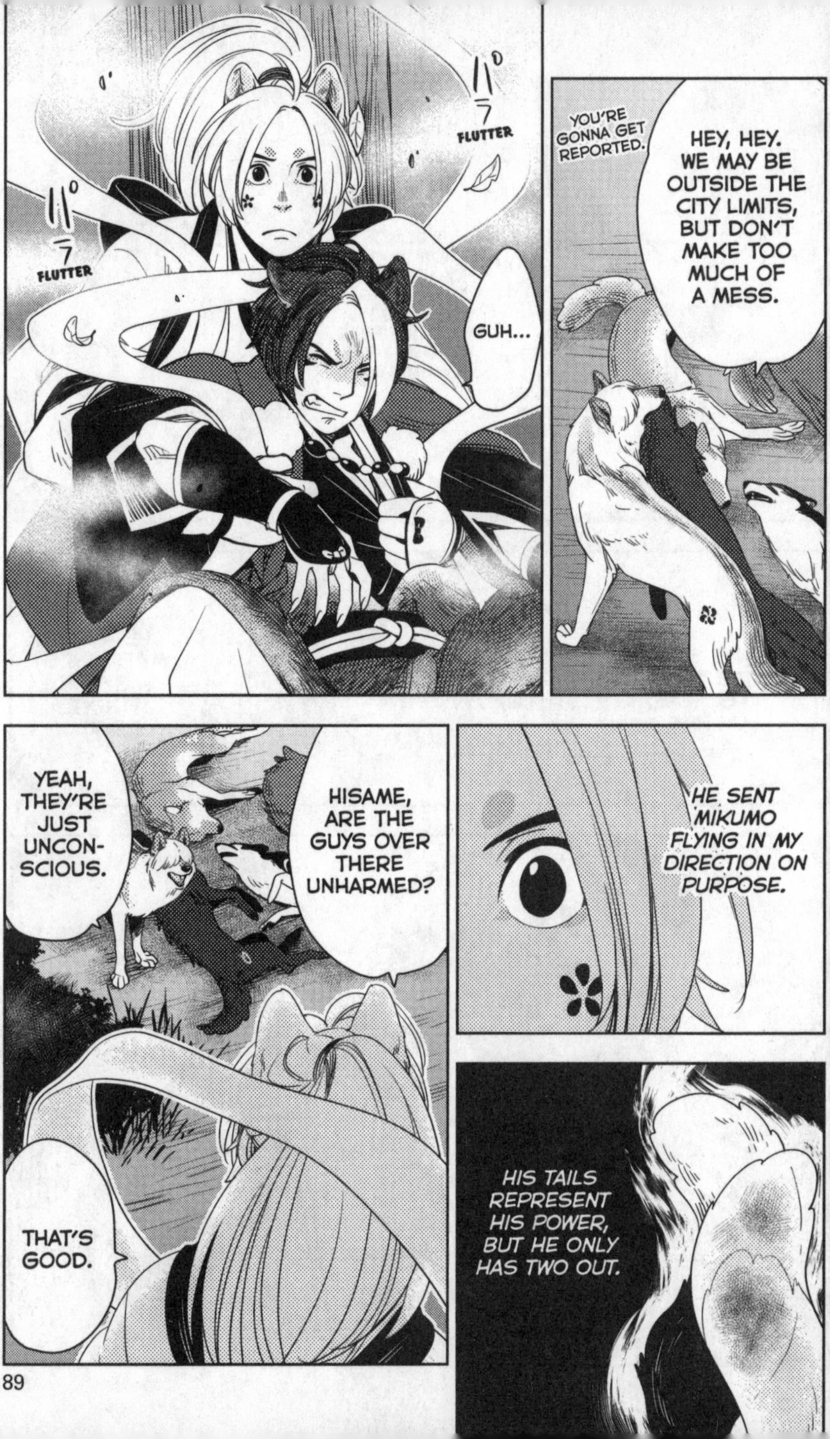
HEY, HEY. WE MAY BE OUTSIDE THE CITY LIMITS, BUT DON'T MAKE TOO MUCH OF A MESS.
YOU'RE GONNA GET REPORTED.
FLUTTER
FLUTTER
GUH...
HE SENT MIKUMO FLYING IN MY DIRECTION ON PURPOSE.
HIS TAILS REPRESENT HIS POWER, BUT HE ONLY HAS TWO OUT.
HISAME, ARE THE GUYS OVER THERE UNHARMED?
YEAH, THEY'RE JUST UNCON-SCIOUS.
THAT'S GOOD.

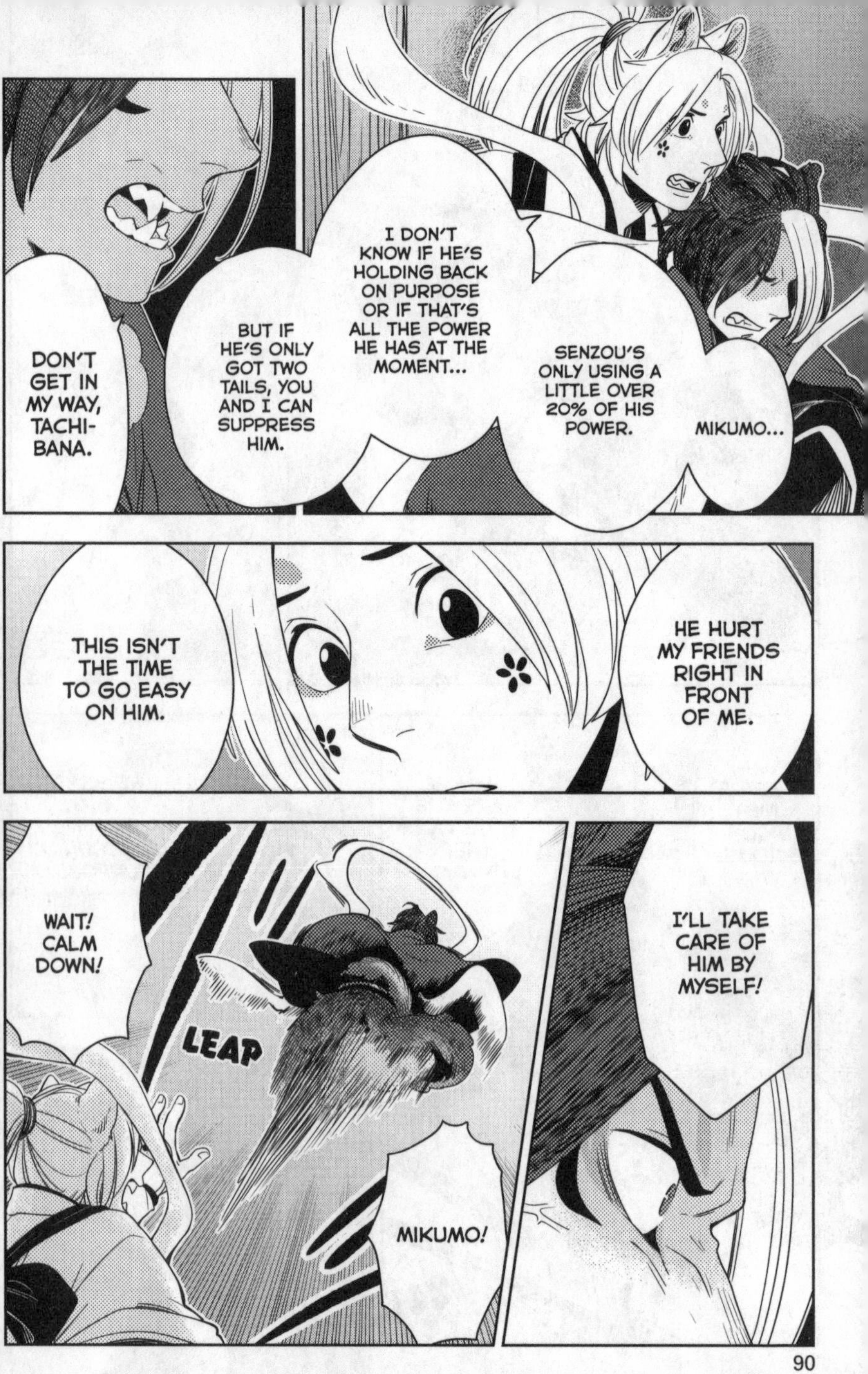
MIKUMO...
SENZOU'S ONLY USING A LITTLE OVER 20% OF HIS POWER.
I DON'T KNOW IF HE'S HOLDING BACK ON PURPOSE OR IF THAT'S ALL THE POWER HE HAS AT THE MOMENT...
BUT IF HE'S ONLY GOT TWO TAILS, YOU AND I CAN SUPPRESS HIM.
DON'T GET IN MY WAY, TACHI-BANA.
HE HURT MY FRIENDS RIGHT IN FRONT OF ME.
THIS ISN'T THE TIME TO GO EASY ON HIM.
I'LL TAKE CARE OF HIM BY MYSELF!
WAIT! CALM DOWN!
LEAP
MIKUMO!

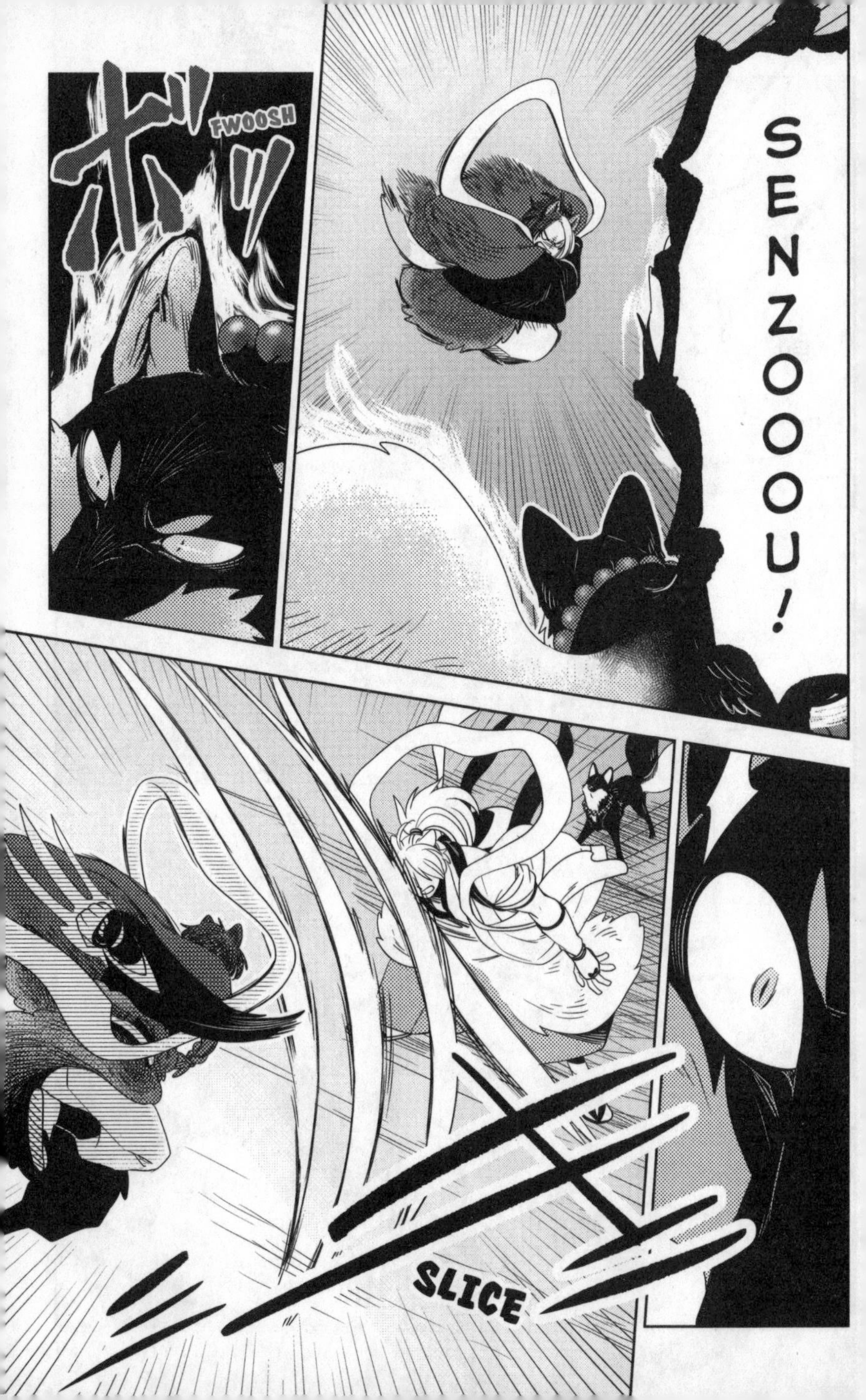
SENZOOOU!
ボッ
FWOOSH
SLICE

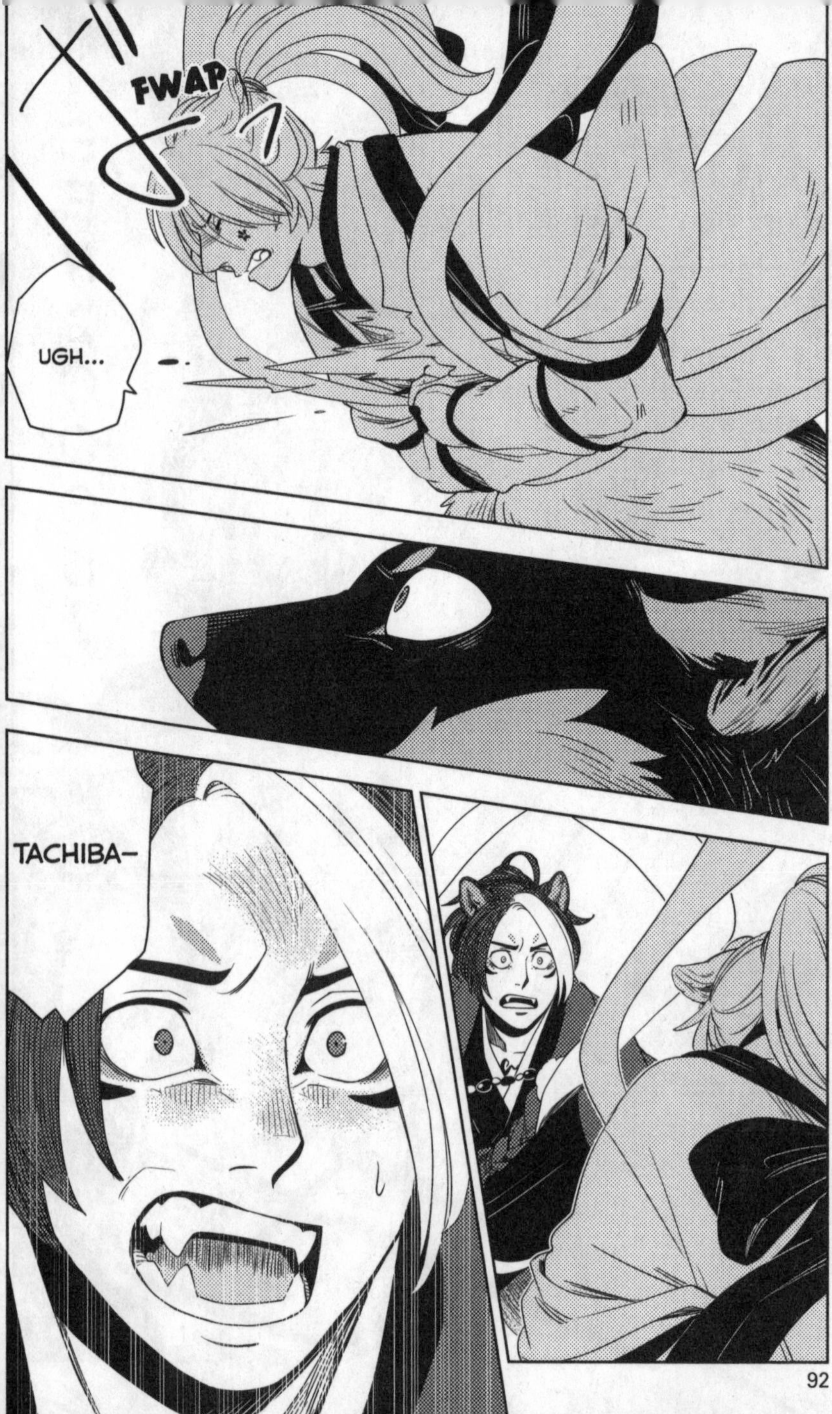
FWAP
UGH...
TACHIBA-

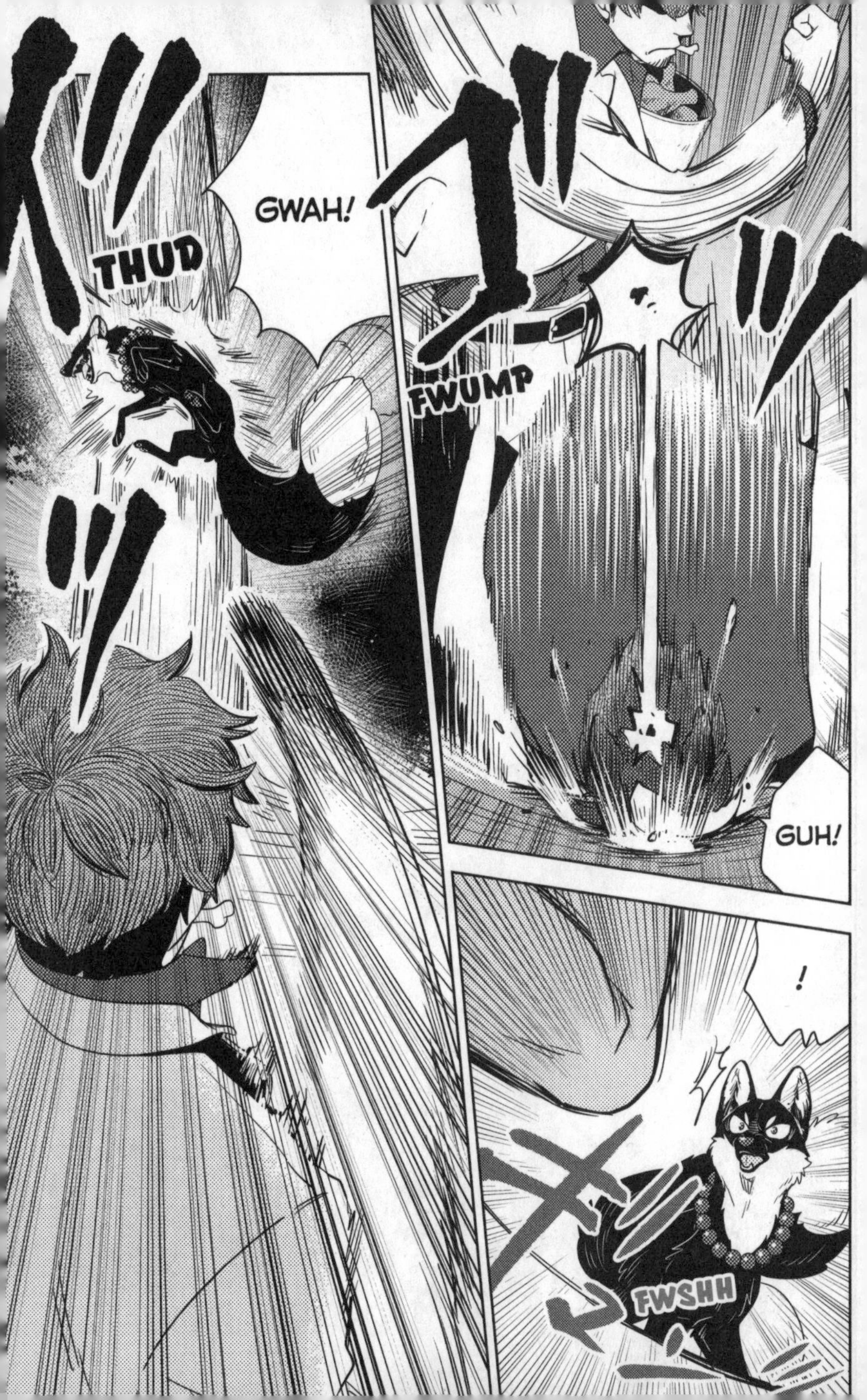
FWUMP
GUH!
!
FWSHH
GWAH!
THUD

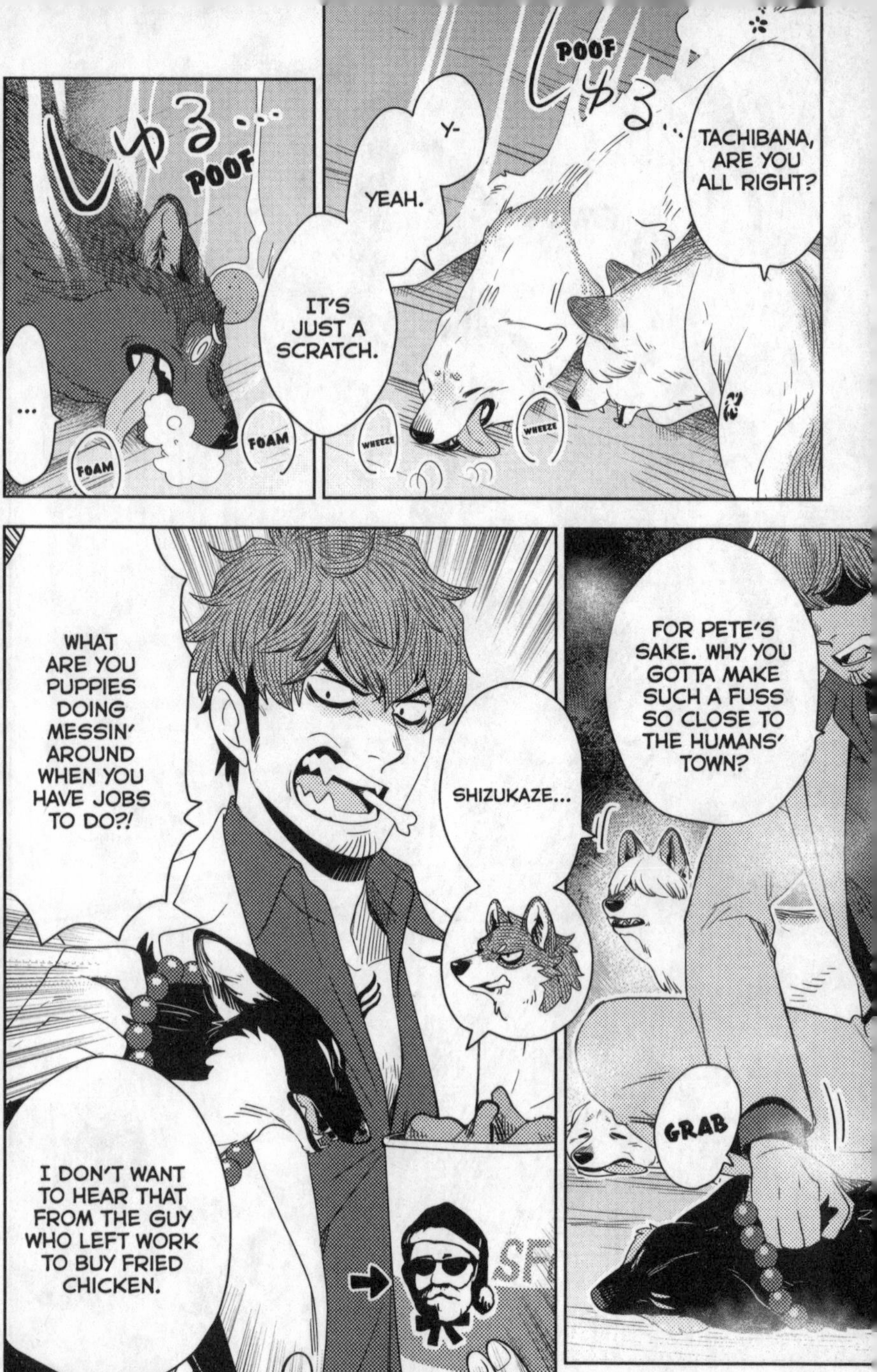
しゅる...
POOF
TACHIBANA, ARE YOU ALL RIGHT?
Y-
YEAH.
IT'S JUST A SCRATCH.
WHEEZE
WHEEZE
しゅる...
POOF
...
FOAM
FOAM
FOR PETE'S SAKE. WHY YOU GOTTA MAKE SUCH A FUSS SO CLOSE TO THE HUMANS' TOWN?
GRAB
WHAT ARE YOU PUPPIES DOING MESSIN' AROUND WHEN YOU HAVE JOBS TO DO?!
SHIZUKAZE...
I DON'T WANT TO HEAR THAT FROM THE GUY WHO LEFT WORK TO BUY FRIED CHICKEN.

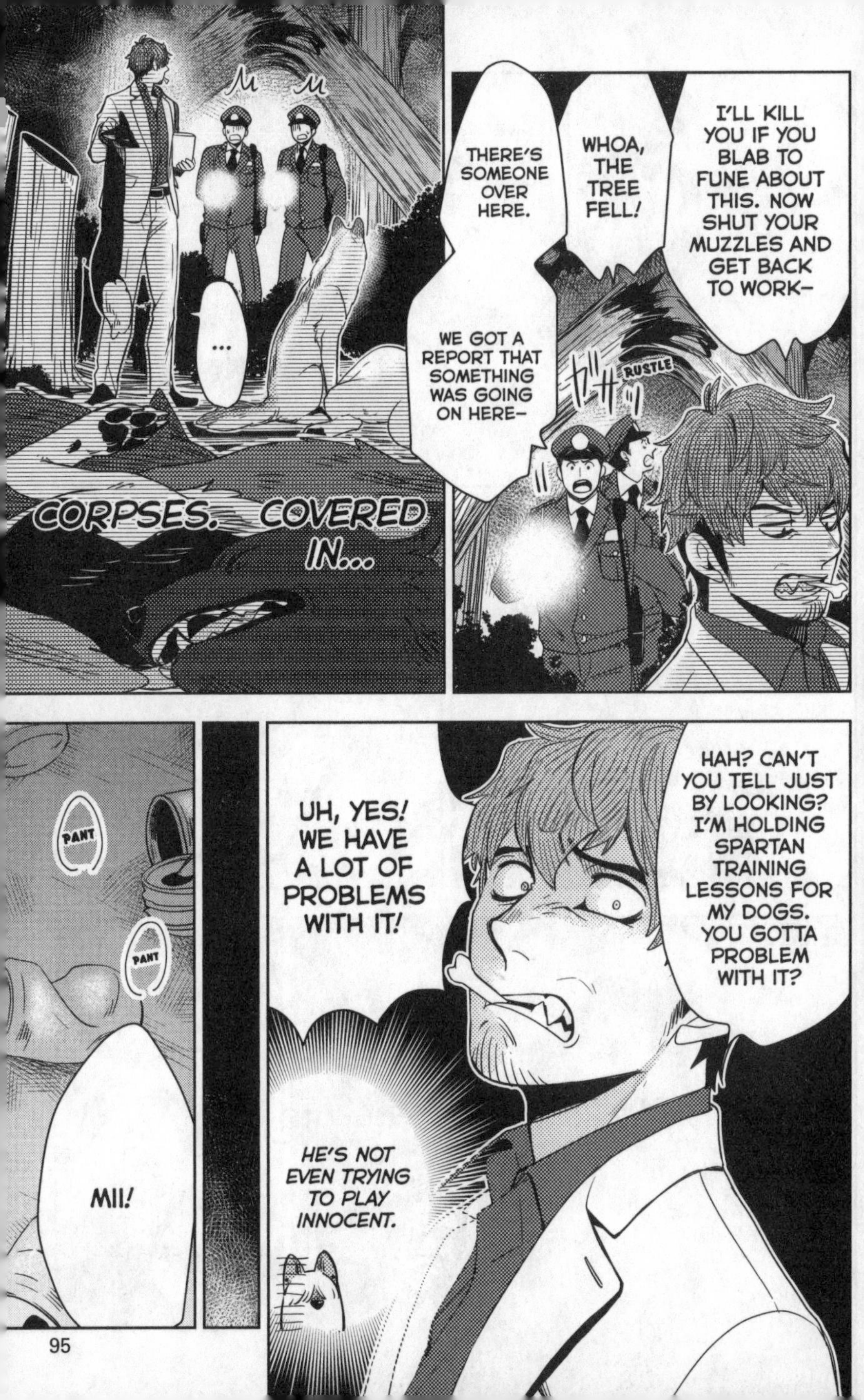
I'LL KILL YOU IF YOU BLAB TO FUNE ABOUT THIS. NOW SHUT YOUR MUZZLES AND GET BACK TO WORK–
WHOA, THE TREE FELL!
THERE'S SOMEONE OVER HERE.
RUSTLE
WE GOT A REPORT THAT SOMETHING WAS GOING ON HERE–
...
CORPSES. COVERED IN...
HAH? CAN'T YOU TELL JUST BY LOOKING? I'M HOLDING SPARTAN TRAINING LESSONS FOR MY DOGS. YOU GOTTA PROBLEM WITH IT?
UH, YES! WE HAVE A LOT OF PROBLEMS WITH IT!
HE'S NOT EVEN TRYING TO PLAY INNOCENT.
PANT
PANT
MII!

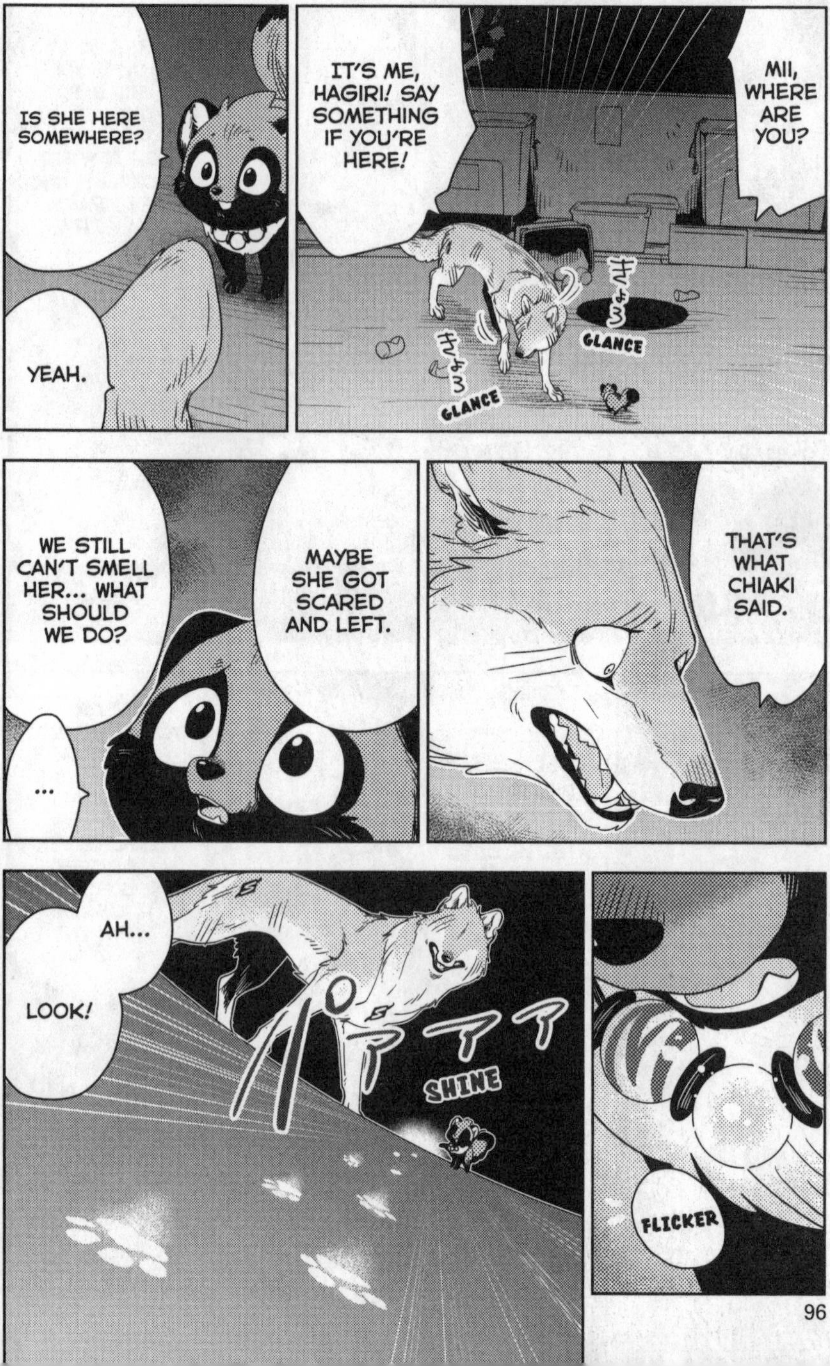

MII, WHERE ARE YOU?
IT'S ME, HAGIRI! SAY SOMETHING IF YOU'RE HERE!
きょろ
GLANCE
きょろ
GLANCE
IS SHE HERE SOMEWHERE?
YEAH.
THAT'S WHAT CHIAKI SAID.
MAYBE SHE GOT SCARED AND LEFT.
WE STILL CAN'T SMELL HER... WHAT SHOULD WE DO?
...
FLICKER
AH...
LOOK!
パァァァ
SHINE

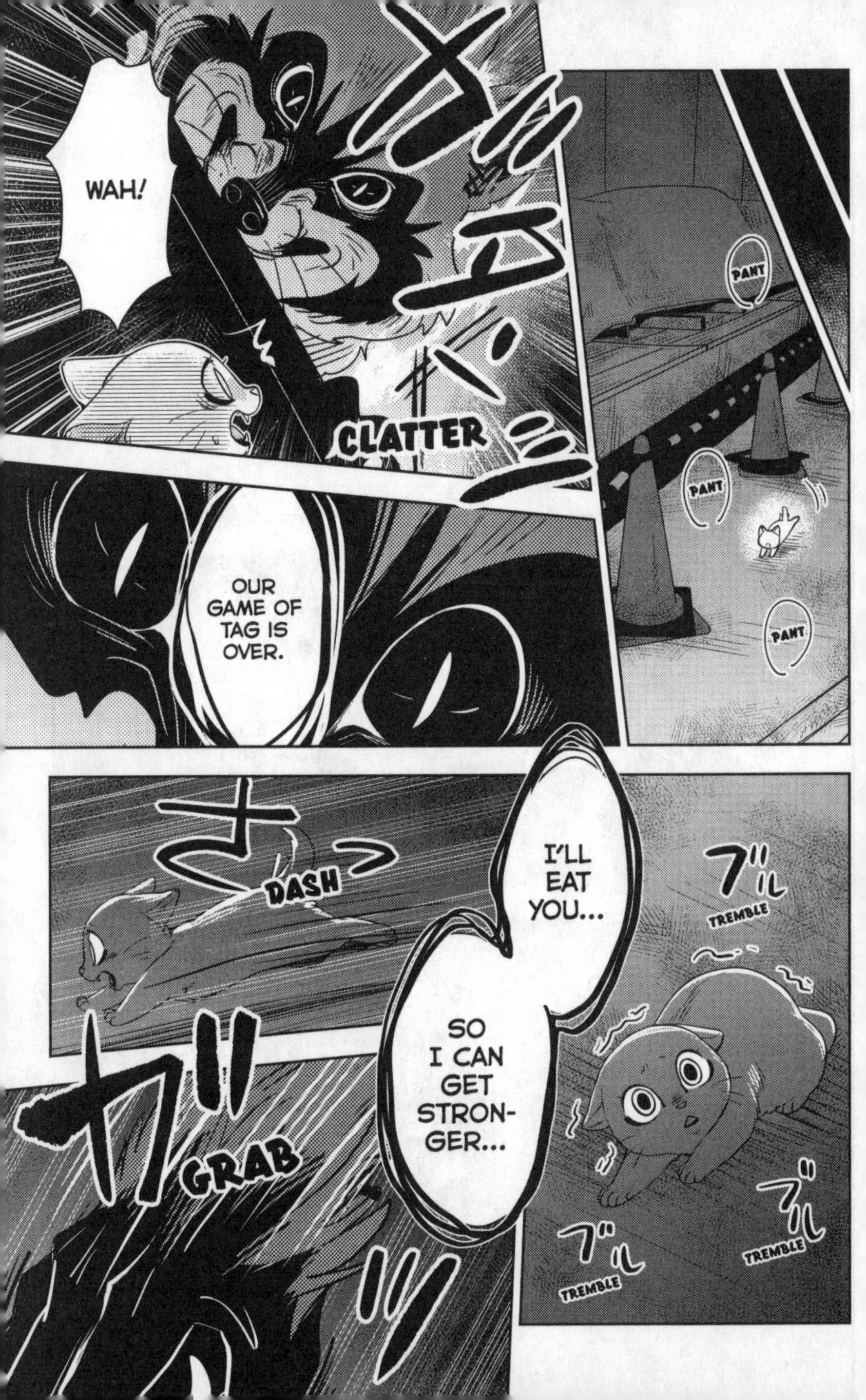
PANT
PANT
PANT
WAH!
CLATTER
OUR GAME OF TAG IS OVER.
TREMBLE
TREMBLE
TREMBLE
I'LL EAT YOU...
SO I CAN GET STRONGER...
DASH
GRAB

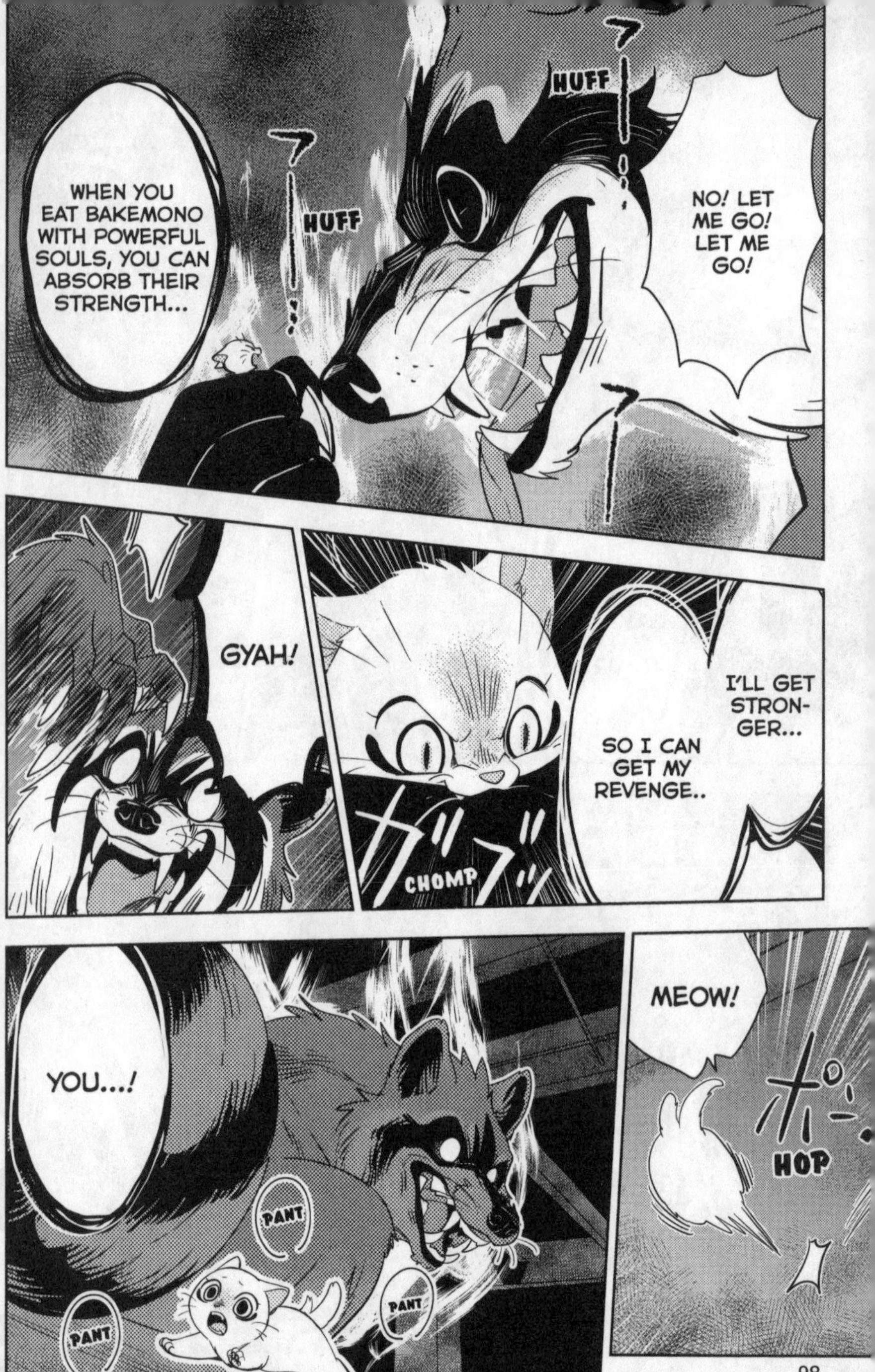
NO! LET ME GO! LET ME GO!
HUFF
HUFF
WHEN YOU EAT BAKEMONO WITH POWERFUL SOULS, YOU CAN ABSORB THEIR STRENGTH...
I'LL GET STRON-GER...
SO I CAN GET MY REVENGE..
CHOMP
GYAH!
MEOW!
HOP
YOU...!
PANT
PANT
PANT

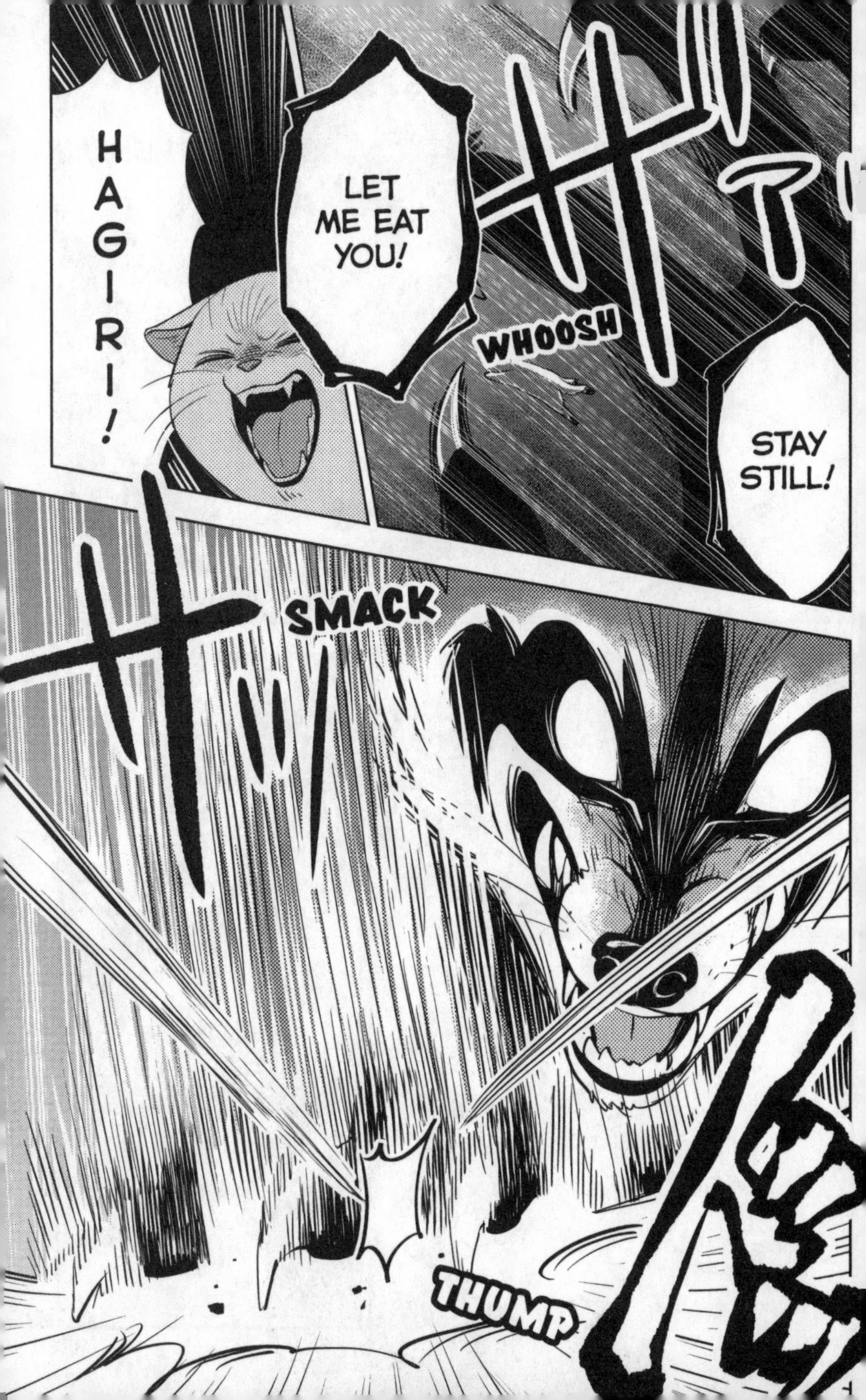
STAY STILL!
WHOOSH
LET ME EAT YOU!
HAGIRI!
SMACK
THUMP

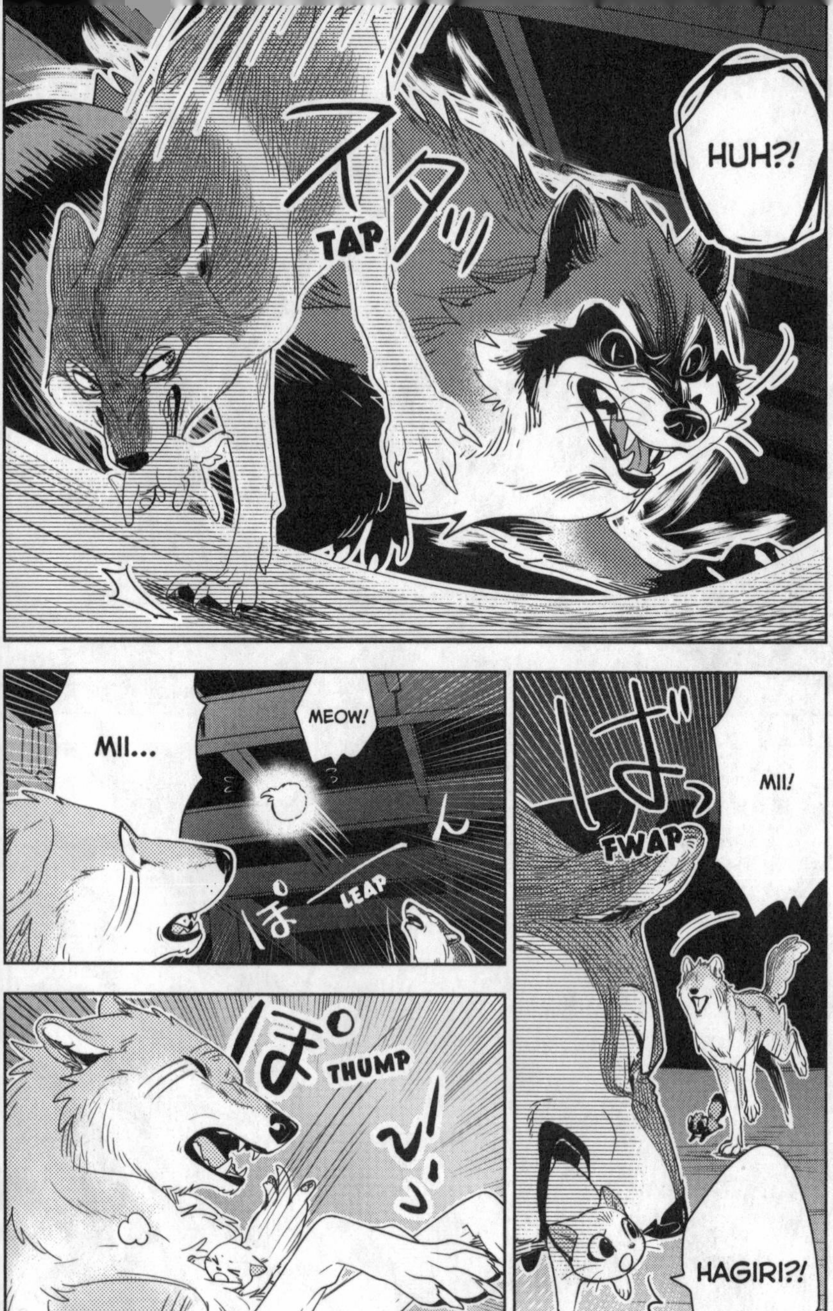

HUH?!
TAP
MII!
FWAP
HAGIRI?!
MEOW!
MII...
LEAP
THUMP

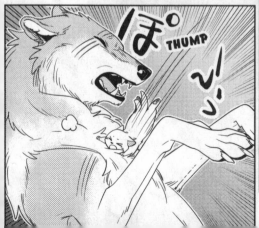

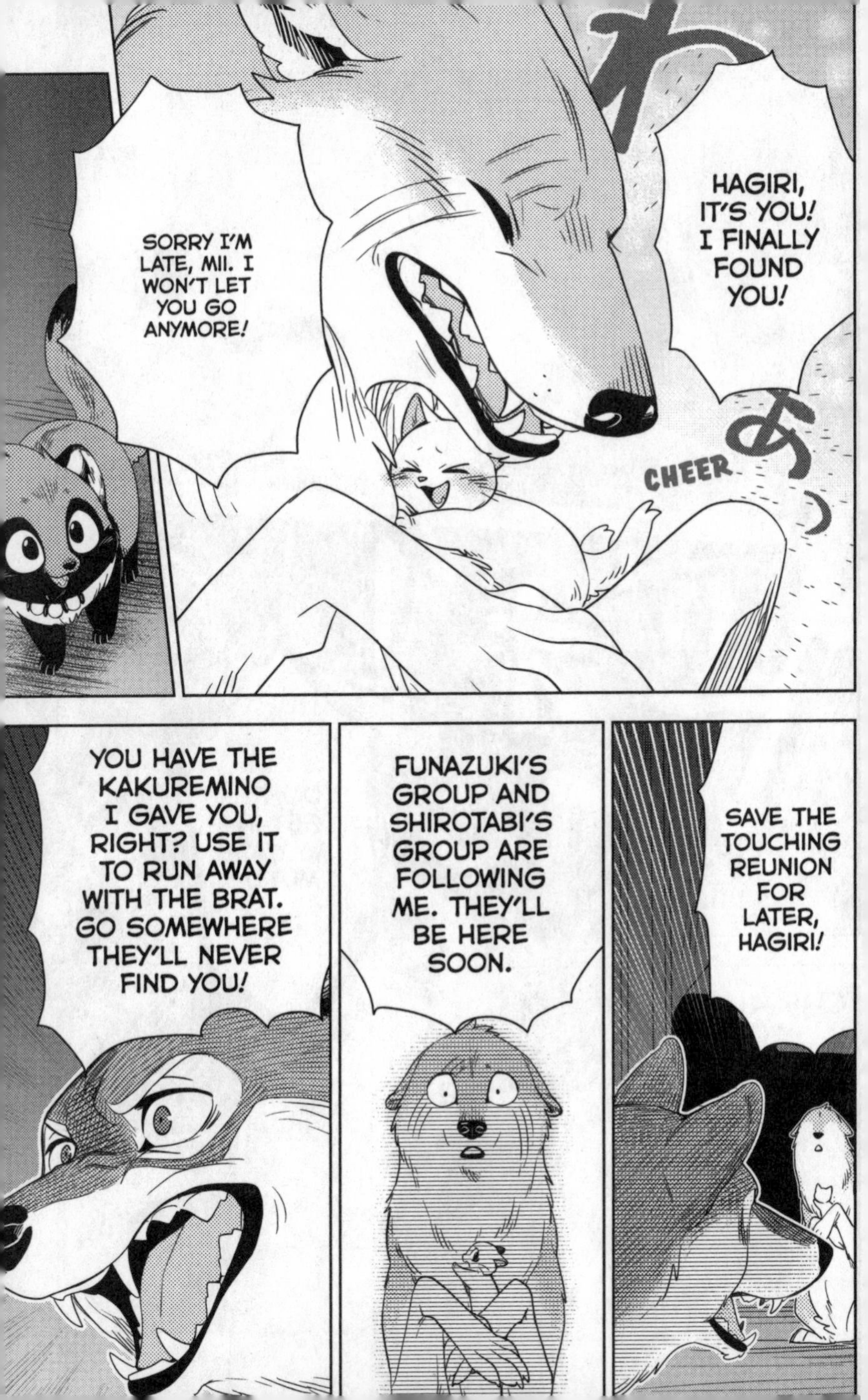
HAGIRI, IT'S YOU! I FINALLY FOUND YOU!
CHEER
SORRY I'M LATE, MII. I WON'T LET YOU GO ANYMORE!
SAVE THE TOUCHING REUNION FOR LATER, HAGIRI!
FUNAZUKI'S GROUP AND SHIROTABI'S GROUP ARE FOLLOWING ME. THEY'LL BE HERE SOON.
YOU HAVE THE KAKUREMINO I GAVE YOU, RIGHT? USE IT TO RUN AWAY WITH THE BRAT. GO SOMEWHERE THEY'LL NEVER FIND YOU!

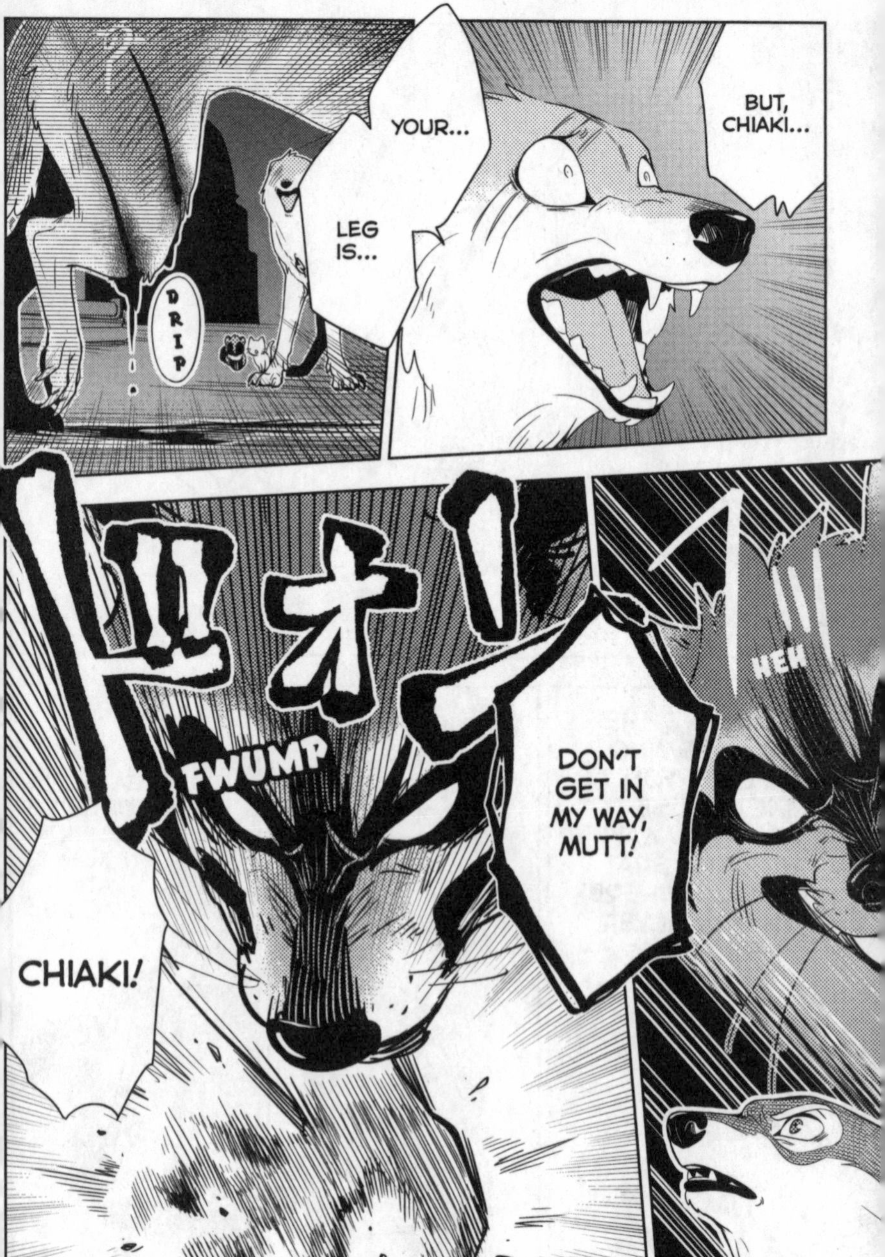
BUT, CHIAKI...
YOUR...
LEG IS...
DRIP
HEH
DON'T GET IN MY WAY, MUTT!
FWUMP
CHIAKI!

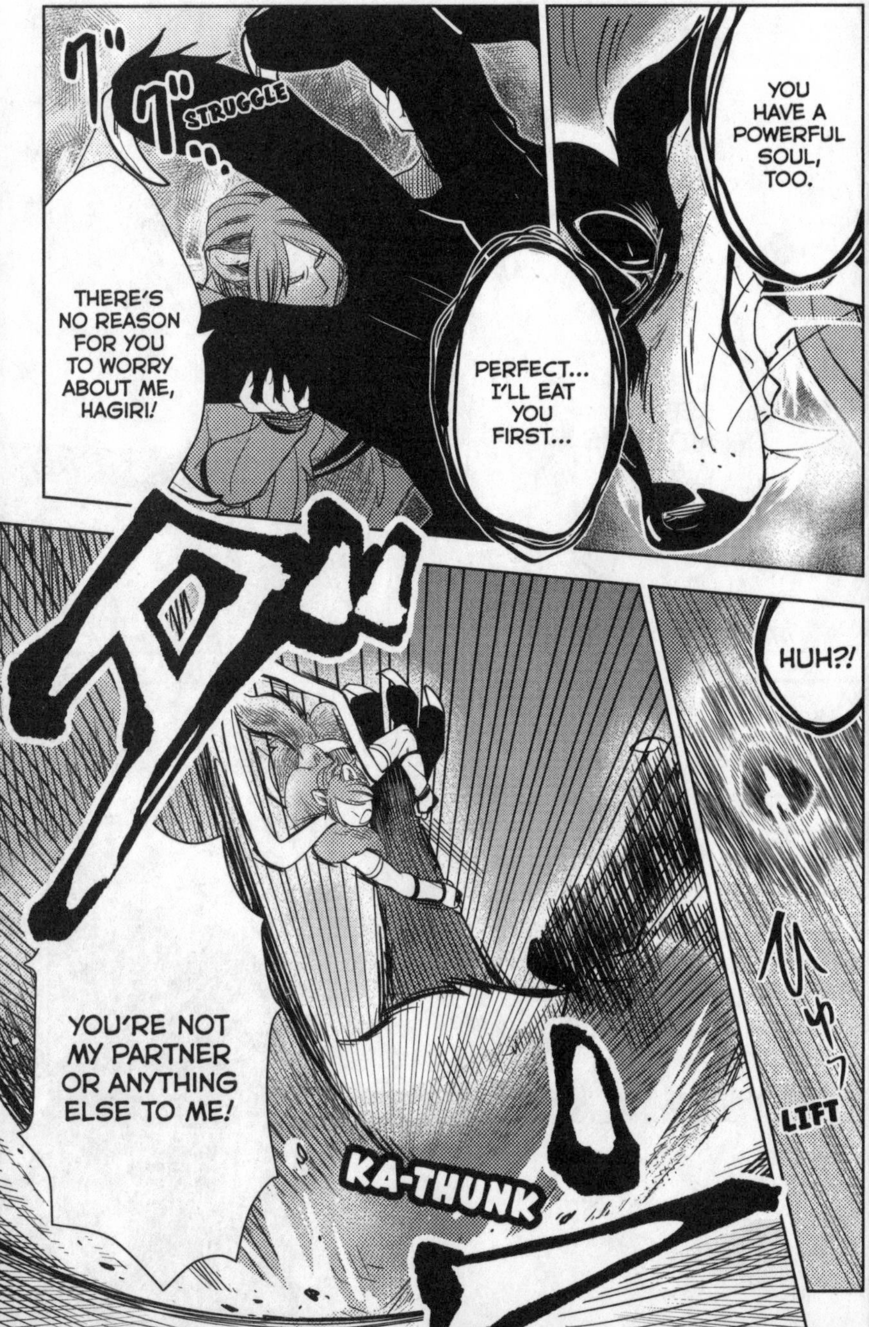
YOU HAVE A POWERFUL SOUL, TOO.
PERFECT... I'LL EAT YOU FIRST...
STRUGGLE
THERE'S NO REASON FOR YOU TO WORRY ABOUT ME, HAGIRI!
HUH?!
LIFT
YOU'RE NOT MY PARTNER OR ANYTHING ELSE TO ME!
KA-THUNK

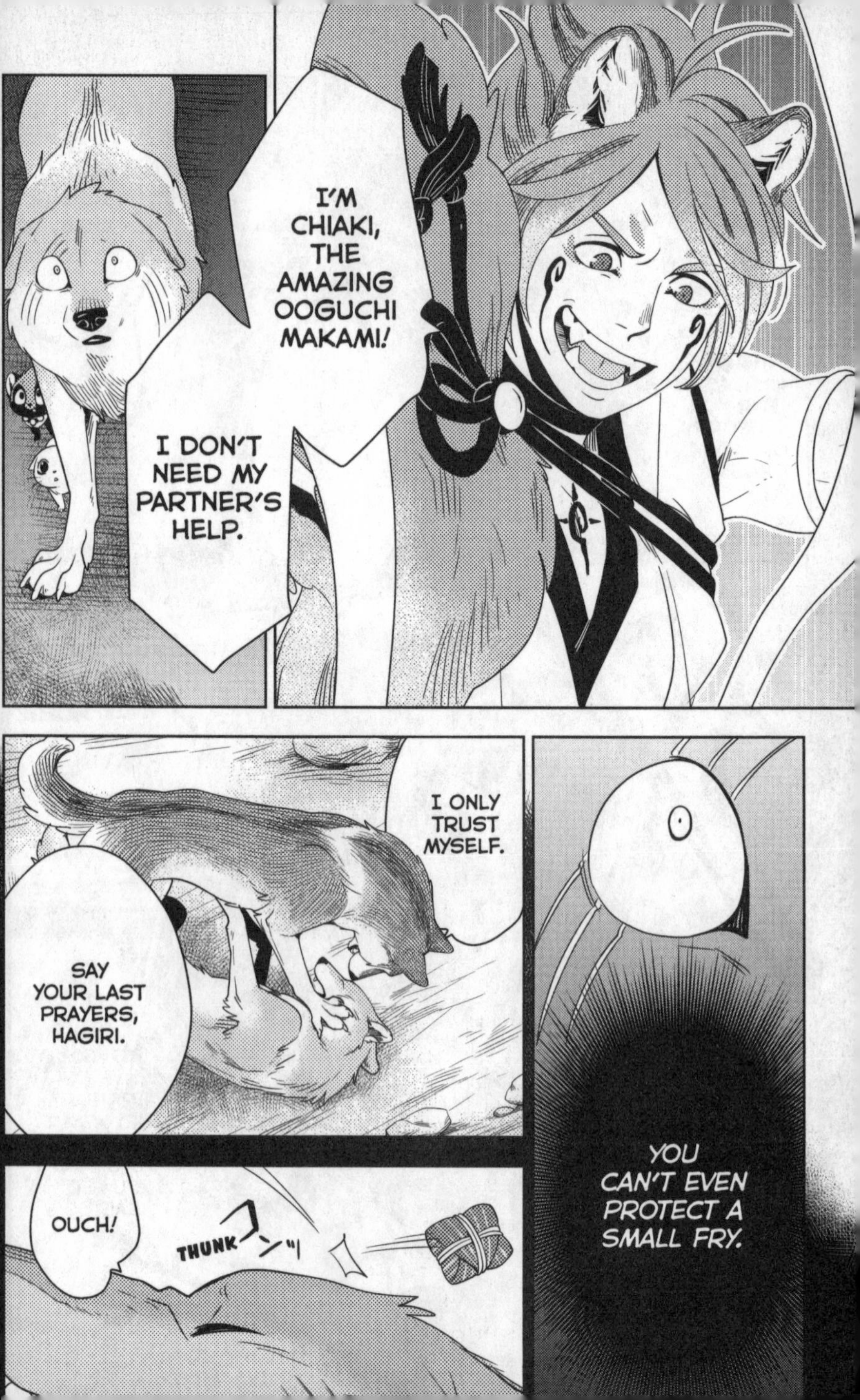
I'M CHIAKI, THE AMAZING OOGUCHI MAKAMI!
I DON'T NEED MY PARTNER'S HELP.
YOU CAN'T EVEN PROTECT A SMALL FRY.
I ONLY TRUST MYSELF.
SAY YOUR LAST PRAYERS, HAGIRI.
THUNK
OUCH!

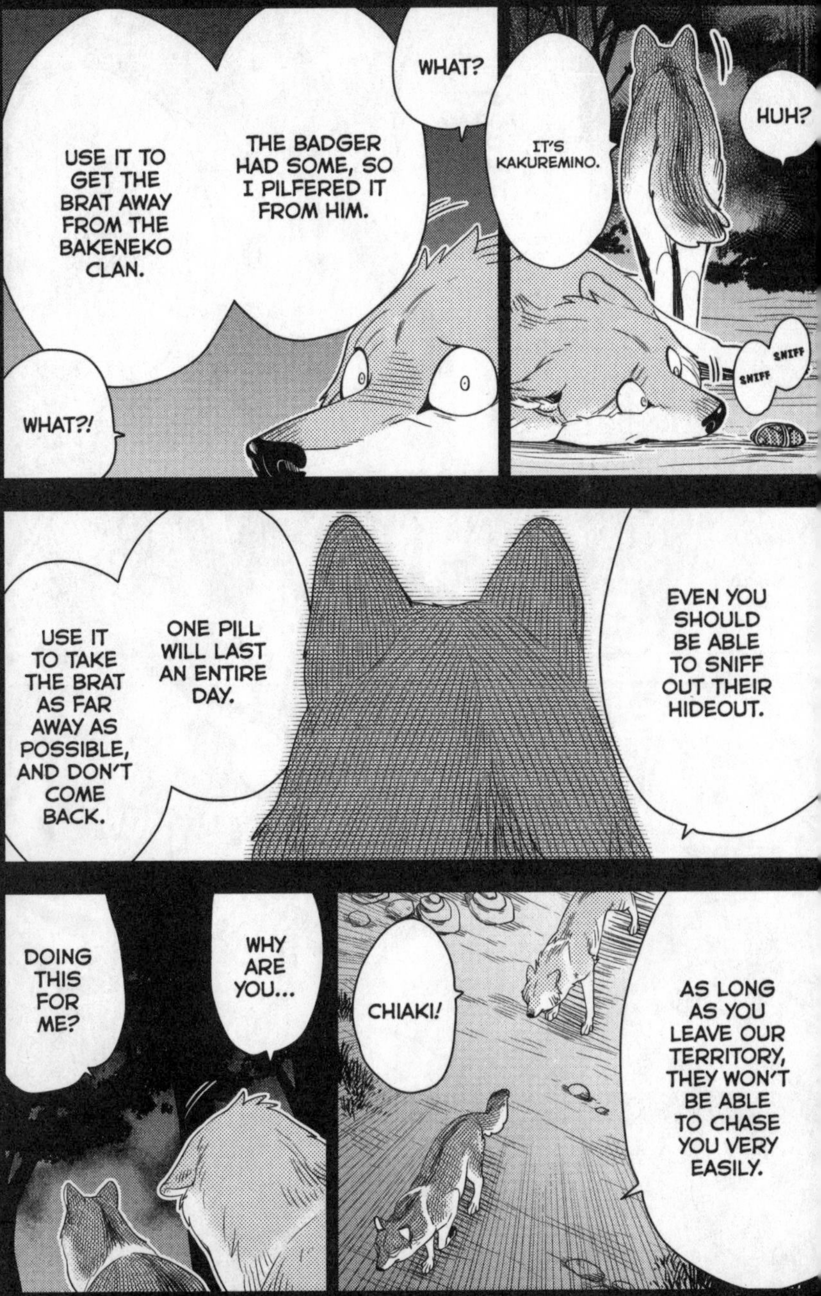
HUH?
IT'S KAKUREMINO.
SNIFF
SNIFF
WHAT?
THE BADGER HAD SOME, SO I PILFERED IT FROM HIM.
USE IT TO GET THE BRAT AWAY FROM THE BAKENEKO CLAN.
WHAT?!
EVEN YOU SHOULD BE ABLE TO SNIFF OUT THEIR HIDEOUT.
ONE PILL WILL LAST AN ENTIRE DAY.
USE IT TO TAKE THE BRAT AS FAR AWAY AS POSSIBLE, AND DON'T COME BACK.
AS LONG AS YOU LEAVE OUR TERRITORY, THEY WON'T BE ABLE TO CHASE YOU VERY EASILY.
CHIAKI!
WHY ARE YOU...
DOING THIS FOR ME?

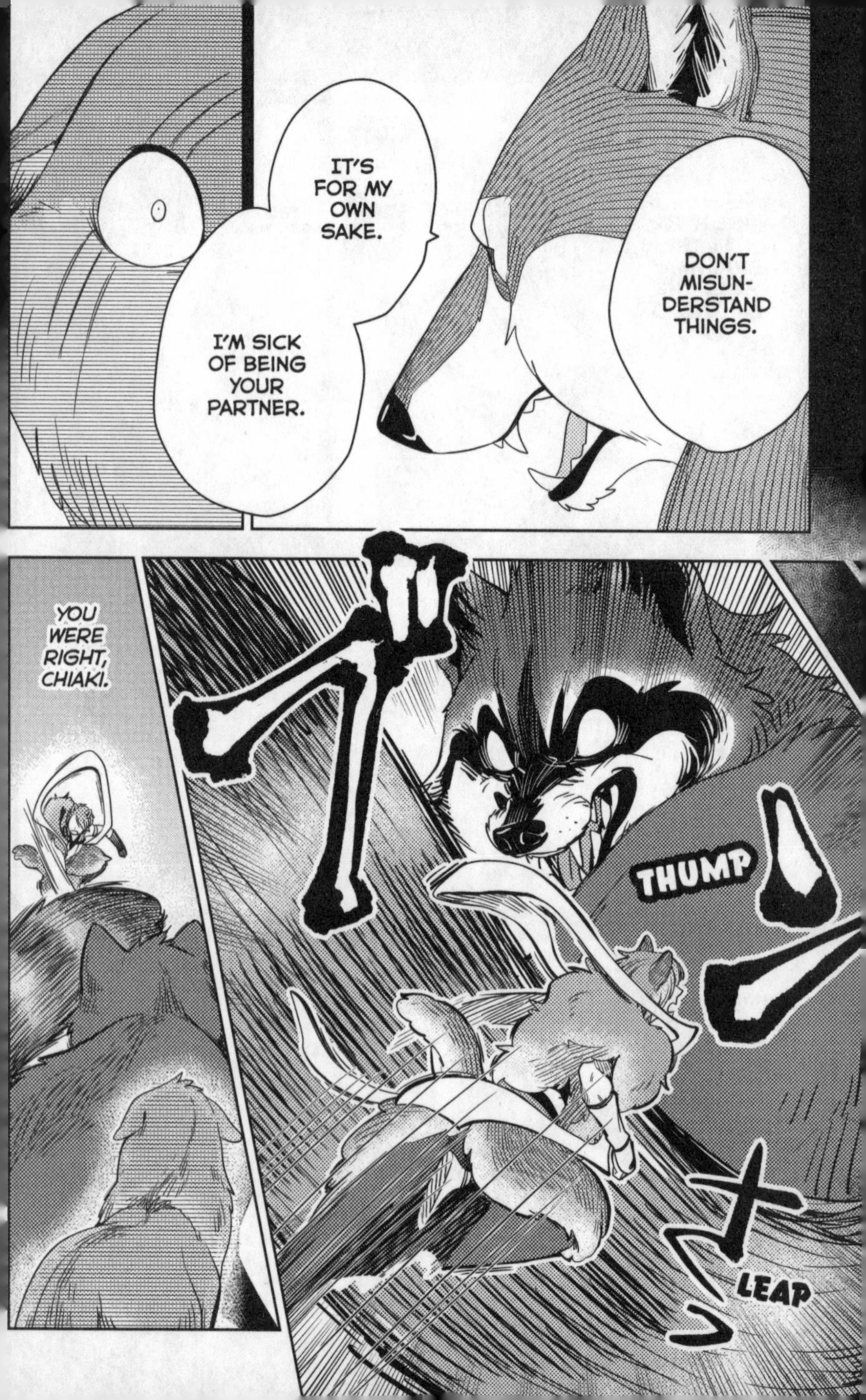
DON'T MISUN-DERSTAND THINGS.
IT'S FOR MY OWN SAKE.
I'M SICK OF BEING YOUR PARTNER.
THUMP
LEAP
YOU WERE RIGHT, CHIAKI.

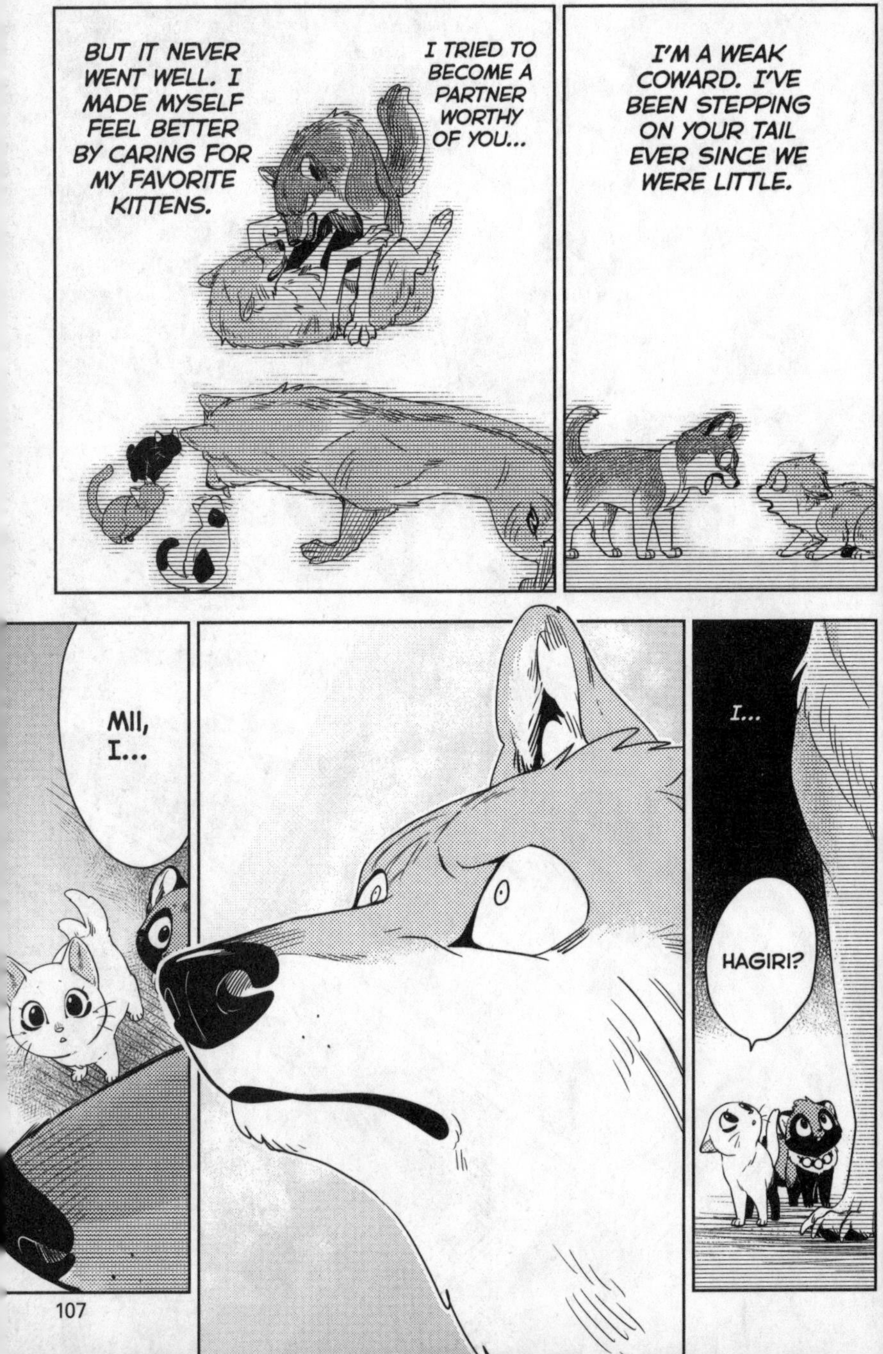
I'M A WEAK COWARD. I'VE BEEN STEPPING ON YOUR TAIL EVER SINCE WE WERE LITTLE.
I TRIED TO BECOME A PARTNER WORTHY OF YOU...
BUT IT NEVER WENT WELL. I MADE MYSELF FEEL BETTER BY CARING FOR MY FAVORITE KITTENS.
I...
HAGIRI?
MII, I...

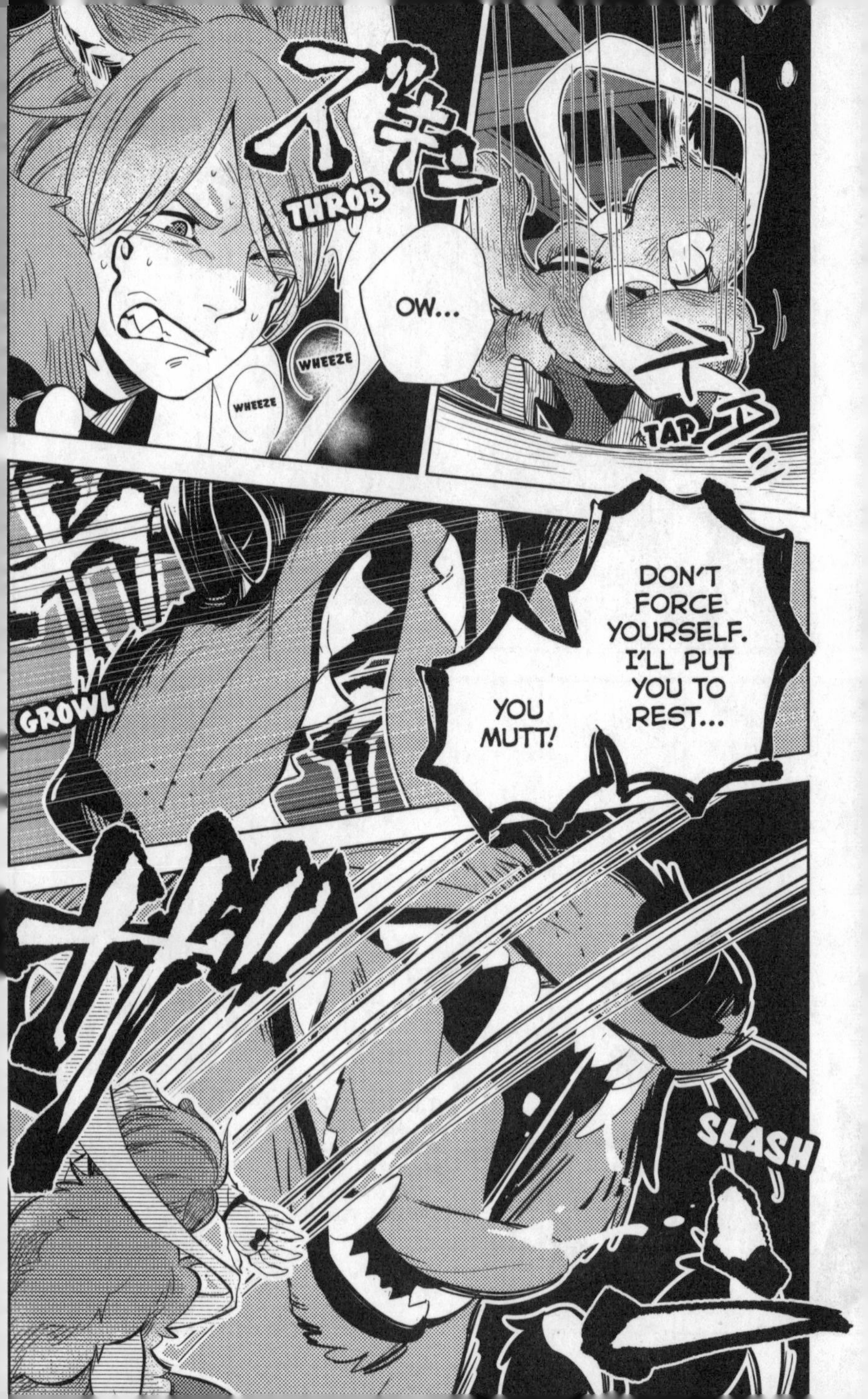

OW...
TAP
THROB
WHEEZE
WHEEZE
DON'T FORCE YOURSELF. I'LL PUT YOU TO REST...
YOU MUTT!
GROWL
SLASH

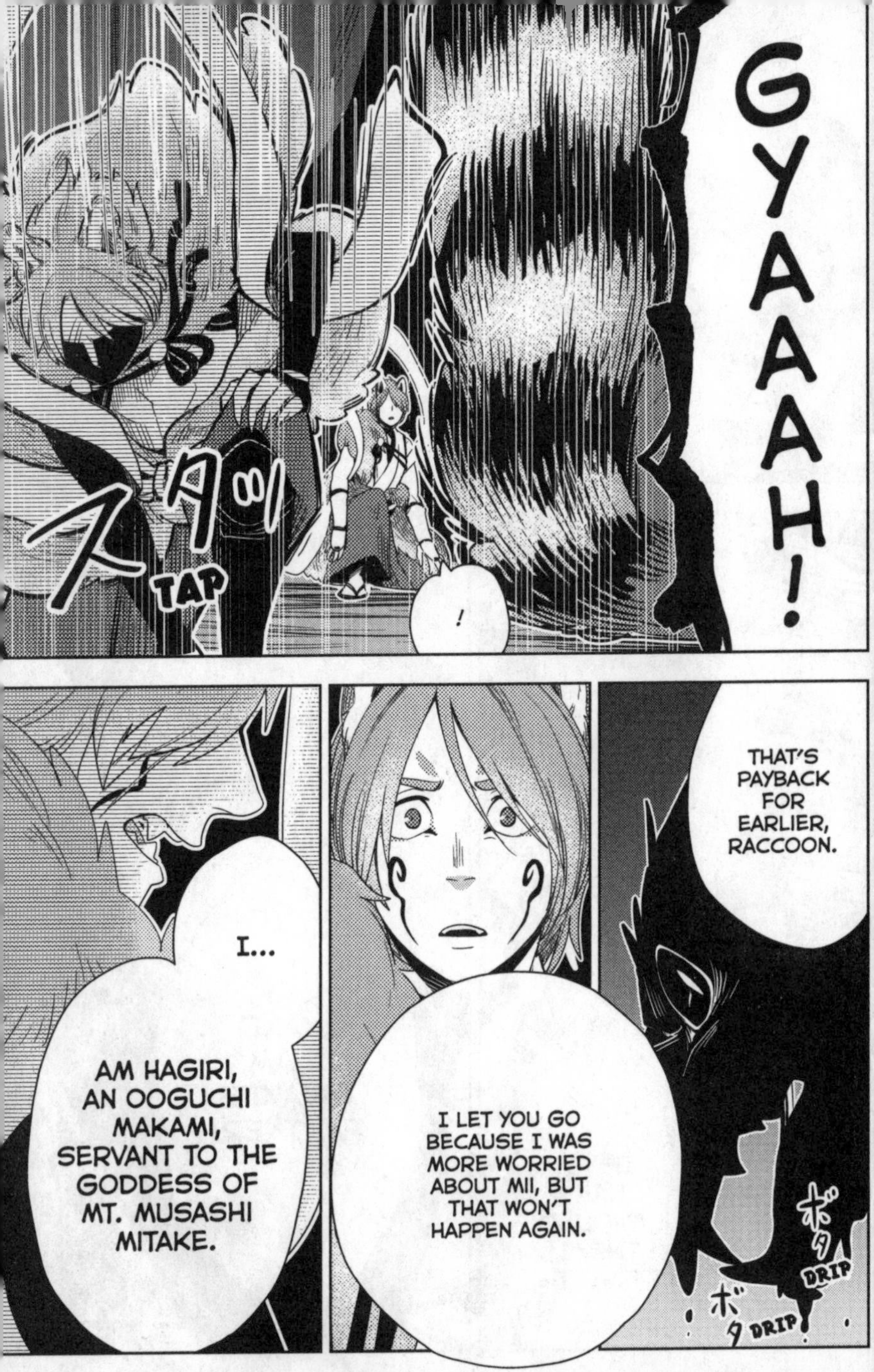
GYAAAH!
!
スタッ
TAP
THAT'S PAYBACK FOR EARLIER, RACCOON.
ボタ
DRIP
ボタ
DRIP
DRIP
I LET YOU GO BECAUSE I WAS MORE WORRIED ABOUT MII, BUT THAT WON'T HAPPEN AGAIN.
I...
AM HAGIRI, AN OOGUCHI MAKAMI, SERVANT TO THE GODDESS OF MT. MUSASHI MITAKE.

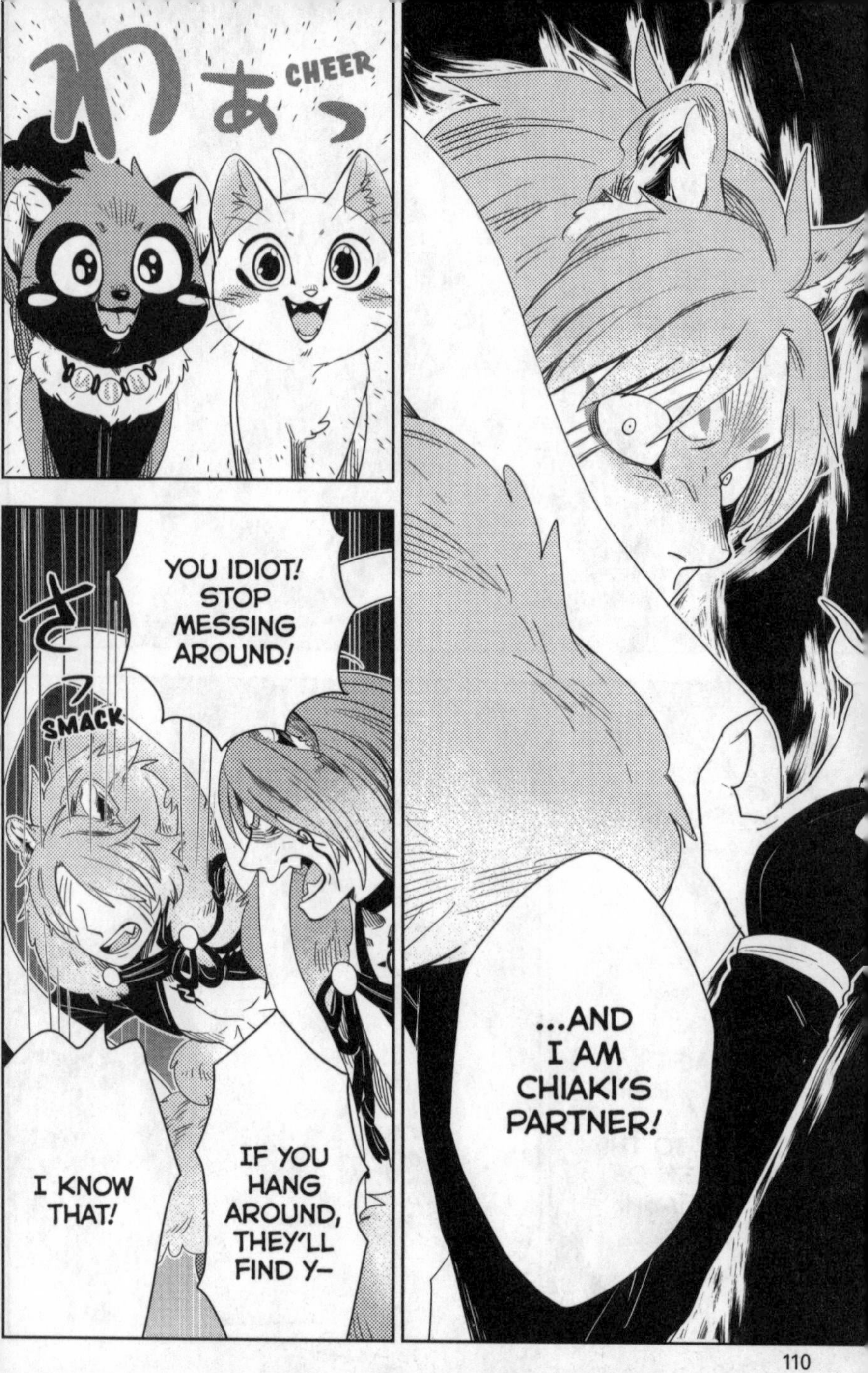
...AND I AM CHIAKI'S PARTNER!
わあっ
CHEER
さっ
SMACK
YOU IDIOT! STOP MESSING AROUND!
IF YOU HANG AROUND, THEY'LL FIND Y—
I KNOW THAT!

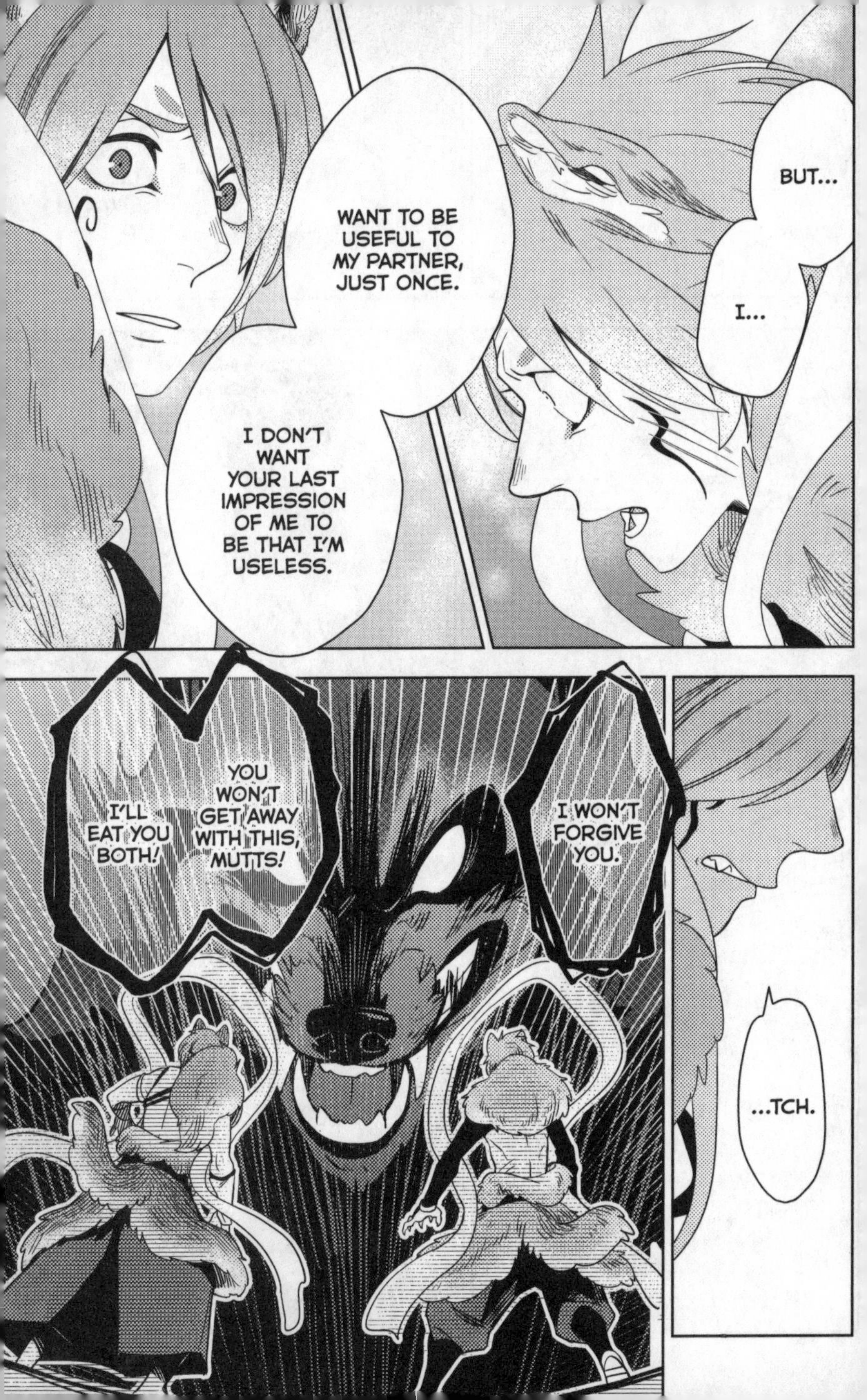
BUT...
I...
WANT TO BE USEFUL TO MY PARTNER, JUST ONCE.
I DON'T WANT YOUR LAST IMPRESSION OF ME TO BE THAT I'M USELESS.
...TCH.
I WON'T FORGIVE YOU.
YOU WON'T GET AWAY WITH THIS, MUTTS!
I'LL EAT YOU BOTH!

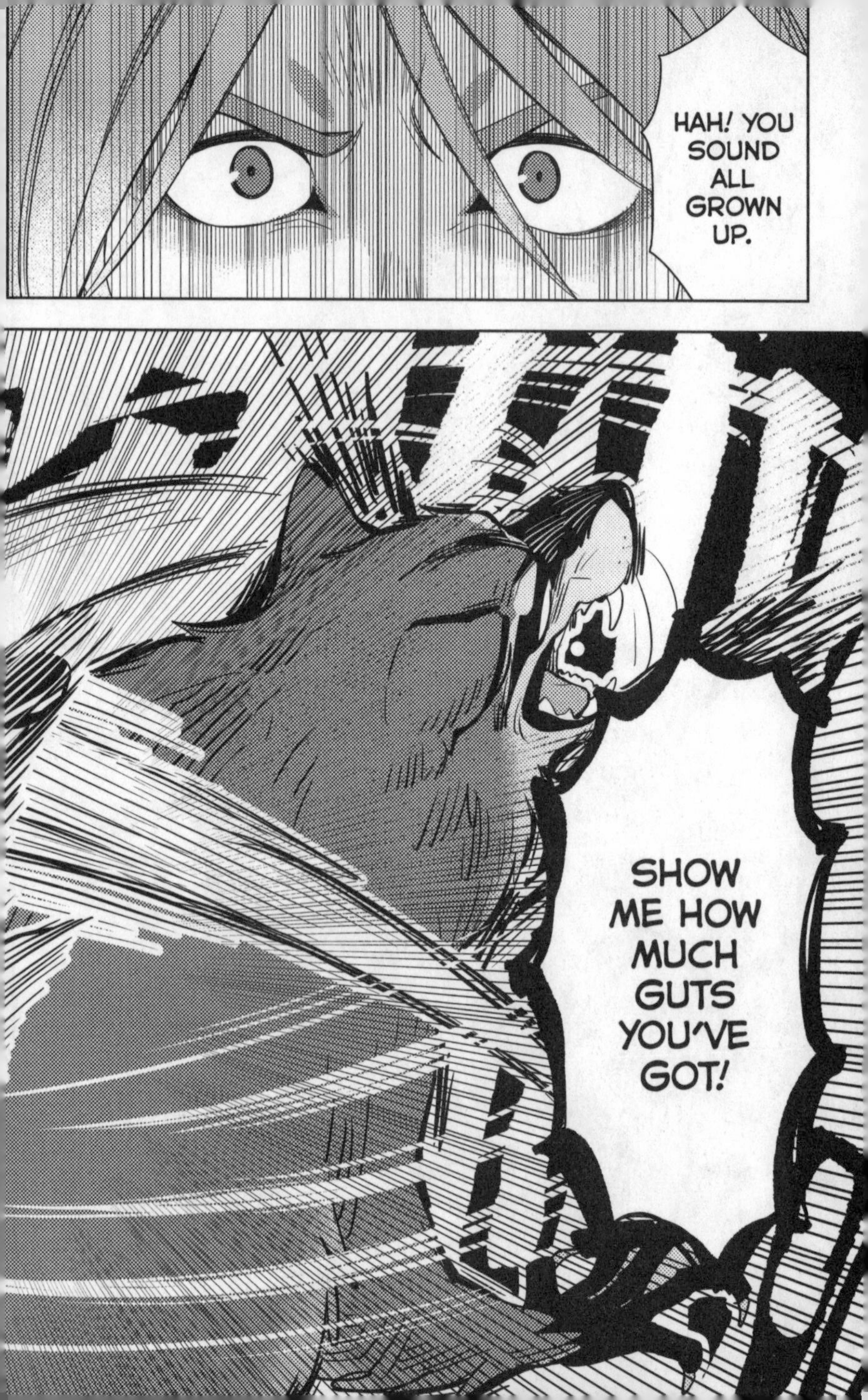
HAH! YOU SOUND ALL GROWN UP.
SHOW ME HOW MUCH GUTS YOU'VE GOT!

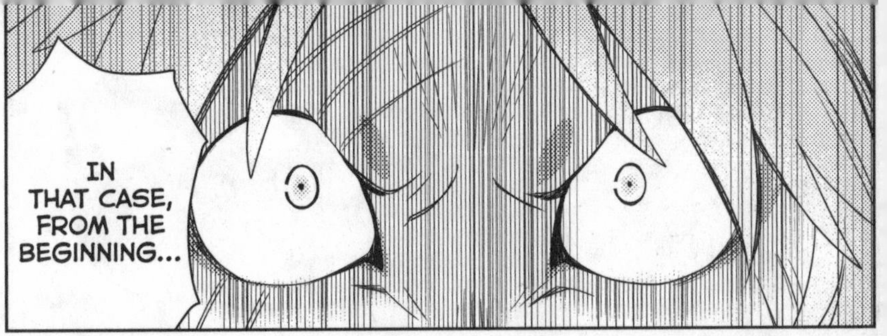
IN THAT CASE, FROM THE BEGINNING...
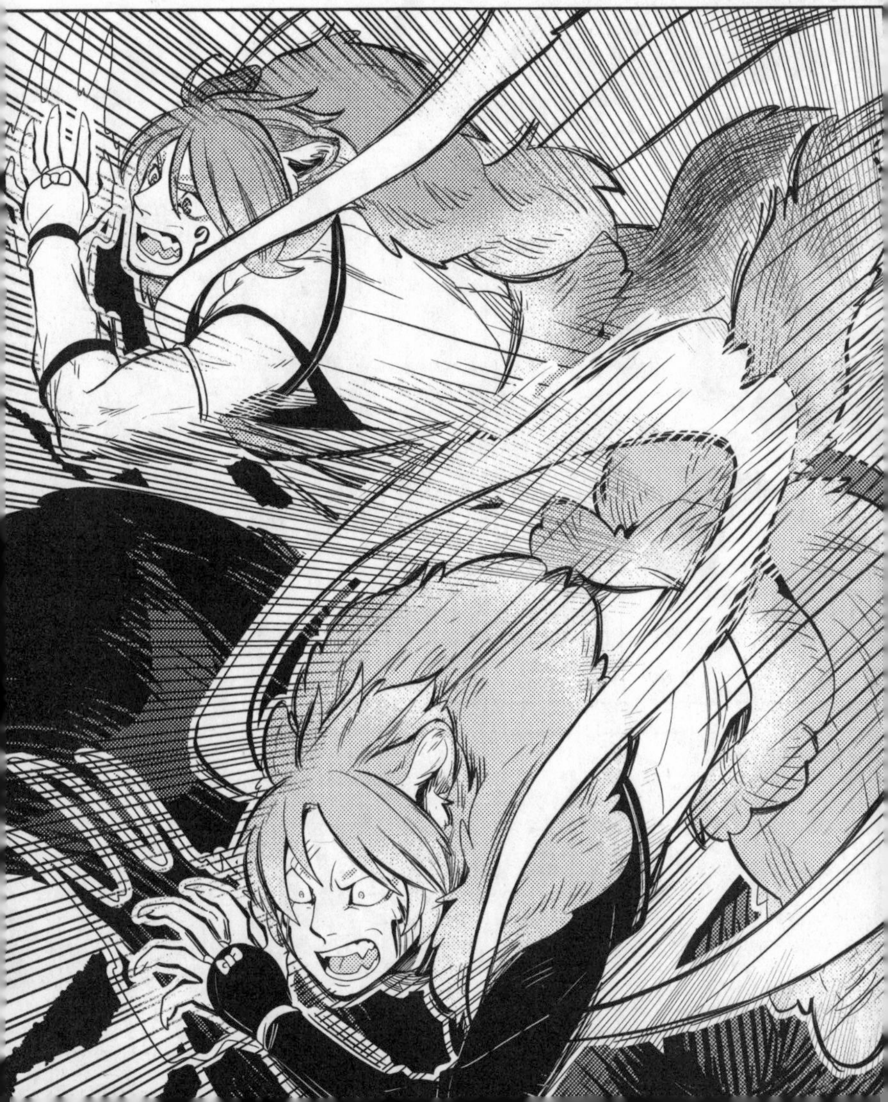

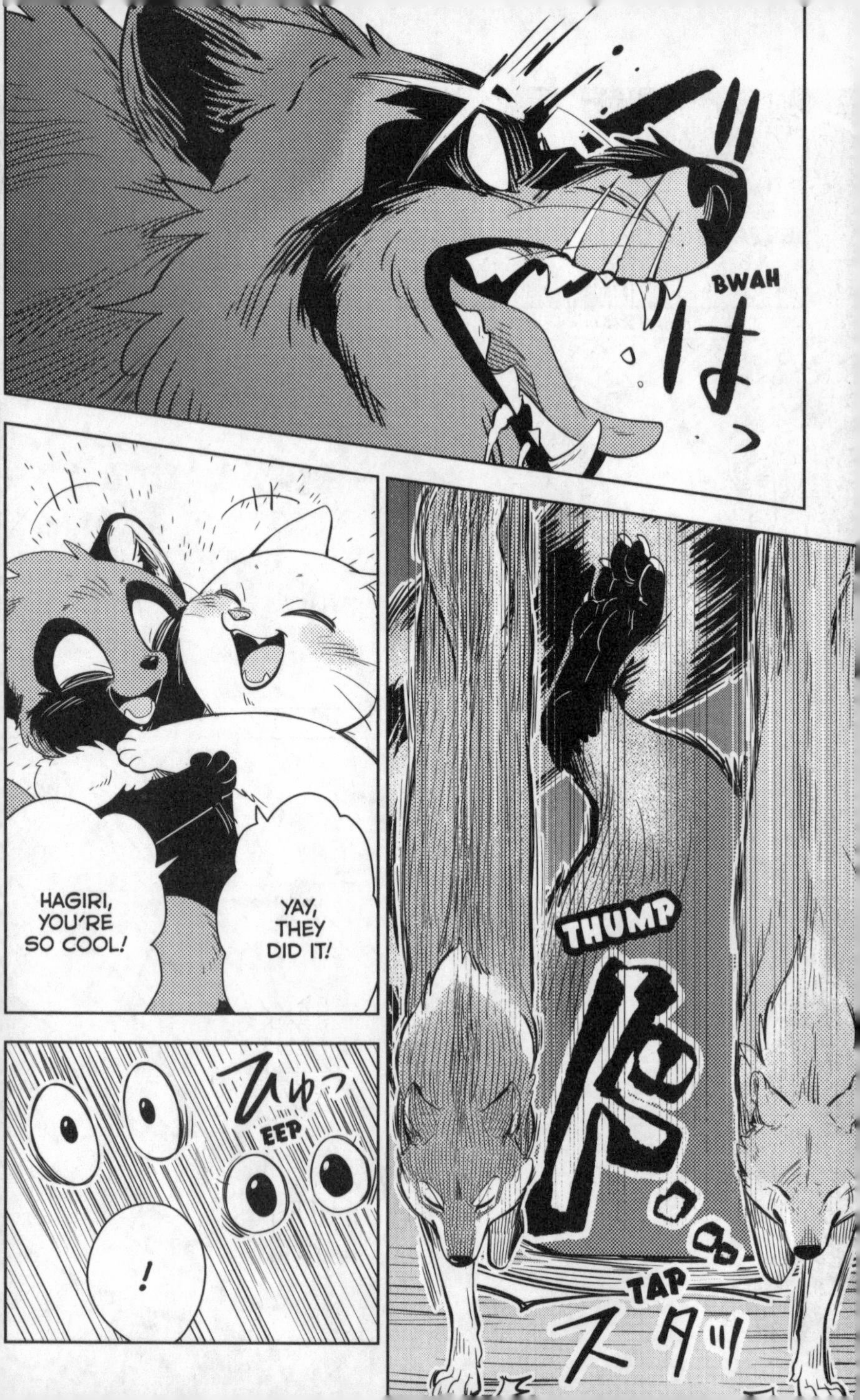
BWAH
はっ
THUMP
TAP
スタッ
YAY, THEY DID IT!
HAGIRI, YOU'RE SO COOL!
ひゅっ
EEP
!

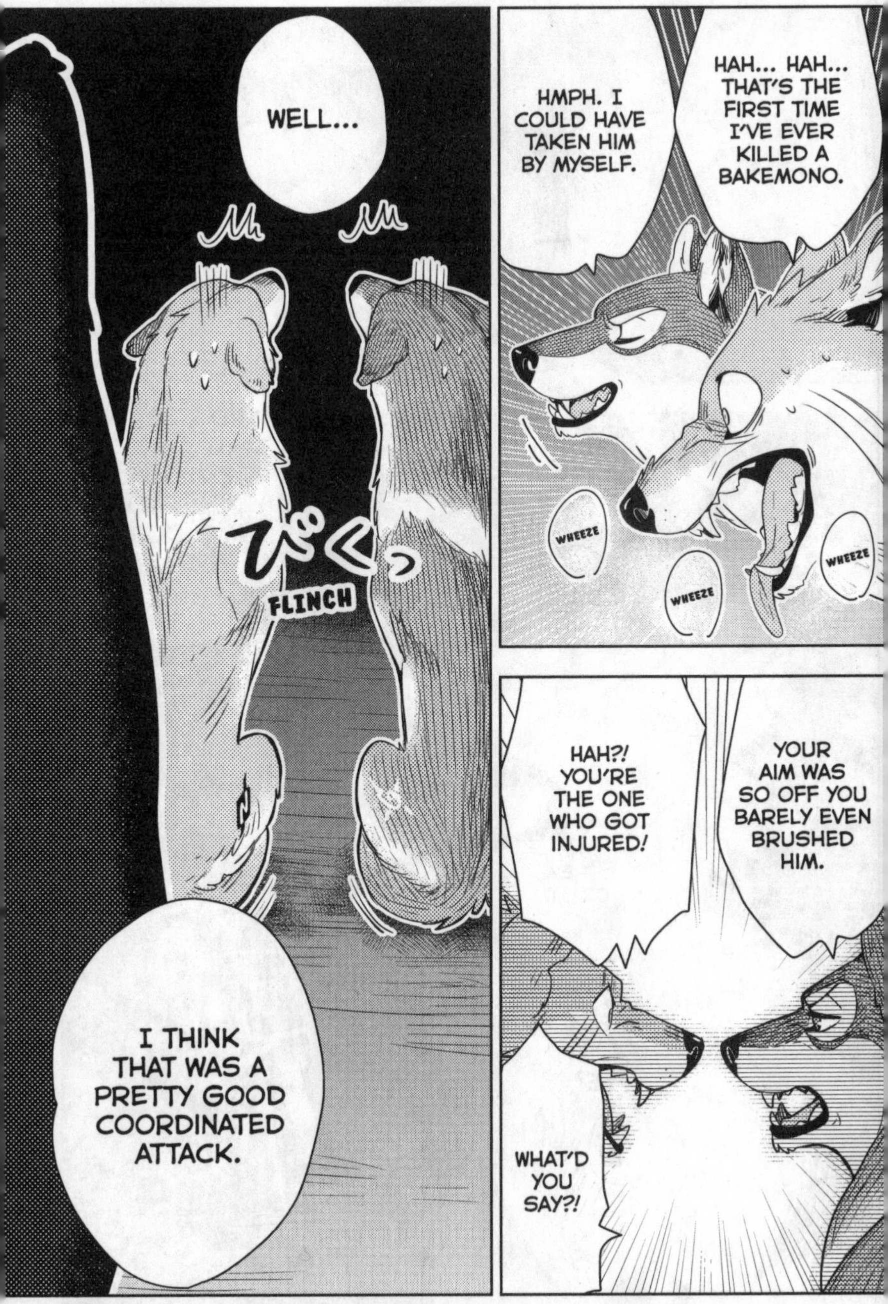
HAH... HAH... THAT'S THE FIRST TIME I'VE EVER KILLED A BAKEMONO.
HMPH. I COULD HAVE TAKEN HIM BY MYSELF.
WHEEZE
WHEEZE
WHEEZE
YOUR AIM WAS SO OFF YOU BARELY EVEN BRUSHED HIM.
HAH?! YOU'RE THE ONE WHO GOT INJURED!
WHAT'D YOU SAY?!
WELL...
ぴくっ
FLINCH
I THINK THAT WAS A PRETTY GOOD COORDINATED ATTACK.

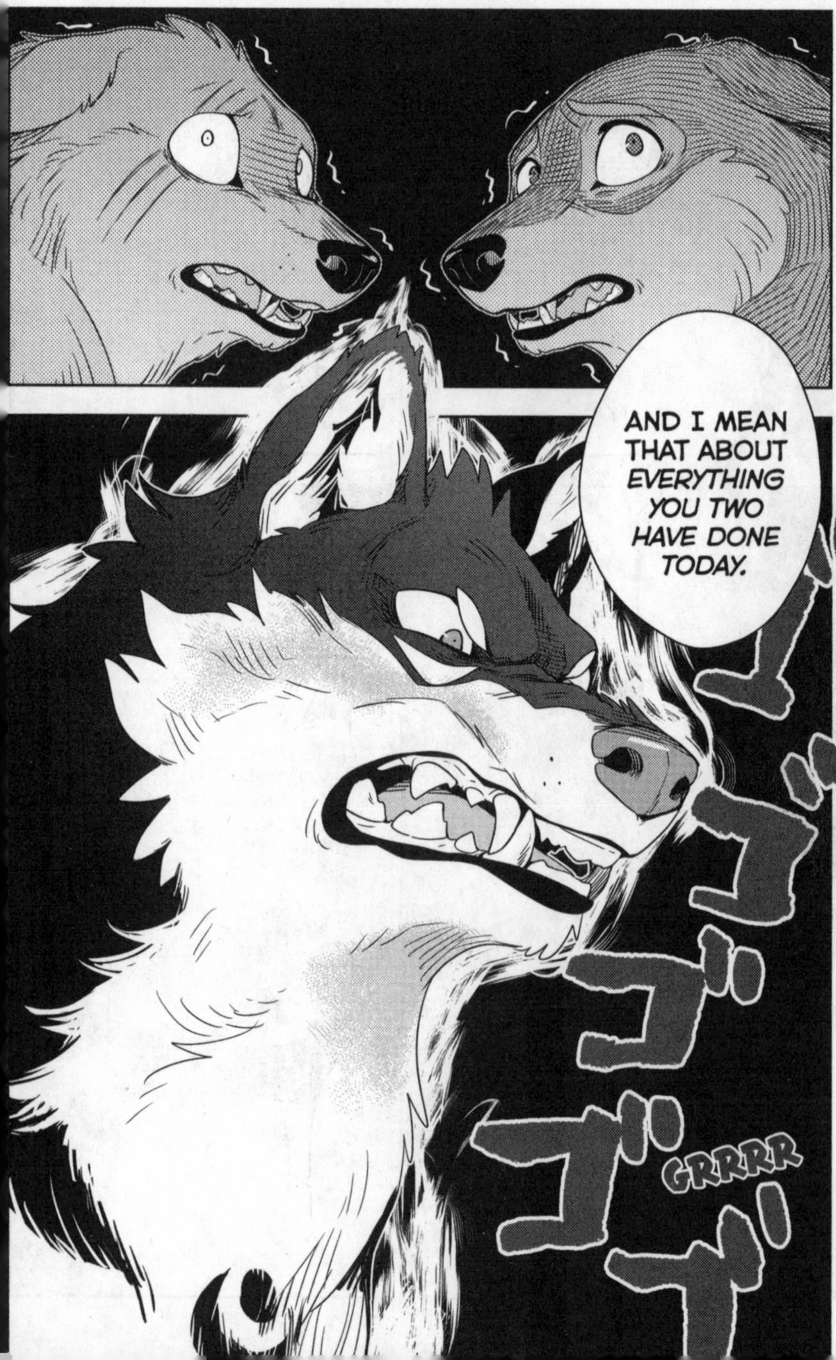
AND I MEAN THAT ABOUT EVERYTHING YOU TWO HAVE DONE TODAY.
ゴゴゴゴ
GRRRR

Chapter 18

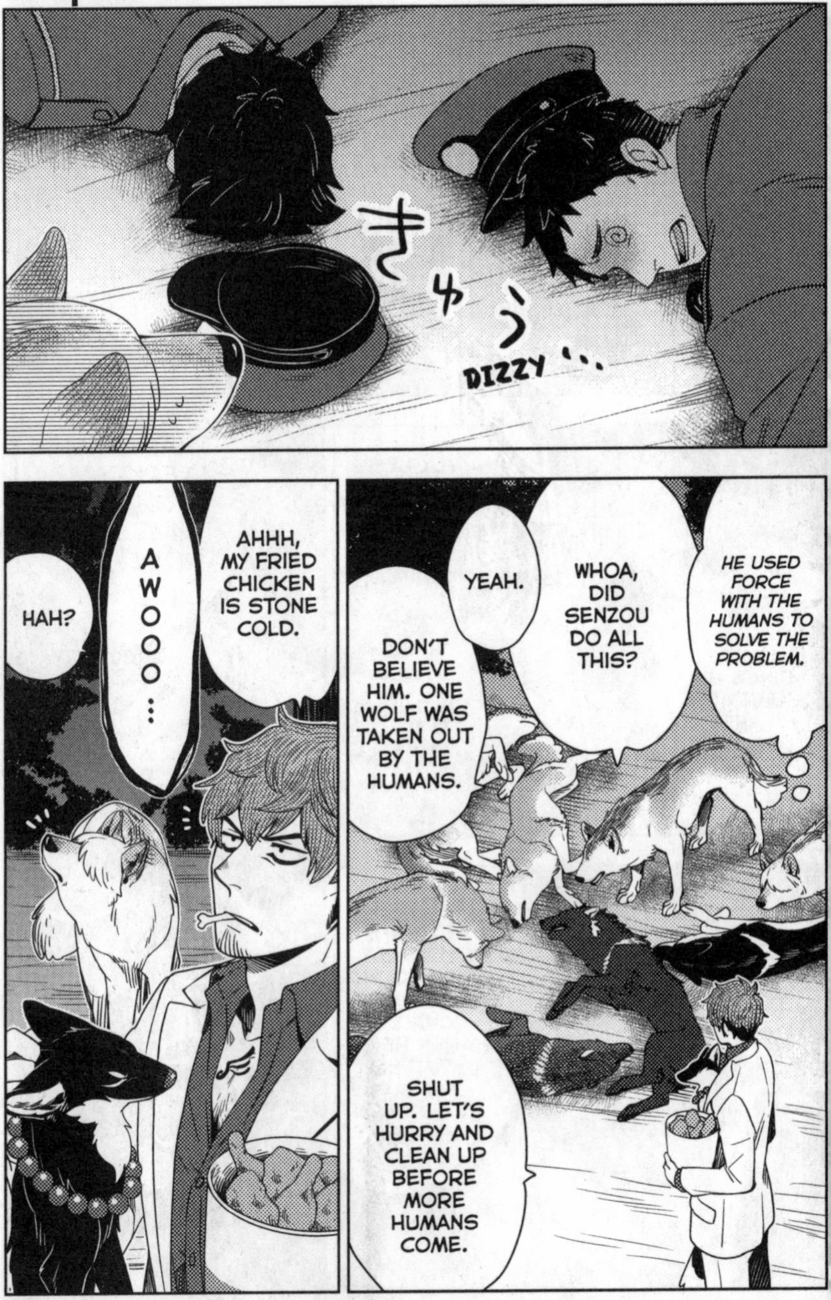
きゅう
DIZZY...
HE USED FORCE WITH THE HUMANS TO SOLVE THE PROBLEM.
WHOA, DID SENZOU DO ALL THIS?
YEAH.
DON'T BELIEVE HIM. ONE WOLF WAS TAKEN OUT BY THE HUMANS.
SHUT UP. LET'S HURRY AND CLEAN UP BEFORE MORE HUMANS COME.
AHHH, MY FRIED CHICKEN IS STONE COLD.
AWOOOO...
HAH?

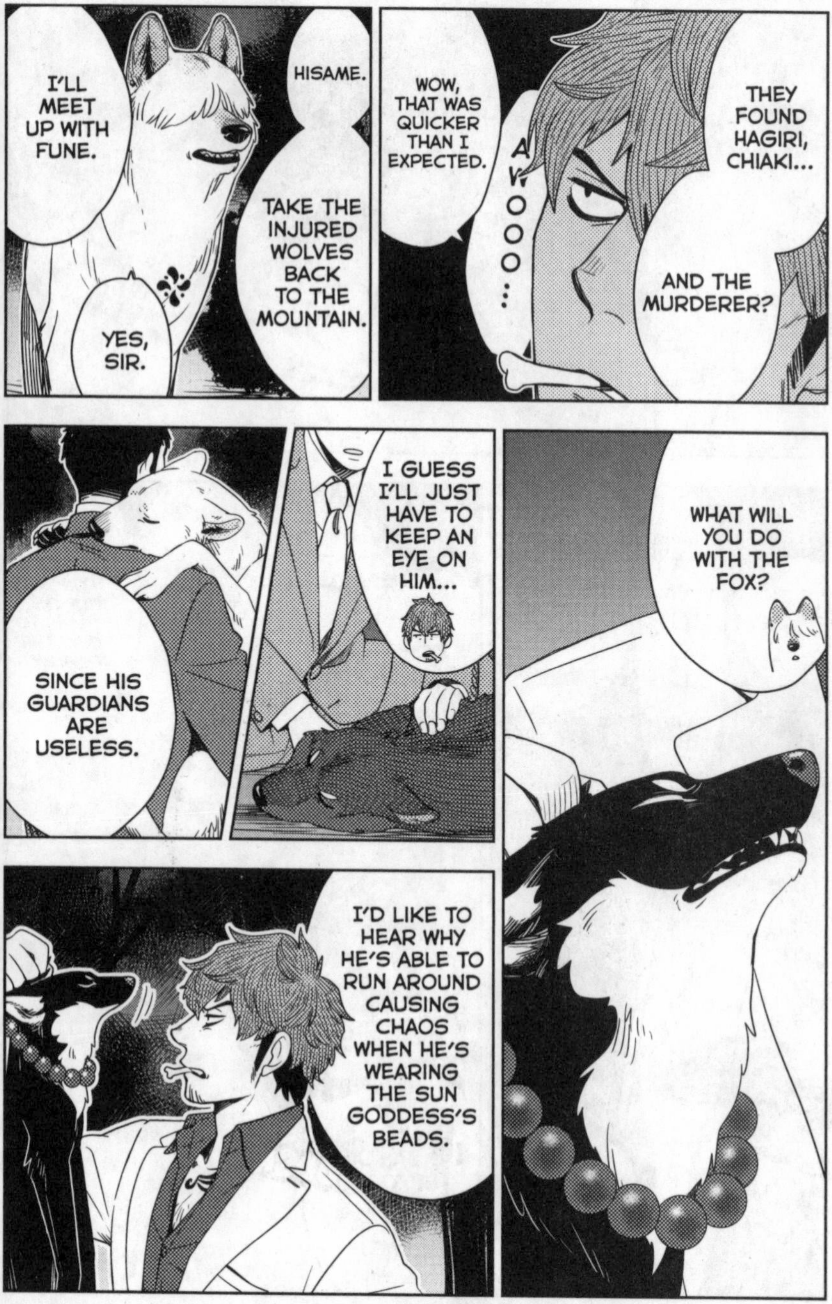
THEY FOUND HAGIRI, CHIAKI...
WOW, THAT WAS QUICKER THAN I EXPECTED.
AWOOO...
AND THE MURDERER?
HISAME.
TAKE THE INJURED WOLVES BACK TO THE MOUNTAIN.
I'LL MEET UP WITH FUNE.
YES, SIR.
WHAT WILL YOU DO WITH THE FOX?
I GUESS I'LL JUST HAVE TO KEEP AN EYE ON HIM...
SINCE HIS GUARDIANS ARE USELESS.
I'D LIKE TO HEAR WHY HE'S ABLE TO RUN AROUND CAUSING CHAOS WHEN HE'S WEARING THE SUN GODDESS'S BEADS.

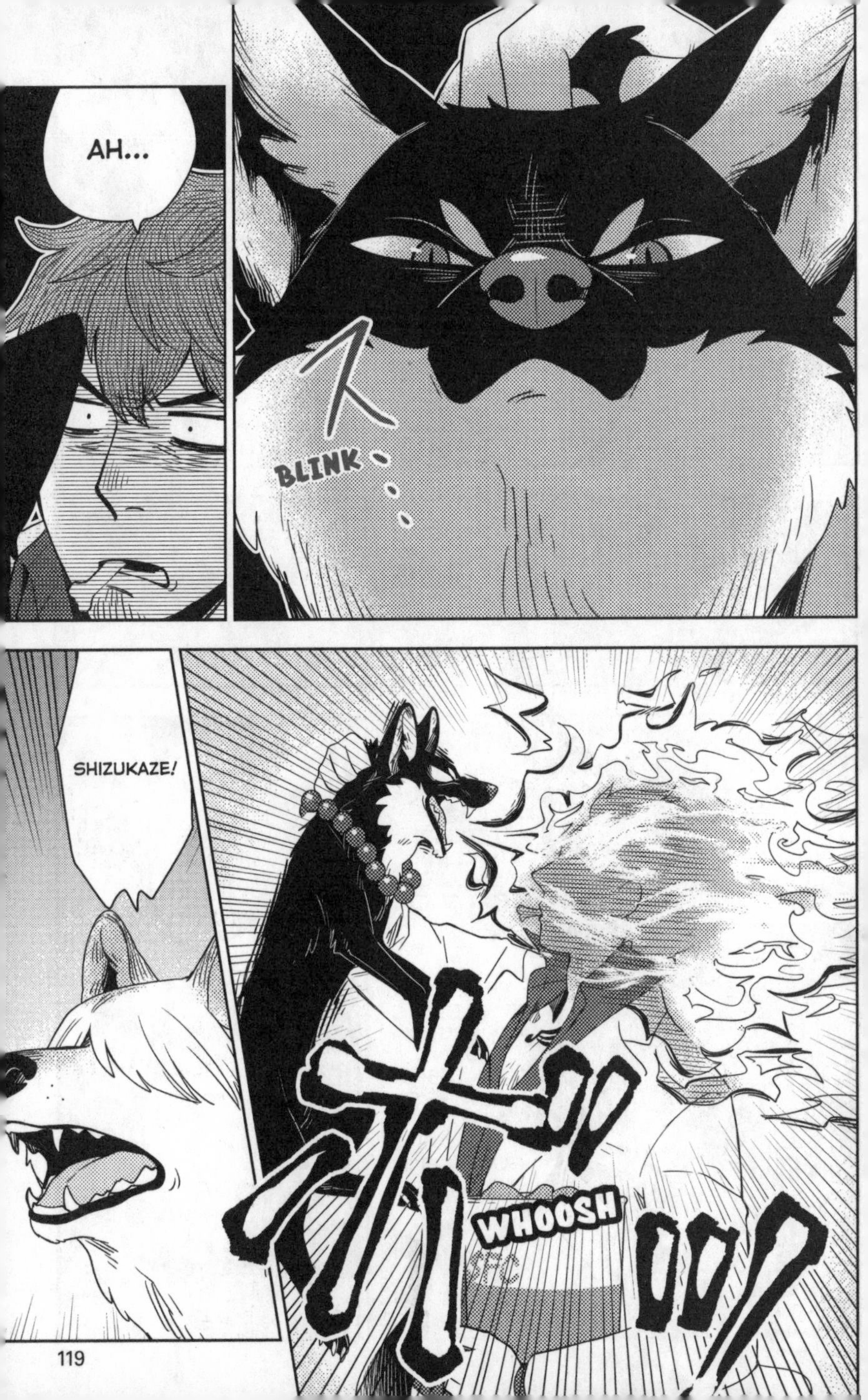
BLINK
AH...
WHOOSH
SHIZUKAZE!

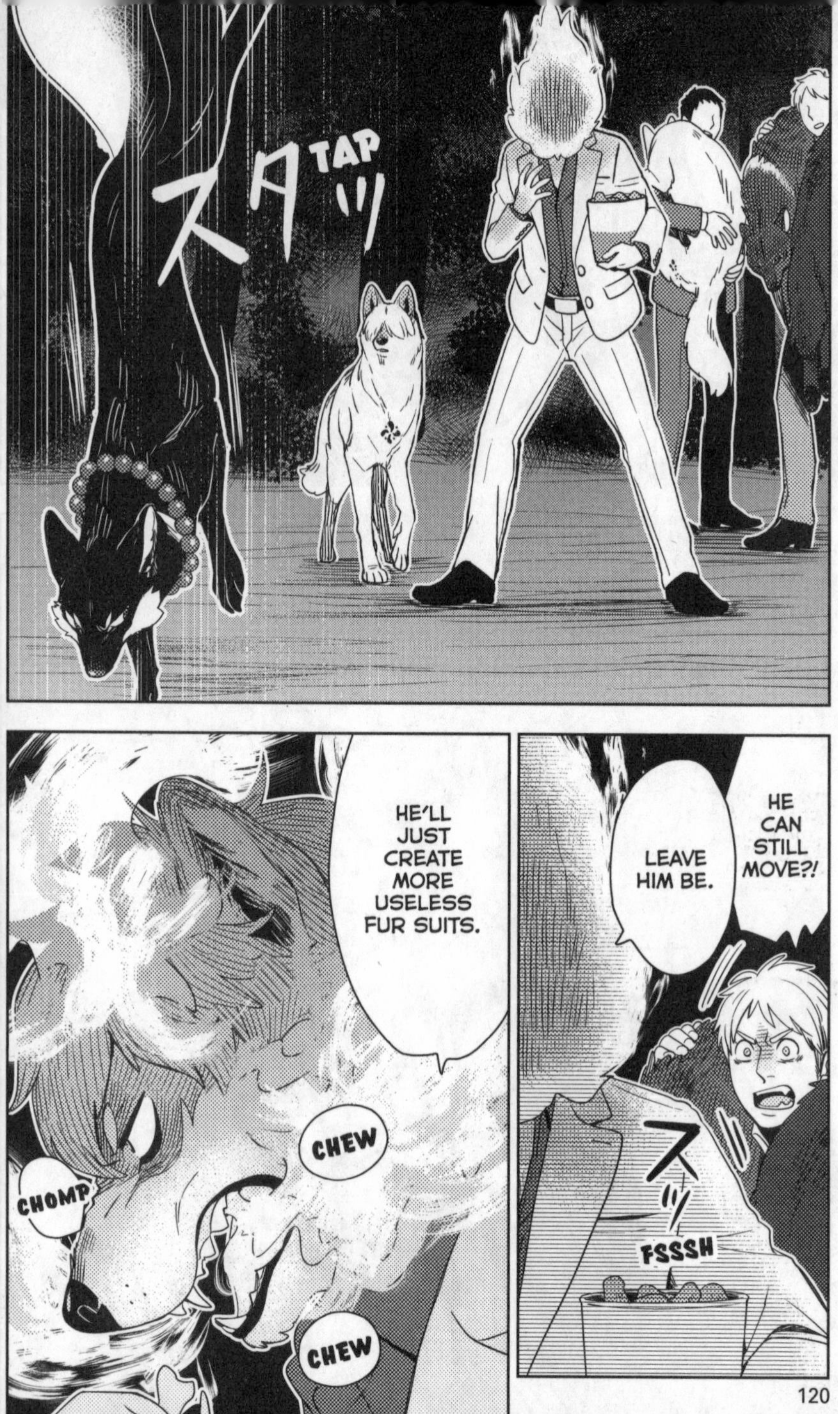
スタッ
TAP
HE CAN STILL MOVE?!
LEAVE HIM BE.
スッ
FSSSH
HE'LL JUST CREATE MORE USELESS FUR SUITS.
CHEW
CHOMP
CHEW

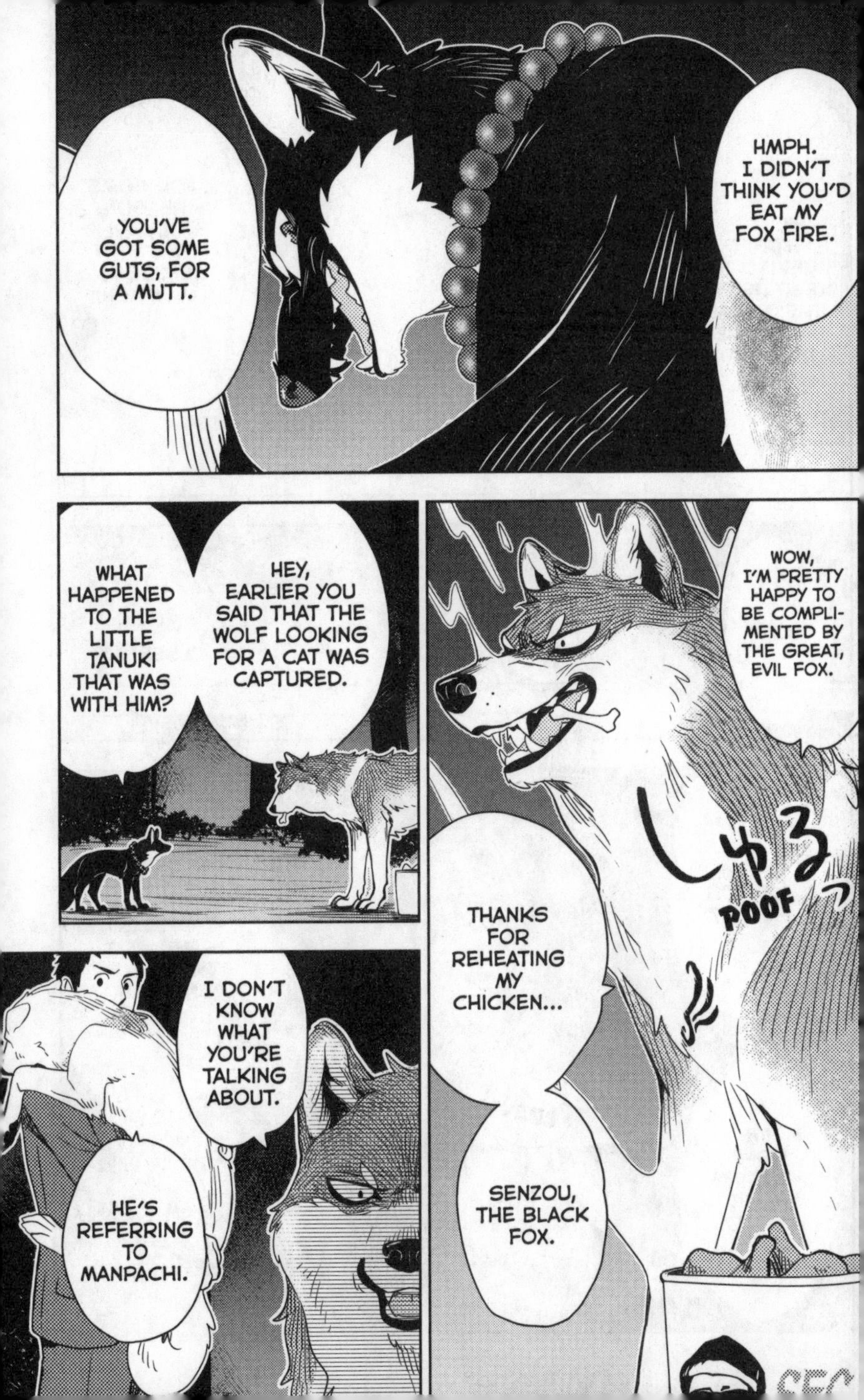
HMPH. I DIDN'T THINK YOU'D EAT MY FOX FIRE.
YOU'VE GOT SOME GUTS, FOR A MUTT.
WOW, I'M PRETTY HAPPY TO BE COMPLI-MENTED BY THE GREAT, EVIL FOX.
しゅる
POOF
THANKS FOR REHEATING MY CHICKEN...
SENZOU, THE BLACK FOX.
HEY, EARLIER YOU SAID THAT THE WOLF LOOKING FOR A CAT WAS CAPTURED.
WHAT HAPPENED TO THE LITTLE TANUKI THAT WAS WITH HIM?
I DON'T KNOW WHAT YOU'RE TALKING ABOUT.
HE'S REFERRING TO MANPACHI.

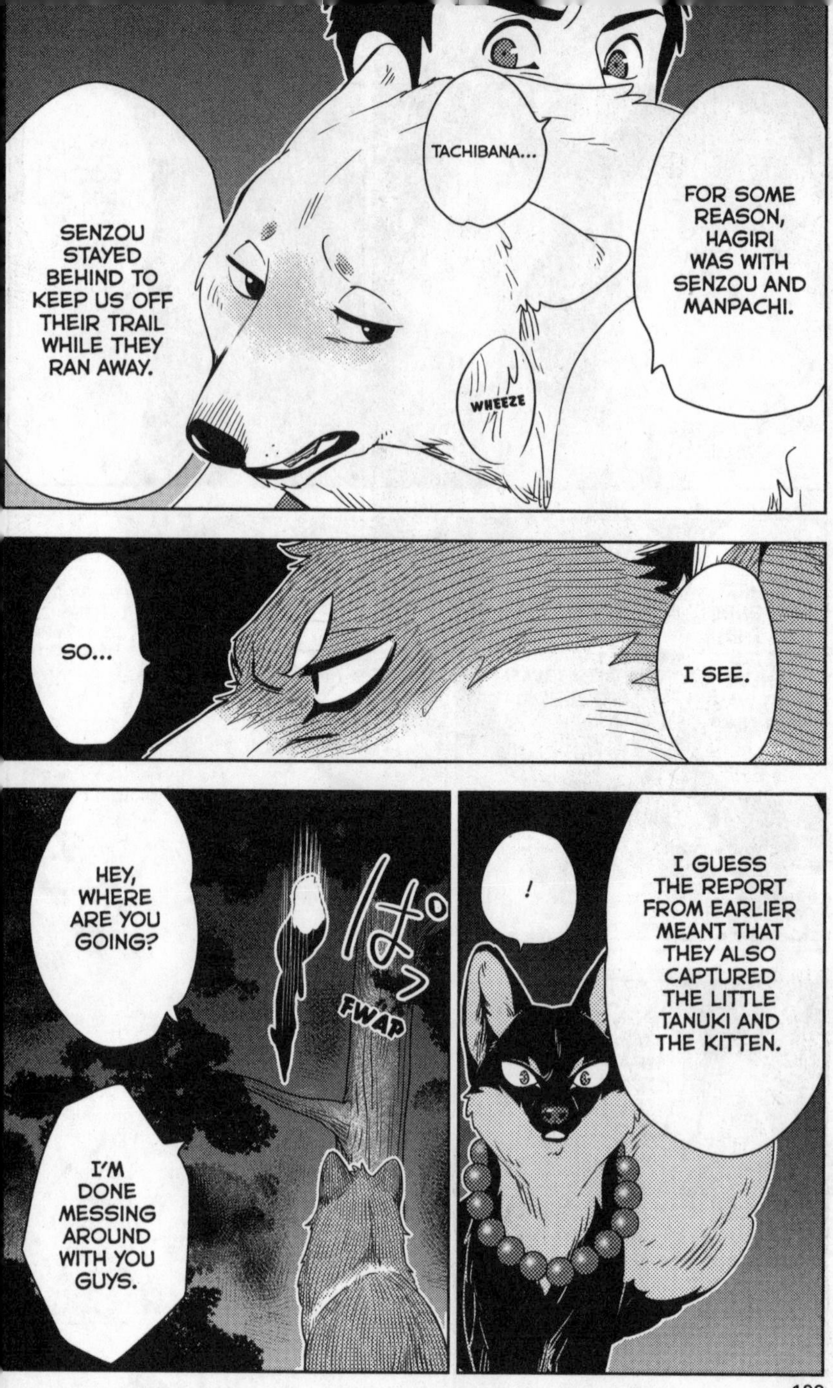
TACHIBANA...
FOR SOME REASON, HAGIRI WAS WITH SENZOU AND MANPACHI.
WHEEZE
SENZOU STAYED BEHIND TO KEEP US OFF THEIR TRAIL WHILE THEY RAN AWAY.
I SEE.
SO...
I GUESS THE REPORT FROM EARLIER MEANT THAT THEY ALSO CAPTURED THE LITTLE TANUKI AND THE KITTEN.
!
HEY, WHERE ARE YOU GOING?
はっ
FWAP
I'M DONE MESSING AROUND WITH YOU GUYS.

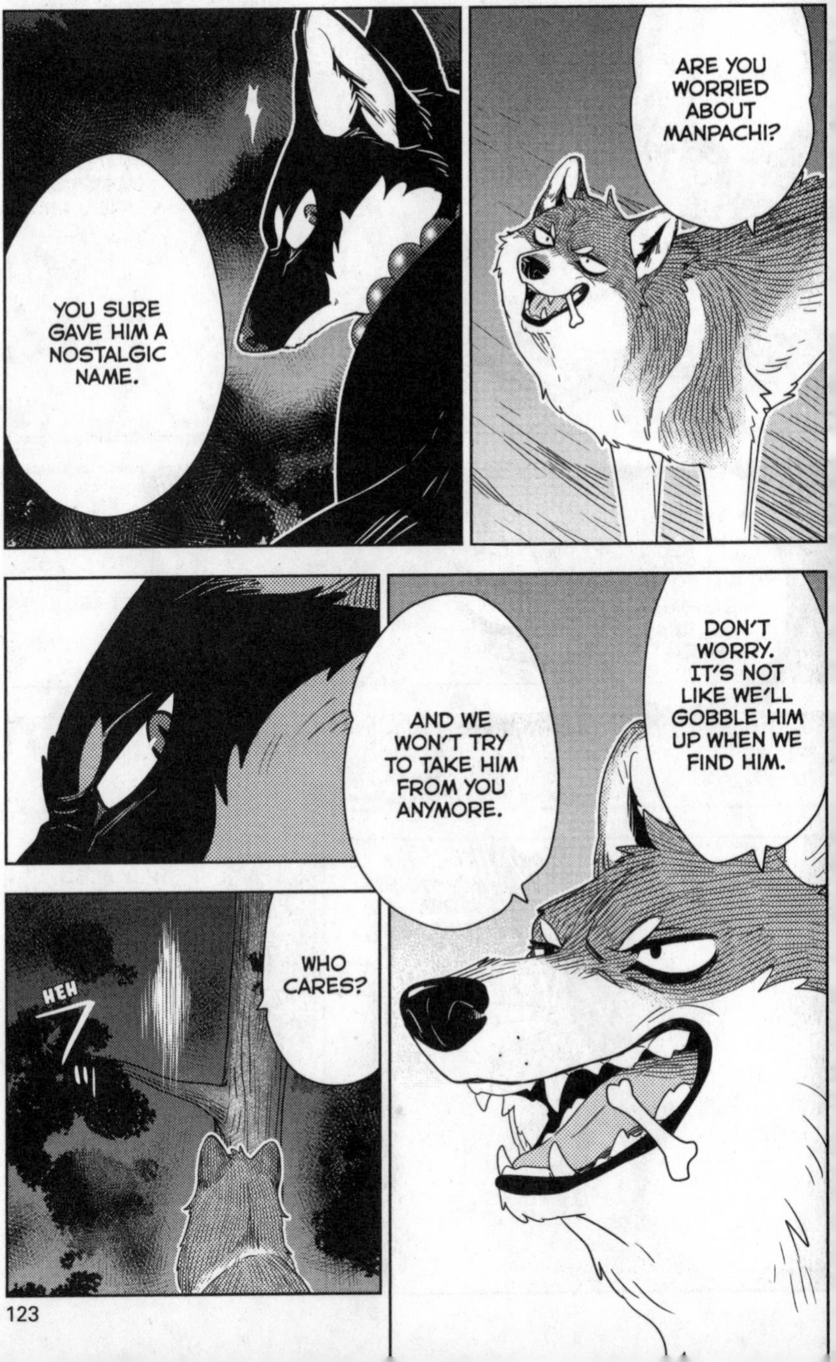
ARE YOU WORRIED ABOUT MANPACHI?
YOU SURE GAVE HIM A NOSTALGIC NAME.
DON'T WORRY. IT'S NOT LIKE WE'LL GOBBLE HIM UP WHEN WE FIND HIM.
AND WE WON'T TRY TO TAKE HIM FROM YOU ANYMORE.
WHO CARES?
HEH

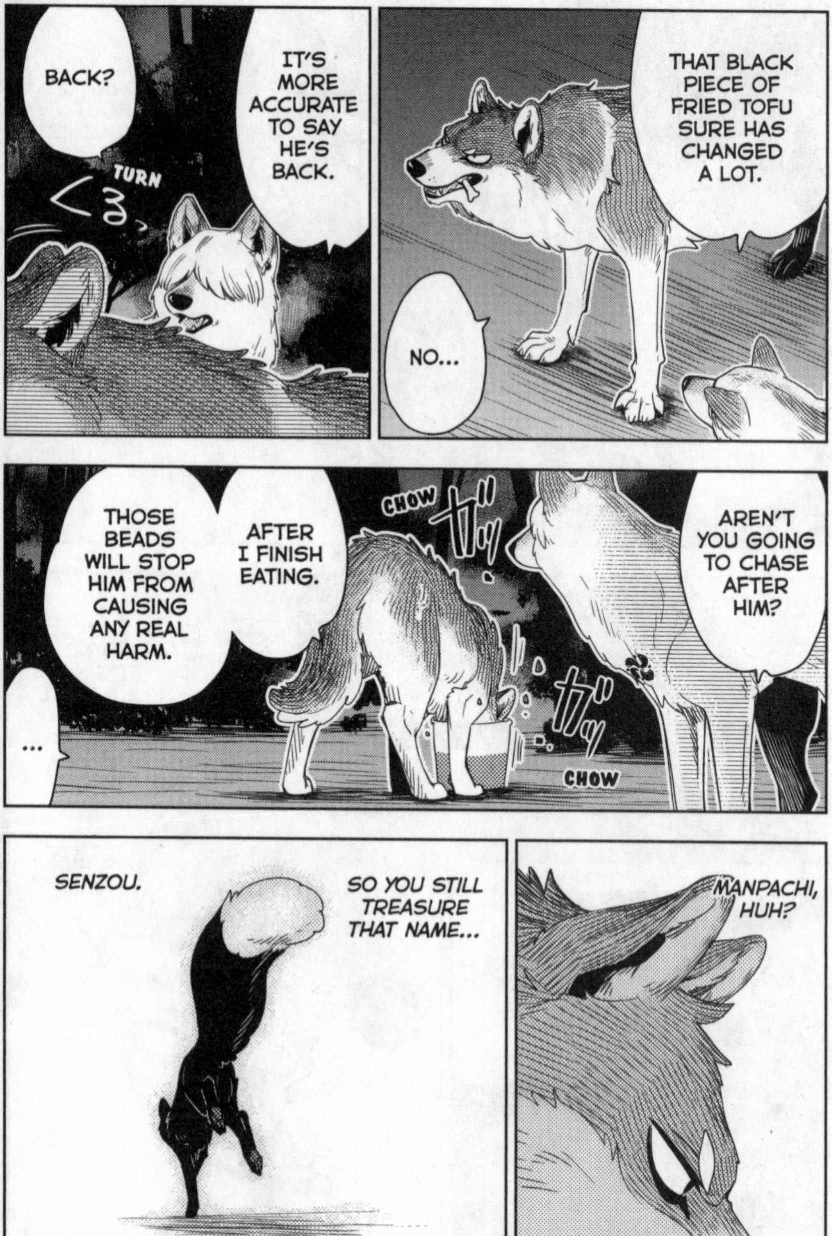
THAT BLACK PIECE OF FRIED TOFU SURE HAS CHANGED A LOT.
NO...
IT'S MORE ACCURATE TO SAY HE'S BACK.
BACK?
TURN
AREN'T YOU GOING TO CHASE AFTER HIM?
CHOW
CHOW
AFTER I FINISH EATING.
THOSE BEADS WILL STOP HIM FROM CAUSING ANY REAL HARM.
...
MANPACHI, HUH?
SO YOU STILL TREASURE THAT NAME...
SENZOU.

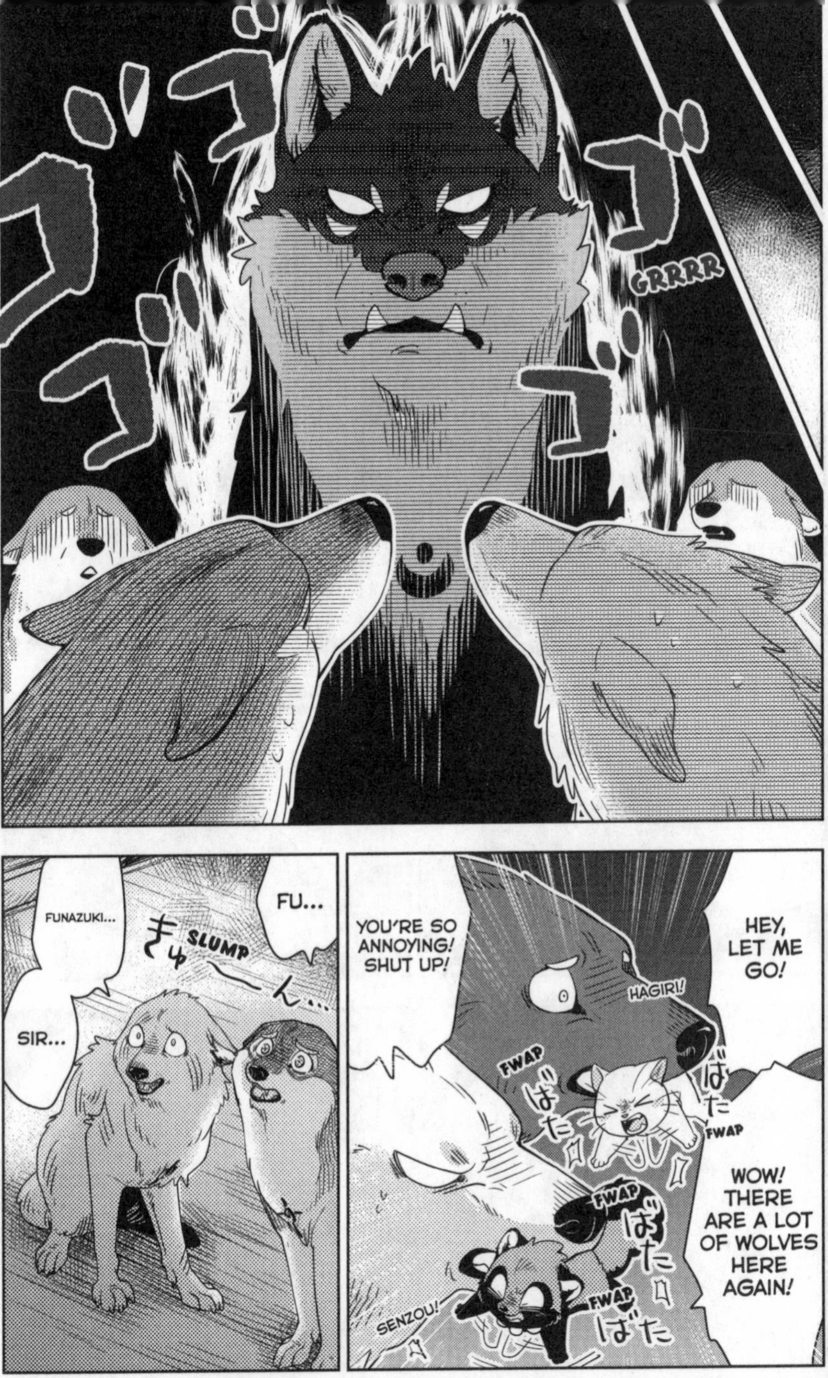
ゴゴゴゴゴ
GRRRR
HEY, LET ME GO!
HAGIRI!
YOU'RE SO ANNOYING! SHUT UP!
FWAP ばた
ばた FWAP
WOW! THERE ARE A LOT OF WOLVES HERE AGAIN!
FWAP ばた
FWAP ばた
SENZOU!
FU...
SIR...
FUNAZUKI...
SLUMP きゅ～ん...

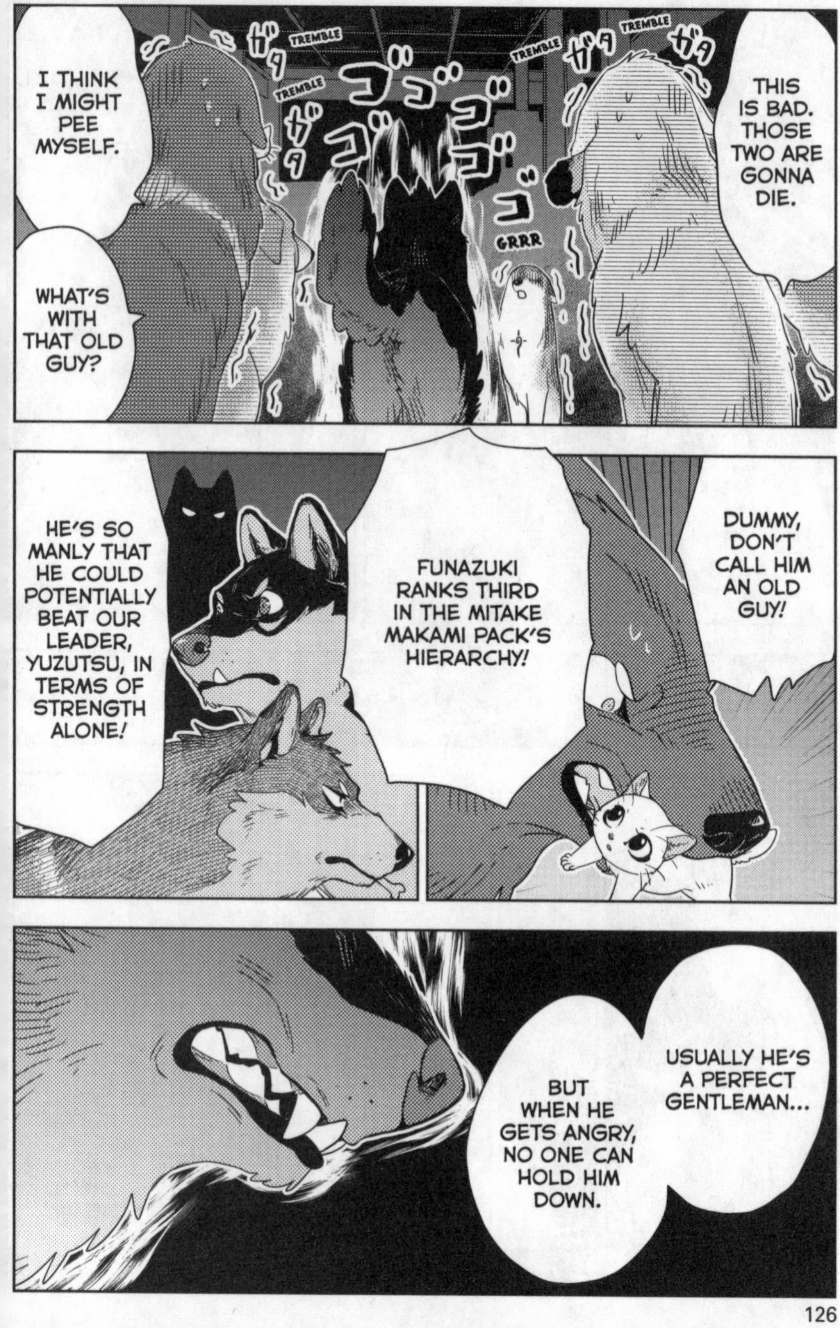
THIS IS BAD. THOSE TWO ARE GONNA DIE.
TREMBLE
TREMBLE
GRRR
TREMBLE
TREMBLE
I THINK I MIGHT PEE MYSELF.
WHAT'S WITH THAT OLD GUY?
DUMMY, DON'T CALL HIM AN OLD GUY!
FUNAZUKI RANKS THIRD IN THE MITAKE MAKAMI PACK'S HIERARCHY!
HE'S SO MANLY THAT HE COULD POTENTIALLY BEAT OUR LEADER, YUZUTSU, IN TERMS OF STRENGTH ALONE!
USUALLY HE'S A PERFECT GENTLEMAN...
BUT WHEN HE GETS ANGRY, NO ONE CAN HOLD HIM DOWN.

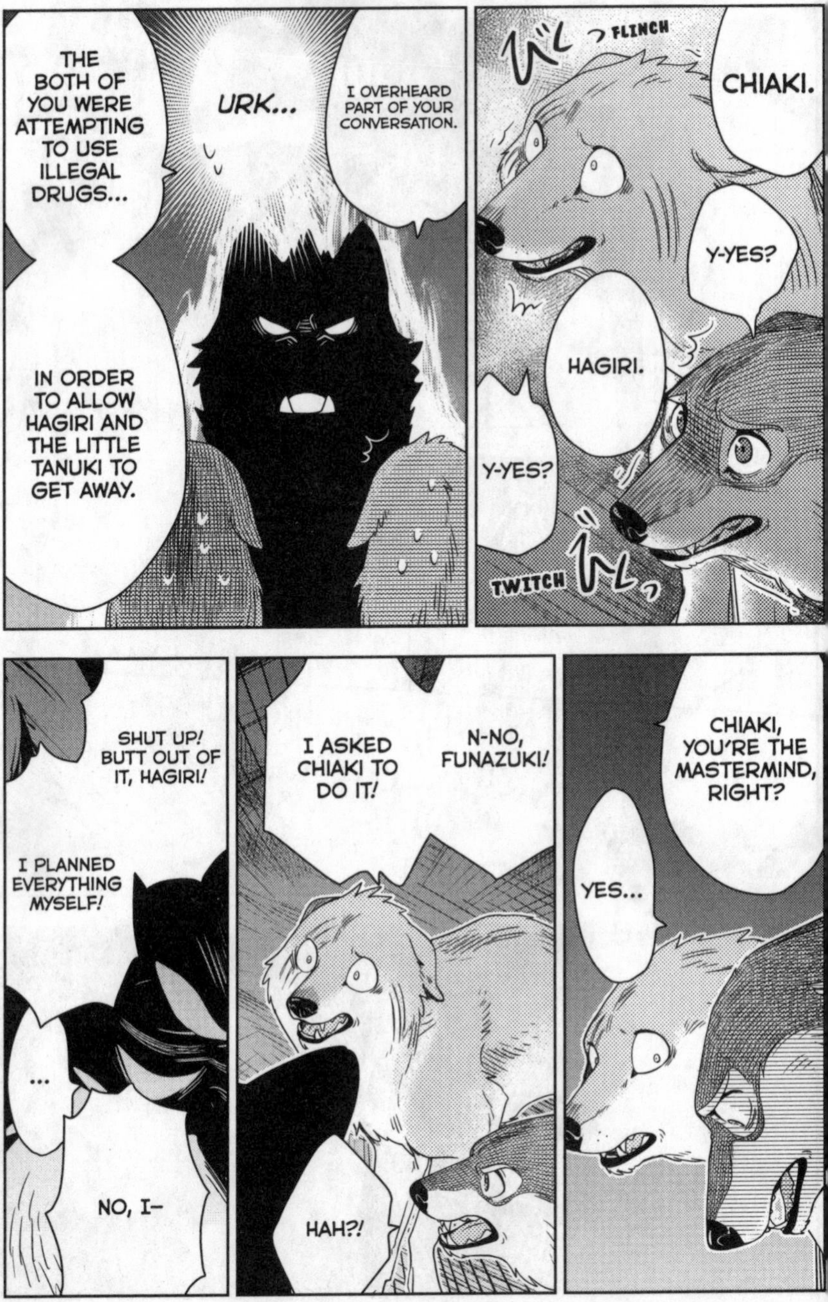
CHIAKI.
FLINCH
Y-YES?
HAGIRI.
Y-YES?
TWITCH
I OVERHEARD PART OF YOUR CONVERSATION.
URK...
THE BOTH OF YOU WERE ATTEMPTING TO USE ILLEGAL DRUGS...
IN ORDER TO ALLOW HAGIRI AND THE LITTLE TANUKI TO GET AWAY.
CHIAKI, YOU'RE THE MASTERMIND, RIGHT?
YES...
N-NO, FUNAZUKI!
I ASKED CHIAKI TO DO IT!
HAH?!
SHUT UP! BUTT OUT OF IT, HAGIRI!
I PLANNED EVERYTHING MYSELF!
...
NO, I–

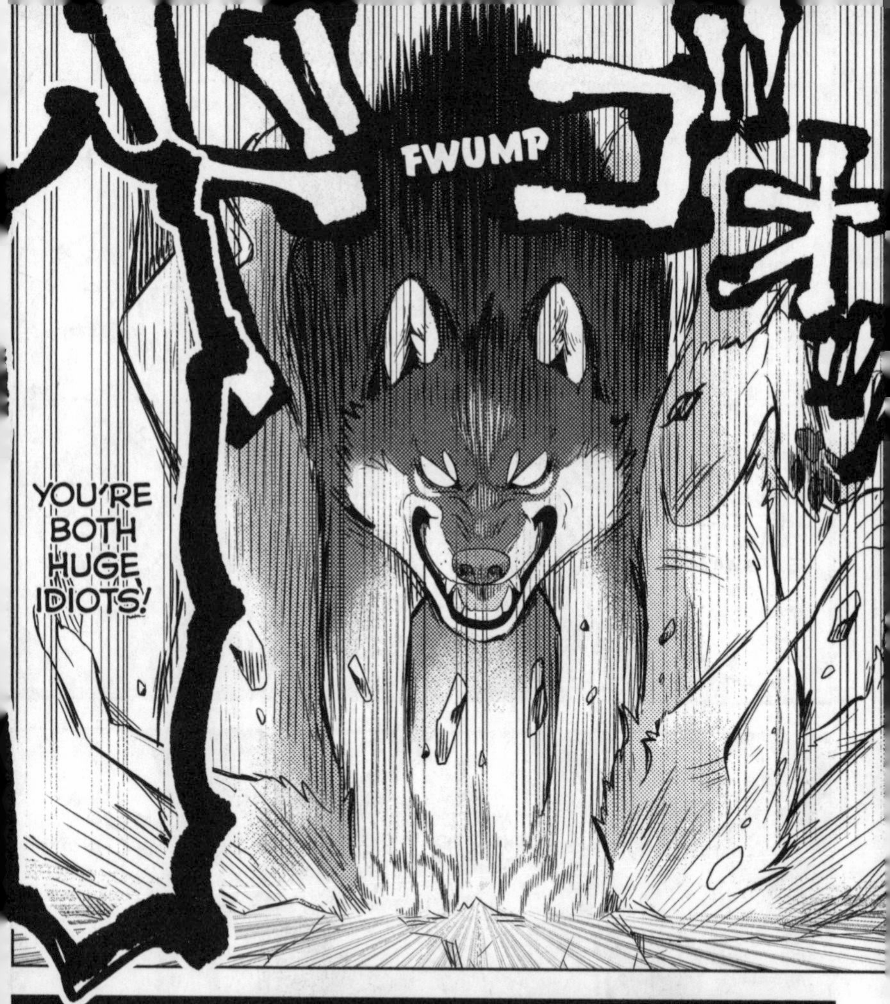
FWUMP
YOU'RE BOTH HUGE IDIOTS!
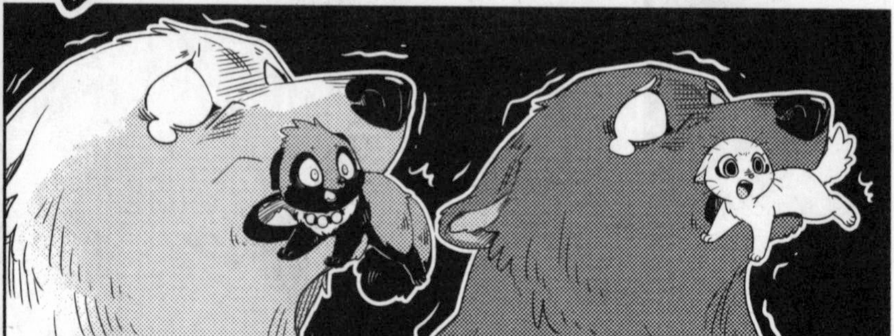

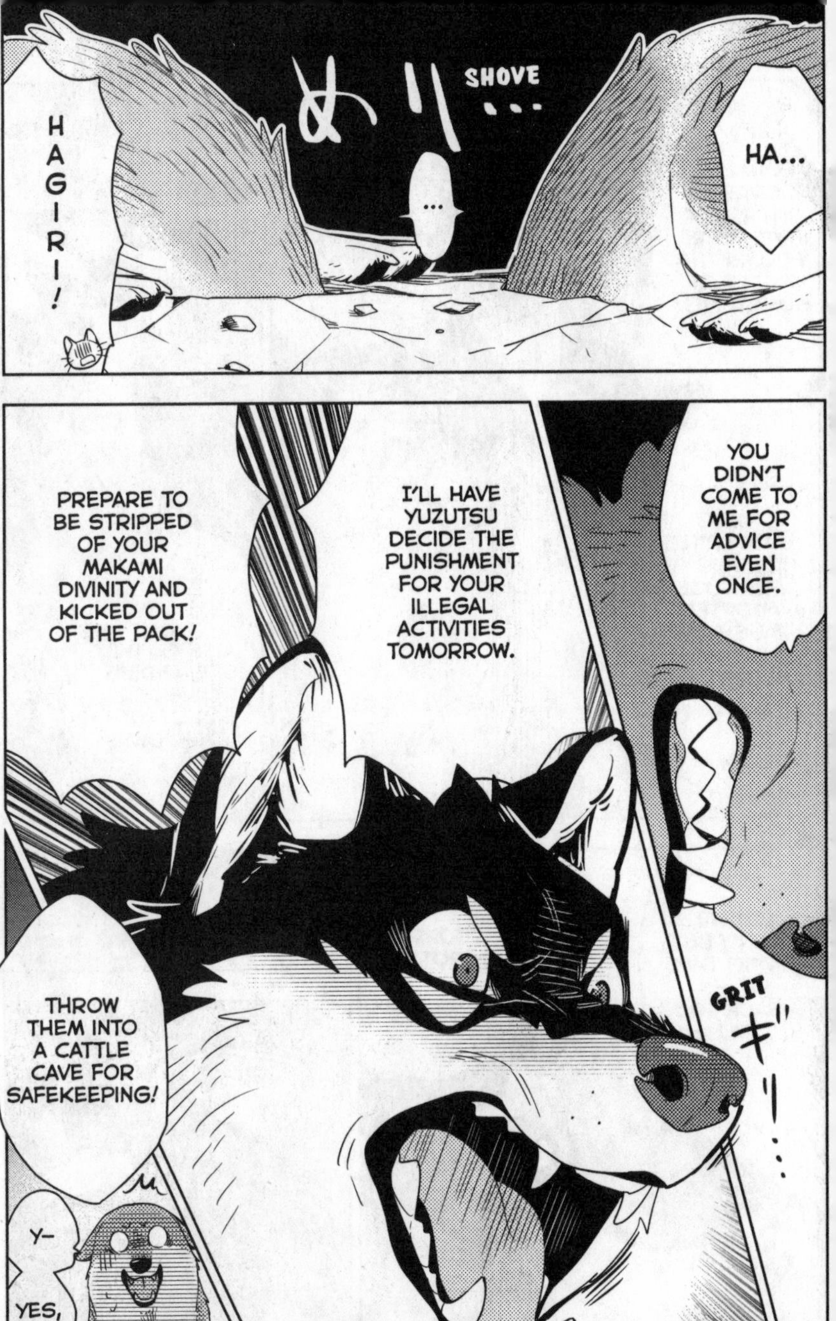
HA...
ぬり
SHOVE...
...
HAGIRI!
YOU DIDN'T COME TO ME FOR ADVICE EVEN ONCE.
GRIT
ギリ…
I'LL HAVE YUZUTSU DECIDE THE PUNISHMENT FOR YOUR ILLEGAL ACTIVITIES TOMORROW.
PREPARE TO BE STRIPPED OF YOUR MAKAMI DIVINITY AND KICKED OUT OF THE PACK!
THROW THEM INTO A CATTLE CAVE FOR SAFEKEEPING!
Y–
YES, SIR!

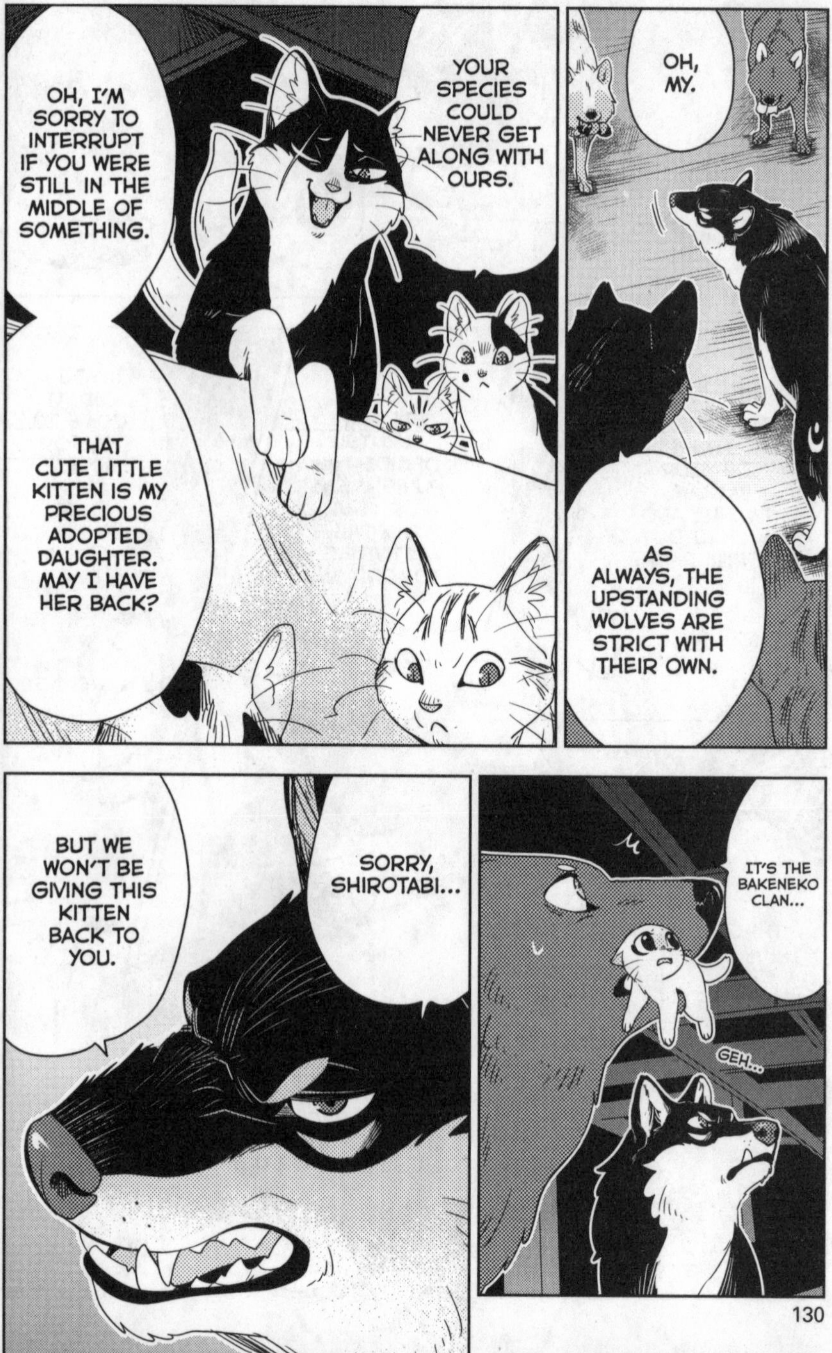
OH, MY.
AS ALWAYS, THE UPSTANDING WOLVES ARE STRICT WITH THEIR OWN.
YOUR SPECIES COULD NEVER GET ALONG WITH OURS.
OH, I'M SORRY TO INTERRUPT IF YOU WERE STILL IN THE MIDDLE OF SOMETHING.
THAT CUTE LITTLE KITTEN IS MY PRECIOUS ADOPTED DAUGHTER. MAY I HAVE HER BACK?
IT'S THE BAKENEKO CLAN...
GEH...
SORRY, SHIROTABI...
BUT WE WON'T BE GIVING THIS KITTEN BACK TO YOU.

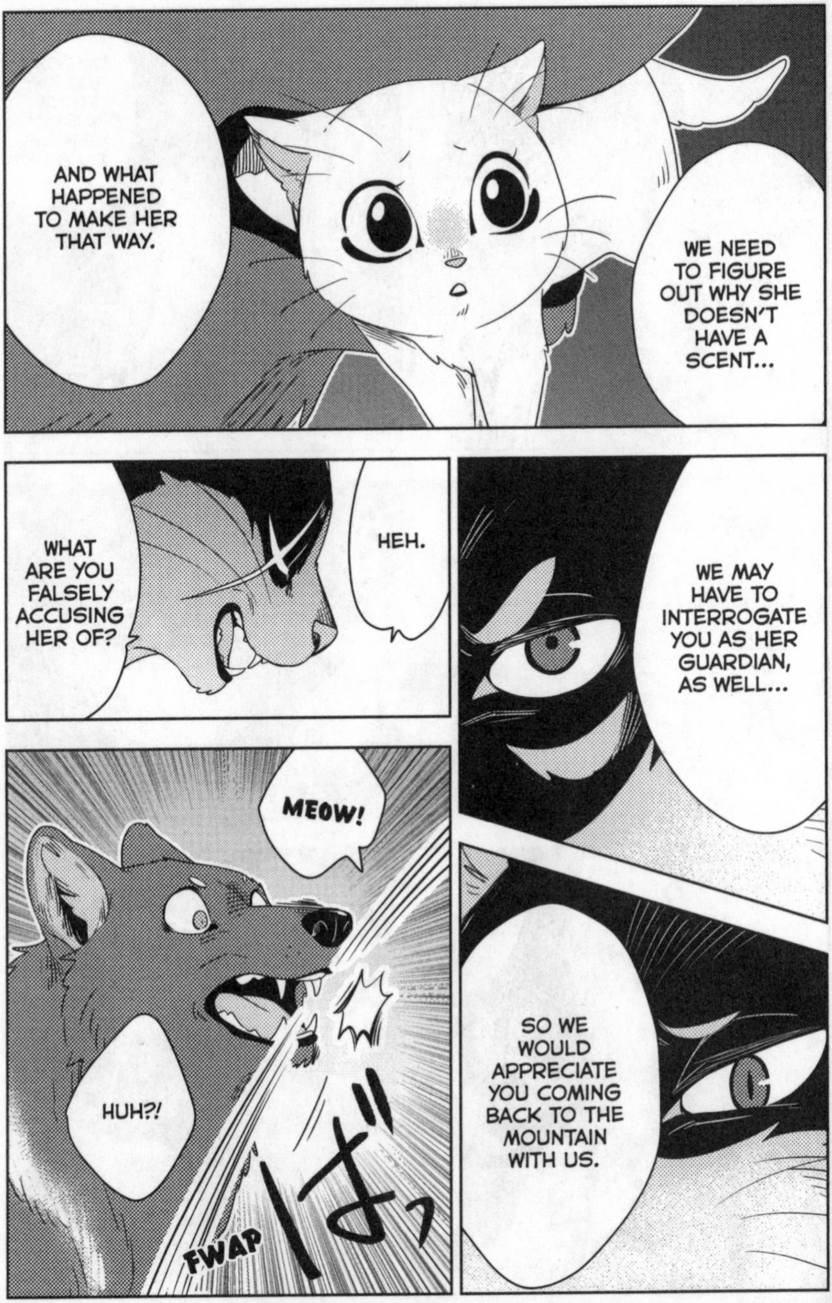
WE NEED TO FIGURE OUT WHY SHE DOESN'T HAVE A SCENT...
AND WHAT HAPPENED TO MAKE HER THAT WAY.
WE MAY HAVE TO INTERROGATE YOU AS HER GUARDIAN, AS WELL...
SO WE WOULD APPRECIATE YOU COMING BACK TO THE MOUNTAIN WITH US.
HEH.
WHAT ARE YOU FALSELY ACCUSING HER OF?
MEOW!
ばっ
FWAP
HUH?!

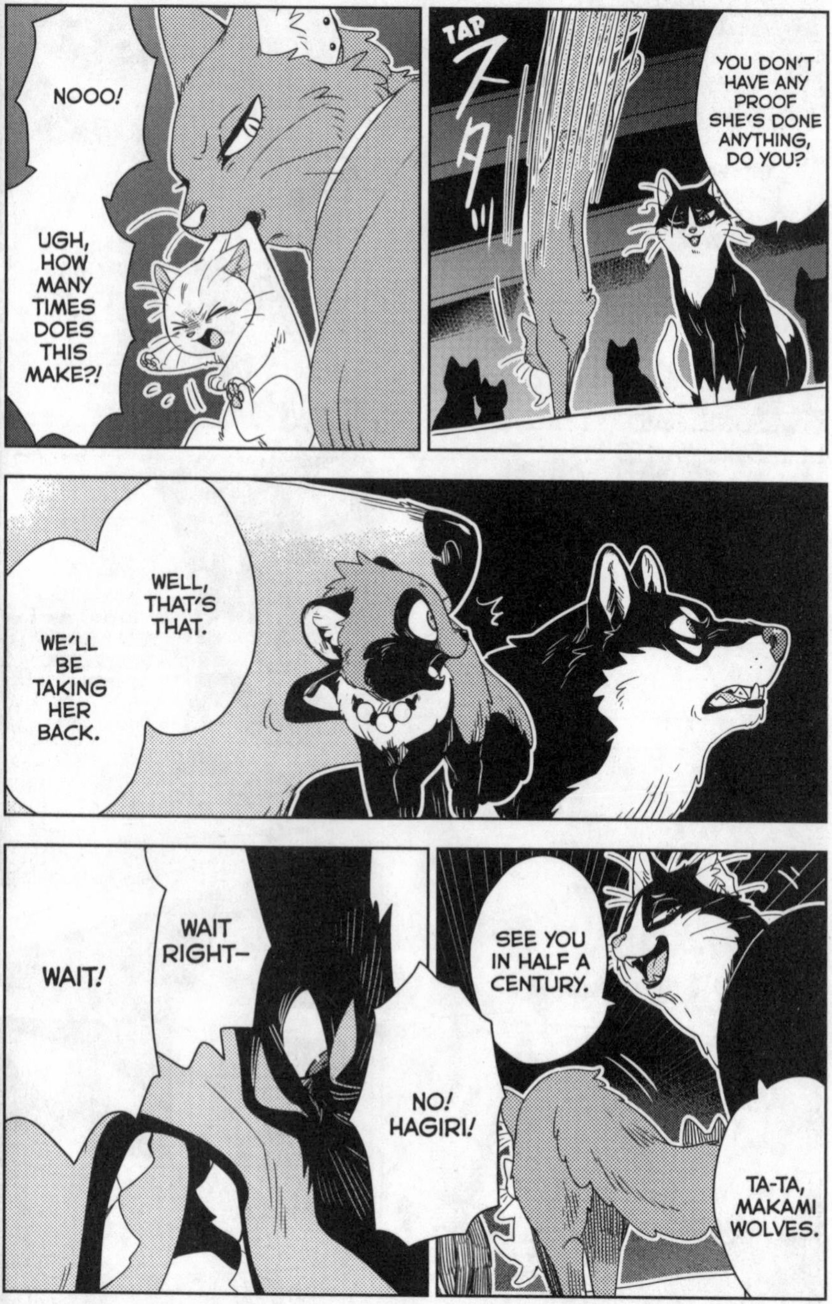
TAP
YOU DON'T HAVE ANY PROOF SHE'S DONE ANYTHING, DO YOU?
NOOO!
UGH, HOW MANY TIMES DOES THIS MAKE?!
WELL, THAT'S THAT.
WE'LL BE TAKING HER BACK.
SEE YOU IN HALF A CENTURY.
TA-TA, MAKAMI WOLVES.
WAIT RIGHT–
WAIT!
NO! HAGIRI!

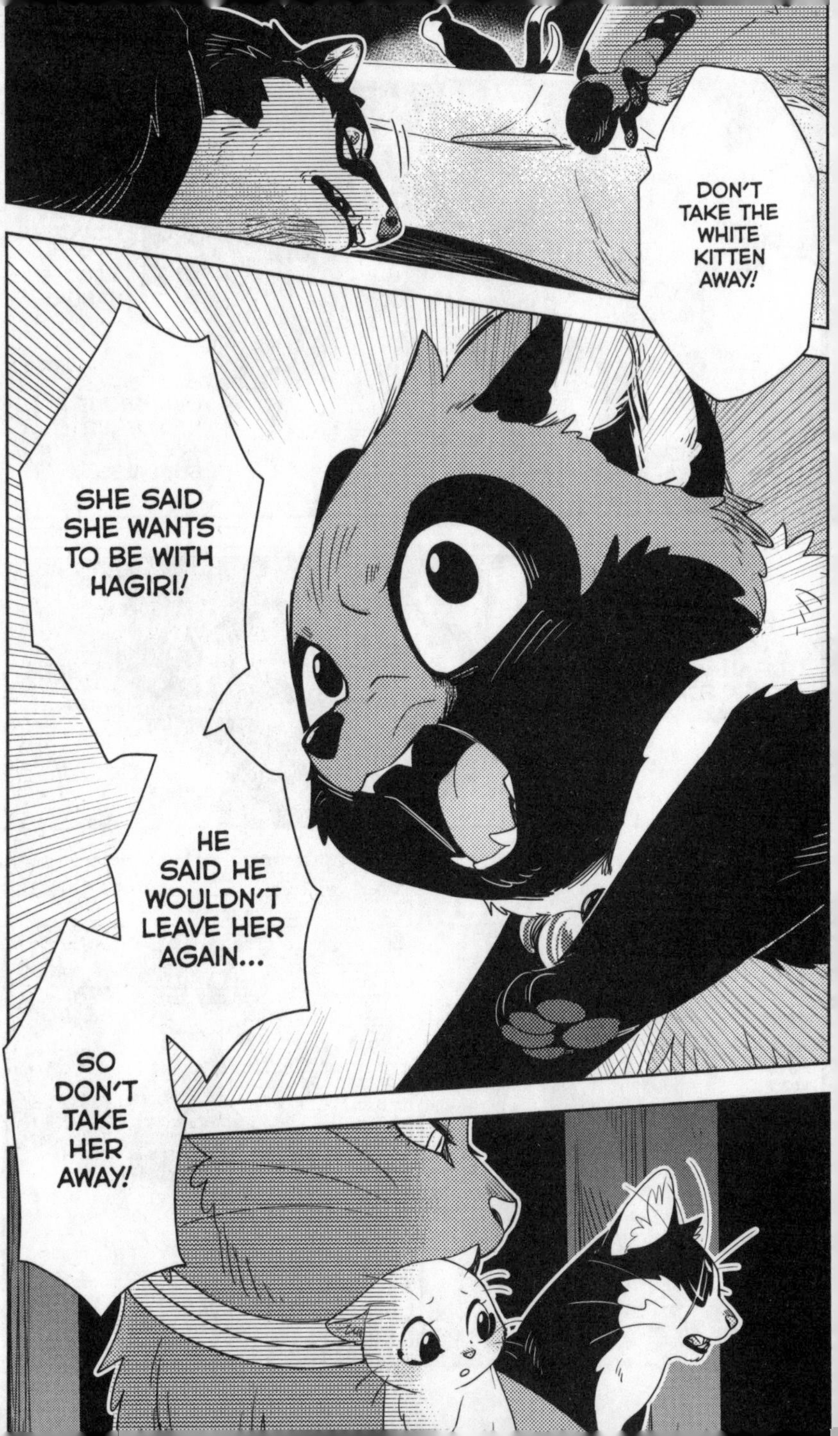
DON'T TAKE THE WHITE KITTEN AWAY!
SHE SAID SHE WANTS TO BE WITH HAGIRI!
HE SAID HE WOULDN'T LEAVE HER AGAIN...
SO DON'T TAKE HER AWAY!

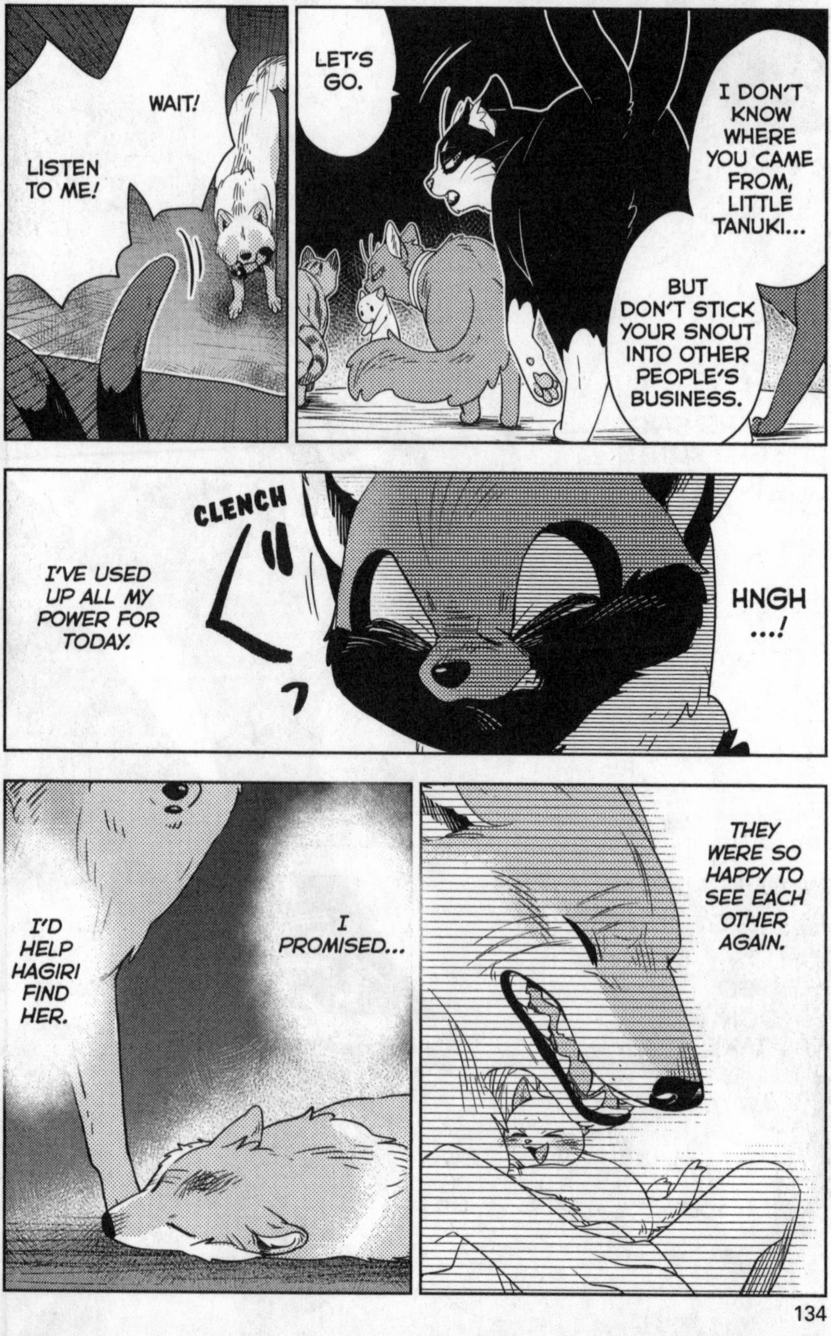
I DON'T KNOW WHERE YOU CAME FROM, LITTLE TANUKI...
BUT DON'T STICK YOUR SNOUT INTO OTHER PEOPLE'S BUSINESS.
LET'S GO.
WAIT!
LISTEN TO ME!
HNGH ...!
CLENCH
I'VE USED UP ALL MY POWER FOR TODAY.
THEY WERE SO HAPPY TO SEE EACH OTHER AGAIN.
I PROMISED...
I'D HELP HAGIRI FIND HER.

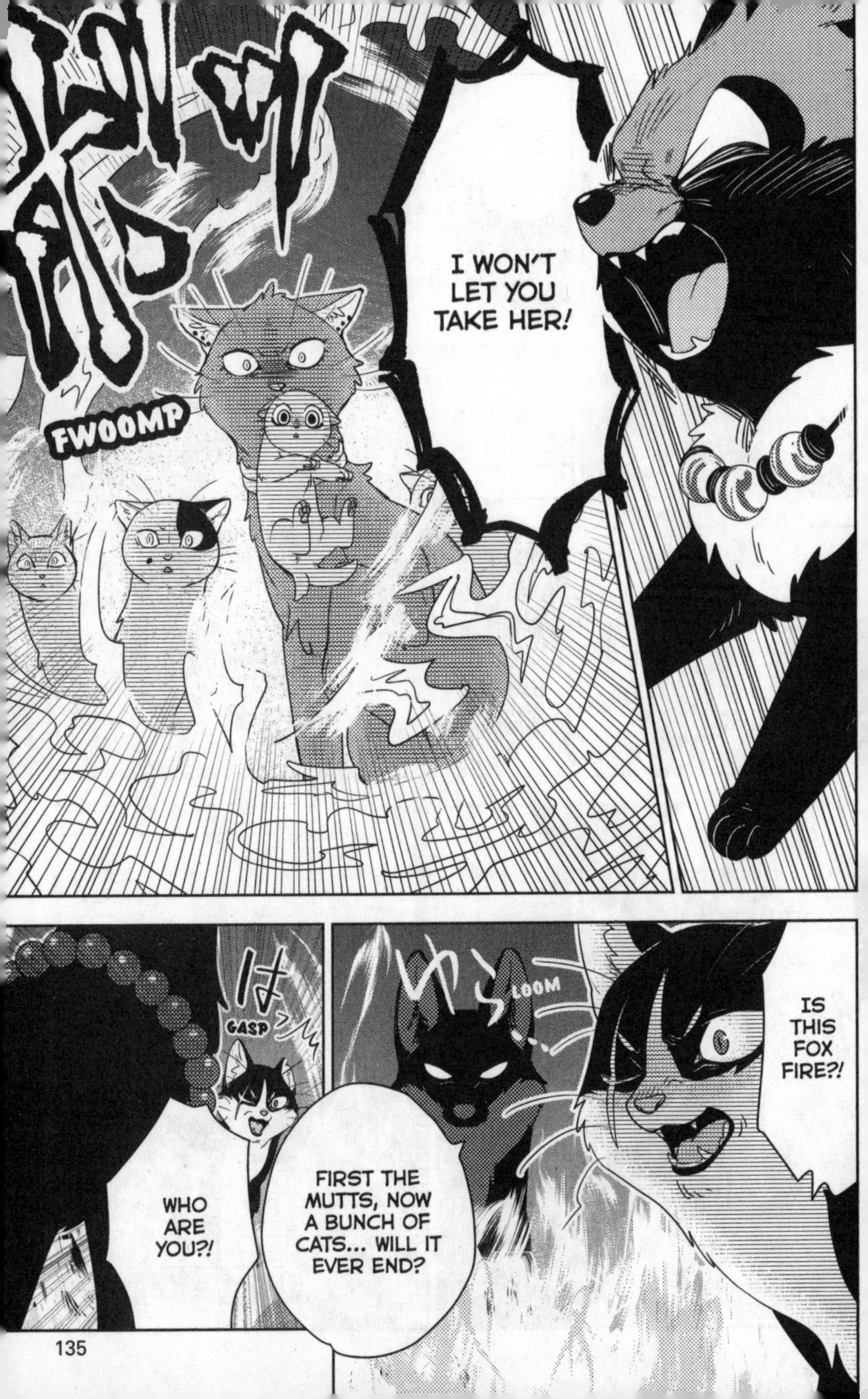
I WON'T LET YOU TAKE HER!
FWOOMP
ゆら
LOOM
IS THIS FOX FIRE?!
FIRST THE MUTTS, NOW A BUNCH OF CATS... WILL IT EVER END?
は
GASP
WHO ARE YOU?!

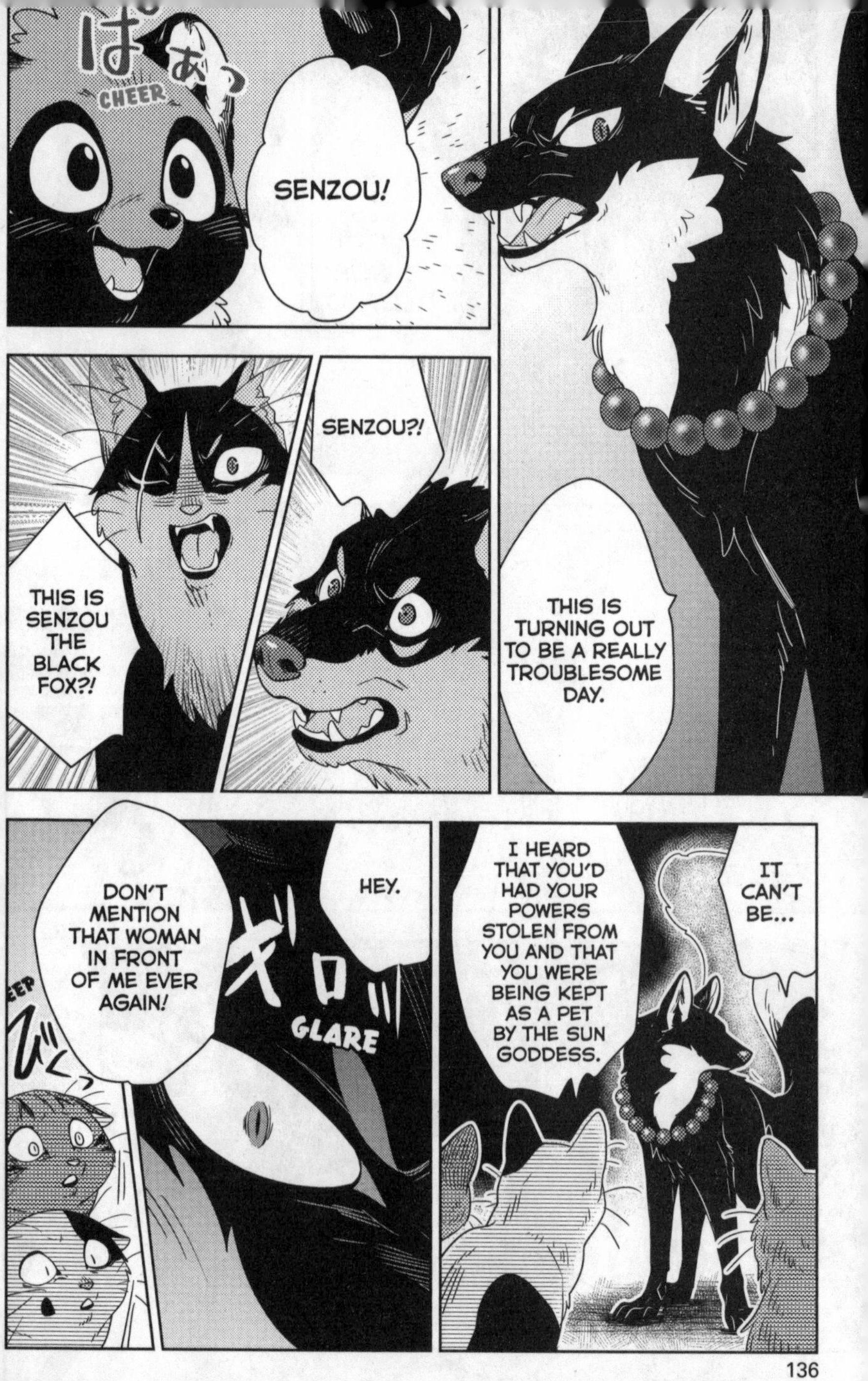
THIS IS TURNING OUT TO BE A REALLY TROUBLESOME DAY.
ぱあっ
CHEER
SENZOU!
SENZOU?!
THIS IS SENZOU THE BLACK FOX?!
IT CAN'T BE...
I HEARD THAT YOU'D HAD YOUR POWERS STOLEN FROM YOU AND THAT YOU WERE BEING KEPT AS A PET BY THE SUN GODDESS.
HEY.
ギロッ
GLARE
DON'T MENTION THAT WOMAN IN FRONT OF ME EVER AGAIN!
びくっ
EEP

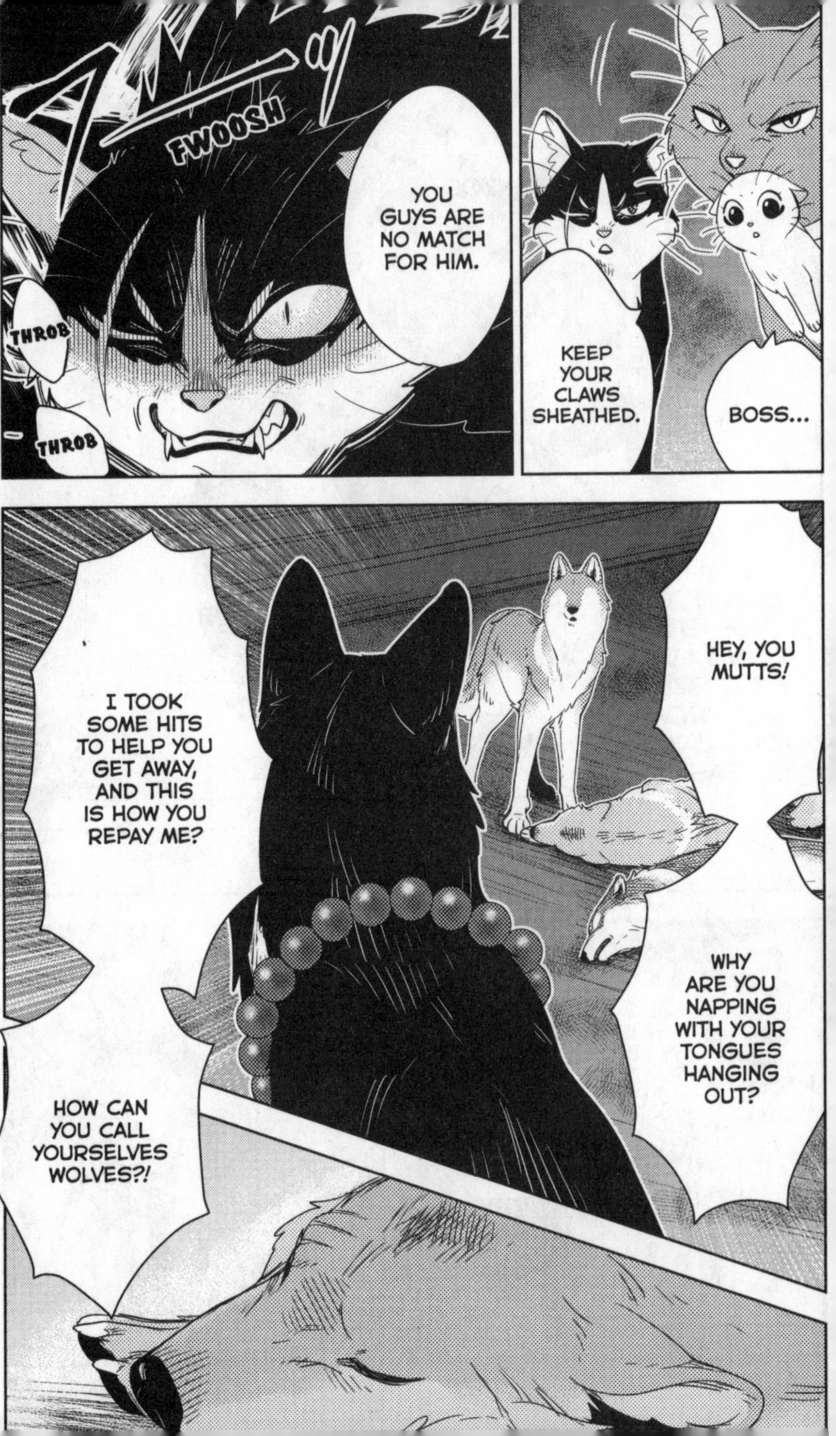
BOSS...
KEEP YOUR CLAWS SHEATHED.
FWOOSH
YOU GUYS ARE NO MATCH FOR HIM.
THROB
THROB
HEY, YOU MUTTS!
WHY ARE YOU NAPPING WITH YOUR TONGUES HANGING OUT?
I TOOK SOME HITS TO HELP YOU GET AWAY, AND THIS IS HOW YOU REPAY ME?
HOW CAN YOU CALL YOURSELVES WOLVES?!

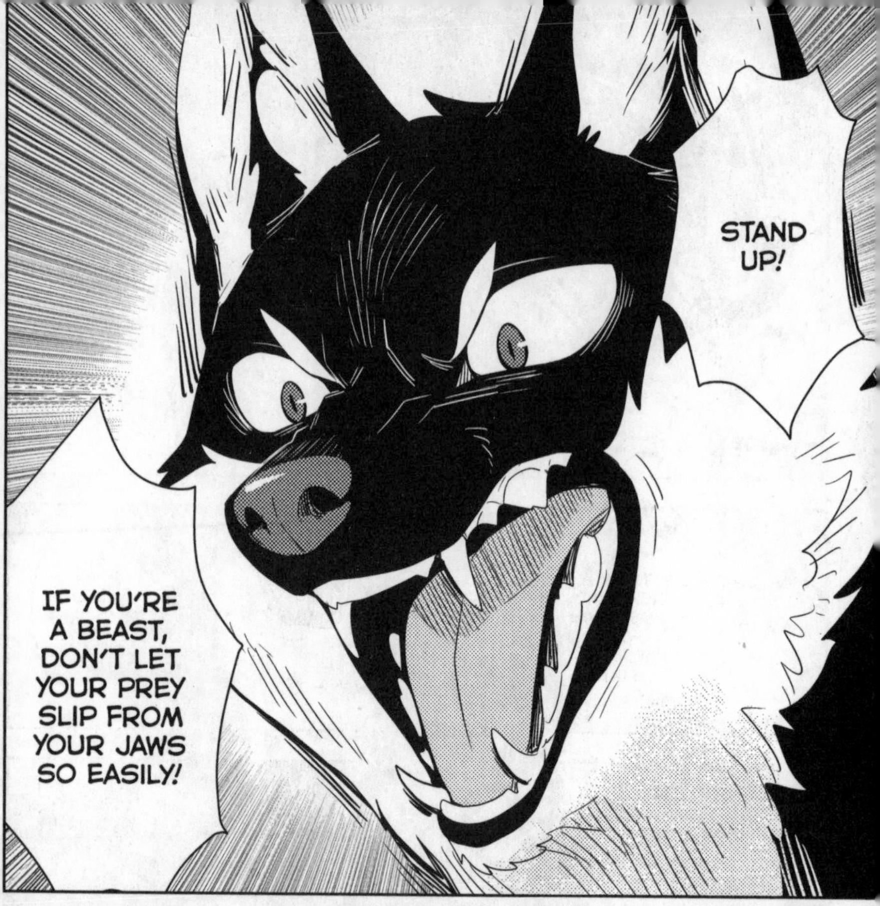
STAND UP!
IF YOU'RE A BEAST, DON'T LET YOUR PREY SLIP FROM YOUR JAWS SO EASILY!

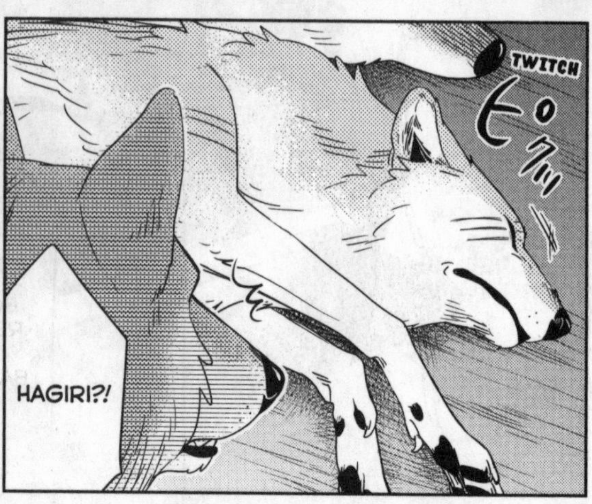
TWITCH
HAGIRI?!

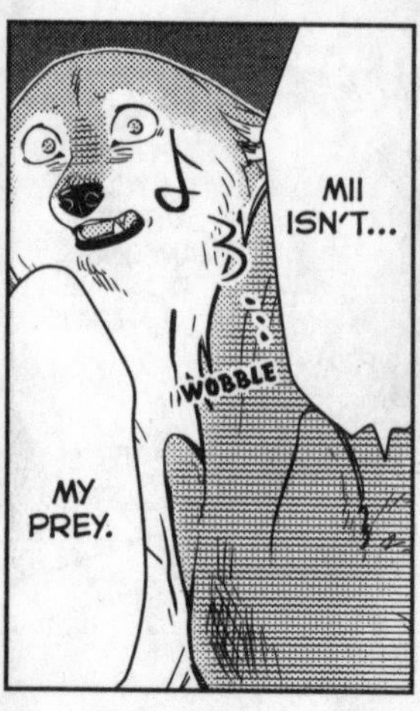
MII ISN'T...
WOBBLE
MY PREY.

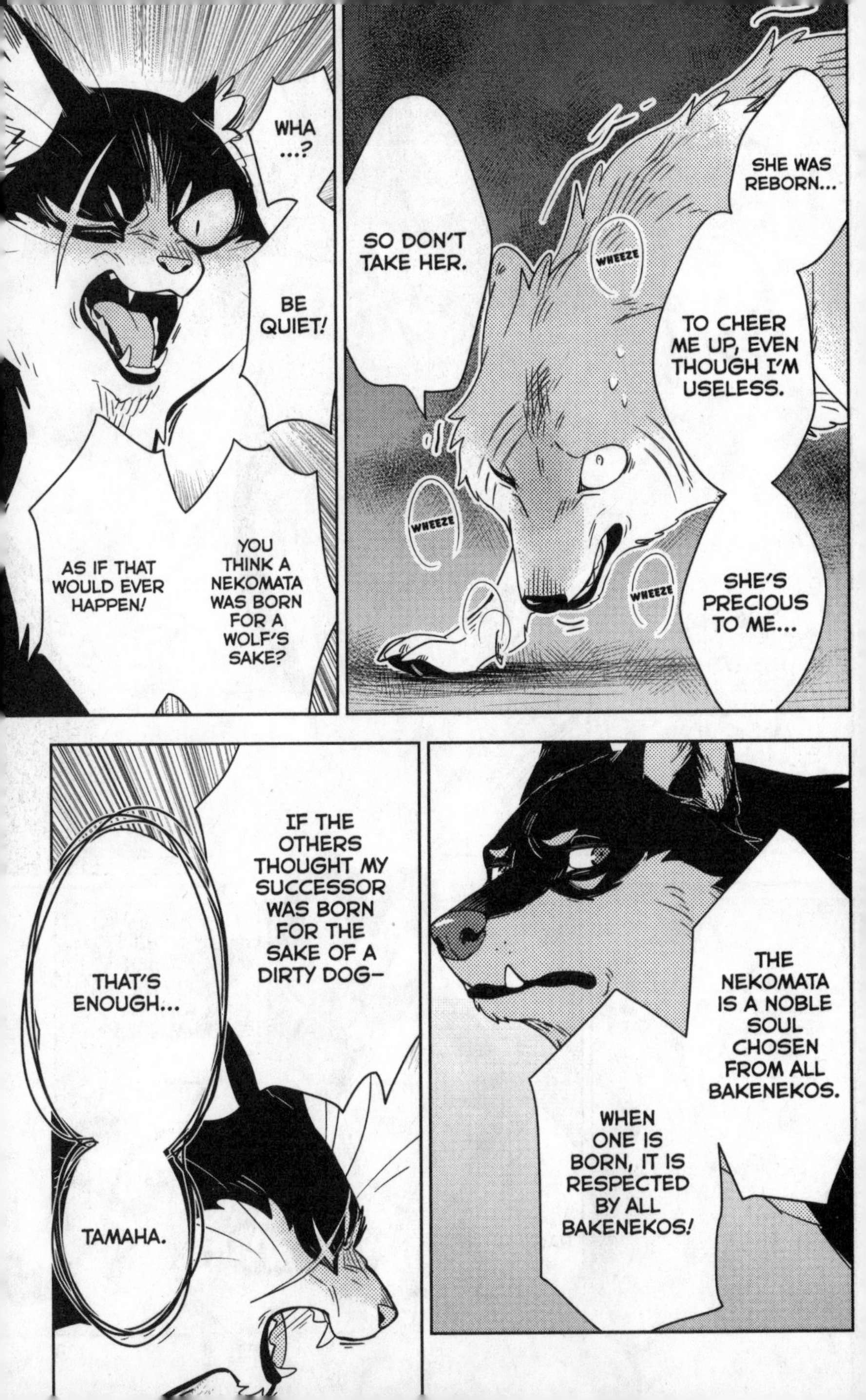
SHE WAS REBORN...
TO CHEER ME UP, EVEN THOUGH I'M USELESS.
WHEEZE
WHEEZE
WHEEZE
SHE'S PRECIOUS TO ME...
SO DON'T TAKE HER.
WHA ...?
BE QUIET!
YOU THINK A NEKOMATA WAS BORN FOR A WOLF'S SAKE?
AS IF THAT WOULD EVER HAPPEN!
THE NEKOMATA IS A NOBLE SOUL CHOSEN FROM ALL BAKENEKOS.
WHEN ONE IS BORN, IT IS RESPECTED BY ALL BAKENEKOS!
IF THE OTHERS THOUGHT MY SUCCESSOR WAS BORN FOR THE SAKE OF A DIRTY DOG–
THAT'S ENOUGH...
TAMAHA.

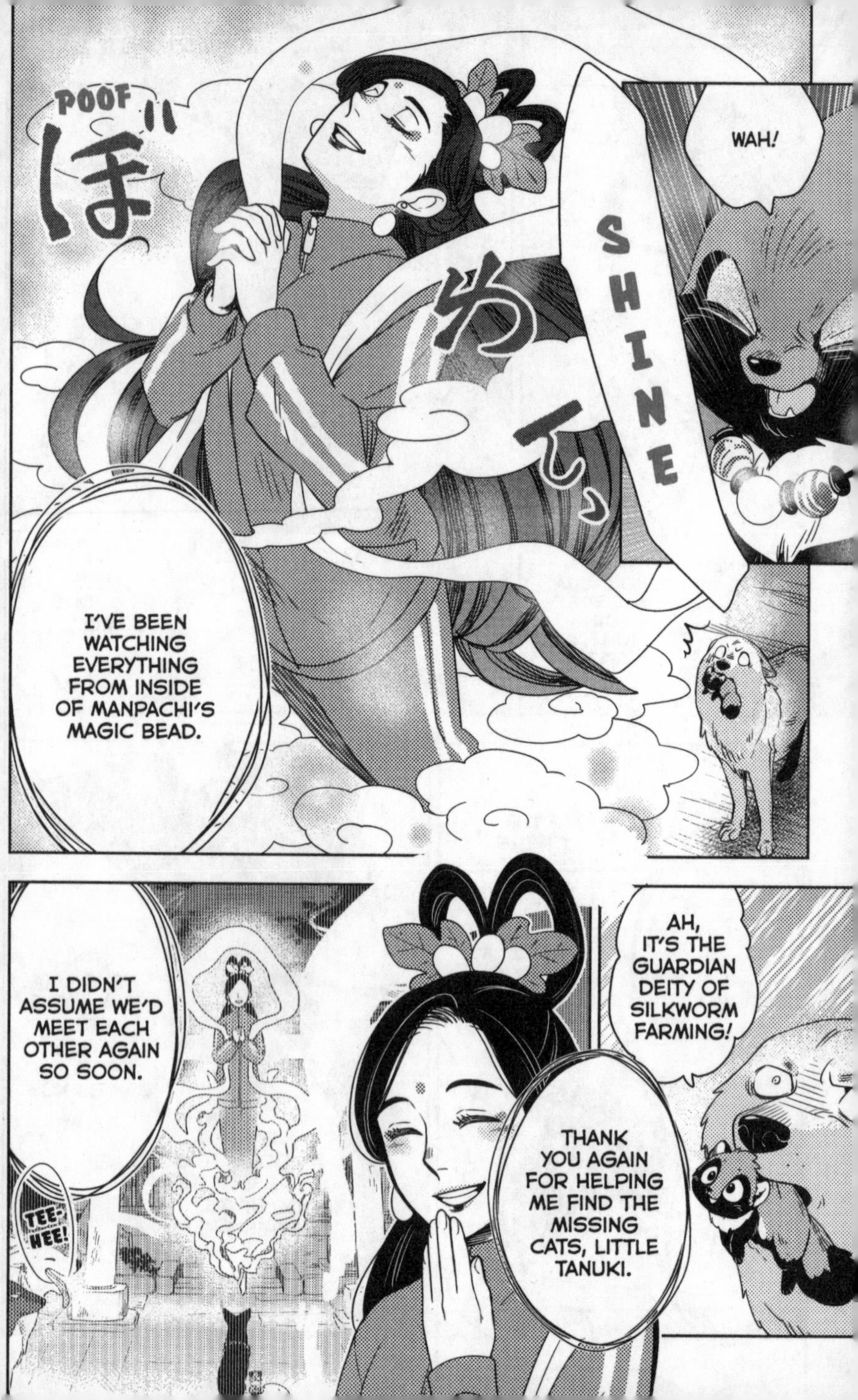
WAH!
SHINE
やてっ
POOF
ぼ
I'VE BEEN WATCHING EVERYTHING FROM INSIDE OF MANPACHI'S MAGIC BEAD.
AH, IT'S THE GUARDIAN DEITY OF SILKWORM FARMING!
THANK YOU AGAIN FOR HELPING ME FIND THE MISSING CATS, LITTLE TANUKI.
I DIDN'T ASSUME WE'D MEET EACH OTHER AGAIN SO SOON.
TEE-HEE!

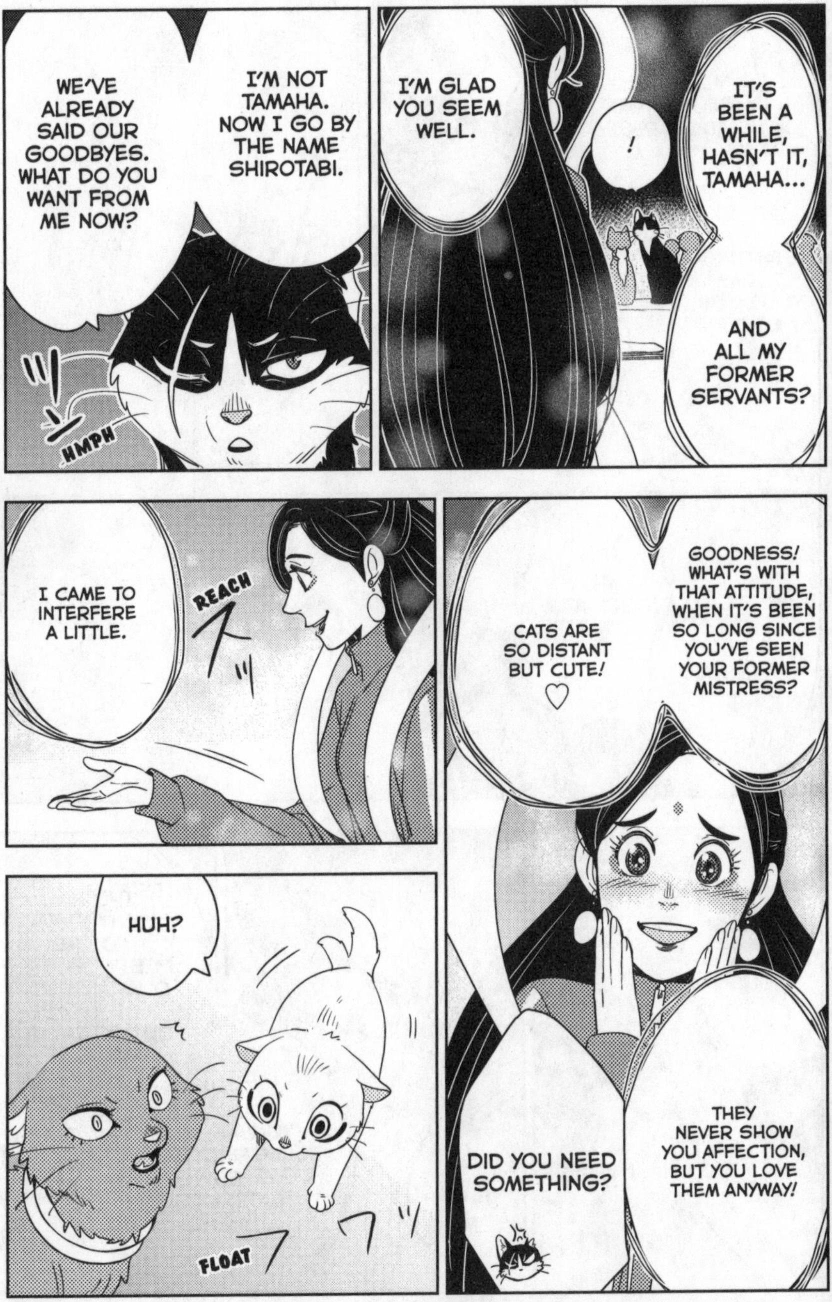
IT'S BEEN A WHILE, HASN'T IT, TAMAHA...
!
I'M GLAD YOU SEEM WELL.
AND ALL MY FORMER SERVANTS?
I'M NOT TAMAHA. NOW I GO BY THE NAME SHIROTABI.
WE'VE ALREADY SAID OUR GOODBYES. WHAT DO YOU WANT FROM ME NOW?
HMPH
GOODNESS! WHAT'S WITH THAT ATTITUDE, WHEN IT'S BEEN SO LONG SINCE YOU'VE SEEN YOUR FORMER MISTRESS?
CATS ARE SO DISTANT BUT CUTE! ♡
THEY NEVER SHOW YOU AFFECTION, BUT YOU LOVE THEM ANYWAY!
DID YOU NEED SOMETHING?
I CAME TO INTERFERE A LITTLE.
REACH
HUH?
FLOAT

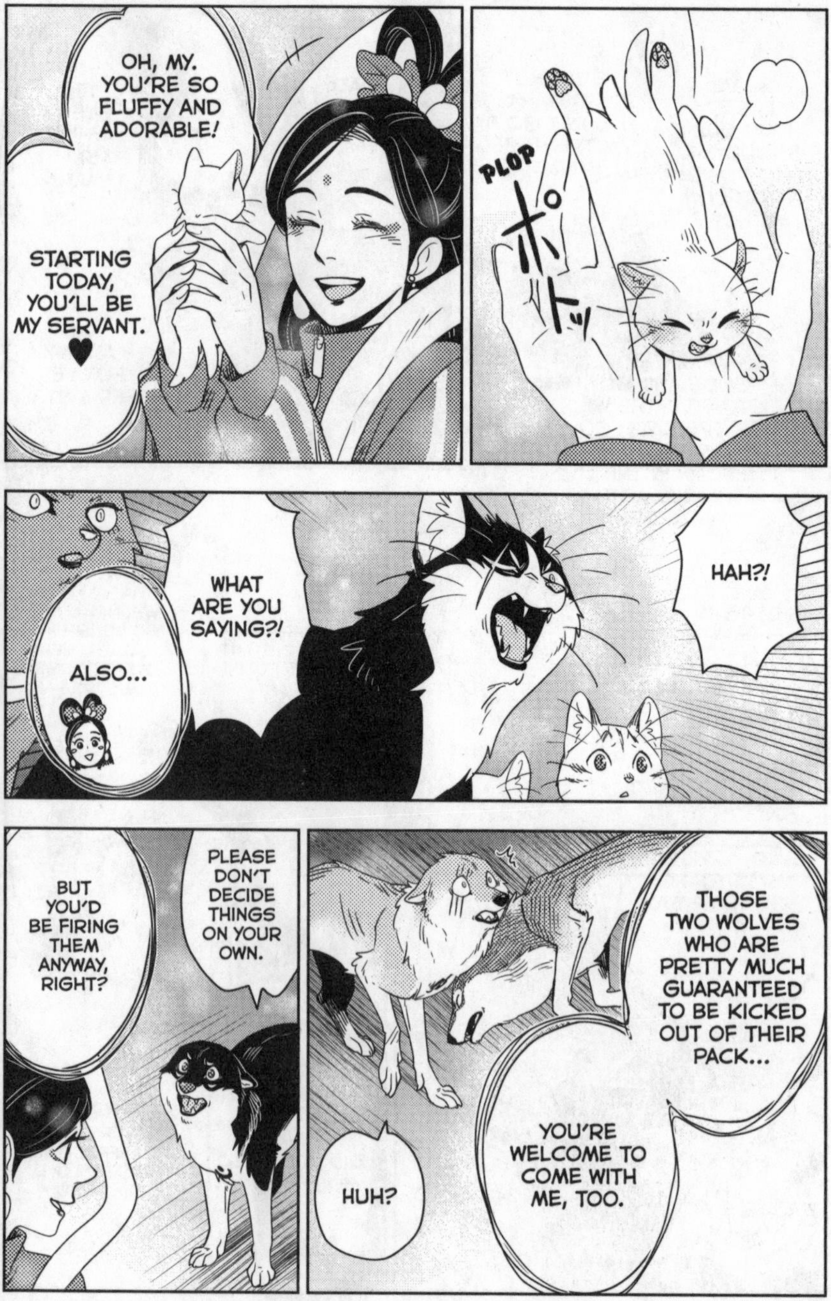
PLOP
ポトッ
OH, MY. YOU'RE SO FLUFFY AND ADORABLE!
STARTING TODAY, YOU'LL BE MY SERVANT. ♥
HAH?!
WHAT ARE YOU SAYING?!
ALSO...
THOSE TWO WOLVES WHO ARE PRETTY MUCH GUARANTEED TO BE KICKED OUT OF THEIR PACK...
YOU'RE WELCOME TO COME WITH ME, TOO.
HUH?
PLEASE DON'T DECIDE THINGS ON YOUR OWN.
BUT YOU'D BE FIRING THEM ANYWAY, RIGHT?

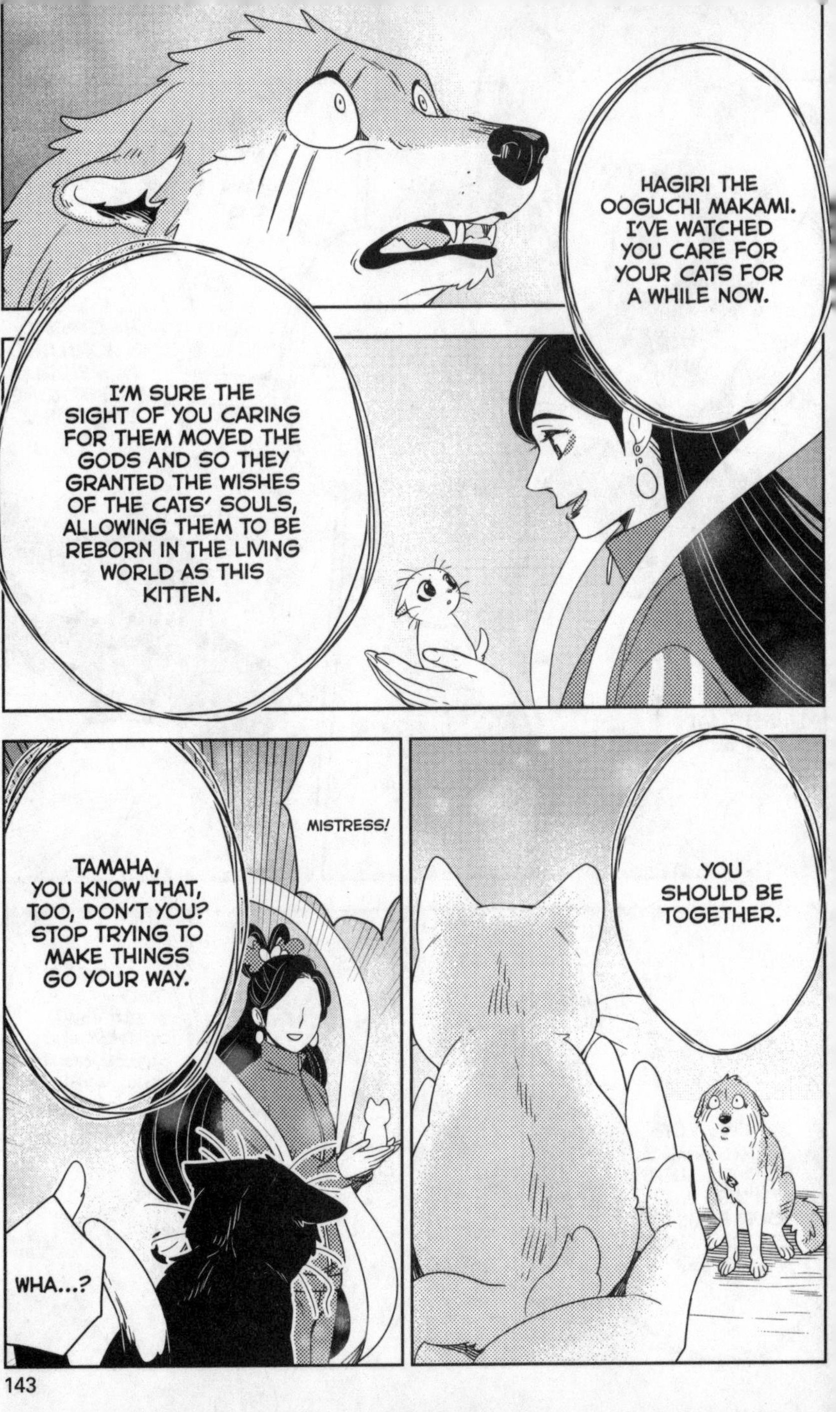
HAGIRI THE OOGUCHI MAKAMI. I'VE WATCHED YOU CARE FOR YOUR CATS FOR A WHILE NOW.
I'M SURE THE SIGHT OF YOU CARING FOR THEM MOVED THE GODS AND SO THEY GRANTED THE WISHES OF THE CATS' SOULS, ALLOWING THEM TO BE REBORN IN THE LIVING WORLD AS THIS KITTEN.
YOU SHOULD BE TOGETHER.
MISTRESS!
TAMAHA, YOU KNOW THAT, TOO, DON'T YOU? STOP TRYING TO MAKE THINGS GO YOUR WAY.
WHA...?

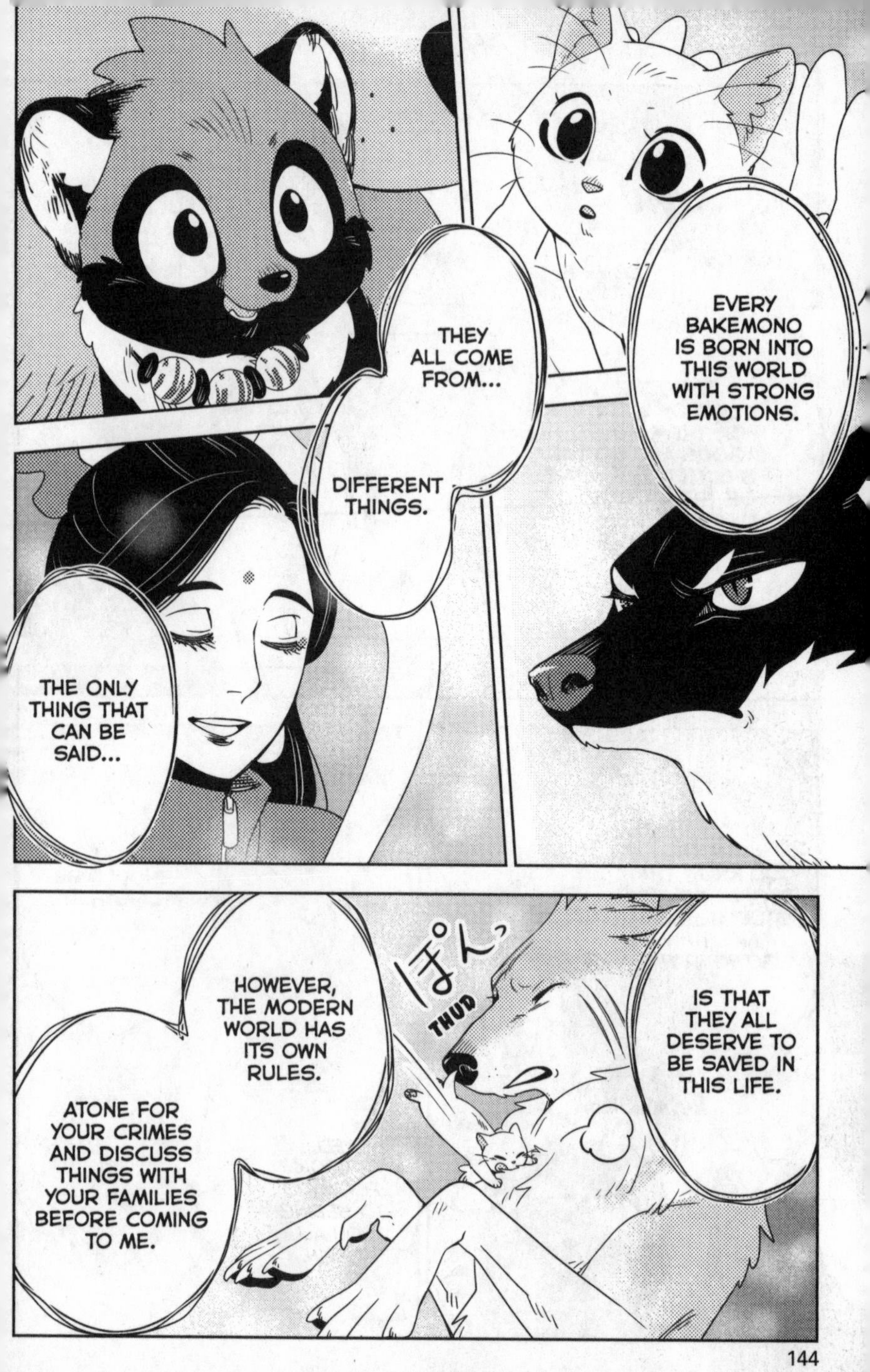
EVERY BAKEMONO IS BORN INTO THIS WORLD WITH STRONG EMOTIONS.
THEY ALL COME FROM...
DIFFERENT THINGS.
THE ONLY THING THAT CAN BE SAID...
IS THAT THEY ALL DESERVE TO BE SAVED IN THIS LIFE.
ぽん
THUD
HOWEVER, THE MODERN WORLD HAS ITS OWN RULES.
ATONE FOR YOUR CRIMES AND DISCUSS THINGS WITH YOUR FAMILIES BEFORE COMING TO ME.

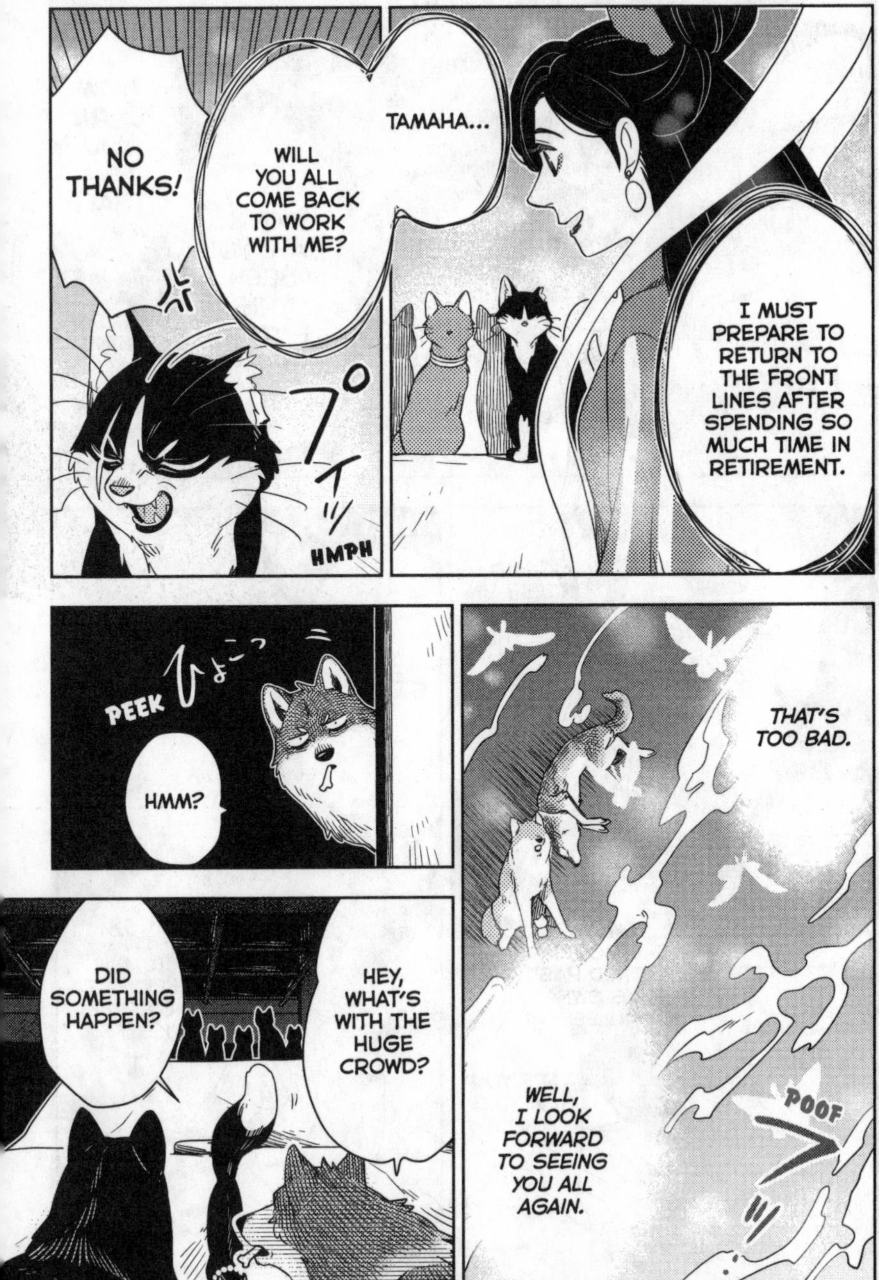
TAMAHA...
I MUST PREPARE TO RETURN TO THE FRONT LINES AFTER SPENDING SO MUCH TIME IN RETIREMENT.
WILL YOU ALL COME BACK TO WORK WITH ME?
NO THANKS!
HMPH
THAT'S TOO BAD.
WELL, I LOOK FORWARD TO SEEING YOU ALL AGAIN.
POOF
PEEK
HMM?
HEY, WHAT'S WITH THE HUGE CROWD?
DID SOMETHING HAPPEN?

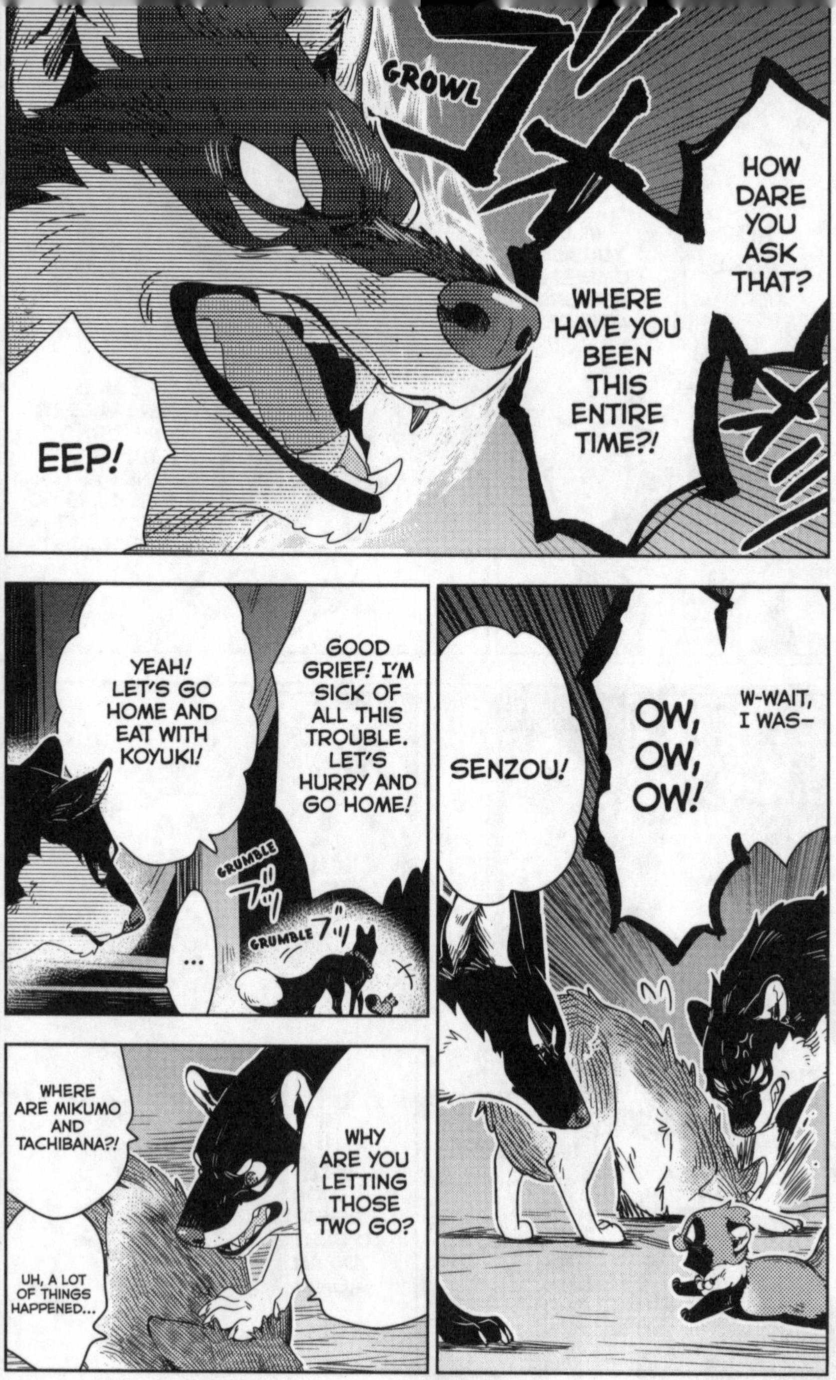
GROWL
HOW DARE YOU ASK THAT?
WHERE HAVE YOU BEEN THIS ENTIRE TIME?!
EEP!
W-WAIT, I WAS—
OW, OW, OW!
SENZOU!
GOOD GRIEF! I'M SICK OF ALL THIS TROUBLE. LET'S HURRY AND GO HOME!
YEAH! LET'S GO HOME AND EAT WITH KOYUKI!
GRUMBLE
GRUMBLE
...
WHY ARE YOU LETTING THOSE TWO GO?
WHERE ARE MIKUMO AND TACHIBANA?!
UH, A LOT OF THINGS HAPPENED...

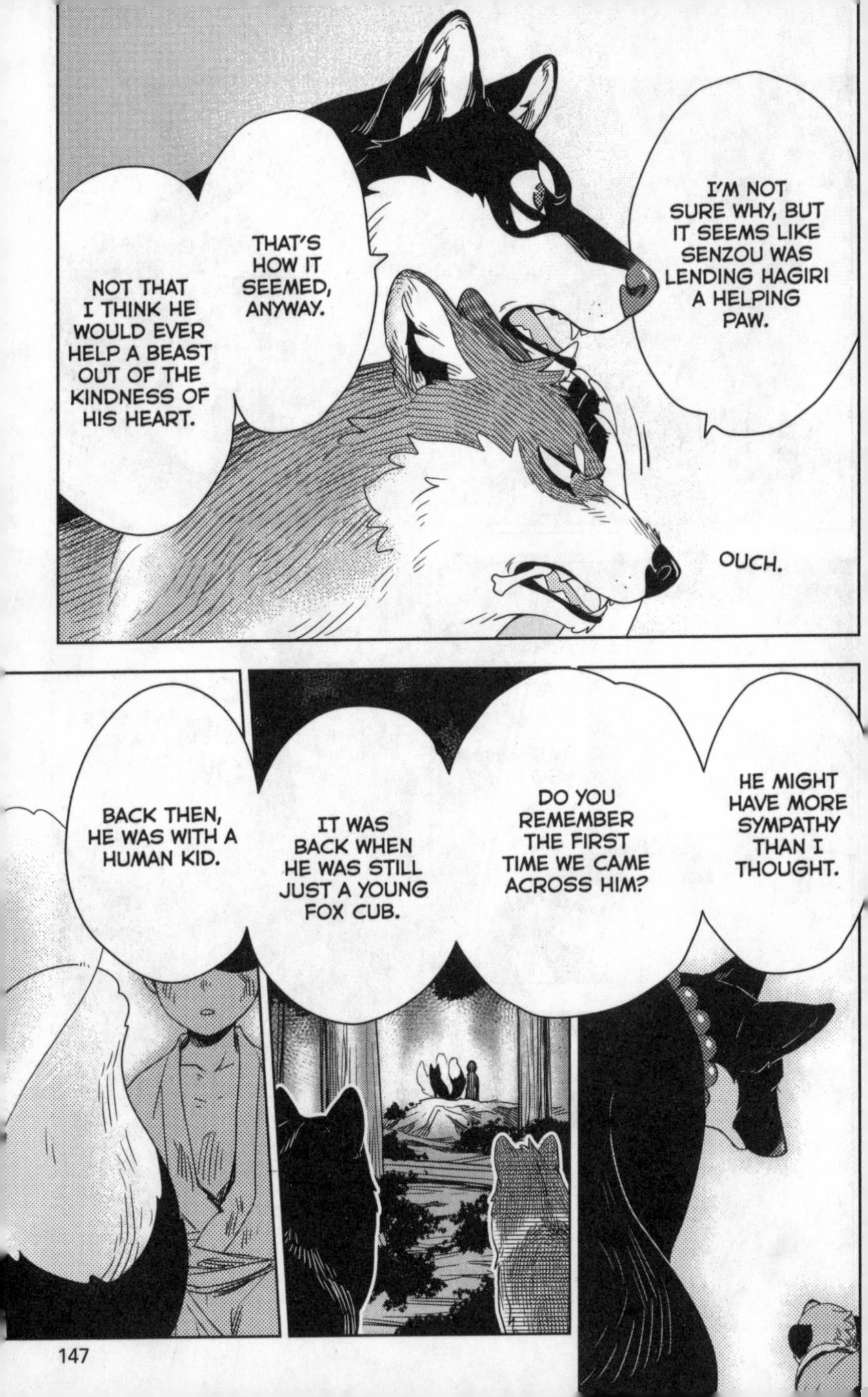
I'M NOT SURE WHY, BUT IT SEEMS LIKE SENZOU WAS LENDING HAGIRI A HELPING PAW.
THAT'S HOW IT SEEMED, ANYWAY.
NOT THAT I THINK HE WOULD EVER HELP A BEAST OUT OF THE KINDNESS OF HIS HEART.
OUCH.
HE MIGHT HAVE MORE SYMPATHY THAN I THOUGHT.
DO YOU REMEMBER THE FIRST TIME WE CAME ACROSS HIM?
IT WAS BACK WHEN HE WAS STILL JUST A YOUNG FOX CUB.
BACK THEN, HE WAS WITH A HUMAN KID.

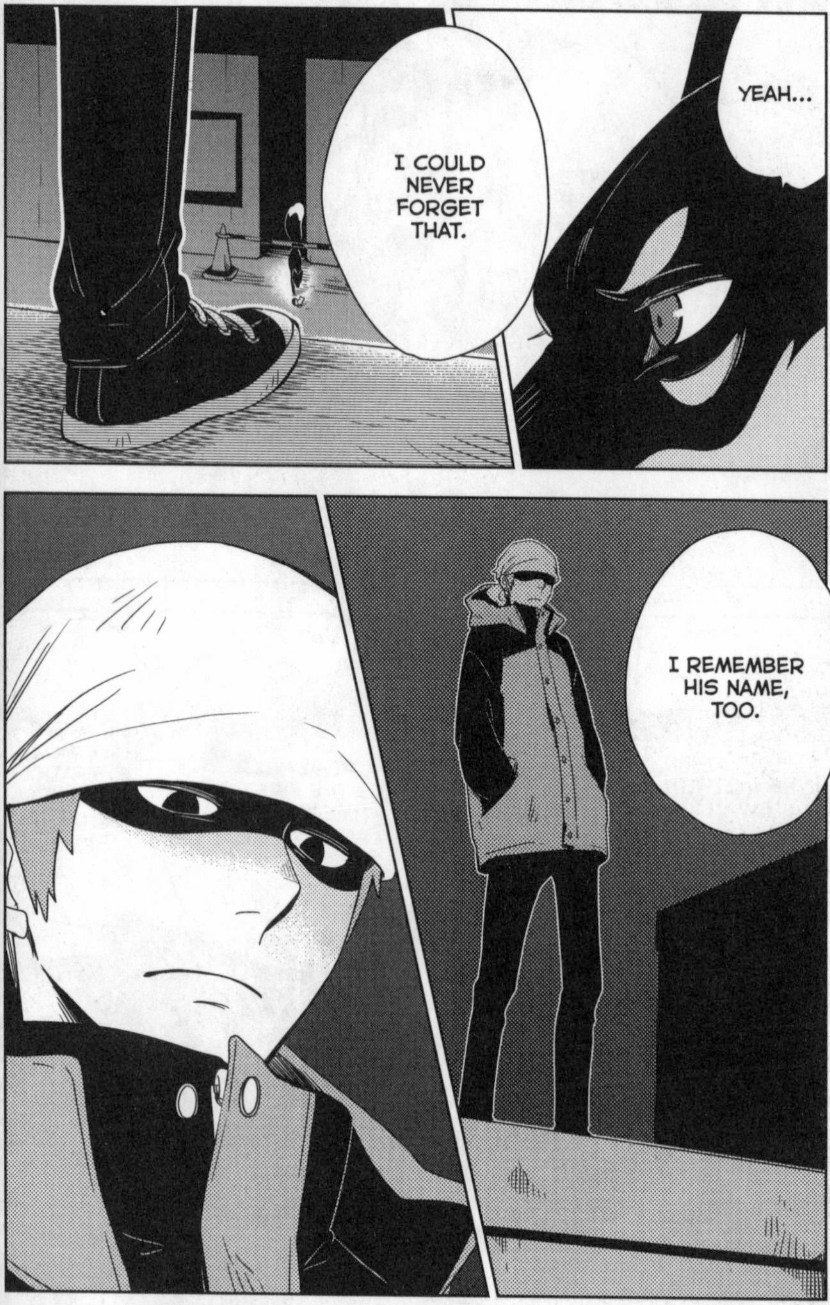
YEAH...
I COULD NEVER FORGET THAT.
I REMEMBER HIS NAME, TOO.

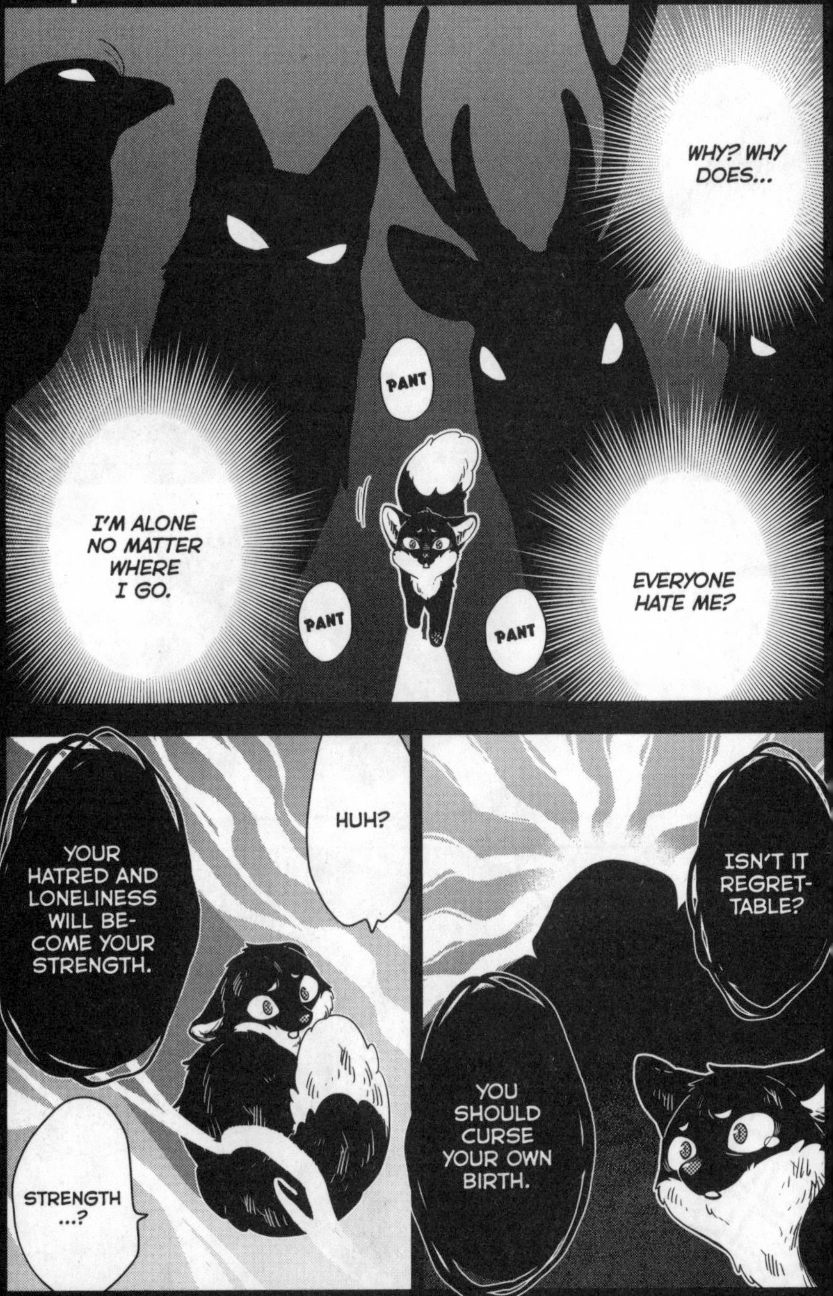
WHY? WHY DOES...
PANT
EVERYONE HATE ME?
PANT
PANT
I'M ALONE NO MATTER WHERE I GO.
ISN'T IT REGRET-TABLE?
YOU SHOULD CURSE YOUR OWN BIRTH.
HUH?
YOUR HATRED AND LONELINESS WILL BE-COME YOUR STRENGTH.
STRENGTH ...?

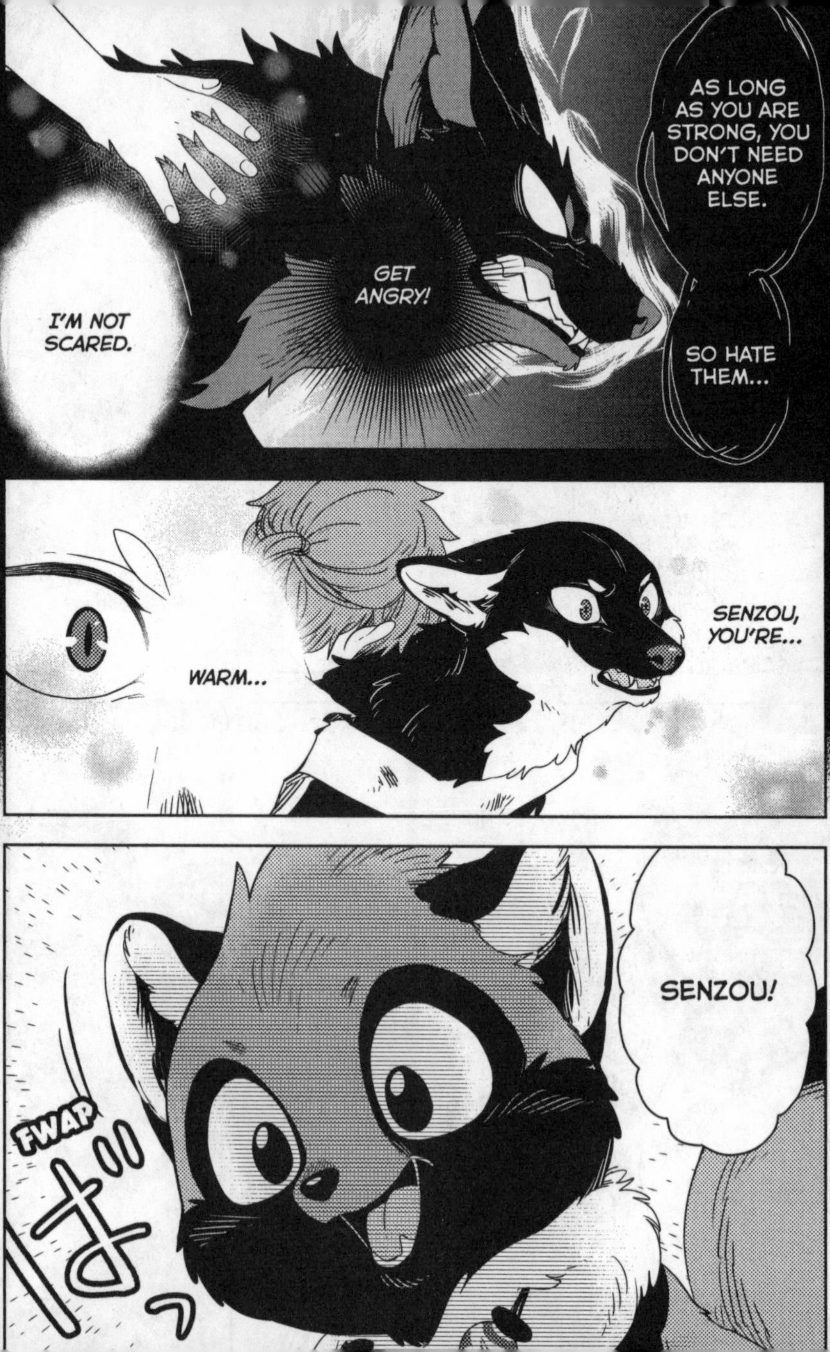
AS LONG AS YOU ARE STRONG, YOU DON'T NEED ANYONE ELSE.
SO HATE THEM...
GET ANGRY!
I'M NOT SCARED.
SENZOU, YOU'RE...
WARM...
SENZOU!
FWAP

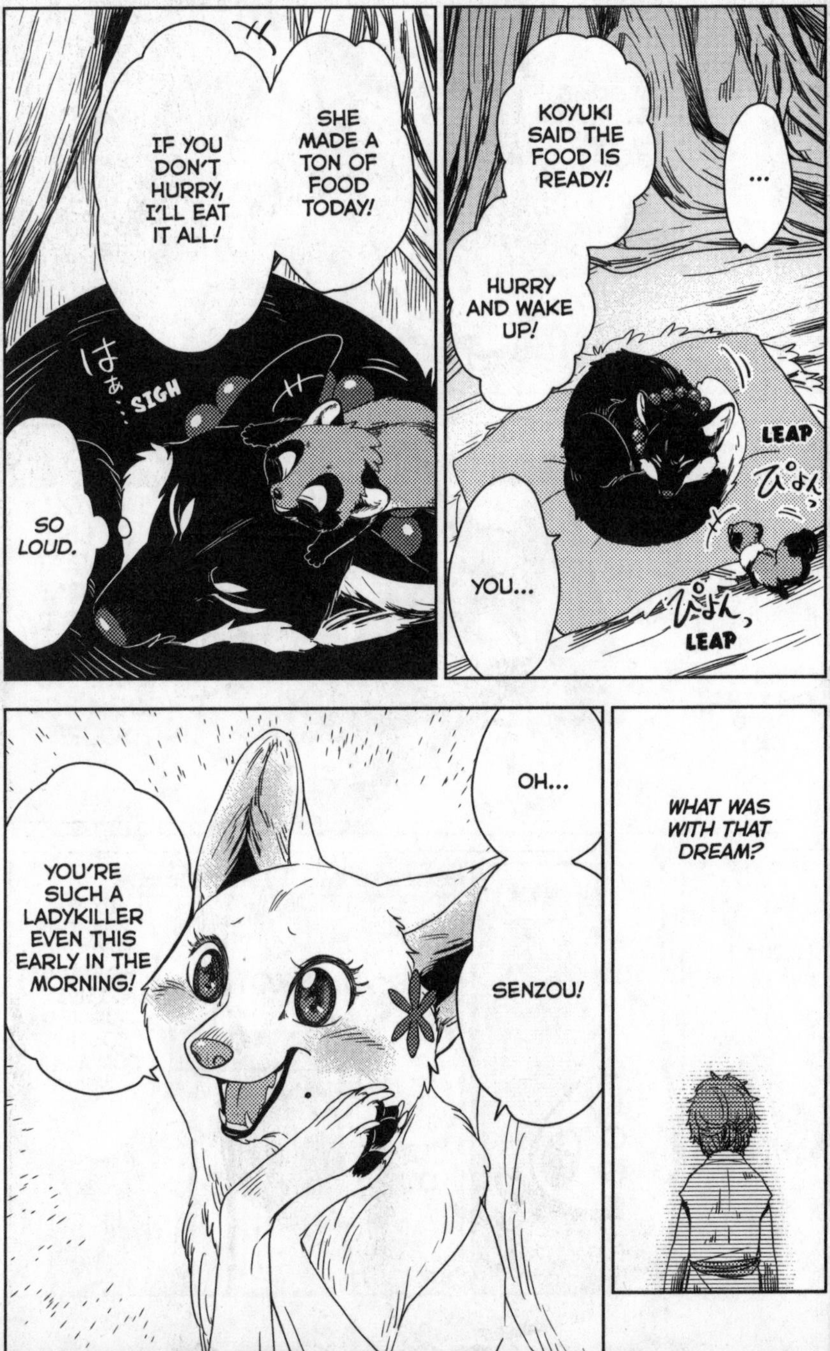
...
KOYUKI SAID THE FOOD IS READY!
HURRY AND WAKE UP!
LEAP
ぴょん
YOU...
ぴょん
LEAP
SHE MADE A TON OF FOOD TODAY!
IF YOU DON'T HURRY, I'LL EAT IT ALL!
はぁ…
SIGH
SO LOUD.
WHAT WAS WITH THAT DREAM?
OH...
SENZOU!
YOU'RE SUCH A LADYKILLER EVEN THIS EARLY IN THE MORNING!

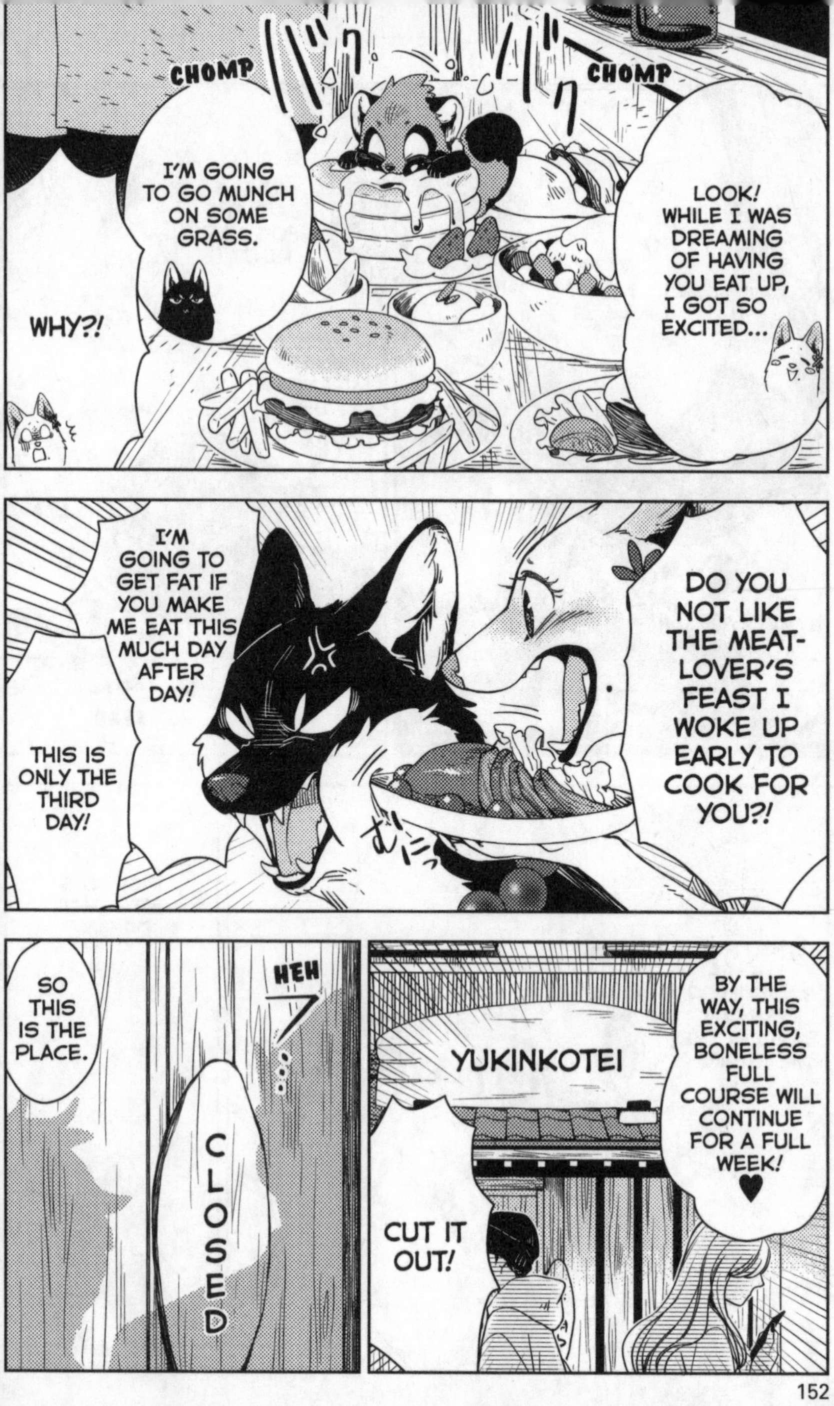
CHOMP
CHOMP
LOOK! WHILE I WAS DREAMING OF HAVING YOU EAT UP, I GOT SO EXCITED...
I'M GOING TO GO MUNCH ON SOME GRASS.
WHY?!
DO YOU NOT LIKE THE MEAT-LOVER'S FEAST I WOKE UP EARLY TO COOK FOR YOU?!
I'M GOING TO GET FAT IF YOU MAKE ME EAT THIS MUCH DAY AFTER DAY!
THIS IS ONLY THE THIRD DAY!
BY THE WAY, THIS EXCITING, BONELESS FULL COURSE WILL CONTINUE FOR A FULL WEEK! ♥
YUKINKOTEI
CUT IT OUT!
HEH
SO THIS IS THE PLACE.
...
CLOSED

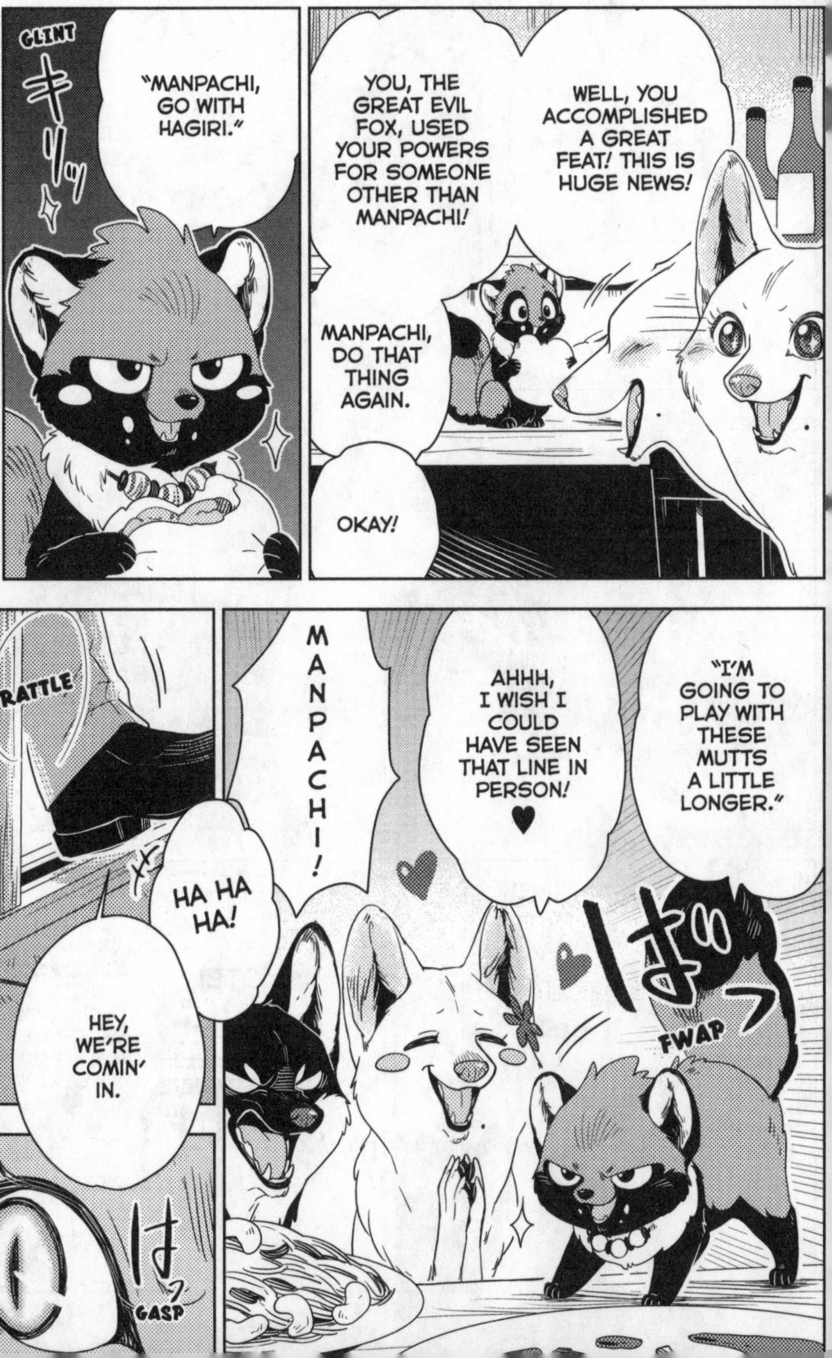
WELL, YOU ACCOMPLISHED A GREAT FEAT! THIS IS HUGE NEWS!
YOU, THE GREAT EVIL FOX, USED YOUR POWERS FOR SOMEONE OTHER THAN MANPACHI!
MANPACHI, DO THAT THING AGAIN.
OKAY!
GLINT
"MANPACHI, GO WITH HAGIRI."
"I'M GOING TO PLAY WITH THESE MUTTS A LITTLE LONGER."
FWAP
AHHH, I WISH I COULD HAVE SEEN THAT LINE IN PERSON! ♥
MANPACHI!
HA HA HA!
RATTLE
HEY, WE'RE COMIN' IN.
GASP

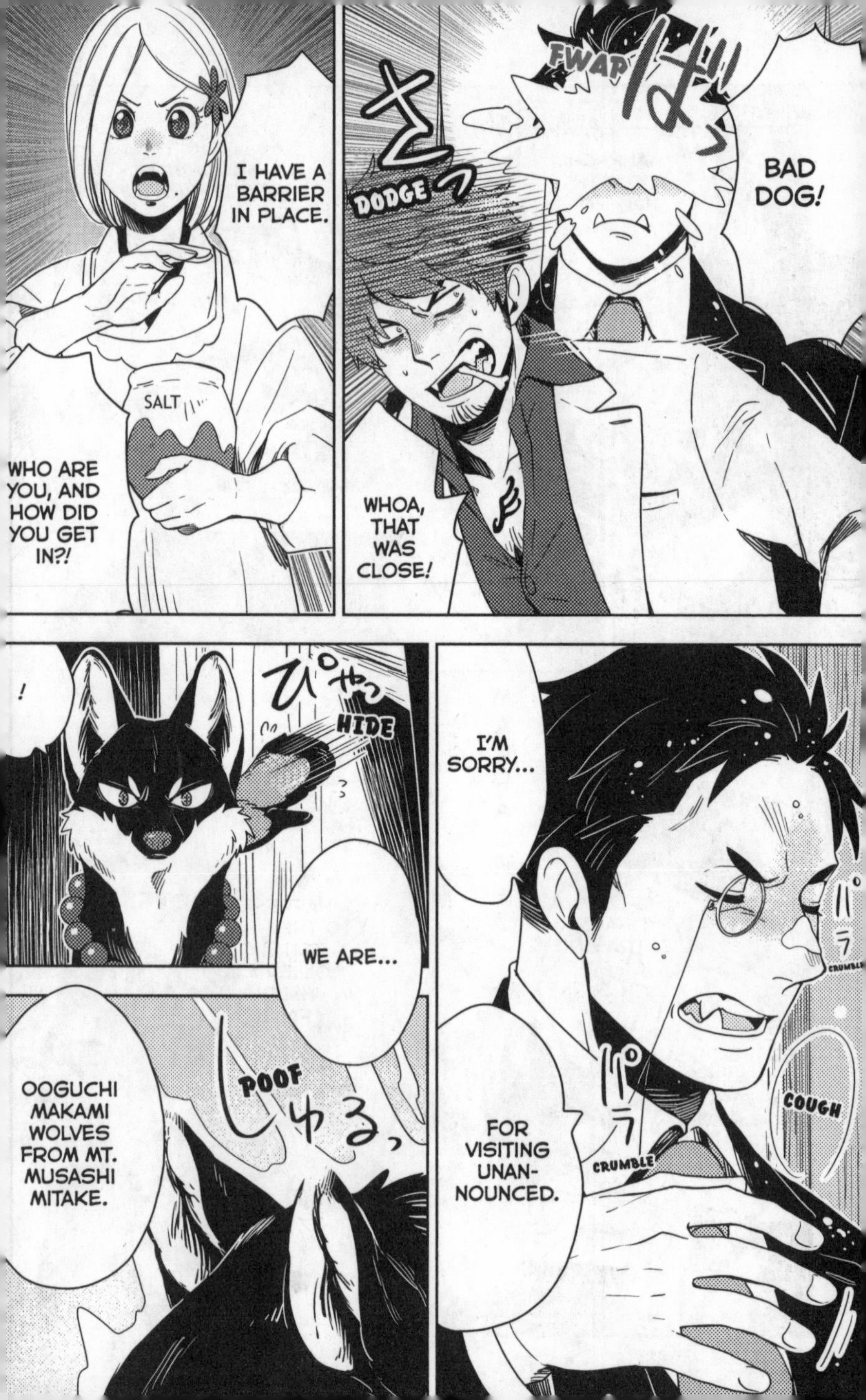
FWAP
BAD DOG!
DODGE
WHOA, THAT WAS CLOSE!
I HAVE A BARRIER IN PLACE.
SALT
WHO ARE YOU, AND HOW DID YOU GET IN?!
I'M SORRY...
CRUMBLE
COUGH
FOR VISITING UNAN-NOUNCED.
CRUMBLE
!
HIDE
WE ARE...
POOF
OOGUCHI MAKAMI WOLVES FROM MT. MUSASHI MITAKE.

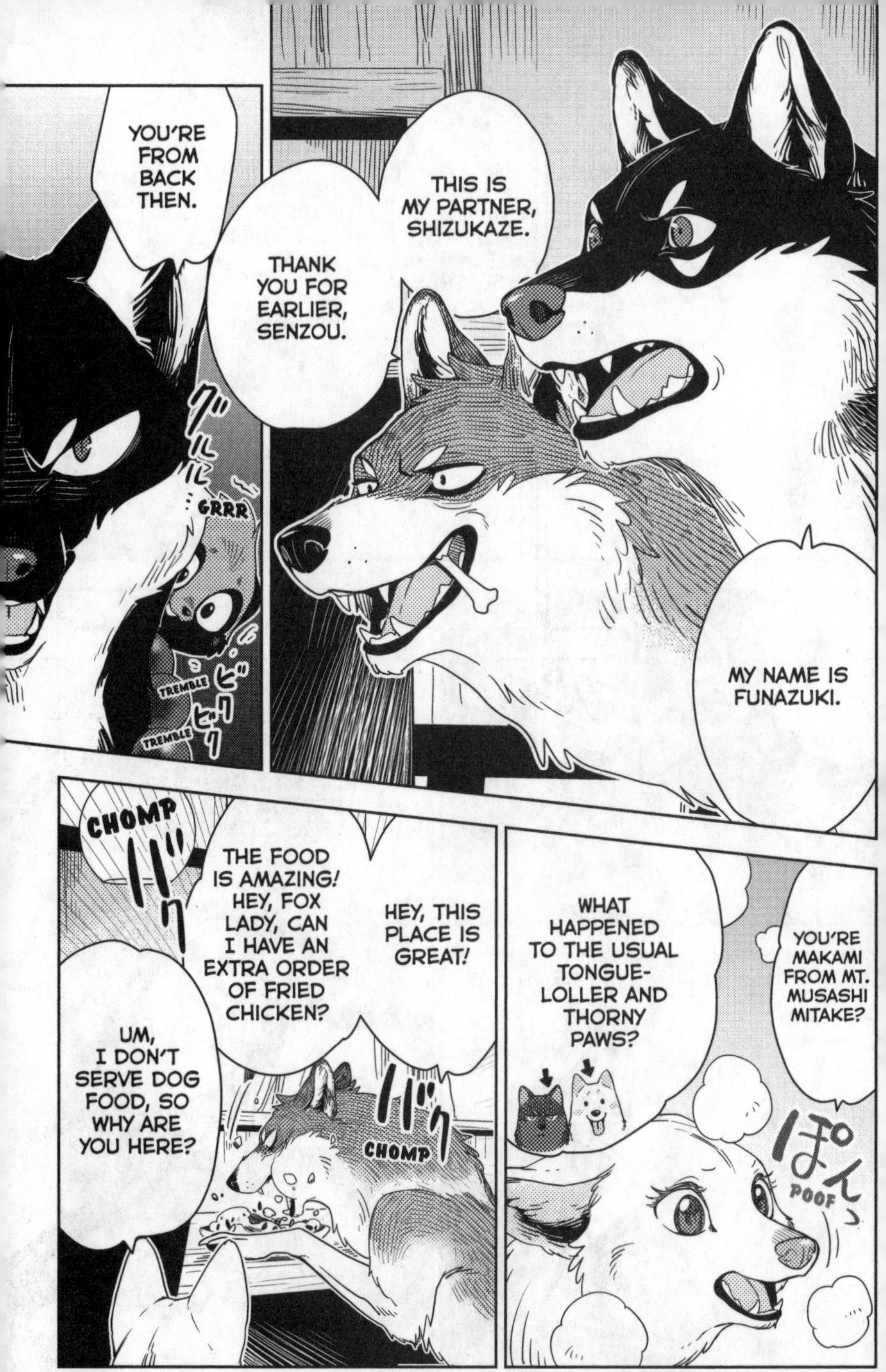
MY NAME IS FUNAZUKI.
THIS IS MY PARTNER, SHIZUKAZE.
THANK YOU FOR EARLIER, SENZOU.
YOU'RE FROM BACK THEN.
GRRR
TREMBLE
TREMBLE
YOU'RE MAKAMI FROM MT. MUSASHI MITAKE?
POOF
WHAT HAPPENED TO THE USUAL TONGUE-LOLLER AND THORNY PAWS?
HEY, THIS PLACE IS GREAT!
THE FOOD IS AMAZING! HEY, FOX LADY, CAN I HAVE AN EXTRA ORDER OF FRIED CHICKEN?
CHOMP
CHOMP
UM, I DON'T SERVE DOG FOOD, SO WHY ARE YOU HERE?

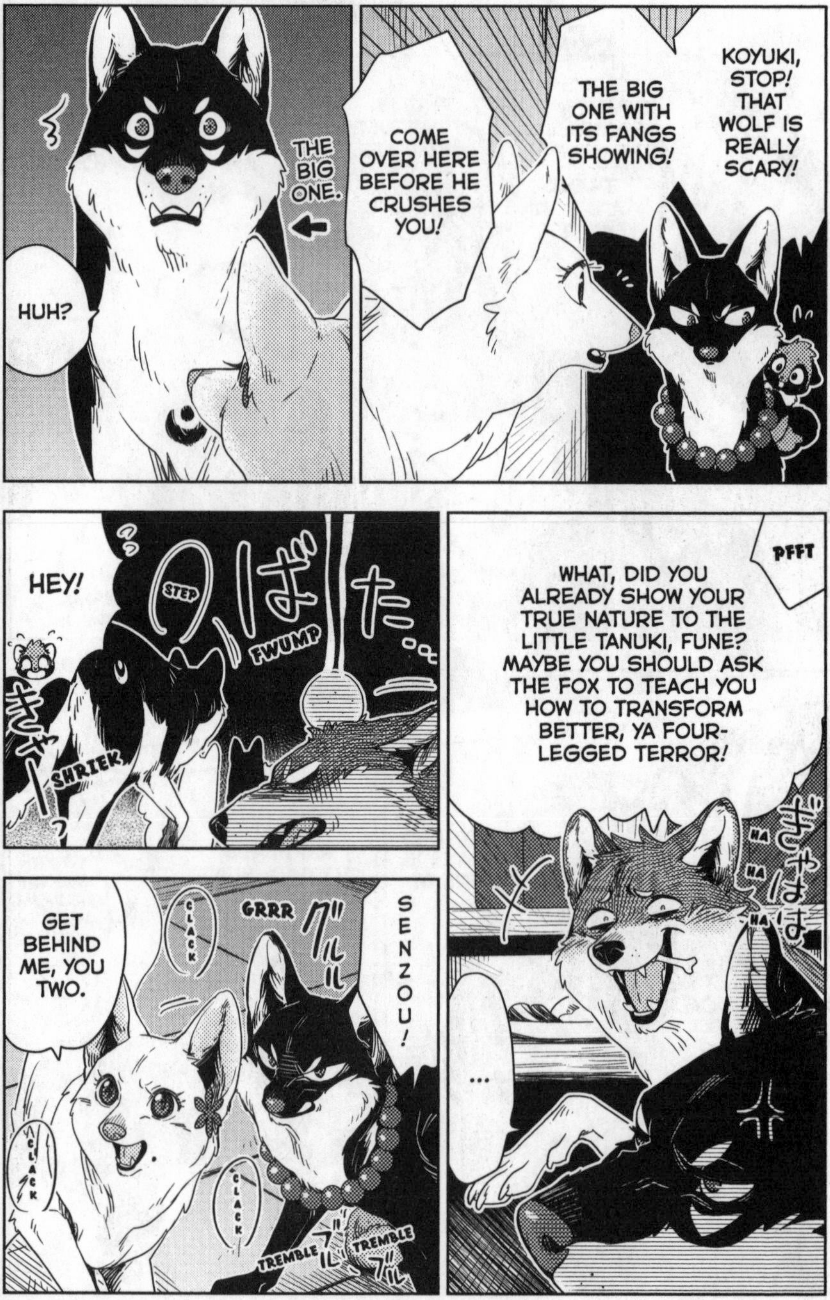
KOYUKI, STOP! THAT WOLF IS REALLY SCARY!
THE BIG ONE WITH ITS FANGS SHOWING!
COME OVER HERE BEFORE HE CRUSHES YOU!
THE BIG ONE.
HUH?
PFFT
WHAT, DID YOU ALREADY SHOW YOUR TRUE NATURE TO THE LITTLE TANUKI, FUNE? MAYBE YOU SHOULD ASK THE FOX TO TEACH YOU HOW TO TRANSFORM BETTER, YA FOUR-LEGGED TERROR!
ぎゃはは
HA
HA
HA
...
HEY!
STEP
ばた
FWUMP
SHRIEK
SENZOU!
GRRR
グルル
GET BEHIND ME, YOU TWO.
CLACK
CLACK
CLACK
TREMBLE
TREMBLE

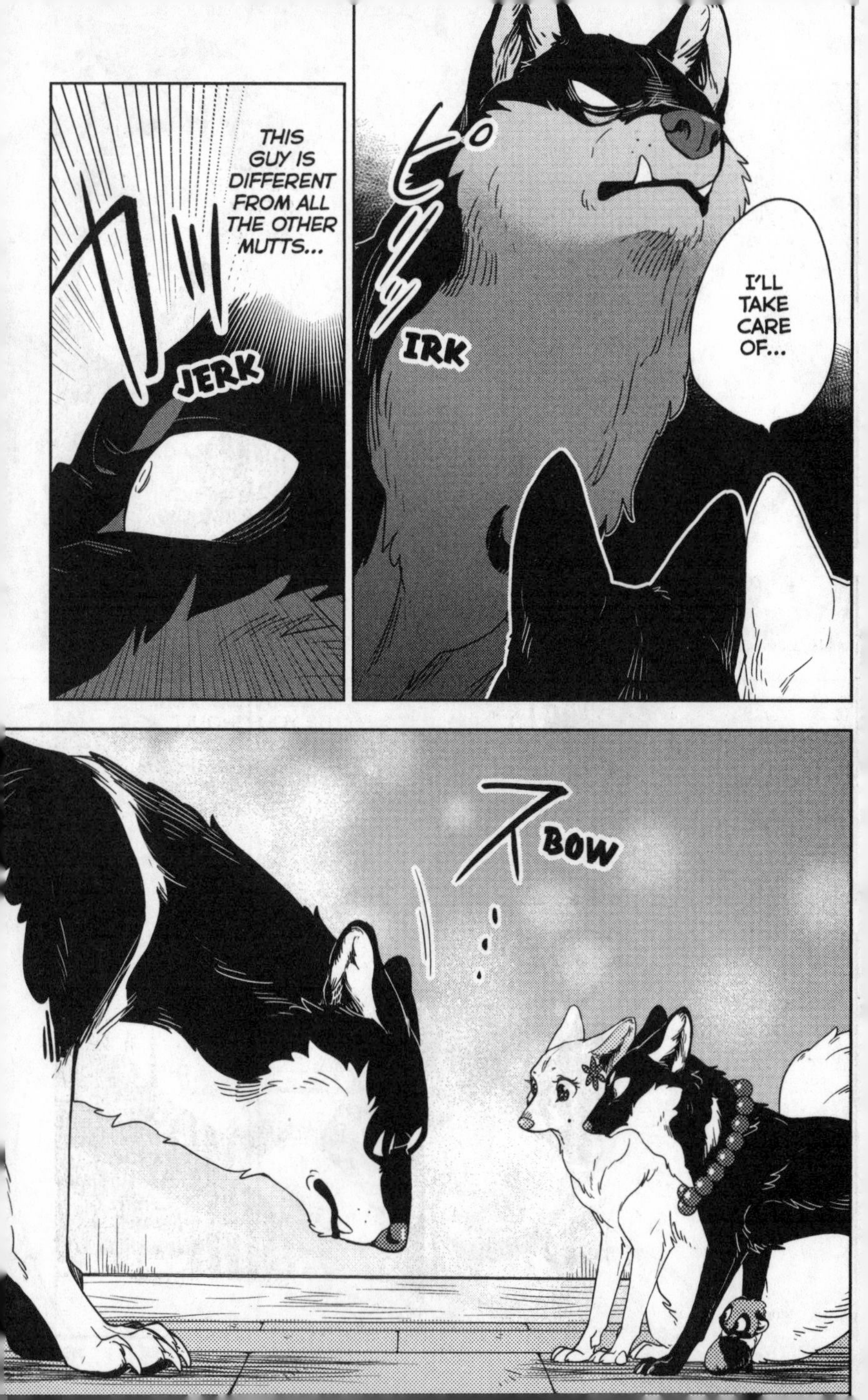
IRK
I'LL TAKE CARE OF...
THIS GUY IS DIFFERENT FROM ALL THE OTHER MUTTS...
JERK
BOW

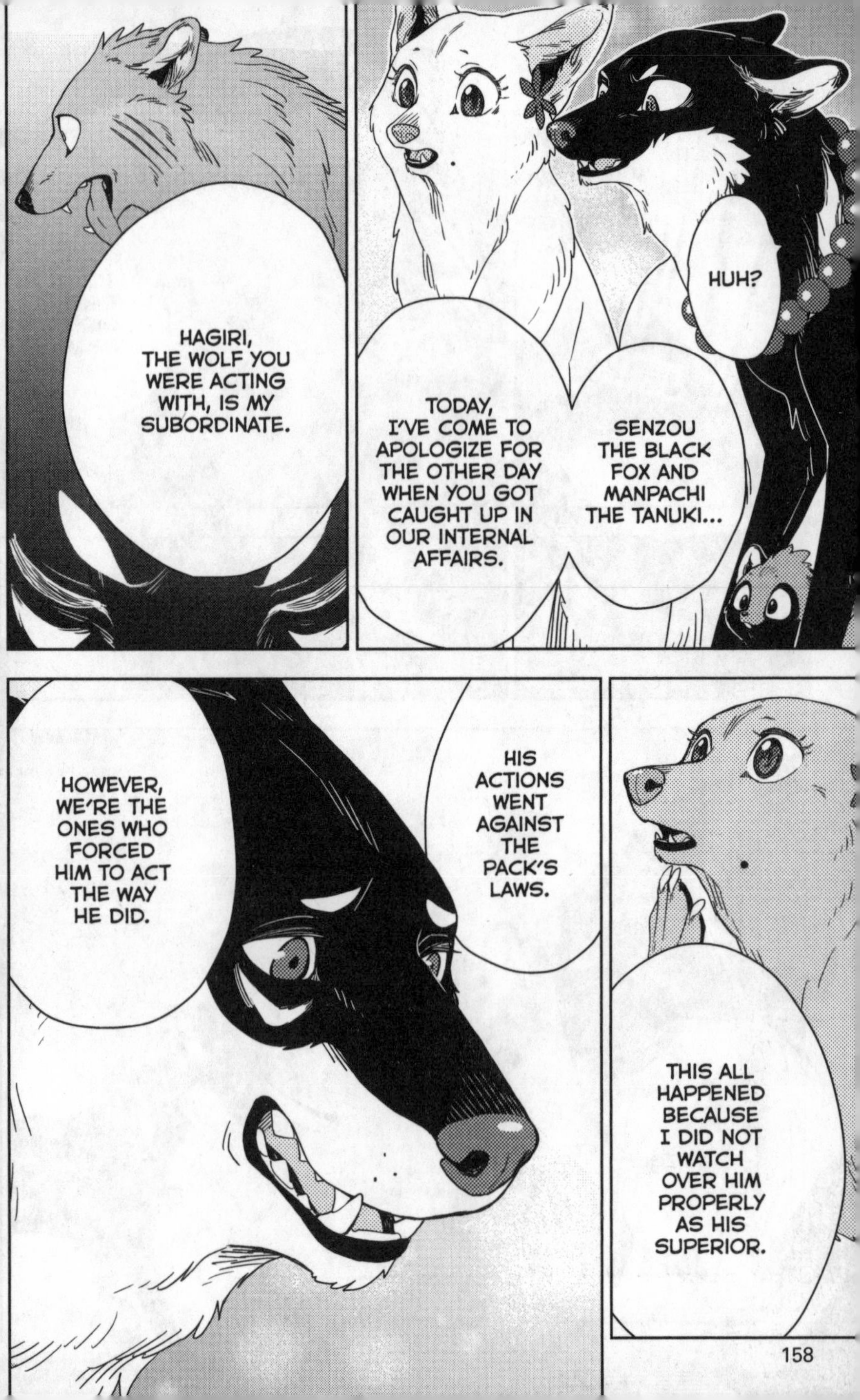
HUH?
SENZOU THE BLACK FOX AND MANPACHI THE TANUKI...
TODAY, I'VE COME TO APOLOGIZE FOR THE OTHER DAY WHEN YOU GOT CAUGHT UP IN OUR INTERNAL AFFAIRS.
HAGIRI, THE WOLF YOU WERE ACTING WITH, IS MY SUBORDINATE.
THIS ALL HAPPENED BECAUSE I DID NOT WATCH OVER HIM PROPERLY AS HIS SUPERIOR.
HIS ACTIONS WENT AGAINST THE PACK'S LAWS.
HOWEVER, WE'RE THE ONES WHO FORCED HIM TO ACT THE WAY HE DID.

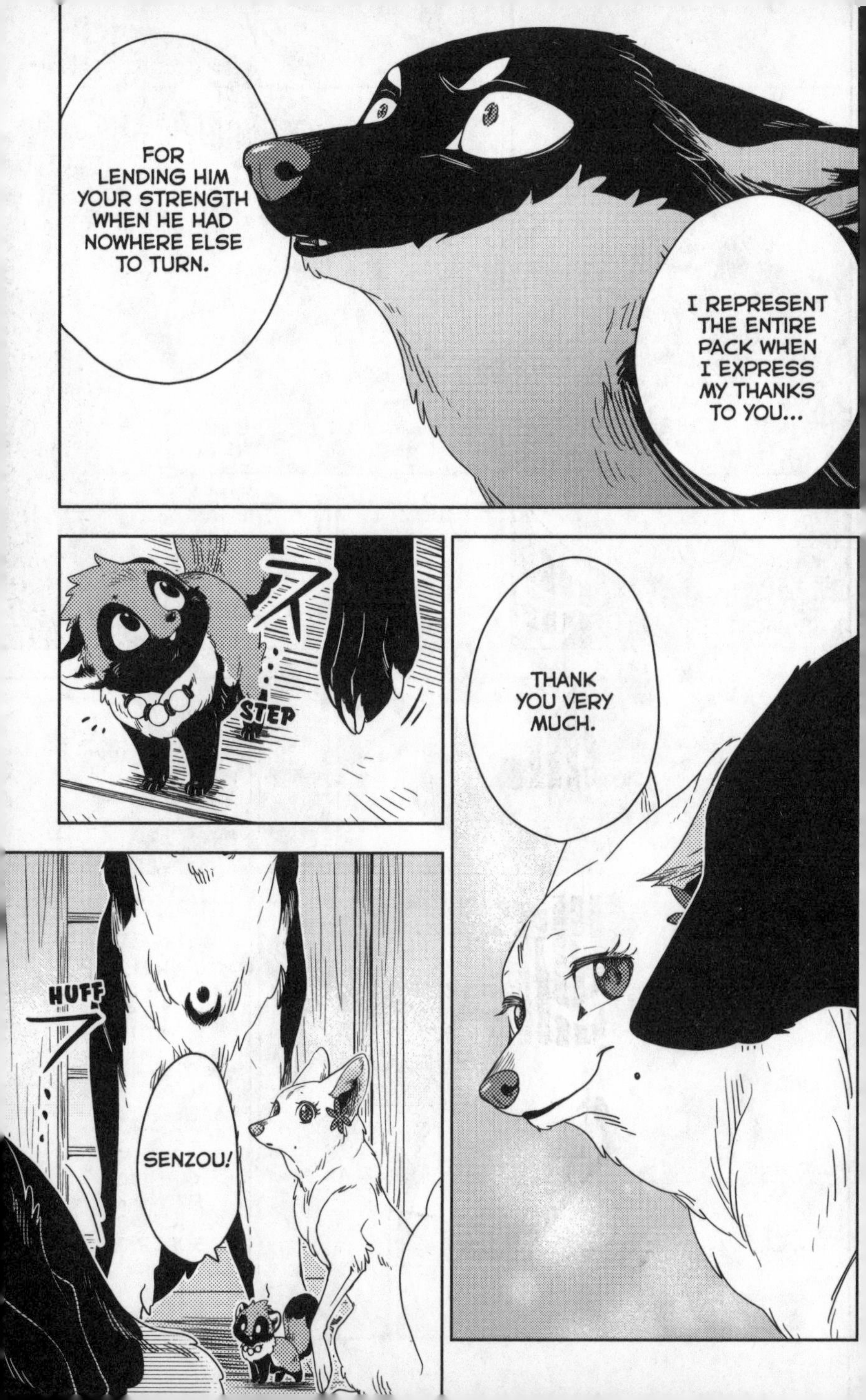
I REPRESENT THE ENTIRE PACK WHEN I EXPRESS MY THANKS TO YOU...
FOR LENDING HIM YOUR STRENGTH WHEN HE HAD NOWHERE ELSE TO TURN.
THANK YOU VERY MUCH.
STEP
HUFF
SENZOU!

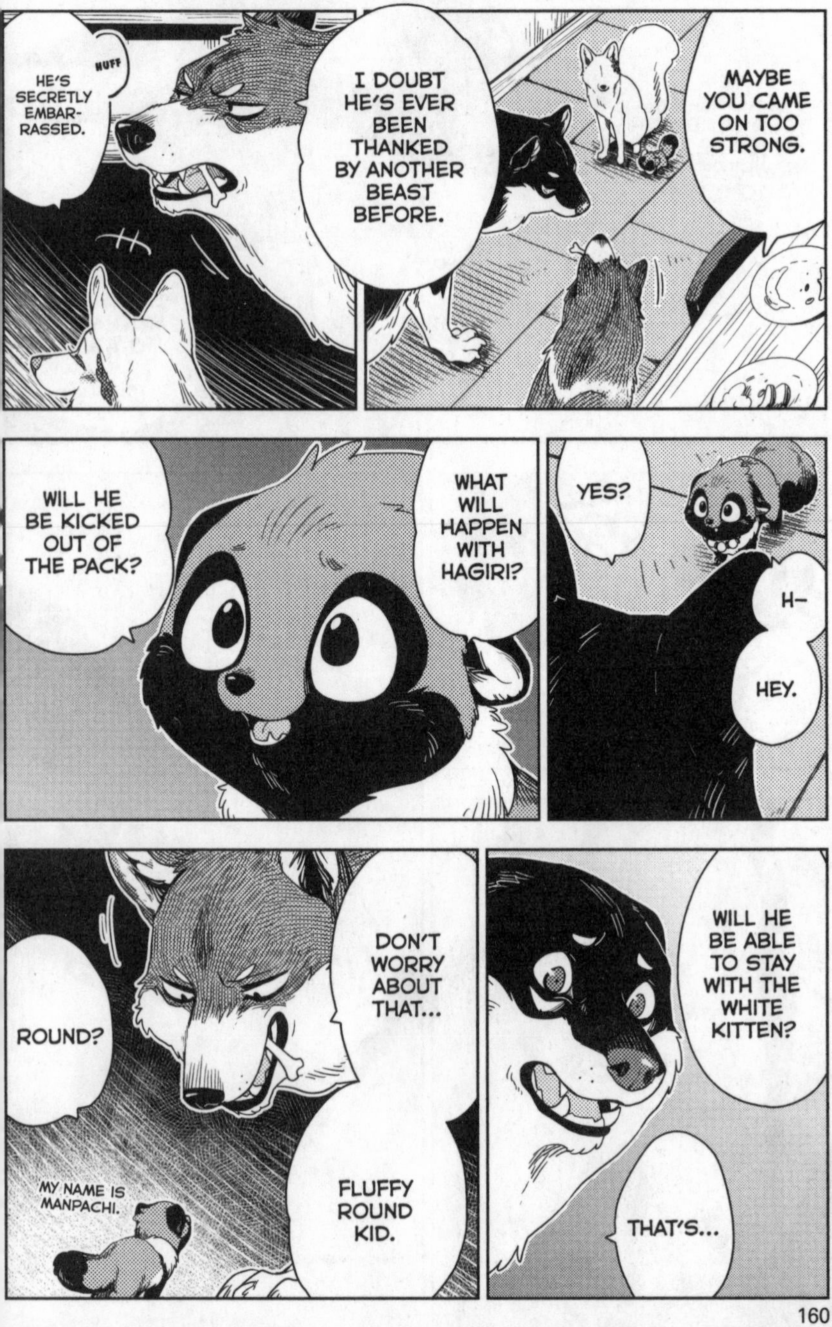
MAYBE YOU CAME ON TOO STRONG.
I DOUBT HE'S EVER BEEN THANKED BY ANOTHER BEAST BEFORE.
HUFF
HE'S SECRETLY EMBARRASSED.
YES?
H–
HEY.
WHAT WILL HAPPEN WITH HAGIRI?
WILL HE BE KICKED OUT OF THE PACK?
WILL HE BE ABLE TO STAY WITH THE WHITE KITTEN?
THAT'S...
DON'T WORRY ABOUT THAT...
FLUFFY ROUND KID.
ROUND?
MY NAME IS MANPACHI.

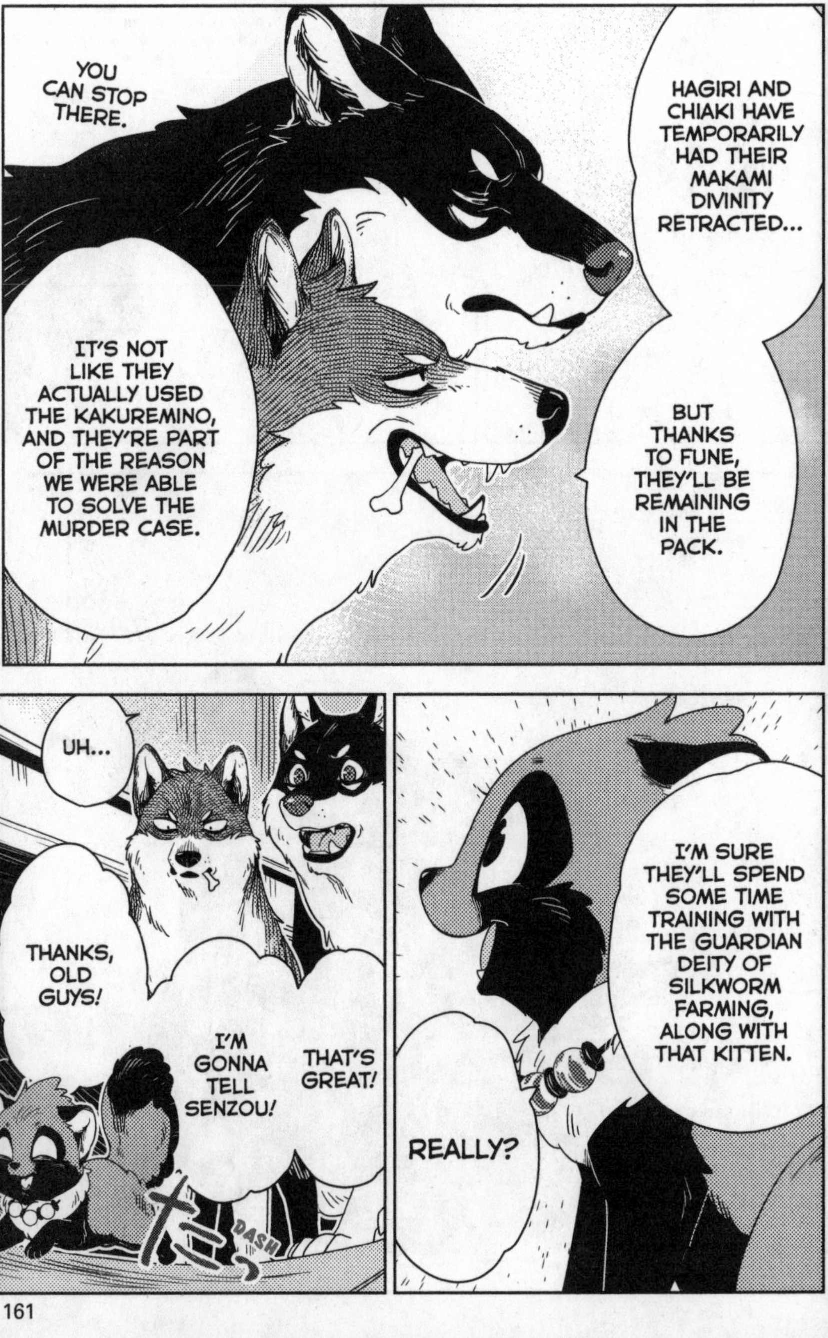
HAGIRI AND CHIAKI HAVE TEMPORARILY HAD THEIR MAKAMI DIVINITY RETRACTED...
BUT THANKS TO FUNE, THEY'LL BE REMAINING IN THE PACK.
YOU CAN STOP THERE.
IT'S NOT LIKE THEY ACTUALLY USED THE KAKUREMINO, AND THEY'RE PART OF THE REASON WE WERE ABLE TO SOLVE THE MURDER CASE.
I'M SURE THEY'LL SPEND SOME TIME TRAINING WITH THE GUARDIAN DEITY OF SILKWORM FARMING, ALONG WITH THAT KITTEN.
REALLY?
UH...
THAT'S GREAT!
I'M GONNA TELL SENZOU!
THANKS, OLD GUYS!
DASH

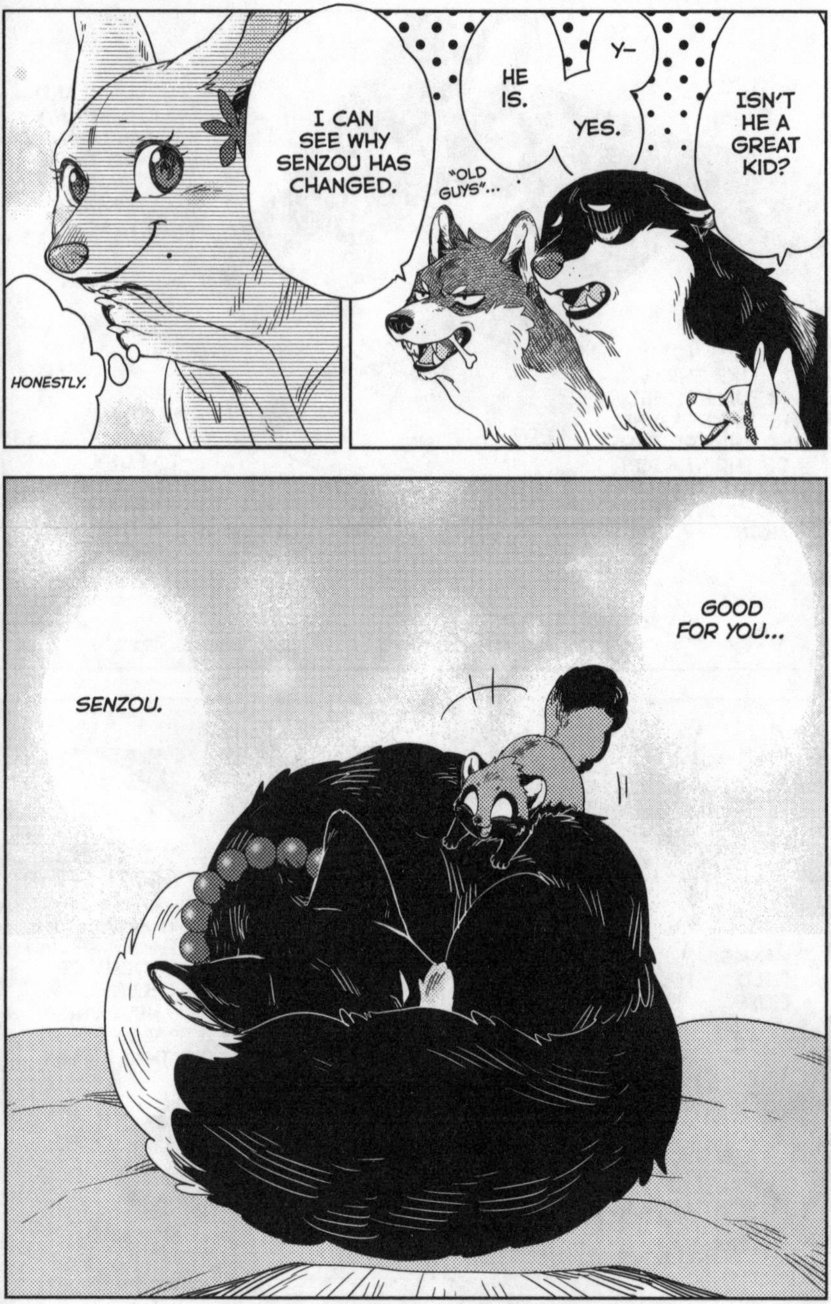
ISN'T HE A GREAT KID?
Y-
YES.
HE IS.
"OLD GUYS"...
I CAN SEE WHY SENZOU HAS CHANGED.
HONESTLY.
GOOD FOR YOU...
SENZOU.

A LITTLE BIT OF

KORISENMAN

**A COLLECTION OF COMIC STRIPS
THE AUTHOR UPLOADED TO SOCIAL MEDIA.**

🐦 twitter.com/tagawa_mi 📷 instagram.com/mi_tagawa

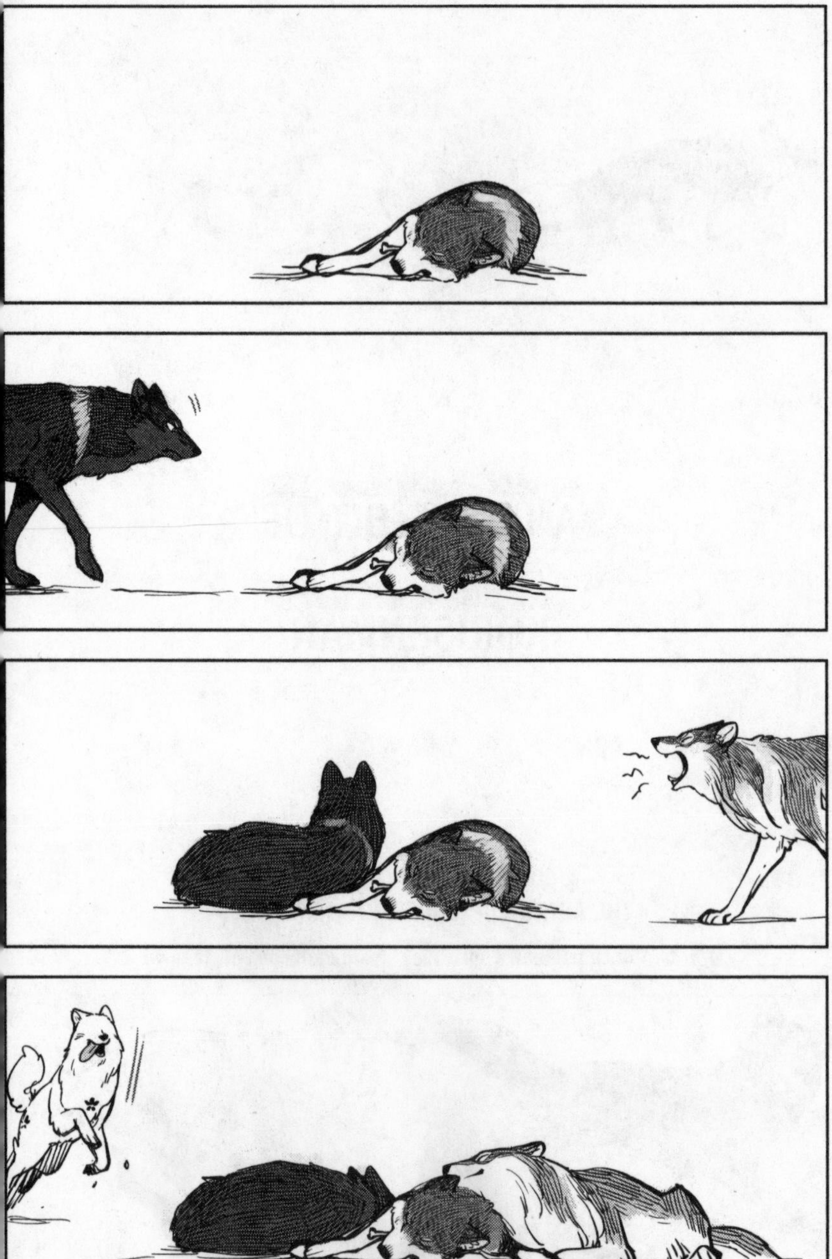

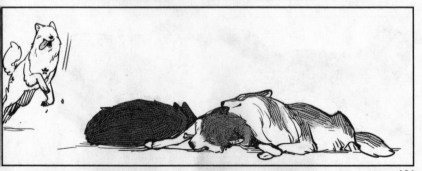

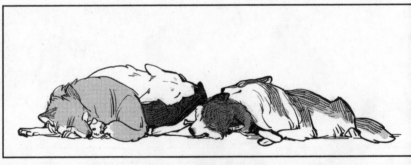

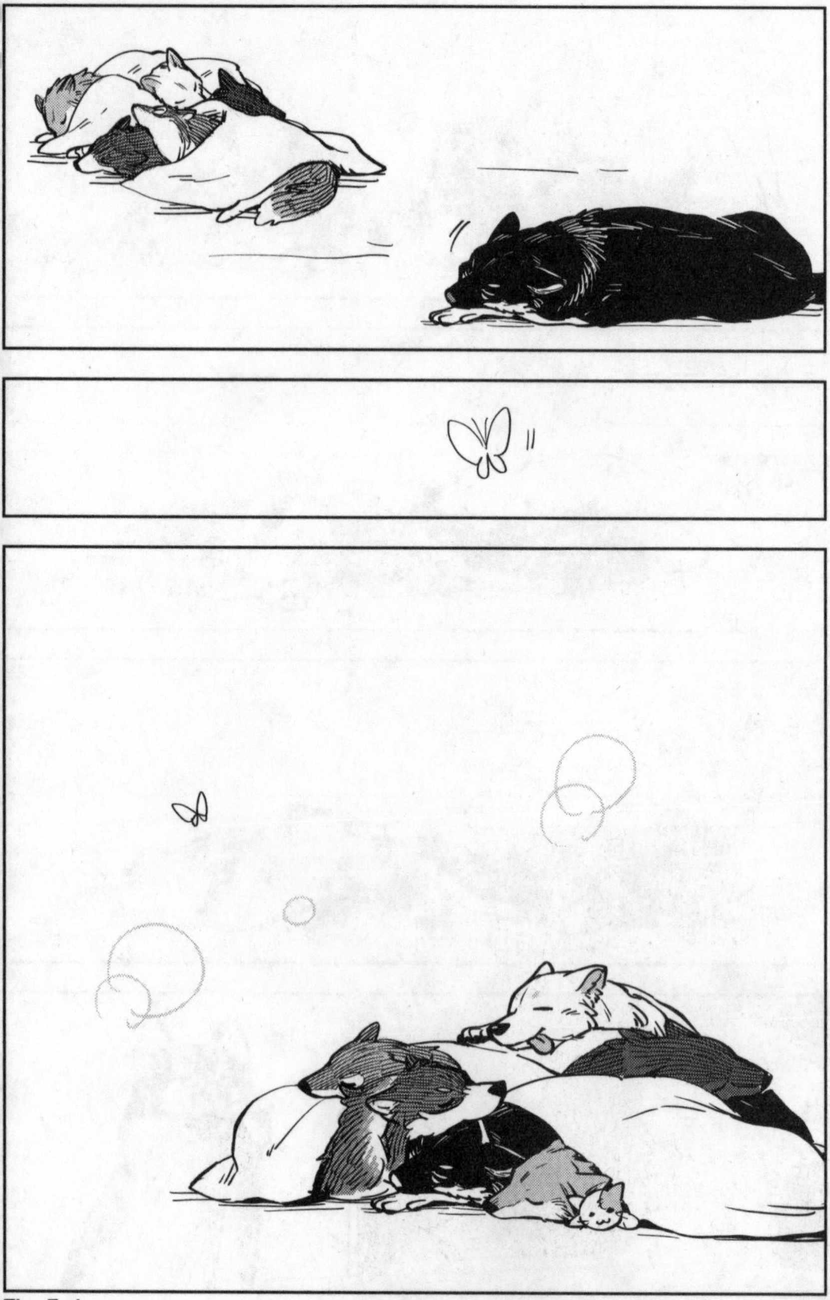

The End

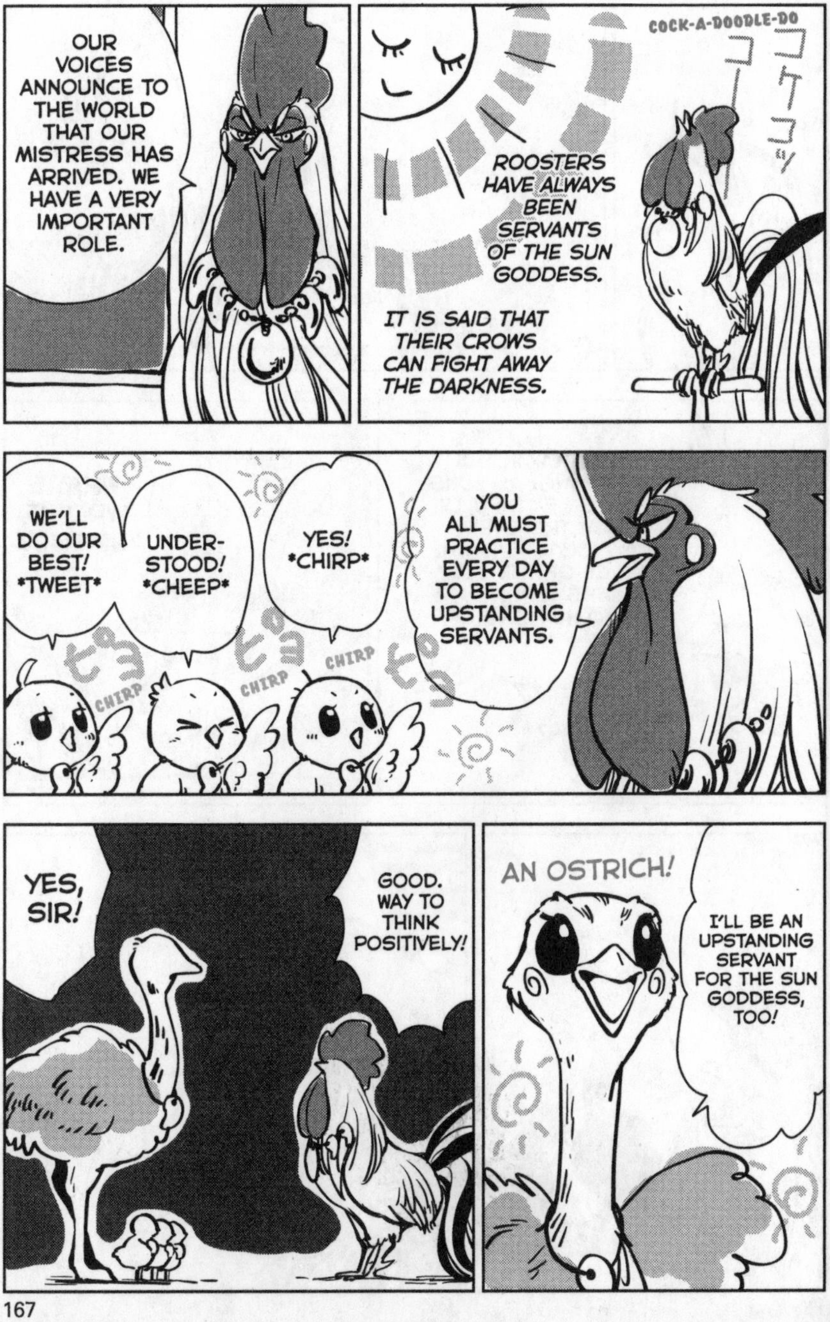
COCK-A-DOODLE-DO
ROOSTERS HAVE ALWAYS BEEN SERVANTS OF THE SUN GODDESS.
IT IS SAID THAT THEIR CROWS CAN FIGHT AWAY THE DARKNESS.
OUR VOICES ANNOUNCE TO THE WORLD THAT OUR MISTRESS HAS ARRIVED. WE HAVE A VERY IMPORTANT ROLE.
YOU ALL MUST PRACTICE EVERY DAY TO BECOME UPSTANDING SERVANTS.
YES! *CHIRP*
UNDER-STOOD! *CHEEP*
WE'LL DO OUR BEST! *TWEET*
CHIRP
CHIRP
CHIRP
AN OSTRICH!
I'LL BE AN UPSTANDING SERVANT FOR THE SUN GODDESS, TOO!
GOOD. WAY TO THINK POSITIVELY!
YES, SIR!

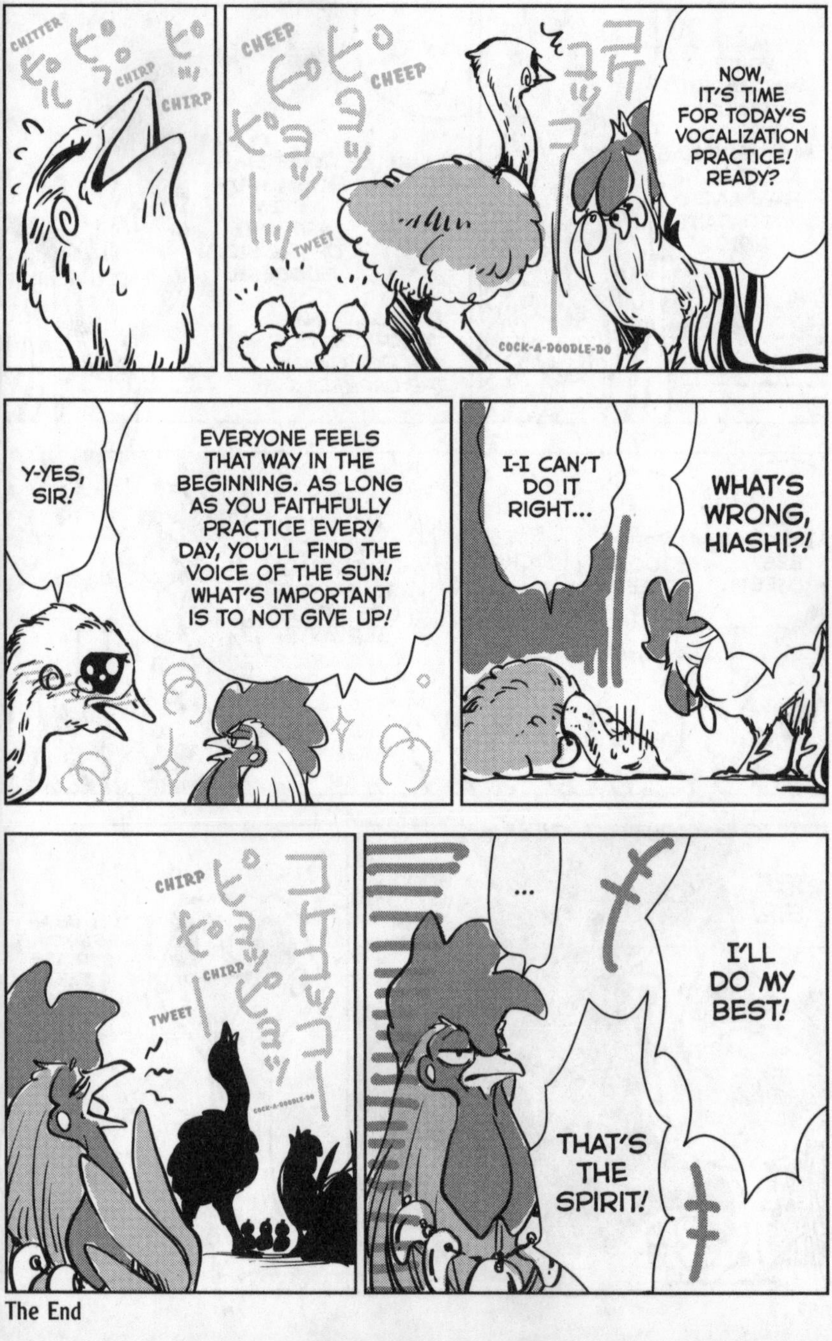
NOW, IT'S TIME FOR TODAY'S VOCALIZATION PRACTICE! READY?
COCK-A-DOODLE-DO
CHEEP
CHEEP
TWEET
CHITTER
CHIRP
CHIRP
WHAT'S WRONG, HIASHI?!
I-I CAN'T DO IT RIGHT...
EVERYONE FEELS THAT WAY IN THE BEGINNING. AS LONG AS YOU FAITHFULLY PRACTICE EVERY DAY, YOU'LL FIND THE VOICE OF THE SUN! WHAT'S IMPORTANT IS TO NOT GIVE UP!
Y-YES, SIR!
I'LL DO MY BEST!
...
THAT'S THE SPIRIT!
COCK-A-DOODLE-DO
CHIRP
CHIRP
TWEET

The End

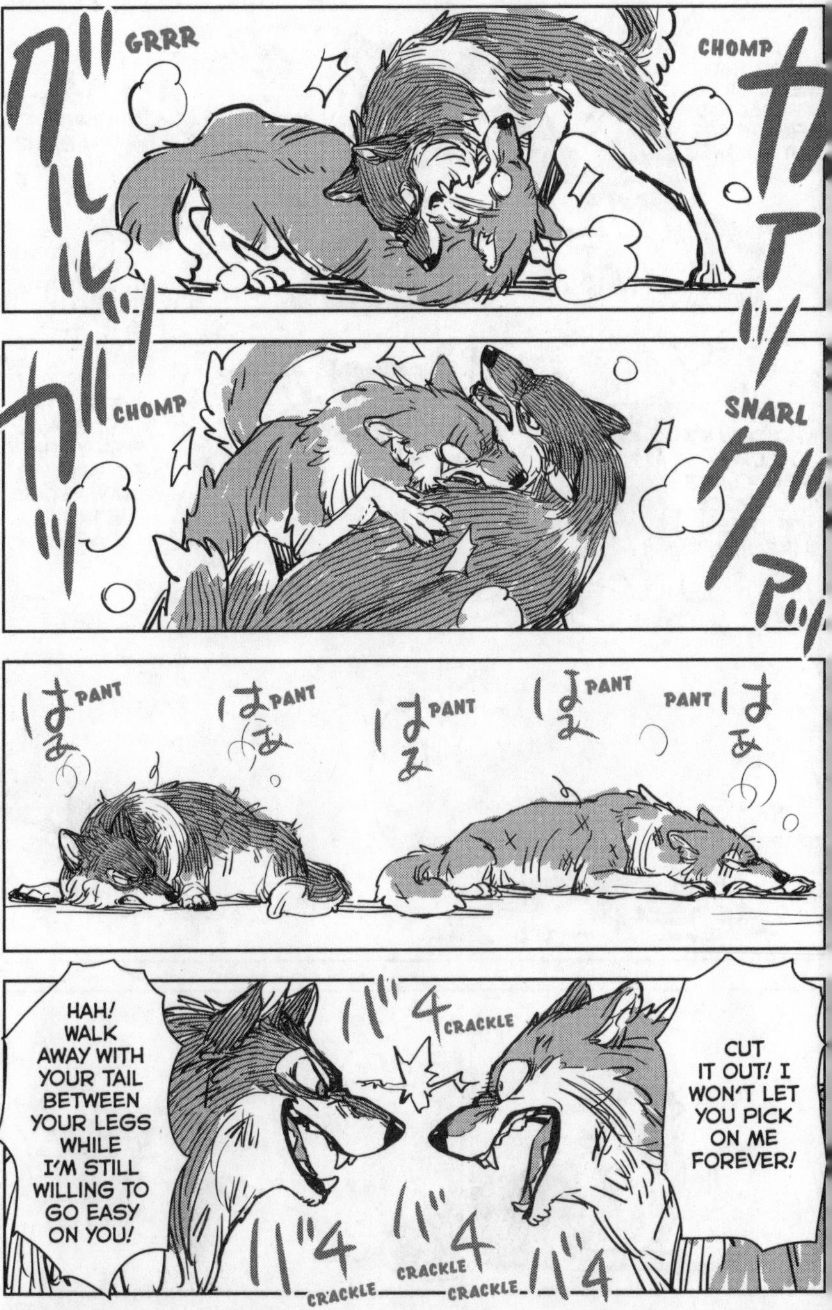

CHOMP
カァッ
GRRR
グルルッ
SNARL
グァッ
CHOMP
ガリッ
PANT
はぁ
PANT
はぁ
PANT
はぁ
PANT
はぁ
PANT
はぁ
CUT IT OUT! I WON'T LET YOU PICK ON ME FOREVER!
CRACKLE
HAH! WALK AWAY WITH YOUR TAIL BETWEEN YOUR LEGS WHILE I'M STILL WILLING TO GO EASY ON YOU!
CRACKLE
CRACKLE
CRACKLE

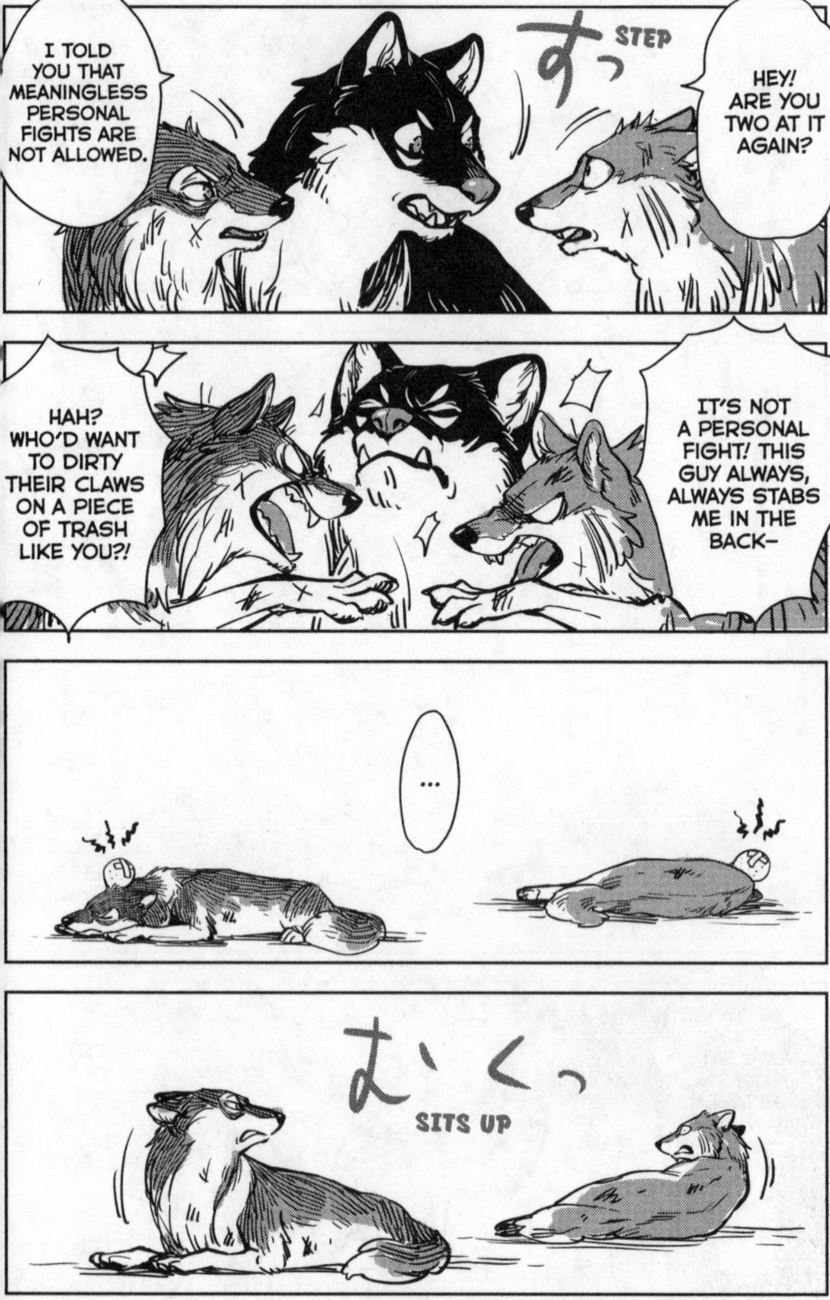

HEY! ARE YOU TWO AT IT AGAIN?
すっ
STEP
I TOLD YOU THAT MEANINGLESS PERSONAL FIGHTS ARE NOT ALLOWED.
IT'S NOT A PERSONAL FIGHT! THIS GUY ALWAYS, ALWAYS STABS ME IN THE BACK–
HAH? WHO'D WANT TO DIRTY THEIR CLAWS ON A PIECE OF TRASH LIKE YOU?!
...
むくっ
SITS UP

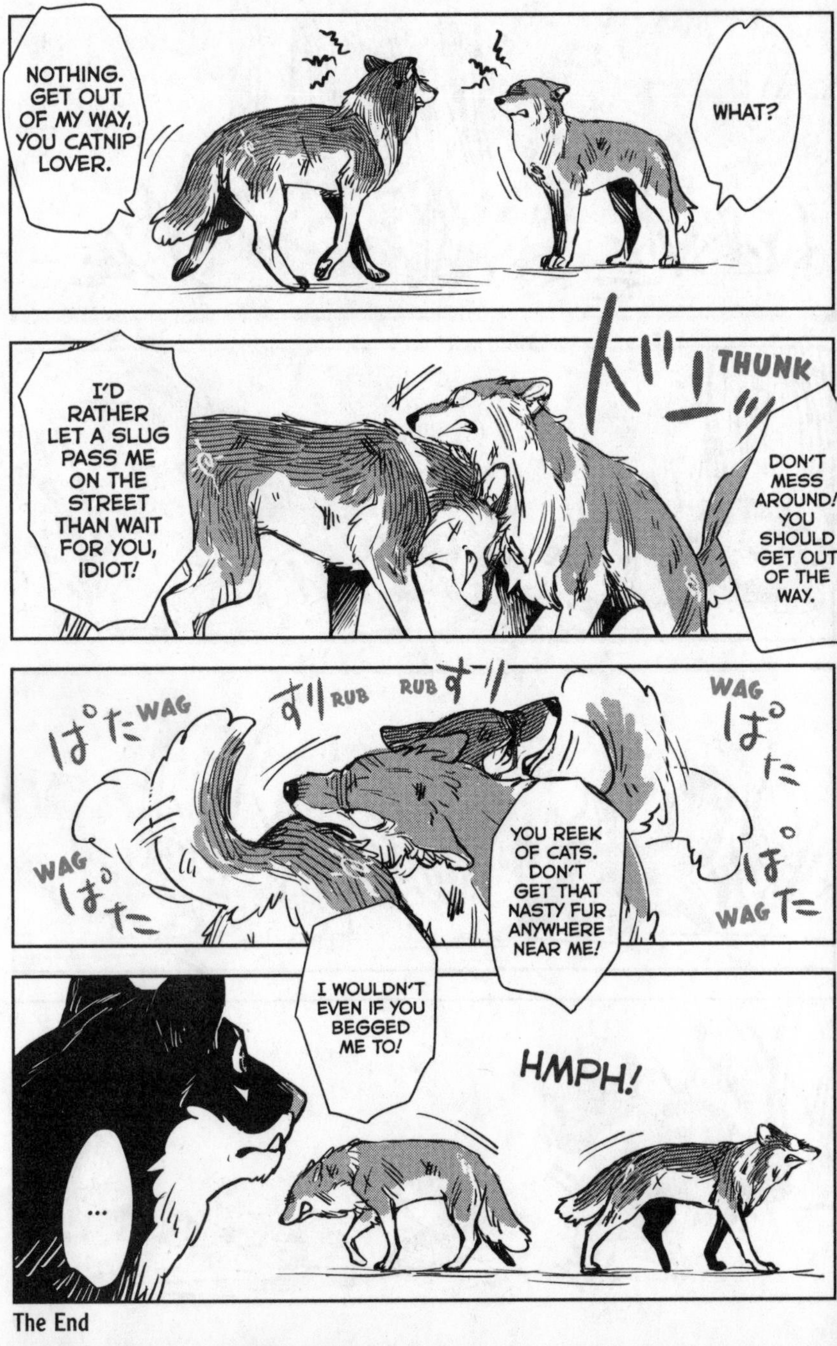
WHAT?
NOTHING. GET OUT OF MY WAY, YOU CATNIP LOVER.
THUNK
DON'T MESS AROUND! YOU SHOULD GET OUT OF THE WAY.
I'D RATHER LET A SLUG PASS ME ON THE STREET THAN WAIT FOR YOU, IDIOT!
WAG ぱた
RUB すり
RUB すり
WAG ぱた
YOU REEK OF CATS. DON'T GET THAT NASTY FUR ANYWHERE NEAR ME!
WAG ぱた
WAG ぱた
I WOULDN'T EVEN IF YOU BEGGED ME TO!
HMPH!
...

The End

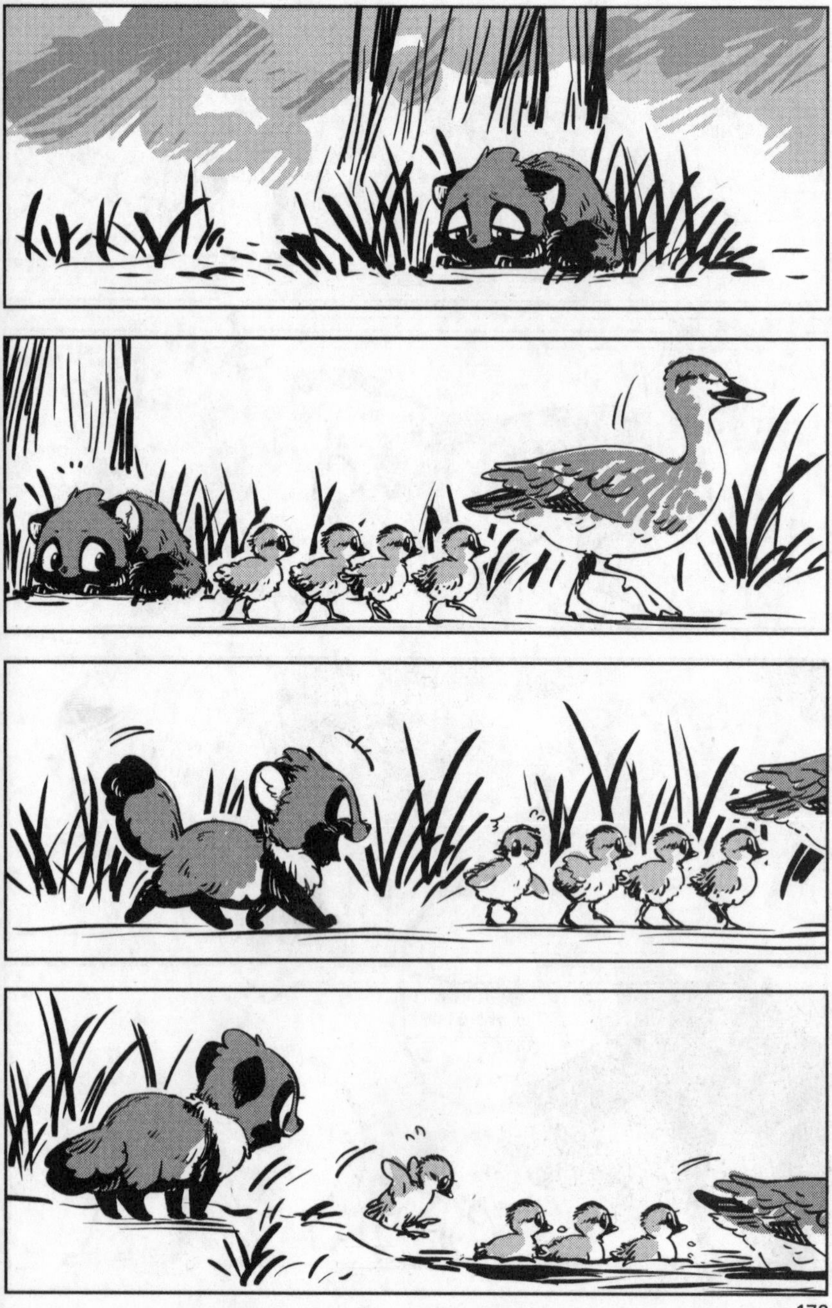

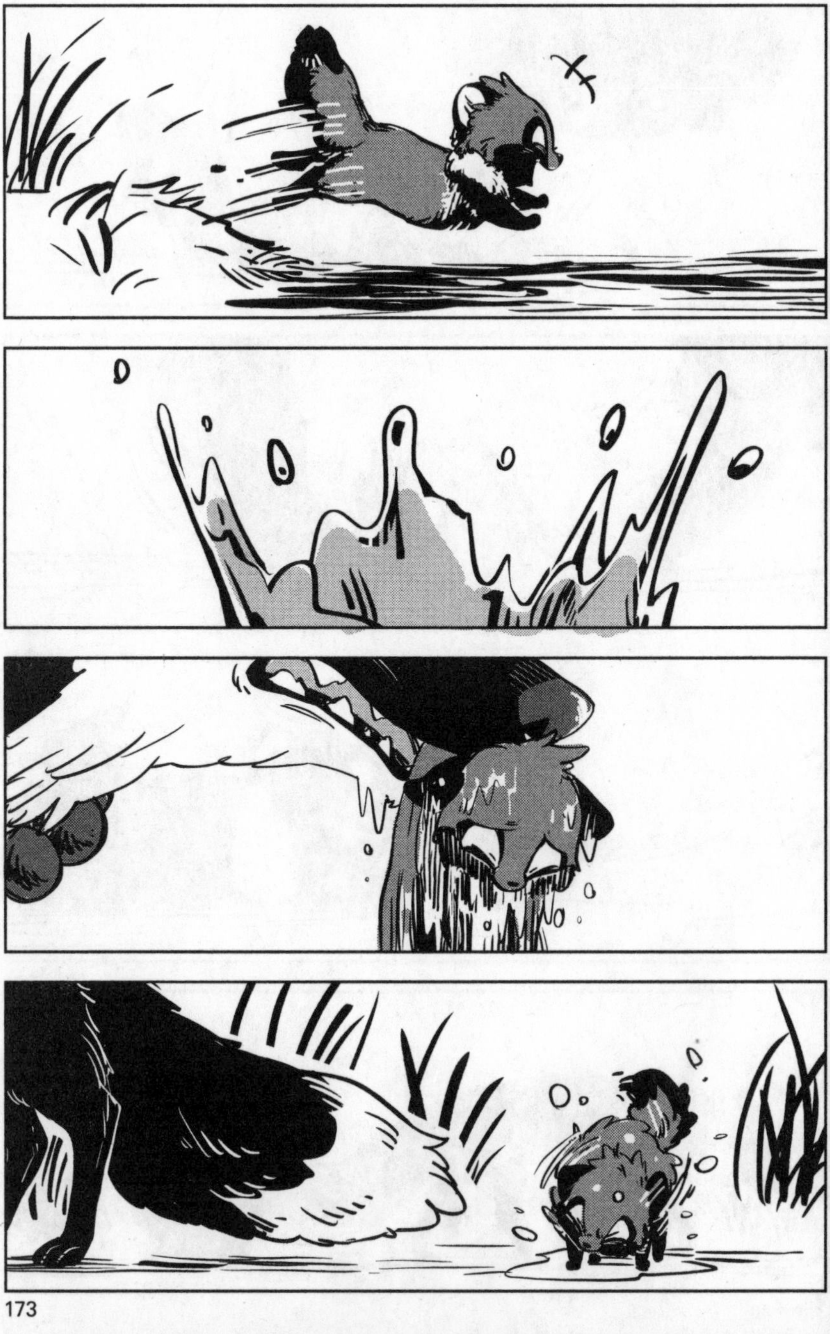

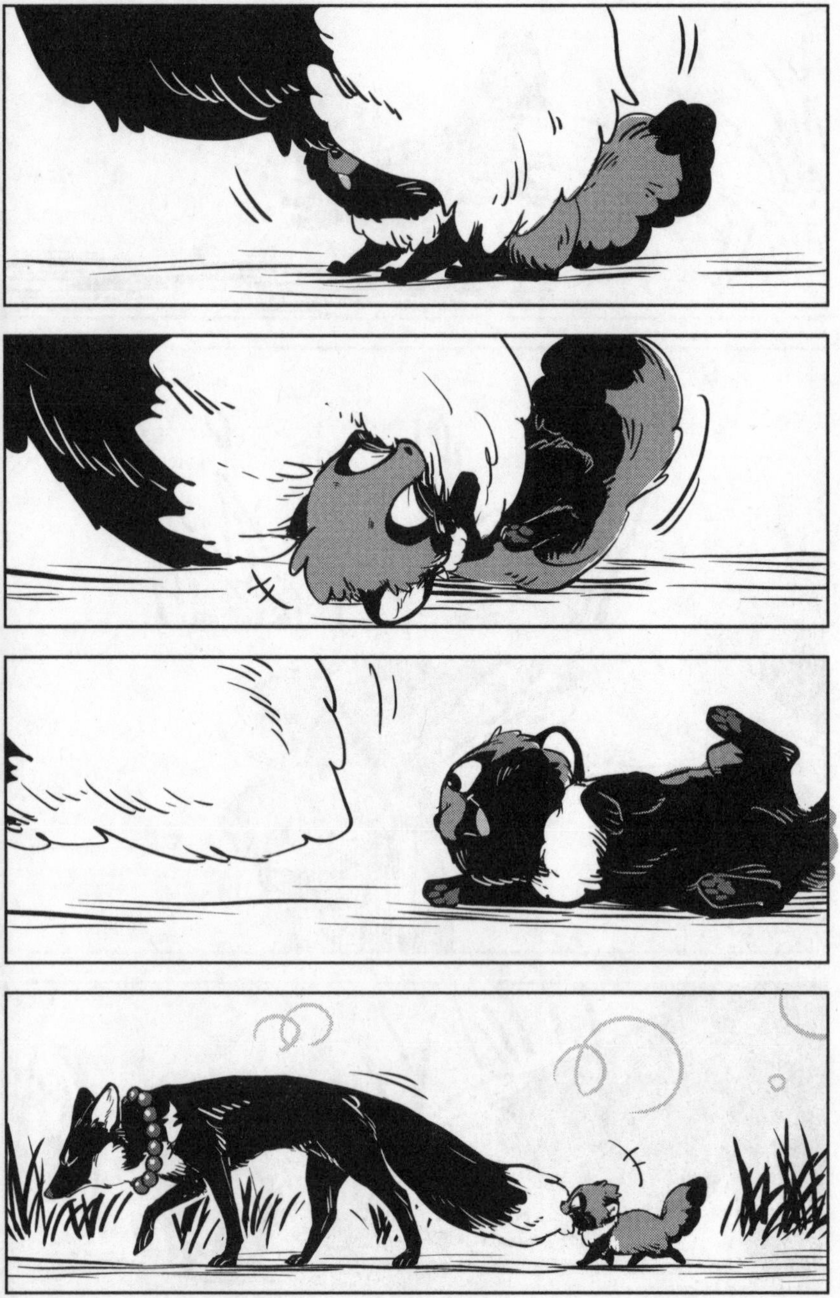

The End

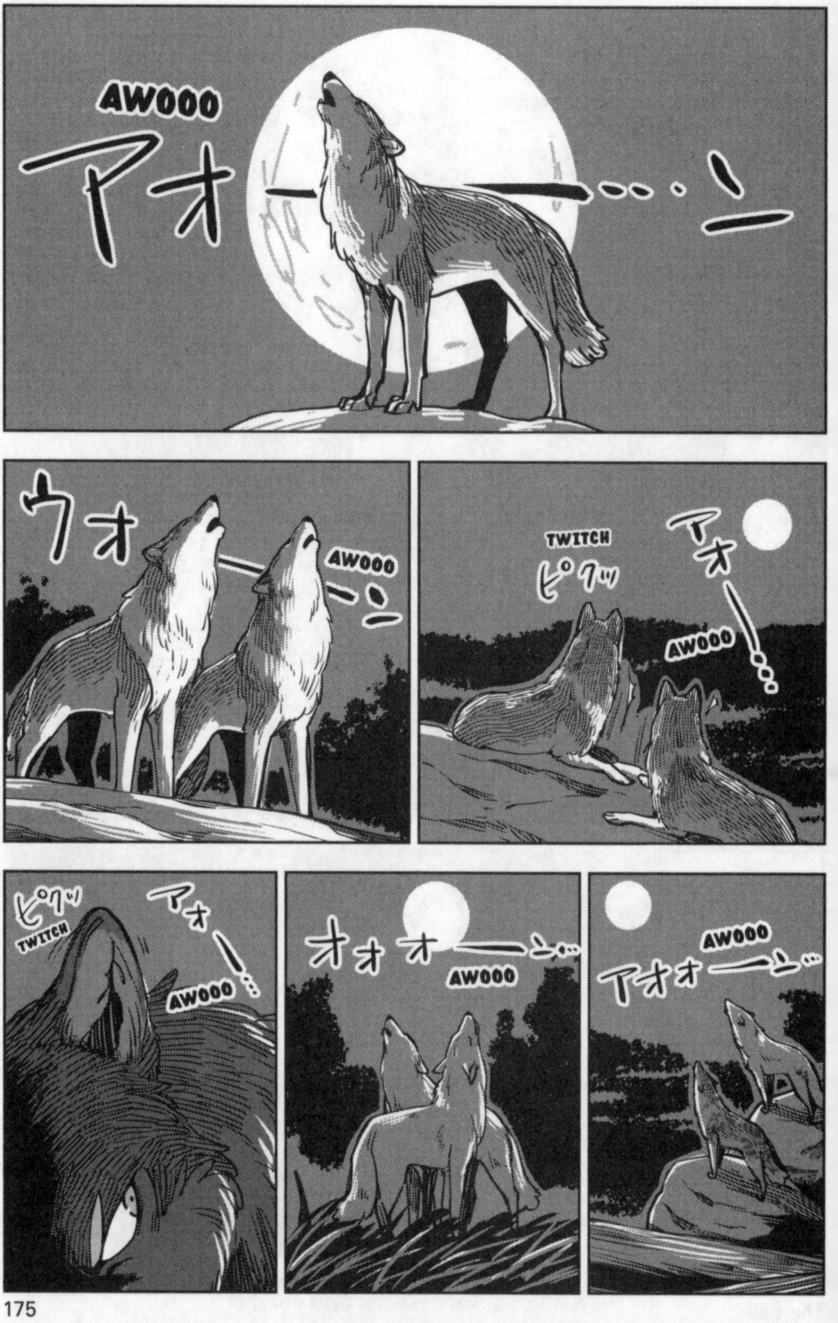
AWOOO
アオーー…ン
アオー…
AWOOO
TWITCH
ピクッ
ウオーン
AWOOO
AWOOO
アオーーン…
オオオーーン…
AWOOO
アオー…
AWOOO
ピクッ
TWITCH

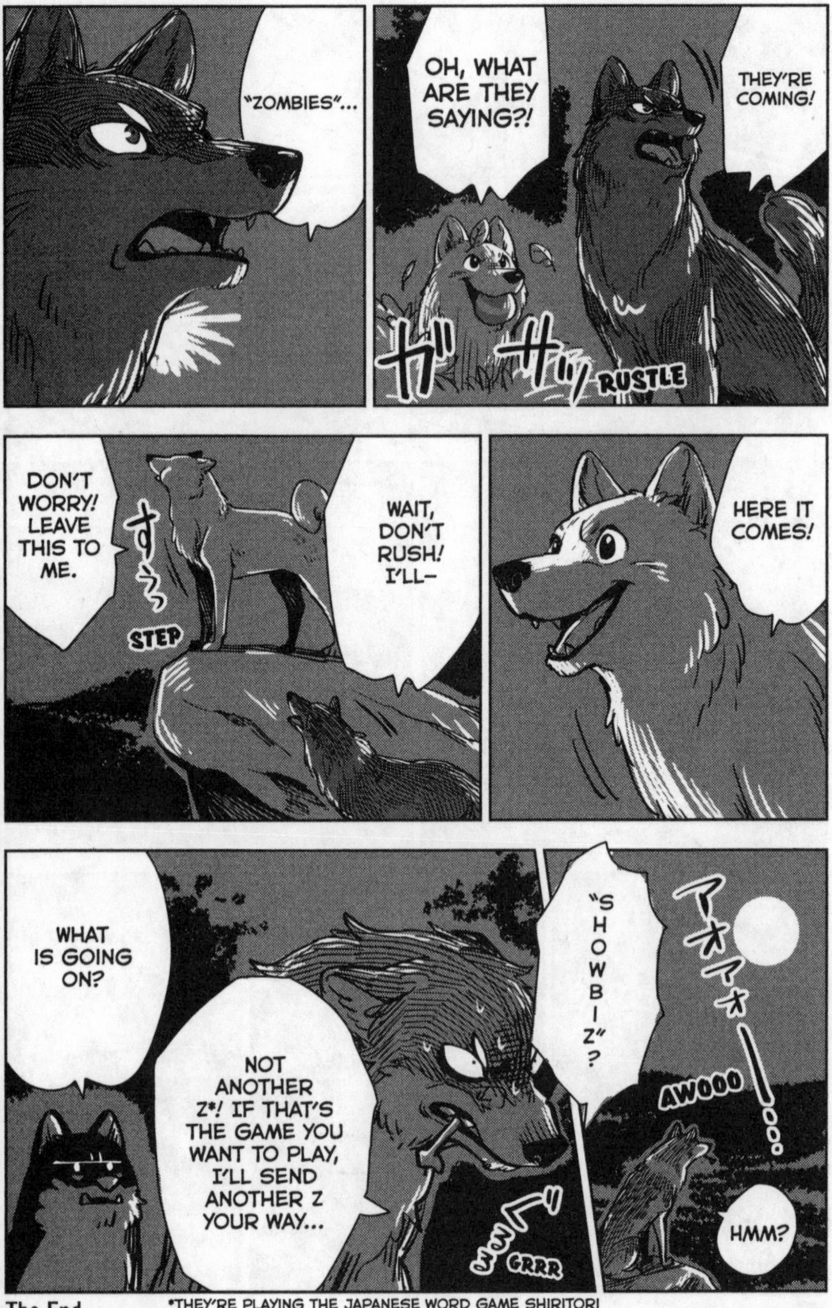
THEY'RE COMING!
OH, WHAT ARE THEY SAYING?!
RUSTLE
"ZOMBIES"...
HERE IT COMES!
WAIT, DON'T RUSH! I'LL–
DON'T WORRY! LEAVE THIS TO ME.
STEP
AWOOO
"SHOWBIZ"?
HMM?
NOT ANOTHER Z*! IF THAT'S THE GAME YOU WANT TO PLAY, I'LL SEND ANOTHER Z YOUR WAY...
GRRR
WHAT IS GOING ON?

The End

*THEY'RE PLAYING THE JAPANESE WORD GAME SHIRITORI

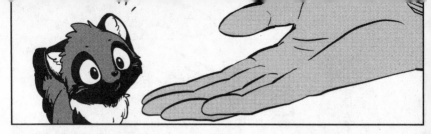

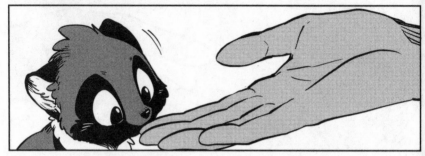

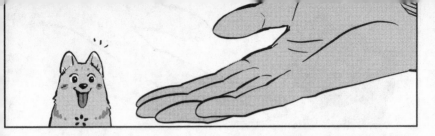

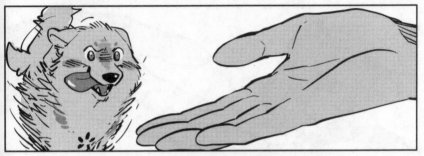

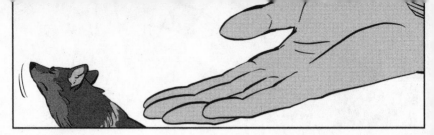

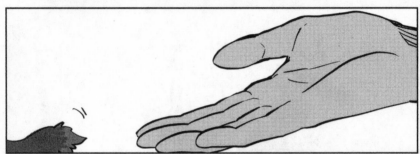

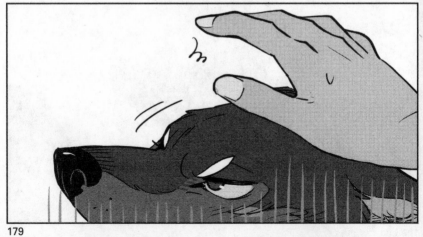

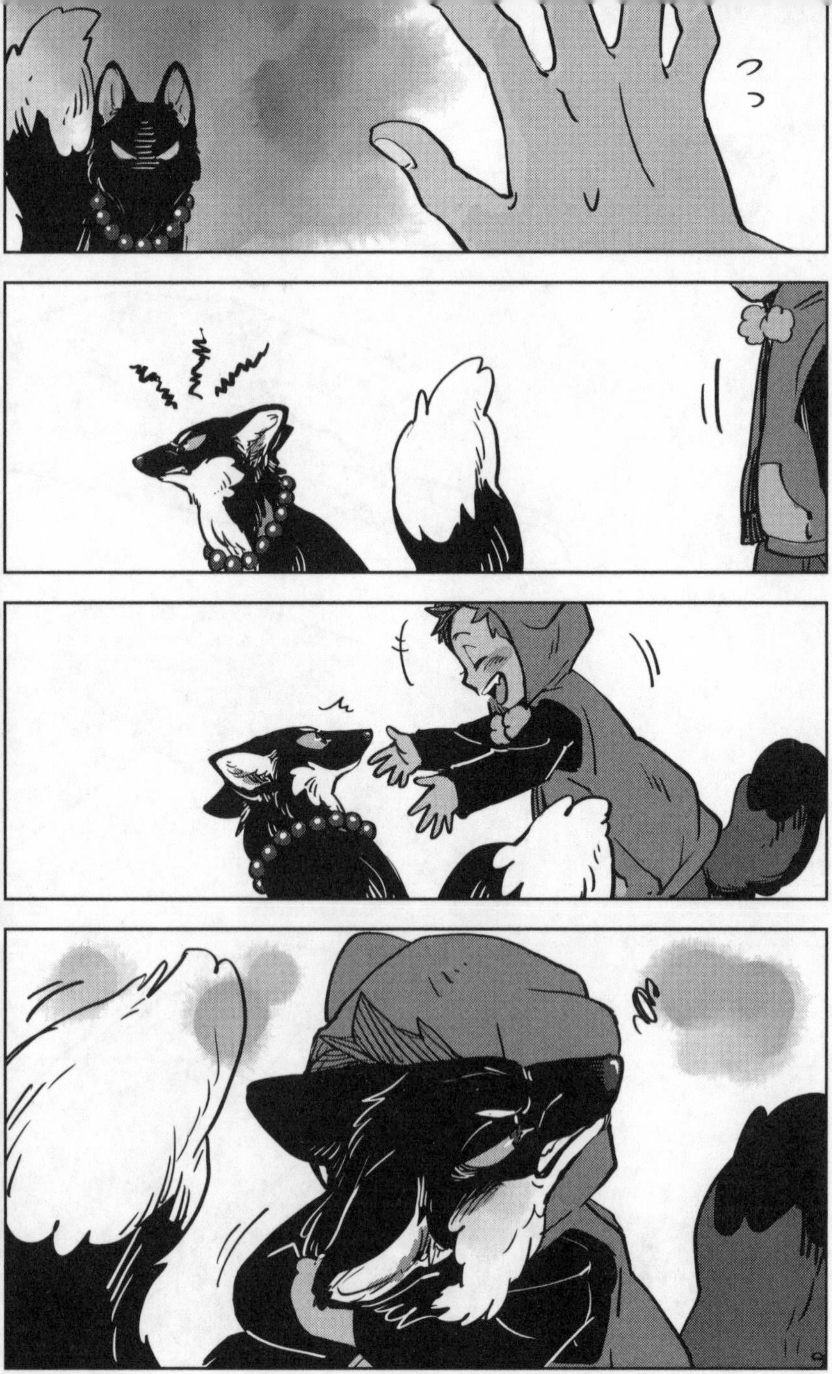

The End

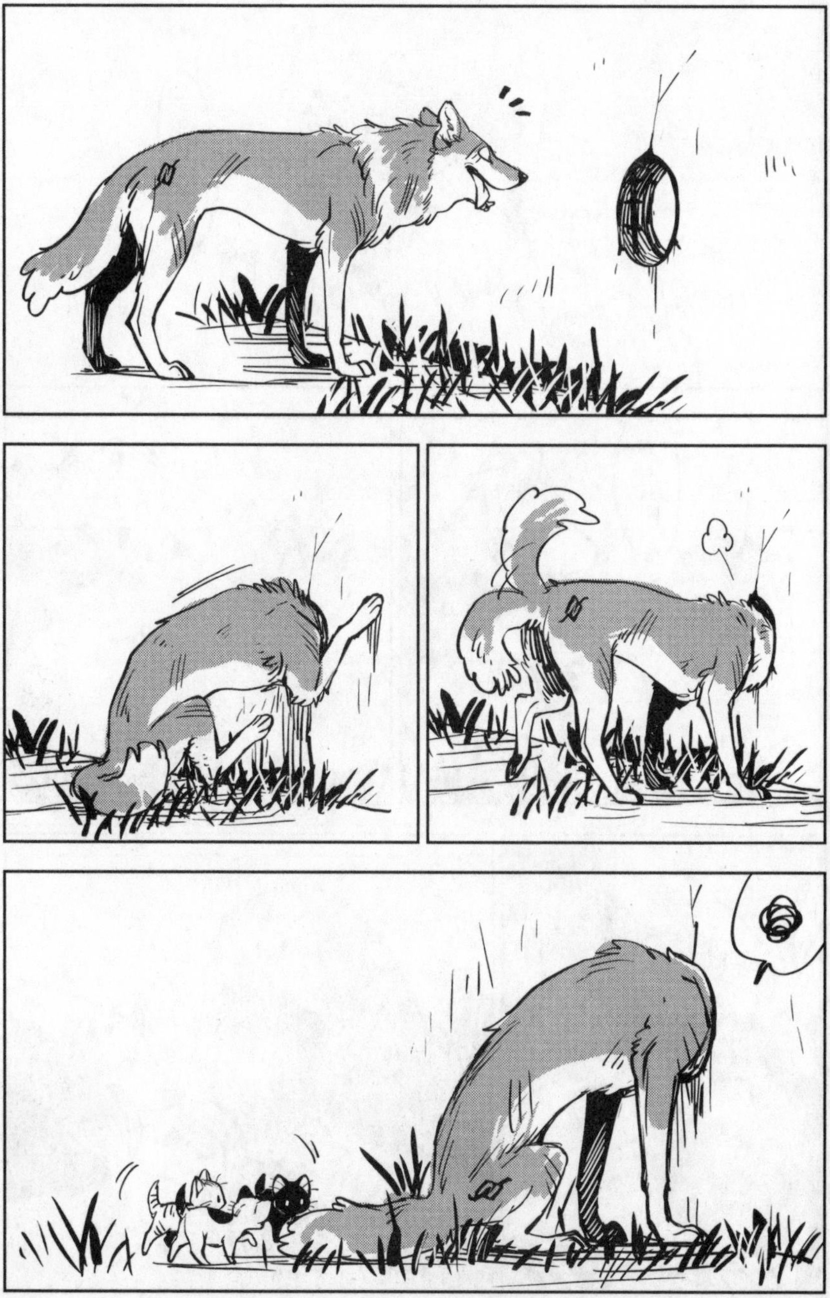

...
PANT
はっ
PANT
はっ
PANT
はっ
SHHH.
?

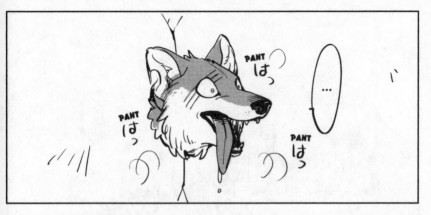

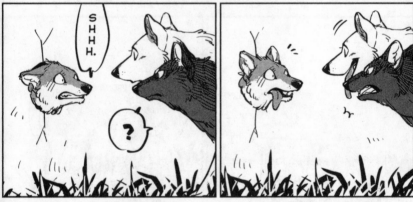

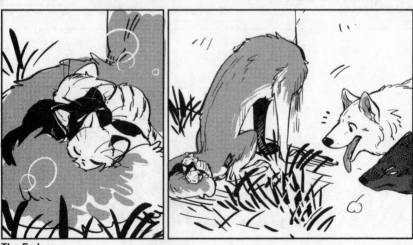

The End

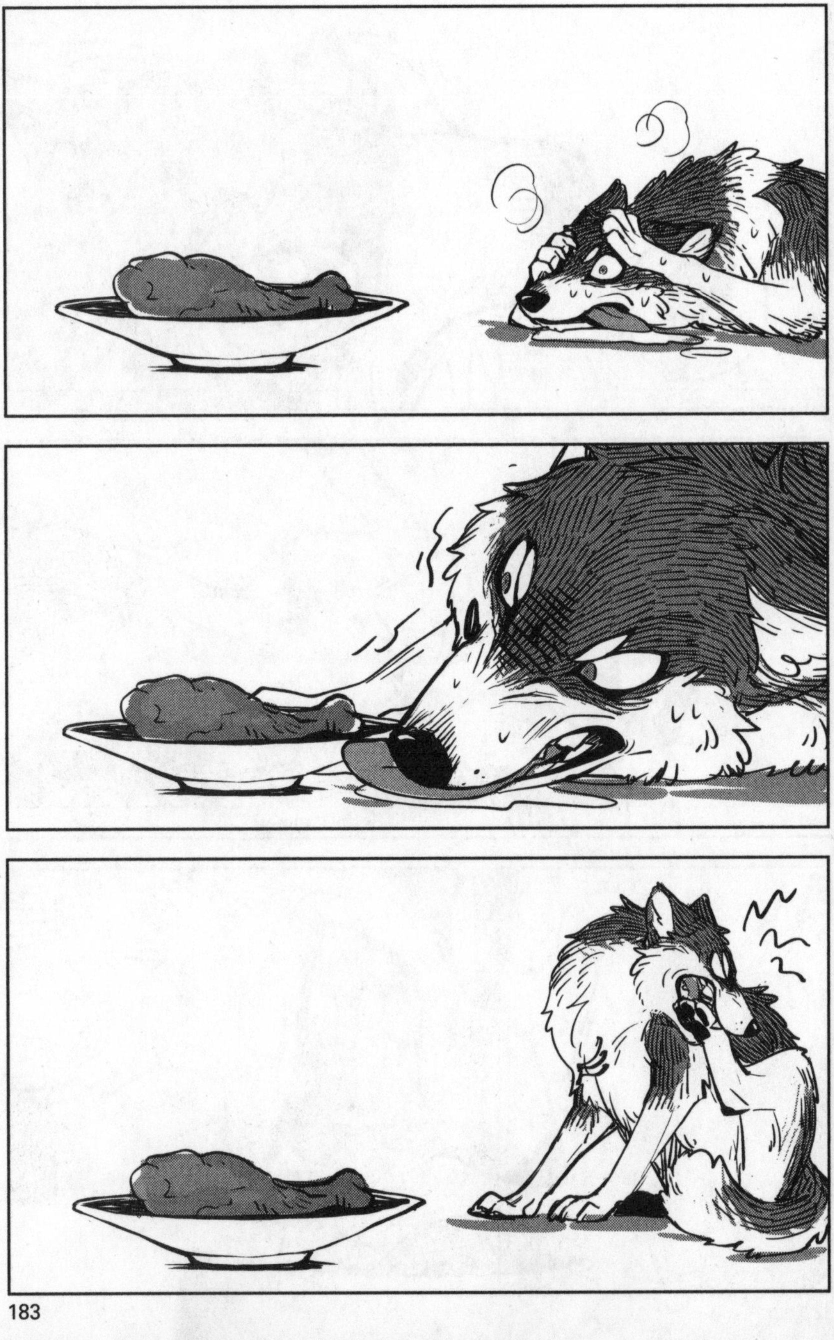

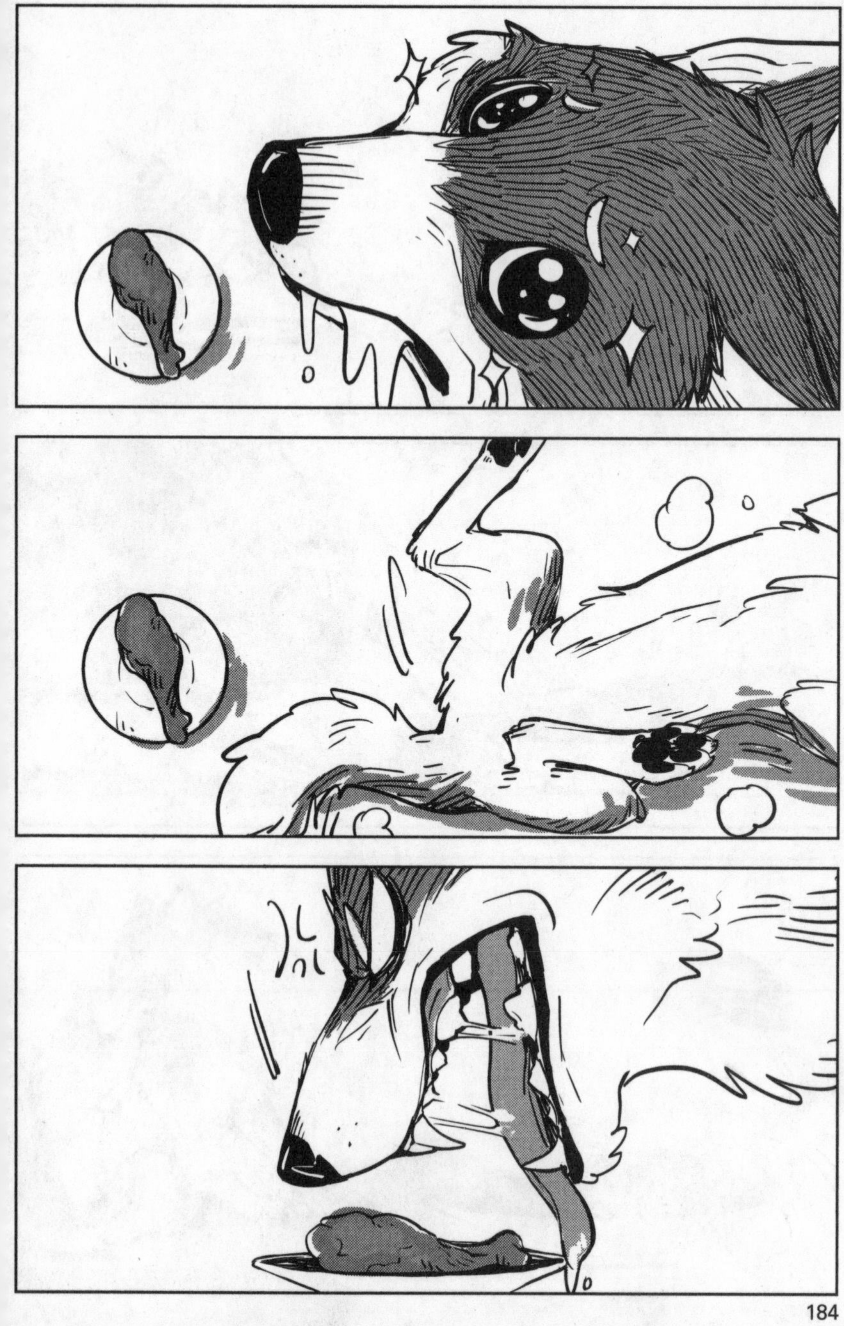

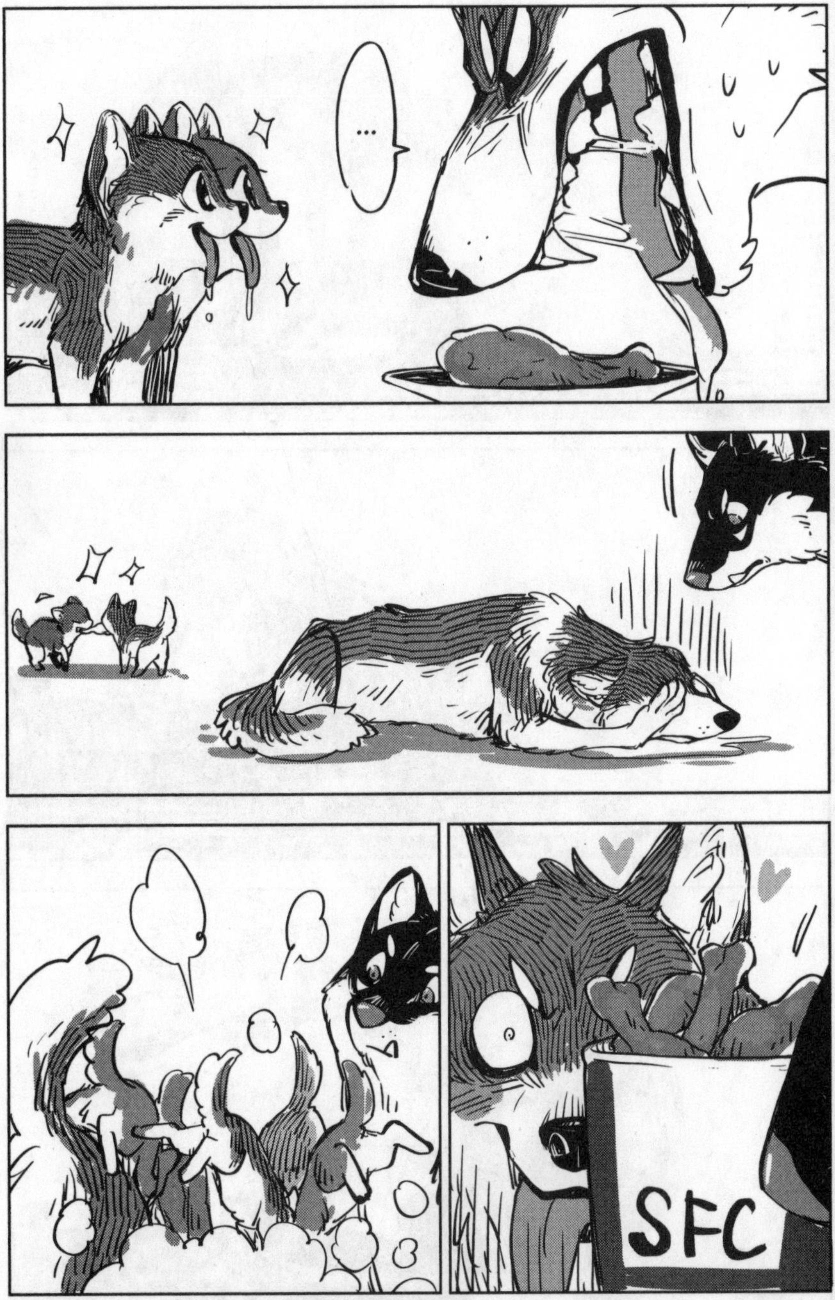
...
SFC

The End

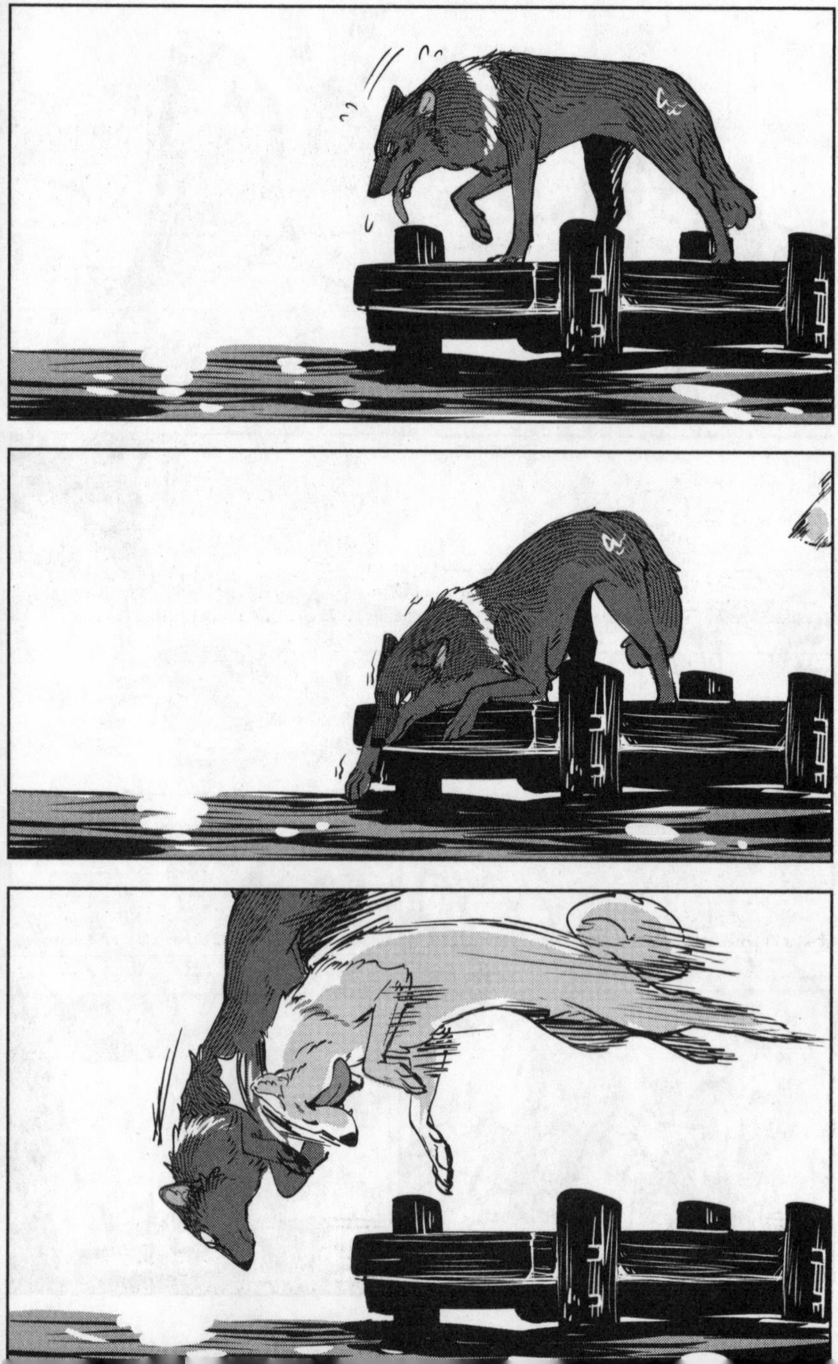

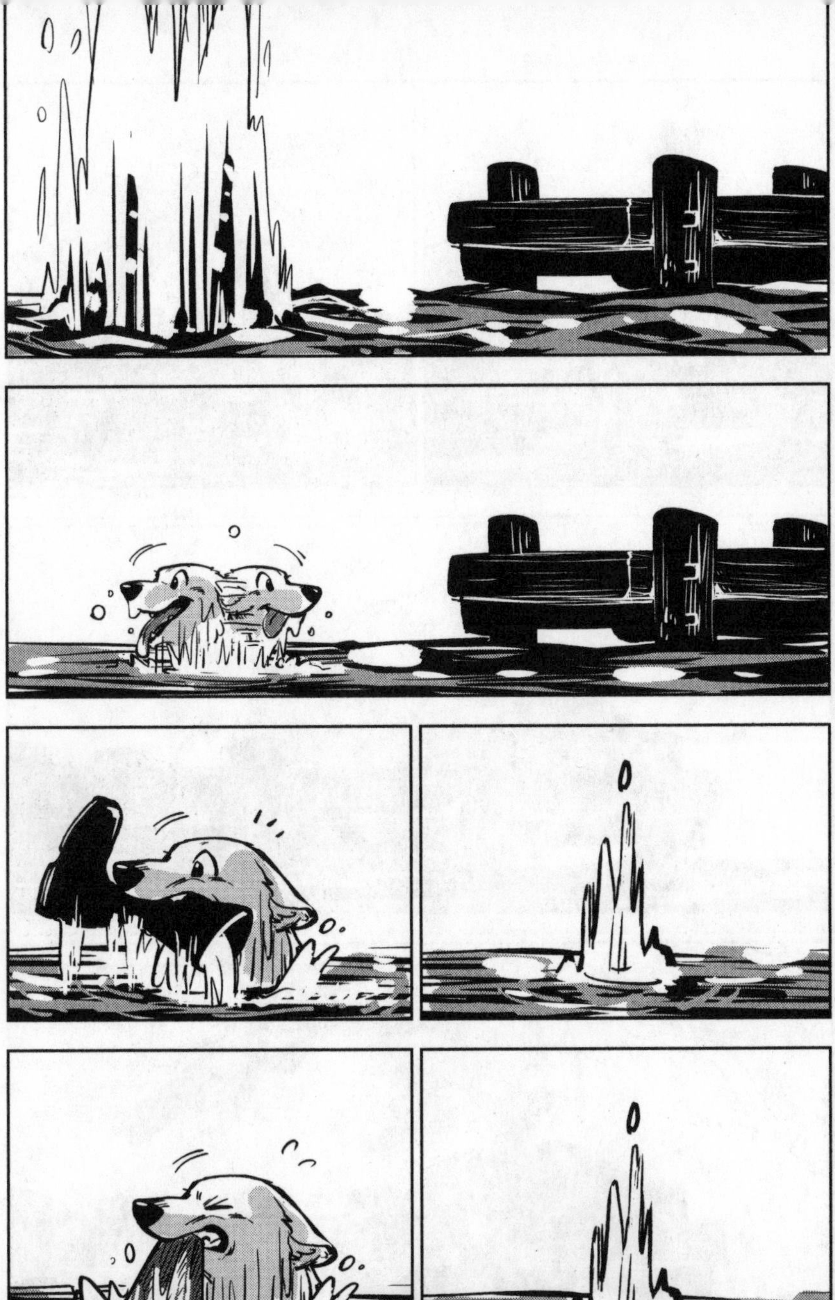

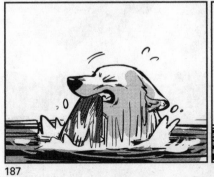

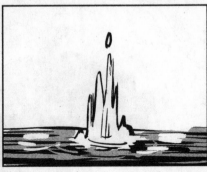

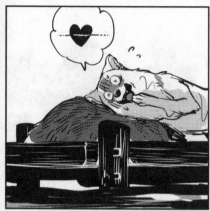

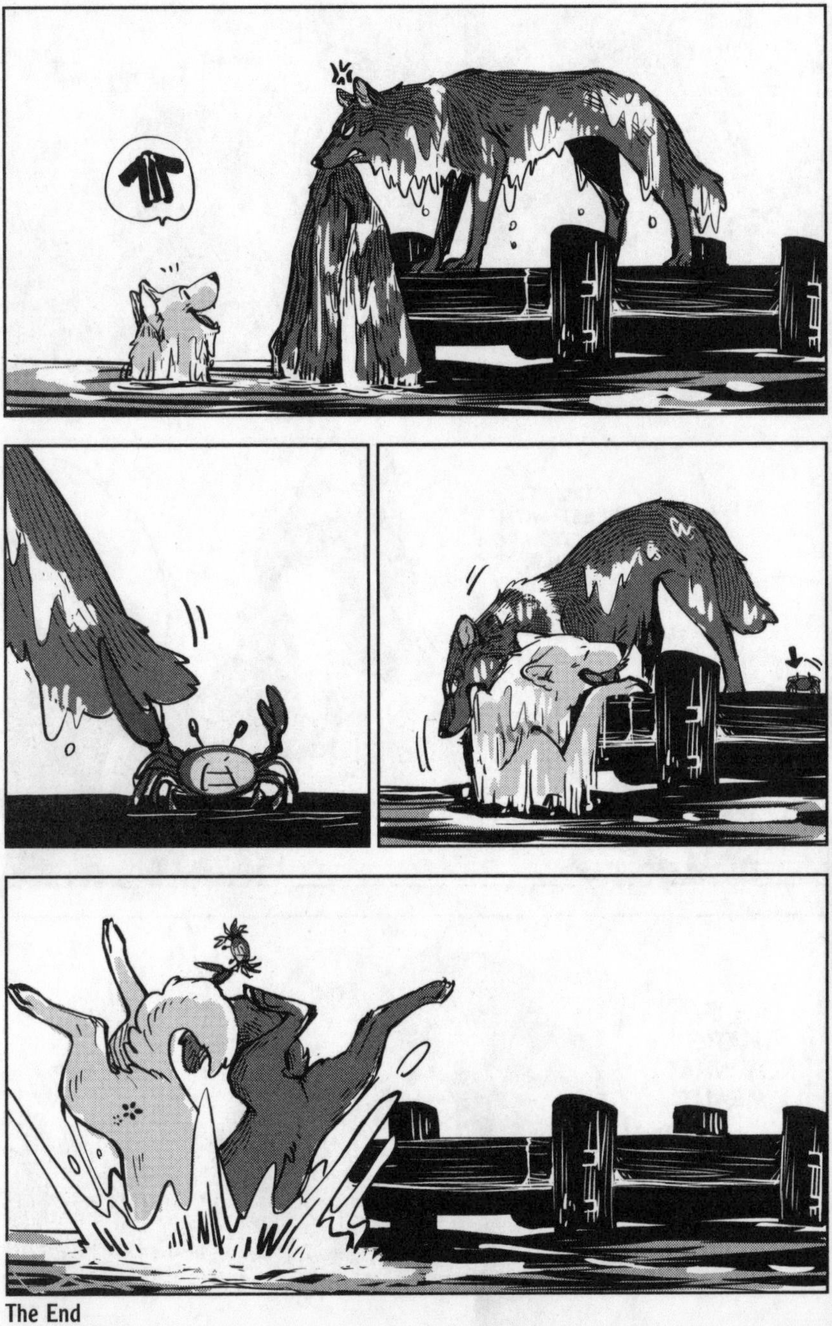

The End

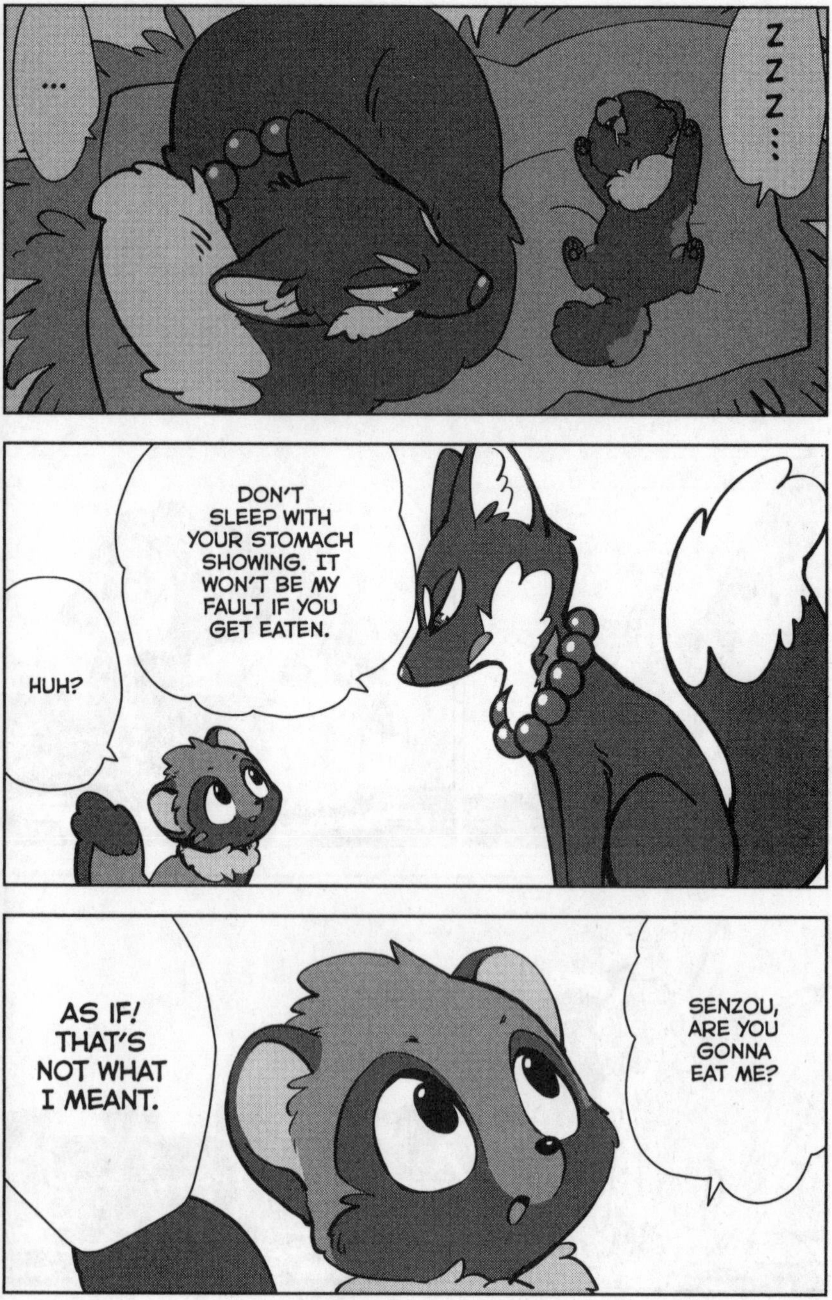
ZZZ...
...
DON'T SLEEP WITH YOUR STOMACH SHOWING. IT WON'T BE MY FAULT IF YOU GET EATEN.
HUH?
SENZOU, ARE YOU GONNA EAT ME?
AS IF! THAT'S NOT WHAT I MEANT.

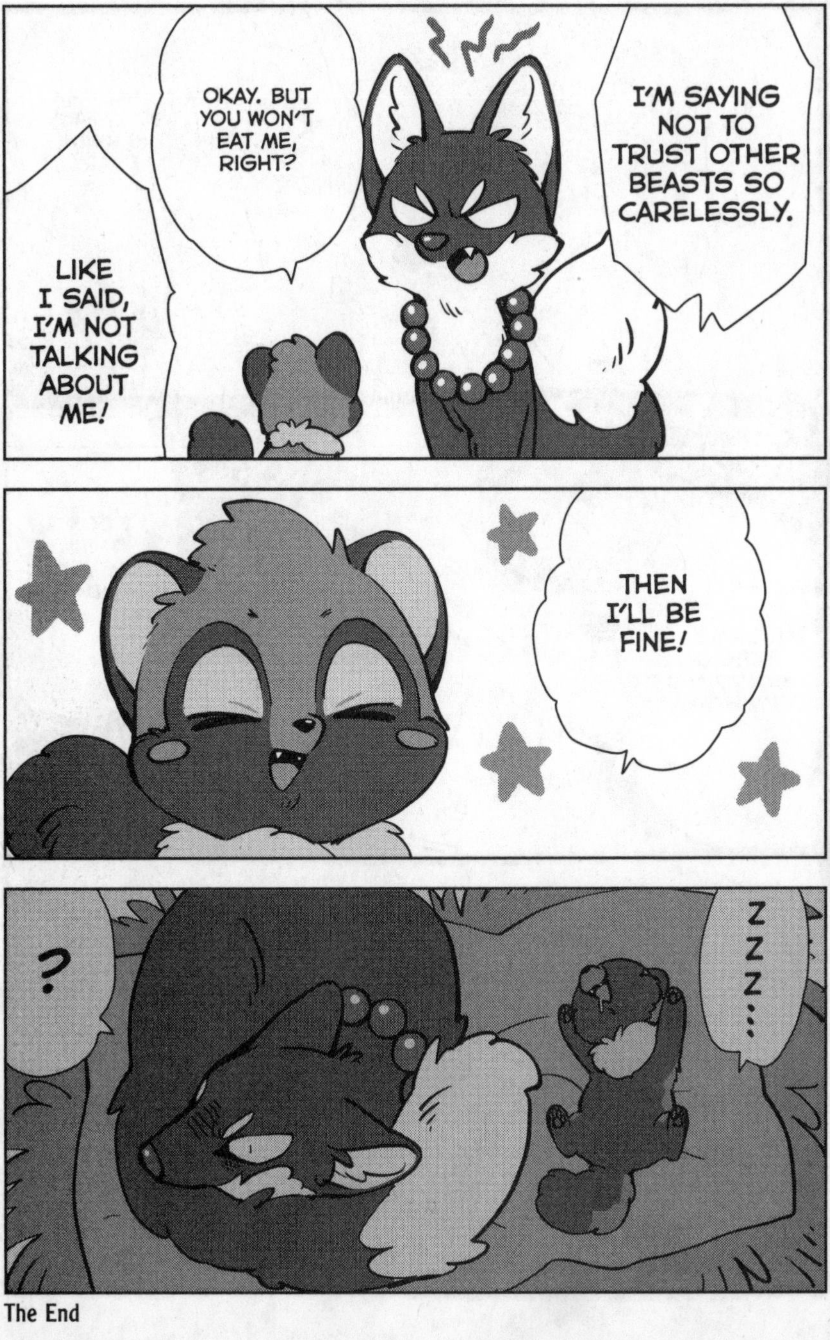
I'M SAYING NOT TO TRUST OTHER BEASTS SO CARELESSLY.
OKAY. BUT YOU WON'T EAT ME, RIGHT?
LIKE I SAID, I'M NOT TALKING ABOUT ME!
THEN I'LL BE FINE!
ZZZ...
?

The End

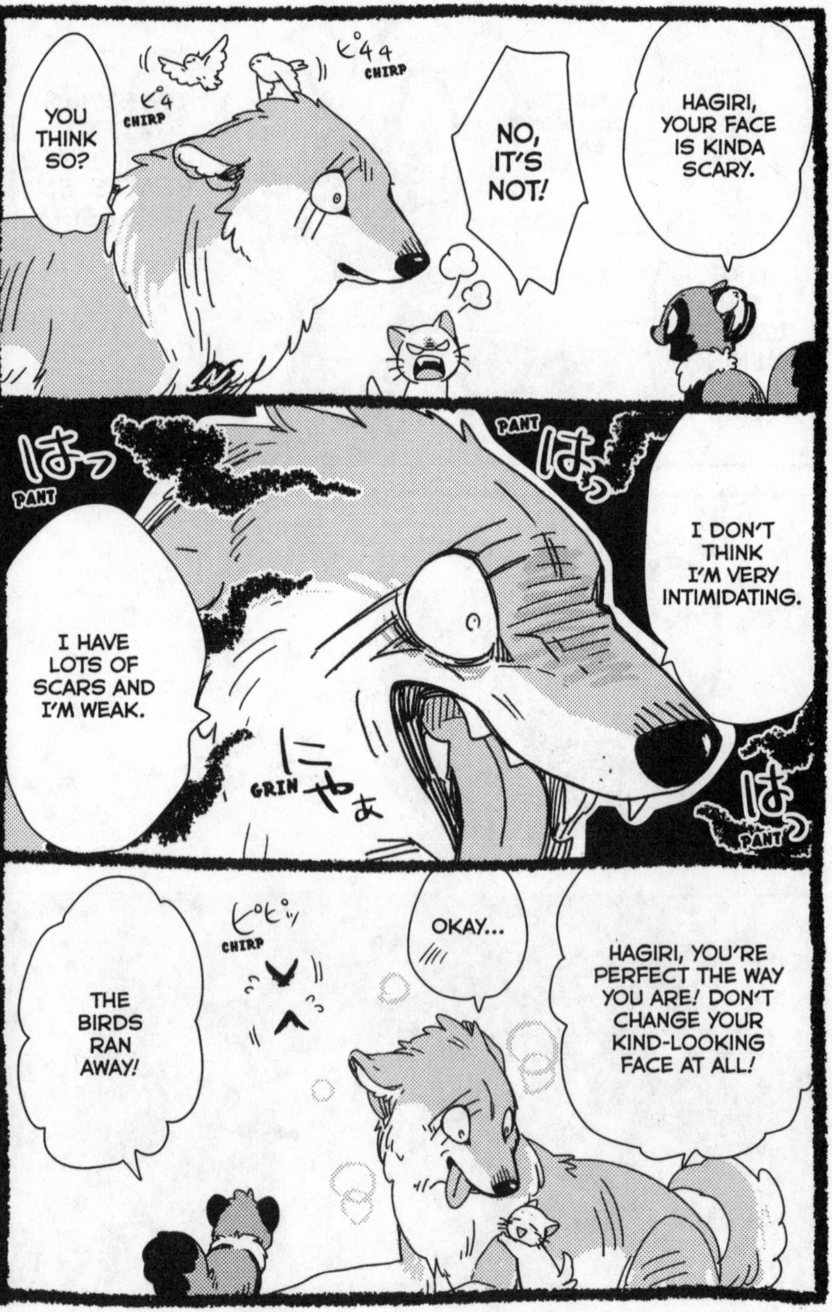
HAGIRI, YOUR FACE IS KINDA SCARY.
NO, IT'S NOT!
CHIRP
CHIRP
YOU THINK SO?
はっ
PANT
I DON'T THINK I'M VERY INTIMIDATING.
はっ
PANT
はっ
PANT
I HAVE LOTS OF SCARS AND I'M WEAK.
にやぁ
GRIN
HAGIRI, YOU'RE PERFECT THE WAY YOU ARE! DON'T CHANGE YOUR KIND-LOOKING FACE AT ALL!
OKAY...
ピピッ
CHIRP
THE BIRDS RAN AWAY!

Thanks to everyone, I was

able to publish volume 3!

Thank you so much!

Please continue

to support the series!

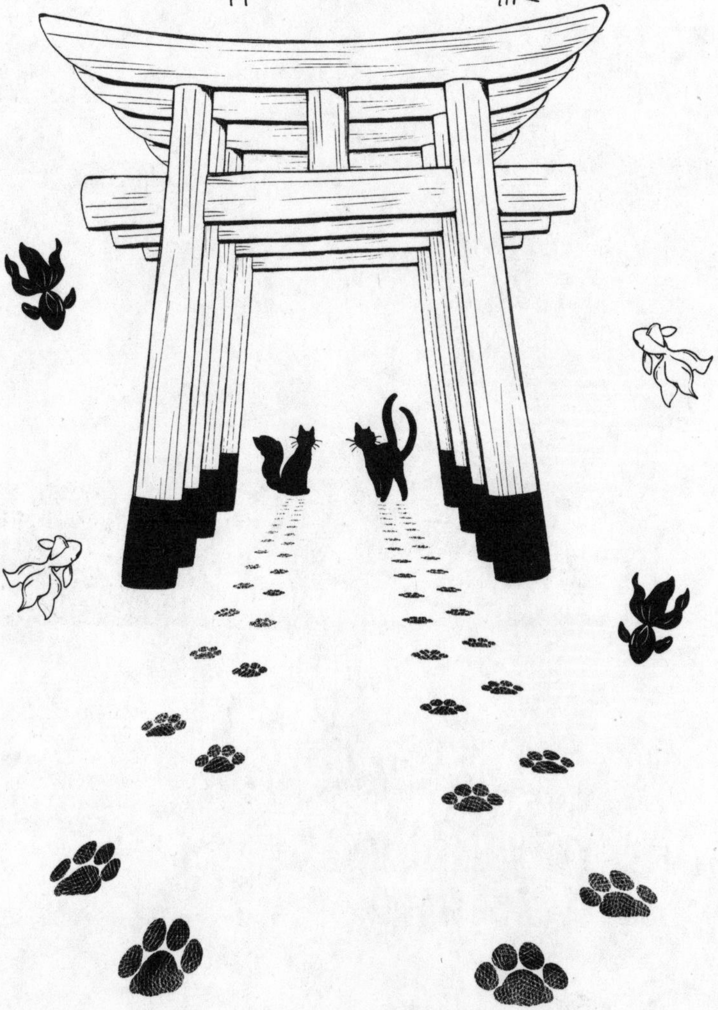

BREATH OF FLOWERS
IN THE LANGUAGE OF FLOWERS, EVERY BLOSSOM IS UNIQUE
BEING A TEEN IS HARD.
IT'S EVEN HARDER
WHEN YOU'RE HIDING A
SECRET...
BREATH OF FLOWERS
Story and Art by CALY
1
TOKYOPOP
BREATH OF FLOWERS
CALY
1
TOKYOPOP
INTERNATIONAL
women of manga
Girls Love / LGBTQ+
© CALY, PIKA EDITION – Editions H2T

©Disney

ORIGINAL JAPAN STORY!

ADORABLE STITCH!

TROPICAL FRUIT (WELL, MANGA FRUIT)!

KID & FAMILY FUN!

TOKYO POP®

DISNEY

DESCENDANTS

Dizzy's NEW FORTUNE

THE NEWEST DESCENDANTS MANGA WITH BRAND-NEW VILLAIN KIDS!

The original Villain Kids have worked hard to prove they deserve to stay in Auradon, and now it's time some of their friends from the Isle of the Lost get that chance too! When Dizzy receives a special invitation from King Ben to join the other VKs at Auradon Prep, at first she's thrilled! But doubt soon creeps in, and she begins to question whether she can truly fit in outside the scrappy world of the Isle.

Bibi & Miyu

When a new student joins her class, Bibi is suspicious. She knows Miyu has a secret, and she's determined to figure it out!

Bibi's journey takes her to Japan, where she learns so many exciting new things! Maybe Bibi and Miyu can be friends, after all!

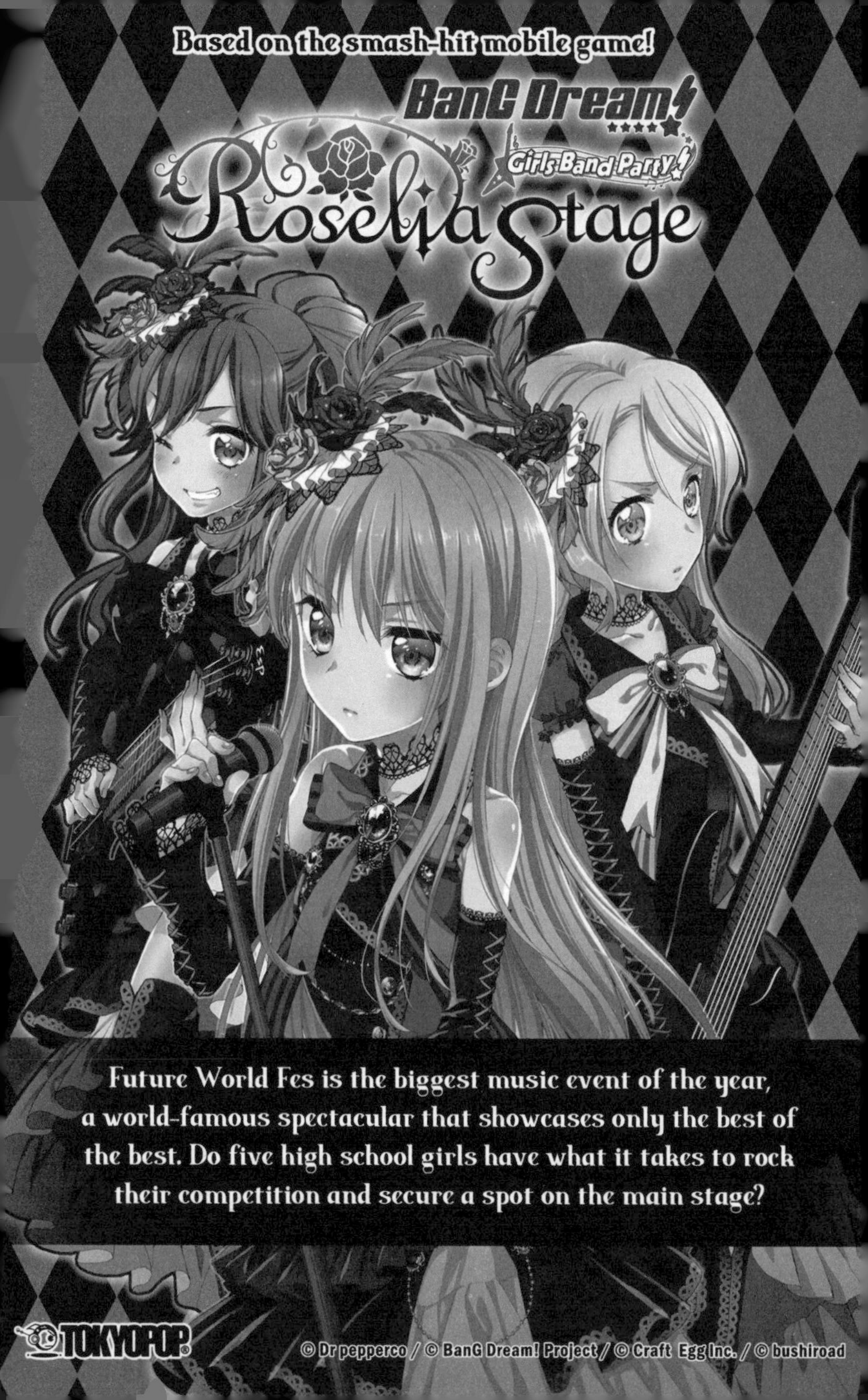
Based on the smash-hit mobile game!
BanG Dream! Girls Band Party!
Roselia Stage
Future World Fes is the biggest music event of the year, a world-famous spectacular that showcases only the best of the best. Do five high school girls have what it takes to rock their competition and secure a spot on the main stage?
TOKYOPOP
© Dr pepperco / © BanG Dream! Project / © Craft Egg Inc. / © bushiroad

GRIMMS manga Tales

The Grimm's Tales reimagined in manga!

Beautiful art by the talented Kei Ishiyama!

Stories from Little Red Riding Hood to Hansel and Gretel!

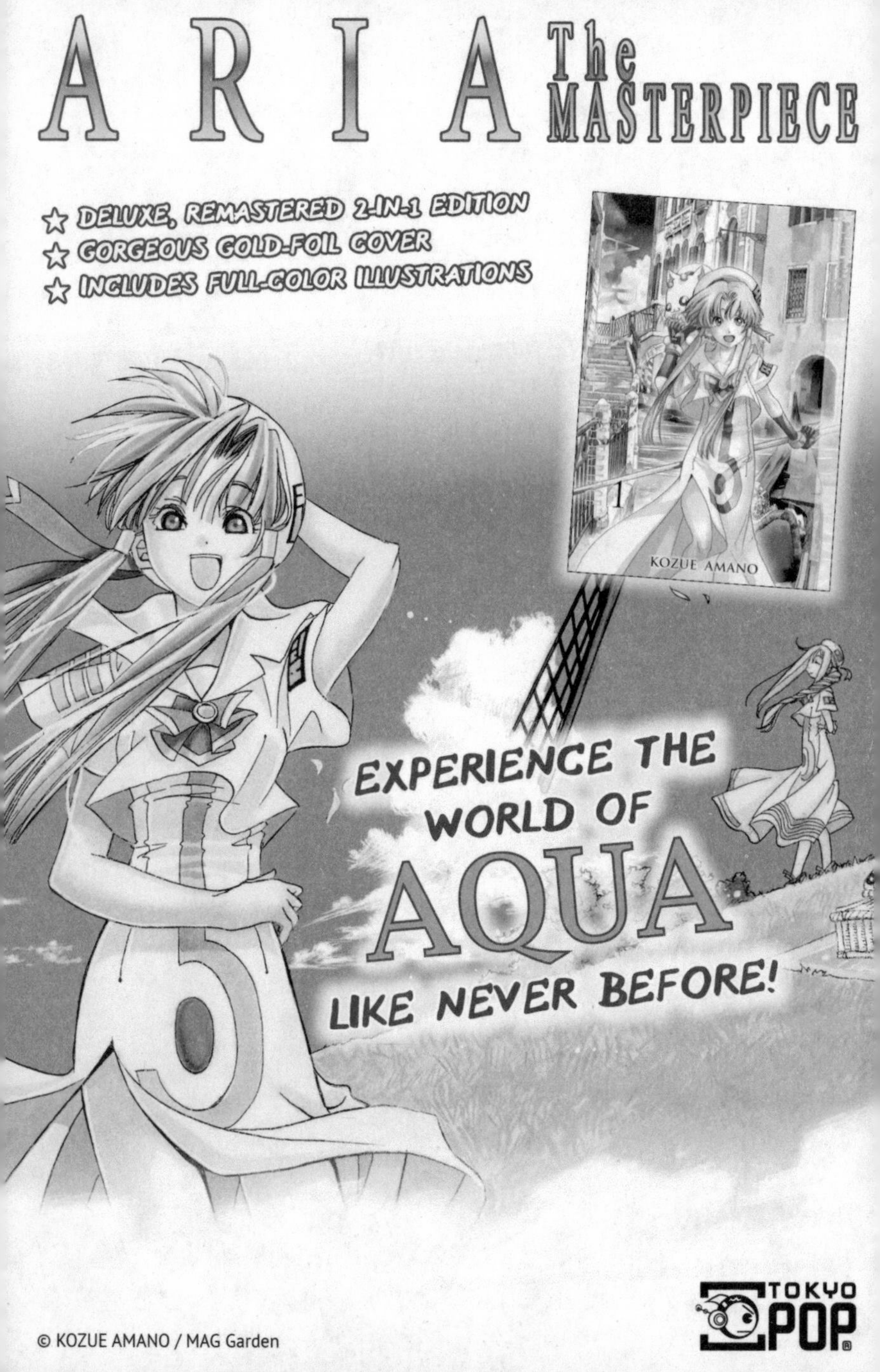
ARIA The MASTERPIECE
☆ DELUXE, REMASTERED 2-IN-1 EDITION
☆ GORGEOUS GOLD-FOIL COVER
☆ INCLUDES FULL-COLOR ILLUSTRATIONS
1
KOZUE AMANO
EXPERIENCE THE WORLD OF AQUA LIKE NEVER BEFORE!
© KOZUE AMANO / MAG Garden
TOKYO POP

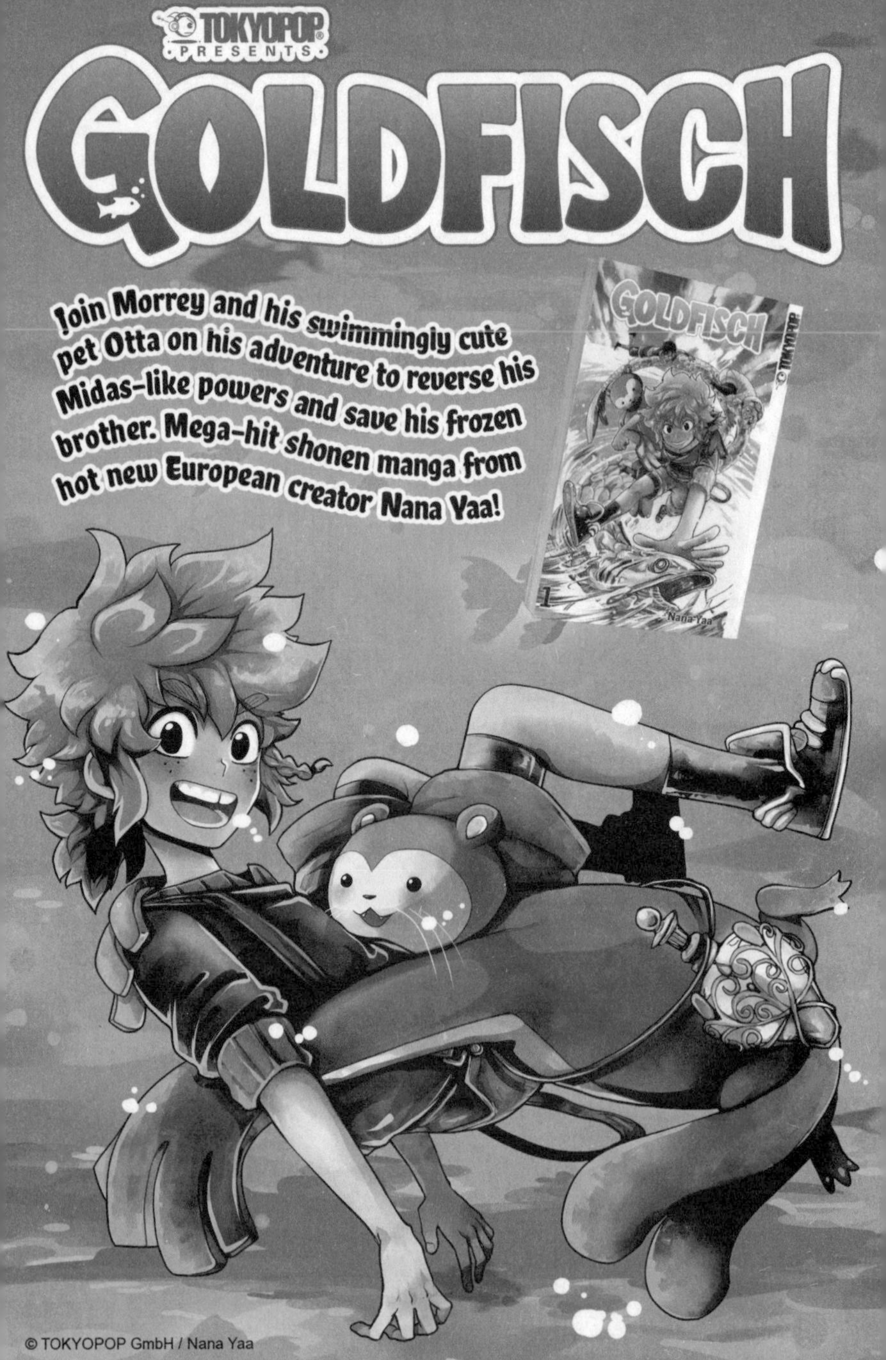
TOKYOPOP
PRESENTS
GOLDFISCH
Join Morrey and his swimmingly cute pet Otta on his adventure to reverse his Midas-like powers and save his frozen brother. Mega-hit shonen manga from hot new European creator Nana Yaa!
GOLDFISCH
TOKYOPOP
1
Nana Yaa

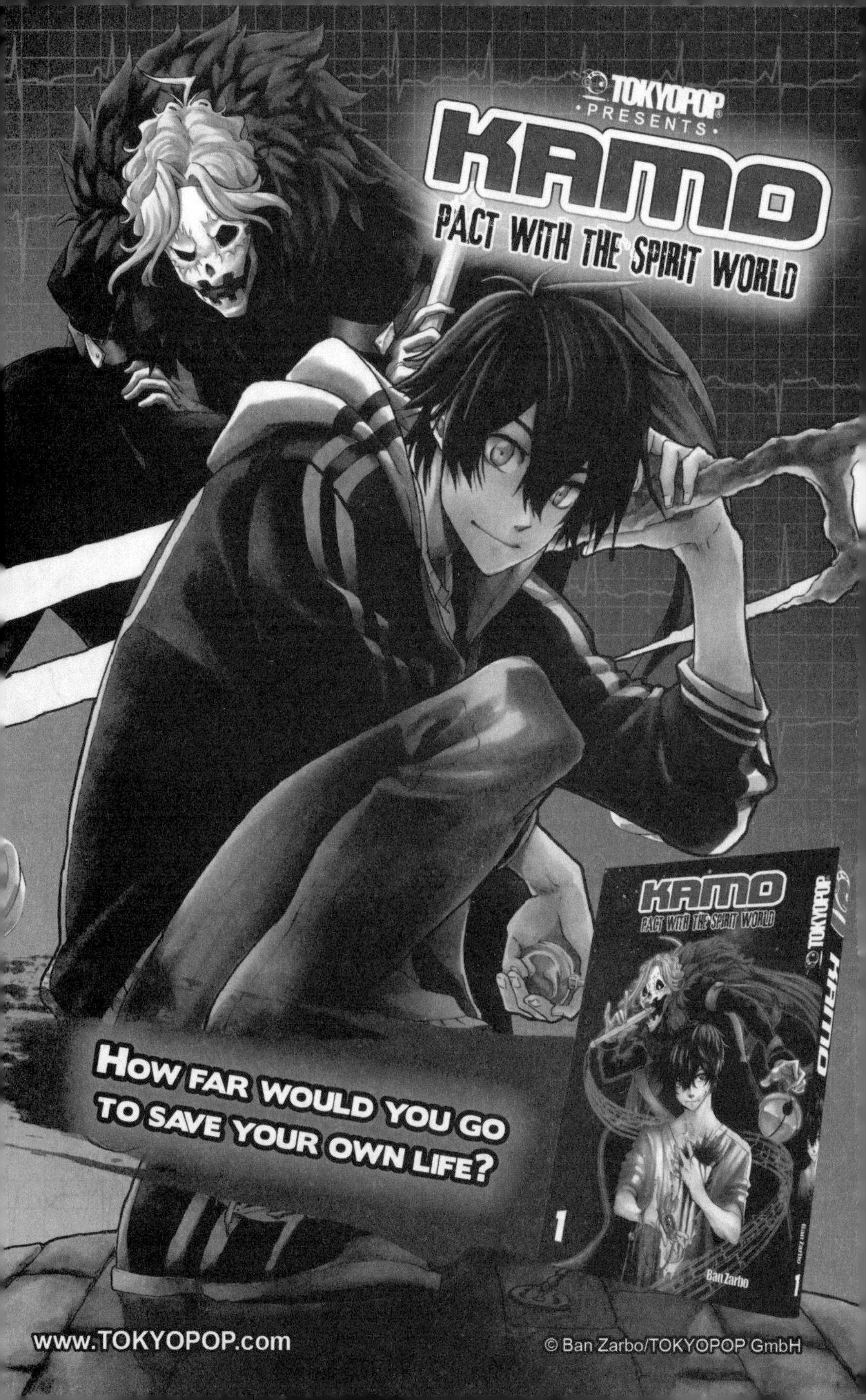

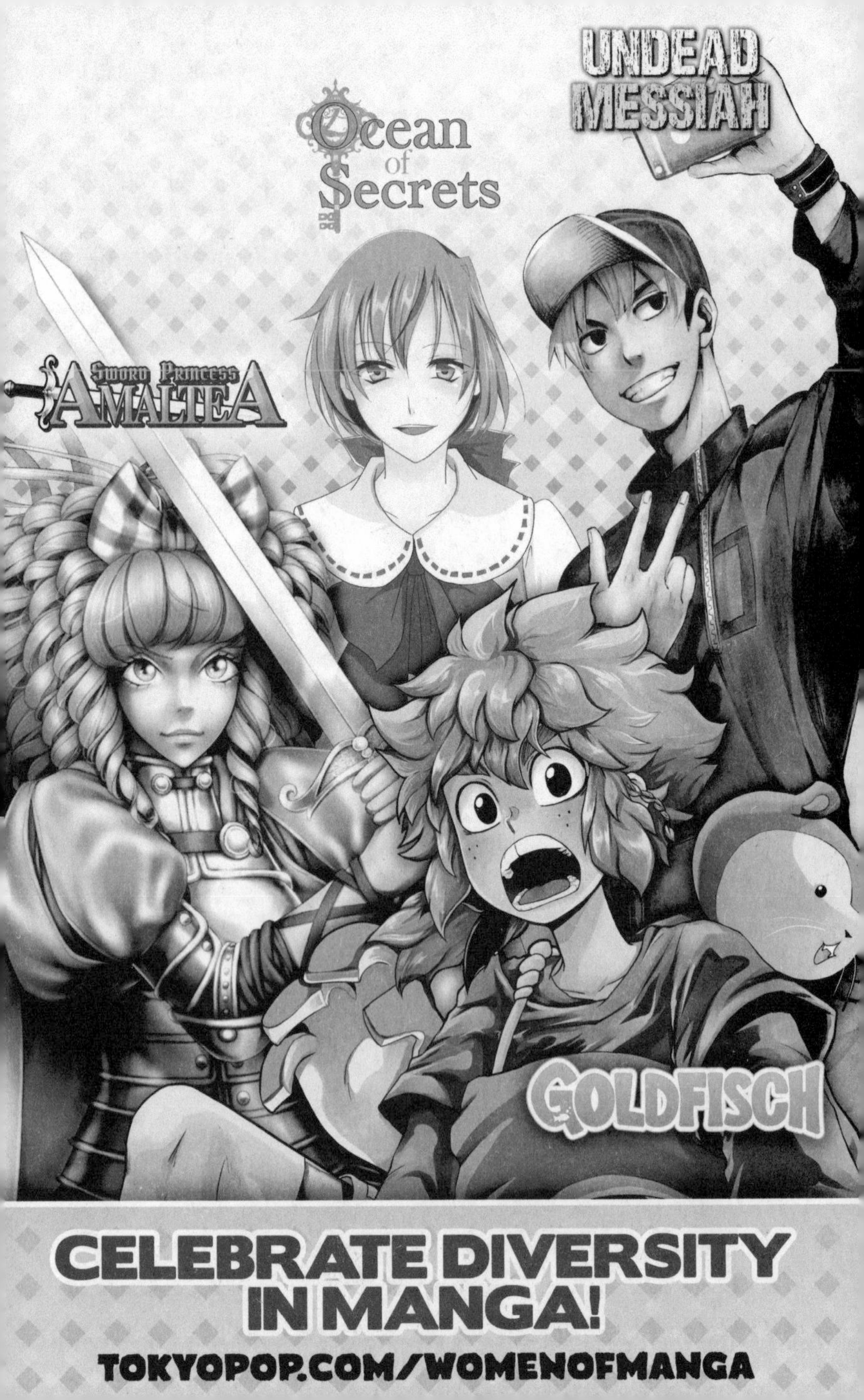
UNDEAD MESSIAH
Ocean of Secrets
SWORD PRINCESS AMALTEA
GOLDFISCH
CELEBRATE DIVERSITY IN MANGA!
TOKYOPOP.COM/WOMENOFMANGA

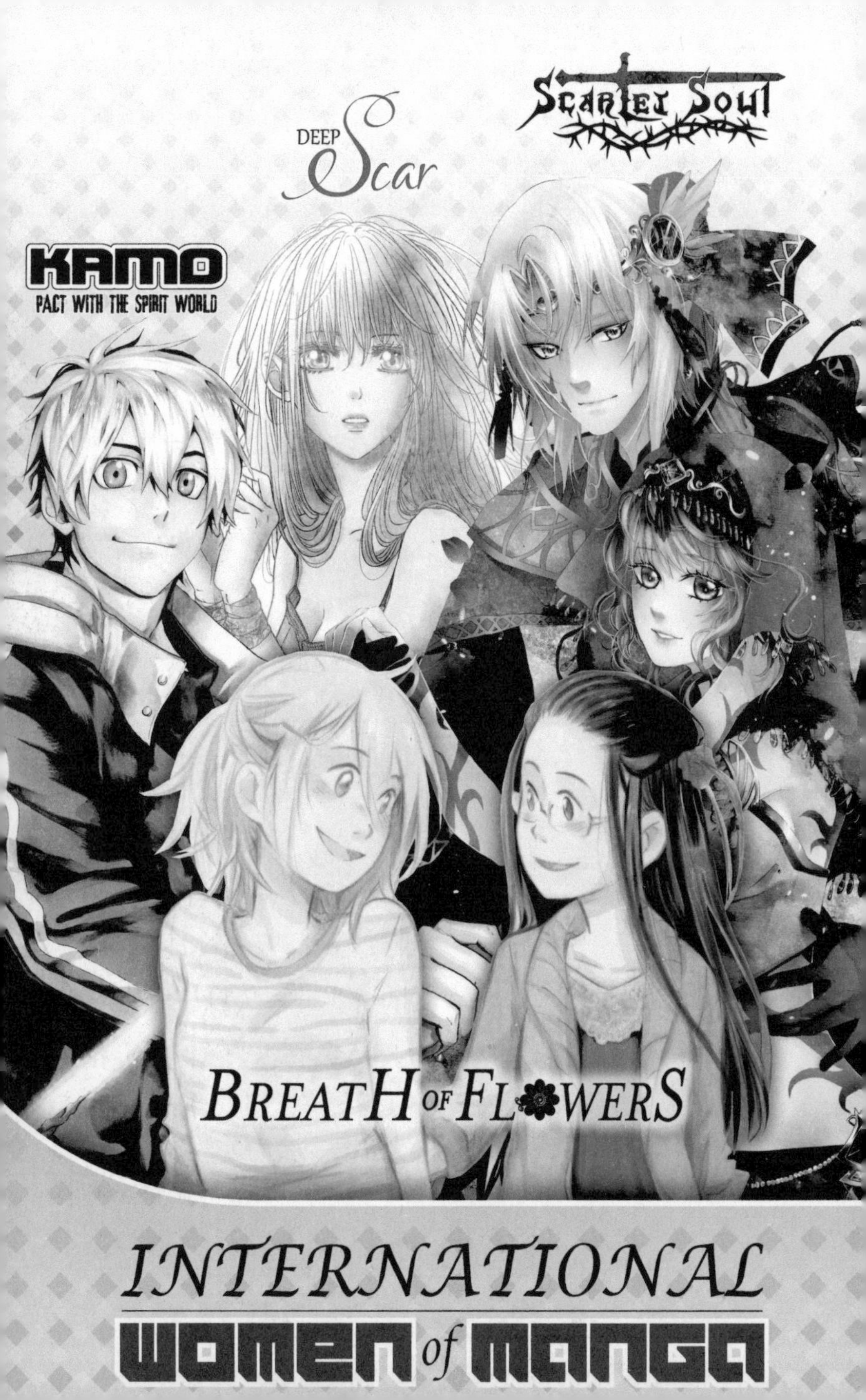
DEEP Scar
Scarlet Soul
KAMO
PACT WITH THE SPIRIT WORLD
BREATH OF FLOWERS
INTERNATIONAL
WOMEN of MANGA

The Fox & Little Tanuki 3
Manga by Mi Tagawa

Editor	-	Lena Atanassova
Translator	-	Katie Kimura
Quality Check	-	Akiko Furuta
Proofreader	-	Massiel Gutierrez
Copy Editor	-	M. Cara Carper
Marketing Associate	-	Kae Winters
Licensing Specialist	-	Arika Yanaka
Cover Design	-	Sol DeLeo
Retouching and Lettering	-	Vibrraant Publishing Studio
Editor-in-Chief & Publisher	-	Stu Levy

A  Manga

TOKYOPOP and 🐸 are trademarks or registered trademarks of TOKYOPOP Inc.

TOKYOPOP Inc.
5200 W. Century Blvd. Suite 705
Los Angeles, 90045

E-mail: info@TOKYOPOP.com
Come visit us online at www.TOKYOPOP.com

f www.facebook.com/TOKYOPOP
🐦 www.twitter.com/TOKYOPOP
📌 www.pinterest.com/TOKYOPOP
📷 www.instagram.com/TOKYOPOP

KORISENMAN volume 3
© 2020 Mi Tagawa

First published in Japan in 2020 by MAG Garden Corporation
English translation rights arranged with MAG Garden Corporation through Tuttle-Mori Agency, Inc, Tokyo

ISBN: 978-1-4278-6740-7
First TOKYOPOP Printing: February 2021
10 9 8 7 6 5 4 3 2 1
Printed in CANADA

STOP

THIS IS THE BACK OF THE BOOK!

How do you read manga-style? It's simple! To learn,
just start in the top right panel and follow the numbers: